The Ground Rules

ROYA CARMEN

OMNIFIC PUBLISHING
LOS ANGELES

Omnific Publishing
1901 Avenue of the Stars, 2nd floor
Los Angeles, CA 90067
www.omnificpublishing.com

First Omnific eBook edition, June 2015
First Omnific trade paperback edition, June 2015

Library of Congress Cataloguing-in-Publication Data

Carmen, Roya.
The Ground Rules / Roya Carmen – 1st ed.
ISBN: 978-1-623422-06-6
1. Marriage — Fiction. 2. Erotica — Fiction.
3. Chicago — Fiction. 4. Swinging — Fiction. I. Title

10 9 8 7 6 5 4 3 2 1

Cover Design by Micha Stone and Amy Brokaw
Interior Book Design by Coreen Montagna

Printed in the United States of America

To my wonderful husband
who always supports my crazy creative pursuits.

Preface

Few words were spoken. Yet I knew. I can't really explain it...physical attraction is a powerful thing, an all-consuming thing. I didn't want it, and I certainly wasn't looking for it, but there it was, nevertheless.

I should have run in the opposite direction. But I didn't. No...I yielded to it.

It's amazing how life can change so easily—veer off the path. A single moment, a decision you make, however insignificant, can change the course of your destiny.

For me, it all started with a pink dress.

Chapter One

The pink dress...

Goodness...my toes are a disgrace. I haven't looked at my feet in a while, and as I stare down at the faded, chipped blue polish on way-too-long toenails, I realize I might be letting myself go.

I really need a pedicure.

I can't remember the last time I gave myself a pedi. Chloe's toes are perfect little shiny red buds—I just did her nails yesterday.

When did my daughter's toenails become more important than mine? Probably about eight years ago or so. I first painted her toenails when she was just a baby—just wanted to see what it would look like.

I suppose that's what happens when you become a mom. One day you have a life. You look hot. Other men (men who are not your husband) want to do wicked things to you.

And then...you're painting your baby's tiny toenails.

I sigh as Chloe wraps one of my colorful scarves around her neck, her dark brown curls caught under the silk. We're playing dress-up.

She twirls in front of the wall mirror. "Do I look grown-up, Mommy?" Her gorgeous eyes gaze at me intently. "Well, do I?"

"Yes, sweetie. You look very sophisticated." *Classier than me*, I muse—ghastly toes, shabby sweats, and all. Every time I look at her, I see her father. She looks so much like him—the crazy dark curls, the gorgeous, sleepy, hazel eyes and the slightly off-kilter, devilish smile.

She's precious, standing in my over-sized black pumps and red cocktail dress, a hodge-podge of necklaces draped around her neck.

Her little sister stands on a vanity chair, arms stretched as she reaches for one of my dresses. "How 'bout this one?"

I give Claire the pick of the crop. I never wear them anymore. And I do have a *lot* of dresses—when a pretty one catches my eye, impulse overtakes me. I *never* ask myself, "When am I ever going to wear this?" If I did, I probably wouldn't have this overstuffed closet.

I've taken over the closet, in fact—Gabe's clothing is stuffed in an armoire, but I don't think he minds. He's a simple guy—he wears mostly jeans, T-shirts, and plaid button shirts. He doesn't need a closet.

Well, that's what I tell myself anyway…

I study the dress Claire has picked out—it's one of my favorites, probably *the* favorite. It's a fifties-era dress I spent a small fortune on at one of those posh vintage stores—pink chiffon over taffeta, a corset-like bodice with lacy straps, and a flowing skirt that falls just above the knee.

The pink dress brushes the carpet, hanging off Claire's tiny six-year-old frame. She looks so sweet in it. I can't help but stare. I've only worn it twice—once at the theater, the other time at a wedding. Gabe's oldest brother tied the knot on a beautiful July day, which somehow managed to turn into a torrential downpour. We all got drenched. Gabe and I sprinted to our hotel room, undressed in a fury, and made love. Gabe's wet shirt had been plastered on his body, the tribal tattoo covering half his body peeking through the soaked fabric. It's one of my favorite (very hot) memories.

I looked really nice in that dress.

"You look like a princess," Chloe tells her little sister. Claire, seemingly pleased with this observation, flashes her adorable toothless smile.

The dress seems so small. *Would I still fit into it? No way.* I'm almost thirty-five years old, and I've had two kids. But…I just need to know.

"Claire," I venture softly. "Can you take the dress off?"

She shrugs, tiny brows furrowed. "But you *said* I could wear any of your dresses." She's not taking it off. "It's my favorite," she says with pursed lips. Even when she's being difficult, she still manages to be adorable.

"Well, it's my favorite too actually." I stroke the chiffon between my fingers. "But it does look very nice on you."

She ponders me for a second, and I can almost see her little mind working. She stares at me with those big brown eyes of hers—she's so sweet. "Do you want to wear it?" she asks softly.

"You think I should. You think I could fit into it?"

"For sure," she says with conviction. Well…she's definitely more optimistic than I am because I'm pretty sure I won't fit into that dress.

She wiggles out of it, and I quickly get out of my shabby sweats. I'm down to my undies and undo the side zipper.

"The moment of truth, girls…"

As I carefully slip the dress over my shoulders, I'm surprised. It falls to my knees and seems to still fit. But whether I can zip it up or not is the question. I make it three-quarters of the way there, and the dress fits more snugly than I remember…but it fits!

I kneel down as Chloe assists me in zipping it to the top. "It looks really nice on you," she proclaims as we study my reflection in the mirror.

It does.

I'm happy I still fit into my favorite dress. But on the other hand, I'm a little depressed. I'll probably never get to wear it again. Let's face it—my life is not exactly full of charity balls and glamorous events. Gabe and I don't get out much—our idea of a date night is a hearty meal at the local family restaurant and a movie, or perhaps the occasional dinner with friends.

"Why do you look so sad?" Claire asks, a dash of concern in her sweet voice.

Because Mommy has no life.

I smile to reassure her. "I'm not sad, Claire. It's just…I'm probably never going to wear this dress ever again."

She looks at me like I have three heads. "You're wearing it right now, silly."

I laugh at her. She has a way of making me giggle, and right now, my life is wonderfully perfect—I have her and Chloe, and Gabe.

"You're right, Claire," I pipe up. "I *am* wearing it. We should do something special. We're all dressed up."

"How 'bout a tea party in my room?"

I smile. "Sounds wonderful."

"So tell me, Mirella," Claire starts. "How have you been?" she asks, her sweet voice laced with pomp and circumstance.

Her expression makes me laugh. "Why, I am just divine, Claire. Thank you for asking."

I sit at the tiny yellow table in my vintage pink chiffon dress, nibbling on animal crackers and drinking iced tea. Maybe it wouldn't be such a bad idea to wear the dress somewhere—perhaps Gabe and I could go see a show—it could be a lot of fun. I should talk to him about it.

And there it is…that "defining moment" wrapped up cleverly into an "ordinary moment."

What if we hadn't been in that closet playing dress-up? What if Claire hadn't picked out *that* dress? What if it hadn't fit? What if…

Claire is having quite the battle with her taco. Every time she bites into it, cheese covered ground beef spills onto her plate. At this rate, she'll never get any of it into her little stomach. The sight makes me laugh.

Gabe rolls his eyes and grabs her taco. "You're not holding it right, Claire," he snaps. "The whole thing's falling apart." He rewraps the taco and folds her fingers around it. He proceeds to instruct her exactly how to hold it and eat it. She seems flustered, and she holds that taco like her life depends on it. I feel a little sorry for her. Leave it to Gabe to turn taco night into a stress-inducing exercise.

He spots her shaking bottom lip—a tell-tale sign she's just about to cry.

"I'm sorry, sweetie. I know tacos aren't easy to eat," Gabe tells her.

She wipes a tear off her face with a pudgy finger.

"It's like a lot of things," he says, with a playful pinch of her cheek. "It takes a lot of work to get right. You're doing great."

She smiles up at him—she's already forgiven him.

Gabe is not as easy-going as I am. I don't think anyone is. Gabe says I'm the most patient person he's ever known. And I guess that's a good thing since I'm a kindergarten teacher. Handling two girls is nothing compared to handling twenty-two five-year olds at school all day.

When the whole taco drama is over, I take advantage of a few precious seconds of silence to talk to Gabe about my idea for "date night." We've had date nights before, but this would be something a little more special.

"I was thinking we should go out, just the two of us," I suggest between bites of my taco. "You never did take me out for Mother's Day."

"Is there a movie you want to see?"

"Well, I was actually thinking of doing something a little different." I'm a little nervous for some reason—I'm not sure why—it's not like I'm asking for a trip to Paris.

"I thought we could dress up and go to the city to see a show."

I spot a scowl for a fraction of a second. The theater is not his thing, but he'll go to great lengths to make me happy. "I guess we could," he finally says. "We could go someplace nice for dinner too."

We sit in silence for a beat. The girls munch on their tacos as they listen to us. They seem curious.

"It'd be sweet to go to some grown-up place for a change," he adds with a smile. "Somewhere posh and fancy, where they serve you a spoonful of food on a big-ass plate and charge you an arm and a leg." He's up for it because he knows that's what I like.

"Yes, somewhere where there are no kiddie menus, after-meal toys, and brown paper covered tables you can doodle on."

"*What?*" Gabe teases. "But you love doodling on the table."

I laugh—he's right. "I'm going to wear my little pink vintage dress," I tell him, stunned by the excitement in my voice. "You know the one?"

"Oh yeah...I *know* the one," he says with a sly smile. "The one I'll be taking off at the end of the night."

I laugh and give him one of those "children *are* in the room" looks. And I'm reminded why I love him so much.

He *will* be taking it off and I get a little giddy at the idea. Almost twenty years together, and he still wants me.

Chapter Two

It seems like fate, doesn't it?

I've bought tickets on-line for the show, and Gabe says he's got dinner under control.

My dark hair is curled and pinned into a retro style. I'm not much for makeup, but I've put on a little liquid liner, mascara, and red lipstick. Standing in front of the mirror in my pink chiffon vintage dress, I'm happy with the results—it's very "fifties pin-up girl." I find myself smiling, but just as soon as my gap-toothed smile appears, it fades. Gabe says the gap gives me character, but what does he know—he loves me unconditionally.

As I peek at myself one last time, it's clear the outfit needs a little something. I pull out my extensive collection of vintage brooches.

Claire sits on the vanity chair—she's been watching me for the longest time, quiet as a mouse. "You look pretty, Mommy," she finally says. Her sweet voice unexpectedly brings out emotion in me, and my eyes tear up. I can't cry and ruin my eye makeup. And then I wonder why I'm so emotional—it's just a night out, for crying out loud.

I show Claire my brooch collection, displayed on wine-red velvet fabric in an old Victorian frame—a little craft project I worked on not long ago. "Which one?"

She points at the amber and pink jeweled owl. "I like that one. I think it would go nice with your dress."

I agree. "I think so too. The colors match, don't they?"

As I pin the brooch just over my heart, I'm pretty happy with the final outcome.

When I finally make it downstairs, Gabe takes one look at me and says, "Wow!"

I smile shyly at him. "You look nice too," I reply, eyeing him from top to bottom. The man is a looker—always has been. His six-foot-three frame looks fantastic in dark pants and a black-striped dress shirt. I almost never get to see him dressed up, and I love it when I do. There's a kind of sexy contrast between the clean-cut outfit and the shaggy dark curls and week-old scruff.

God, I want him right now.

He kisses me softly on the cheek.

"You look like a million bucks," he says. "I've told Caroline all she needs to know, and I've set up dinner for her to feed the kids." Caroline is our babysitter—absolutely the sweetest girl you'll ever meet. We like her because she's nerdy, bookish, and responsible, and will most likely not throw a wild party or scrounge through our underwear drawers…but then, you never know.

As we drive on the interstate in Gabe's beast of a truck to Chicago's downtown, he looks at me again and smiles. I smile back and can only imagine what he's thinking. He slides his hand up my thigh and says softly, "I will *definitely* be taking that dress off tonight."

He's turning me on. He can still turn on the switch, sometimes with just a word or two. "You better keep your eyes on the road before you kill us both," I warn him with a smile.

He smiles and turns away, his eyes focused on the road. I look at him and can't help but sigh a little—my high school sweetheart still does it for me after all these years. We first fell in love our senior year—two seventeen year olds—the popular charming jock and the new girl, a shy bookish sort. It was quite the talk of the school when we got together. Most of the girls were shocked, if not a little jealous too—that a looker like Gabe would fall for plain old me. But then, he's always said it was "love at first sight."

"We need to go pick up the tickets at the box office after dinner," I inform him as we make our way to the restaurant. I'm a little wobbly in my heeled, pink Mary Janes, but I also feel very sexy and sophisticated, so the shoes are worth the effort.

Gabe has arranged for dinner at a restaurant in the theater district. I'm not too familiar with downtown, but he claims it's the place to go—a five star gourmet restaurant specializing in Southern Louisiana cuisine—crawfish, jambalaya, lobster Creole, and the like. I'm not sure if I'll like it, but I'm just happy to be getting away from the usual.

I want to try something new.

The décor is very sleek and contemporary, with none of the old Louisiana charm I expected. Stainless-steel fountains separate the space, and futuristic wave-like lighting fixtures dot the ceiling. Square tables covered in crisp white linens are arranged in perfect symmetry. There are no kids anywhere, and I'm excited at the prospect of spending an evening surrounded by adults, for a change.

Gabe walks up to the hostess who smiles warmly at us. Her large Bohemian earrings dangle as she tilts her head and asks, "Reservations?"

"Yes, under Keates," Gabe tells her.

She is extremely tall—as tall as Gabe, and she must be wearing very high heels behind that hostess podium. Her sleek black dress hugs her perfectly, and her long, shiny dark hair falls like a cascade of silky ribbons. And I suddenly feel odd in my quirky vintage dress.

"I apologize. I don't see it," she tells us with a perfect megawatt smile—she doesn't seem sorry at all. "Let me check for a second," she adds. "Please take a seat."

We make our way to the sleek leather banquette lining the wall. Gabe seems irked.

"It's probably just a little snafu," I say.

I spot a couple entering the restaurant, and my attention is instantly drawn to the woman—she's gorgeous, blond, and *all class*—tucked into a fitted, cream, contemporary two-piece suit and super high, expensive-looking cream pumps. She seems at ease and completely comfortable. *How do some women do that? How do they wear heels that high, suits that tight, and* still *manage to look comfy and put-together, moving with the grace of a ballerina?* She doesn't notice me staring at her, or rather "gawking" might be a more accurate word. I'm glad she's so self-centered and unaware of her surroundings—she doesn't see me at all—I could be invisible as far as she's concerned.

Then my attention shifts to her date, but I can't see his face. He's tall and broad-shouldered and has a fabulous head of hair. Of course, he's wearing a classy fitted suit. And I want to vomit a little—people like these two make me a little sick.

"Check out Barbie and Ken over there," Gabe whispers in my ear. And I laugh out loud—I can't help it—he's been thinking the same thing I have. Barbie turns to look at us, and I offer an apologetic smile. Ken doesn't bother turning around.

"Hello Mr. and Mrs. Hanson," the hostess offers, her attention fully devoted to them. "How are you?" she asks in that fake-ish way people do. I get the sense that Ken and Barbie have been here on a regular basis—it's probably just a regular night for them, not a special once-a-year date night, like it is for Gabe and me.

"Table for two?" she asks. And I wonder what the hell happened to us—what about *our* table lady?

Gabe takes my hand in his and smiles at me. "You look nice," he says. He's said it already earlier tonight, but I don't mind. And I don't mind sitting on this comfy banquette with him for a little while.

"Table for four actually," Barbie says. "We're expecting friends."

"Yes, of course," snooty hostess replies. "I do have a table for you. But it isn't quite ready yet," she offers apologetically. "It'll just take a moment."

"That's fine," Barbie says as she and Ken turn toward us. And I see his face. And he's gorgeous—of course. Of course he's gorgeous—he's exactly what I expected.

We instinctively slide over to the far edge of the banquette to make room for them. And for some reason, I don't smile at them. In such circumstances, I would usually smile politely, as most people would, but I kind of hate these people—they seem a little smug. And they have a table waiting for them, which we apparently don't.

Gabe leans back and stares up at the ceiling. "I bet we'll be sitting here awhile." He's already losing his cool.

Barbie smiles warmly at Gabe, and he smiles back—of course he would—she's gorgeous. Ken doesn't smile at either of us—apparently he's not interested in idle chit-chat. Good...we're on the same page.

"How are you?" Barbie asks us with a flawless smile, her lips a soft coral, her teeth perfect and gleaming white.

"Good," Gabe says. "How 'bout yourself?"

"Great. Thank you."

Of course she's great—she has a table.

"It seems real busy tonight," Gabe offers. He's always been good at small talk and meeting new people—I envy that about him. He's a lot more outgoing than I am.

"It's always busy," Barbie points out. "Have you been waiting for a while?"

"Not too long," I offer, awkwardly planting myself into the conversation—yes, *my* gorgeous husband has a wife, lady. I don't really know why I'm being so possessive—I'm a little threatened I suppose—the woman does look like a supermodel, and it's not every day your husband has a conversation with a supermodel.

I catch Ken's eye, and he quickly averts his gaze. He strikes me as a little odd, the strong silent type. I don't think he's said a single word so far. I find myself checking him out—hey, if she can chat up my husband, I can at least sneak a peek at hers. He's truly beautiful in the classic sense—chiseled features, olive skin, dark sleek hair, not a strand out of place—he's as sleek and put-together as his wife. He seems very conservative, but I like his flashy purple shirt and tie. He turns to look at me, and I instinctively turn away and feel myself blush a little.

His phones rings—a traditional ring tone, nothing fun. He answers promptly, his voice quieter and softer than I would have imagined. I look away and pretend not to listen, but in fact, I'm straining to hear every word.

"Hi, Simon. What is it?"

A long pause of silence—no one speaks. Barbie seems curious too.

He rolls his eyes, and then he smiles. He has a nice wide smile—the kind of smile you see on people who seem to have more teeth than the average human. "*Seriously?*" he says. "Well, I'm not surprised, Simon," he adds, shaking his head. "I've known you too long."

"What is it, Weston?" Barbie asks, very curious. So *Ken's* name is *Weston*—I think I like that better.

He smiles at his wife but doesn't answer. "It's not a problem, Simon. Don't worry. We'll do it another time."

"We'll talk later," he finally says before hanging up.

Barbie, who is apparently not a complete idiot, has deduced the obvious. "They're not coming?"

"Nope," he says plainly, his voice soft. "Apparently, Jennifer has sprained her ankle and insisted on going to the emergency room."

Barbie laughs. "She's such a fashionista. She probably did it in those ridiculously high heels she wears."

I glance down at Barbie's pumps, which must have *a least* a four or five inch heel. *Do shoes get higher than that?*

The hostess, who had stepped away, walks back to her podium. "I'm sorry Mr. Keates. I have no record of a reservation in your name."

"What!" Gabe snaps, standing. "But I made a reservation," he tells her, his mouth a hard line. He's peeved and desperately trying to contain himself. "I called a few days ago."

"I'm sorry," the hostess replies—she seems flustered as well. "But there's no indication on my system."

He rakes a hand through his unruly hair. "Well, do you have anything available?" All eyes and ears are on him now, and the situation feels slightly awkward. I look away, mildly mortified. I bet this never happens to Barbie and Ken...Barbie and *Weston*.

"I'm sorry," the hostess says, straight-faced. She seems a little irked now.

Damn, we don't need this. We don't have time for this. We have a show to catch, and we don't have time to scout for another restaurant—all the restaurants in the area are probably just as packed.

"Well, you seem like a very capable woman," Gabe offers, turning on the charm. "I'm sure you can work something out for us."

"I'm sorry," she almost sneers. "There is absolutely nothing I can do."

God...there is no thawing this ice queen. And I suddenly hate her, and I hate this pompous, pretentious restaurant too.

Barbie jumps to her stiletto-ed feet, "Are you sure there's nothing you can do for them?" she asks, her voice silky.

Okay...so Barbie might not be so bad after all.

"I'm sorry, Mrs. Hanson," the hostess insists. "We're at full capacity." Her eyes light up as she adds, "But I have good news for you... your table for four is ready."

Barbie takes a seat back on the banquette. "I have an idea," she blurts out. "You nice folks could have dinner with us," she offers, all smiles.

Us nice folks? She doesn't know us. We've barely spoken five words. I'm not nice. All I've been doing is judging her—and I suddenly feel like a real witch. Barbie's actually nice. As much as I'd like to hate this woman, I can't.

"Our friends have just canceled on us, and we have a table for four," she tells us, but of course, I already knew that from spying on them. "It seems like fate, doesn't it?" she adds cheerfully.

"Well…uh…" Gabe says. He seems taken aback. I don't think I've ever seen Gabe at a loss for words before.

"Thank you," I say nervously—this is a really strange situation. "But I'm sure you don't want to spend your evening with two strangers."

"Nonsense," she says. "You two really don't strike me as sociopaths," she adds with a laugh.

"Thank you," I say and instantly feel like an idiot—this conversation is very odd.

"Well, sociopaths *do* come in many shapes and sizes," her husband points out, his voice soft and languid. He's looking at me. "But regardless…I think we'll live dangerously and take our chances."

And I can't help but smile—a big genuine smile, and I instinctively bring my hand up to cover it. He smiles back, his gaze staying on me for what seems like the longest time, and I can't seem to look away.

My heart does a little flip.

What the hell has gotten into me?

Chapter Three

Yes...I believe that fits.

We follow the hostess to a table.

Barbie and I go first, followed by Gabe and Weston. I still don't know Barbie's name and they don't know ours. I barely take in my surroundings—this seems like such a strange turn of events.

As we reach our table, Weston pulls Barbie's chair back in a very gentlemanly way, and she gingerly perches her bottom on the seat.

I help Gabe with his jacket—he always runs hot.

"Why don't you sit right there," she suggests to Gabe, her eyes pointing to the chair facing her. "I love a good view with my meal," she adds with a wink and a not-so-subtle flirty voice. My jaw practically falls to the floor. I can't believe she's flirting with my husband—the gall of this woman.

Gabe smiles and does as instructed—I think he's a little stunned. And he doesn't pay me any attention—no gentlemanly chair pulling for me. But I can't blame the guy—a supermodel is flirting with him. That surely doesn't happen every day...or week...or *ever*.

I look over at Weston as he takes a seat next to his wife. I'm curious to see what he thinks of all this. He doesn't seem bothered one bit. I get the feeling this is not an unusual occurrence.

I take a seat opposite Weston and smile at the hostess as she leaves us.

"Where are my manners," Barbie blurts out. "I'm Bridget," she offers, extending her perfectly manicured hand to Gabe.

I suppose I can now stop referring to her as "Barbie."

He quickly shakes her hand. "I'm Gabe," he offers. "And this is my wife, Mirella." I like how he sneaks the word "wife" in there, almost as if he's reminding her he's married.

She extends her hand to me, and I take it, surprised by how soft and delicate it feels. And as I smile at her, I am awestruck by her beauty.

I look over at Weston, who gives me a closed-lipped smile. I already know his name because I've been kind of spying on him.

"Weston Hanson," he offers and shakes both our hands in a very business-like way—no smiles, no fanfare.

All the introductions have been made, and there's a tense moment of silence. Weston rearranges his glassware and cutlery, moving it around ever so slightly and lining it up at perfect angles, into flawless symmetry. His behavior is a little odd.

Then I look over my own setting, and it does seem slightly off, and I find myself mirroring his actions and adjusting it. I look up at him, and he smiles at me. His smile is barely discernable—but it is an invitation, nevertheless, to look at him without inhibition.

The whimsical silver fish-shaped clip on his flashy purple tie draws my eye. He looks completely at ease in his dark sleek suit. I don't know much about suits, but I bet his is expensive and custom tailored. His eyes are striking—light green speckled with gold, lined with long dark lashes, unlike anything I have ever seen. And my heart does another little flip. I immediately tell myself to settle down.

"Where are you wonderful people from?" Bridget asks.

"We're from Naperville, born and raised," Gabe explains. "Well, myself anyway…Mirella moved there from Michigan when she was seventeen." Gabe has taken the conversation into his own hands, as he always does. And I'm just fine with that—I'm not much for small talk—I prefer listening.

"How 'bout you folks?" he asks.

Bridget laughs. "We live in Lake Bluff. But we also have a few properties here and there."

Of course.

An almost invisible woman pours water, barely making a dent in our existence. Bridget and Gabe don't see her at all. Weston gives her a warm, "Thank you," as do I.

I find myself listening intently. For some reason, I want to know more about these people. Bridget does all the talking, and Weston listens, like I do, catching my eye every now and then.

And I try not to look at him too much.

I feel odd—part of me is exhilarated, and another part of me just wants to disappear.

Bridget tells Gabe she's a criminal defense lawyer. *Damn, beautiful* and *smart.* I'm not surprised—a woman with that much class has to have some brains.

Gabe tells her about his business, and she seems genuinely interested. Gabe has worked in his family business for almost twenty years, since he was sixteen. His family name is synonymous with quality handcrafted furniture—they've been doing it for over fifty years.

"Do you build the furniture yourself?" Bridget asks.

Gabe laughs. "Oh no. If I built you a chair, it'd probably be missing a leg, and you'd fall off and break your neck."

Bridget laughs heartily.

"We actually work in collaboration with the Mennonite community," he tells her. "They do fantastic work."

"Too bad," she says, giggling a little. "I was kind of picturing you with a circular saw and a sexy tool belt."

Really? This again?

Gabe laughs. "Sorry to disappoint, Bridget."

Yep, these two seem to be getting along very well—famously, in fact. They're completely ignoring us—it seems as if Weston and I are not even in the room.

I'm mildly irked.

Weston smiles, seemingly amused. This doesn't seem to bother him at all.

"What about yourself, Mirella?" he asks—my name flows slowly off his tongue. "What do you do?"

He speaks!

I'm taken aback, and it takes me a second or two to answer him. "Well, I teach kindergarten actually," I say proudly. I may not make as much money as Bridget, but my work is very rewarding.

He smiles and is silent again.

And after what seems like an eternity, he speaks again. "Yes…I believe that fits."

I'm surprised by his words. There's a certain level of intimacy in them. He doesn't know me—we've barely spoken, but he apparently has an opinion on what "fits me."

I'm curious.

I must get to the bottom of it.

I smile. "What do you mean?"

He hesitates a little. "You seem patient, and also kind and young at heart. A fitting personality for a kindergarten teacher."

He doesn't elaborate further.

I'm flattered by his words, but I can't let this go.

"And what makes you say that?" I ask with a smile. "You barely know me."

He clears his throat, not quite looking at me. "I study people," he explains as he fiddles with his sparkling, fish-shaped silver cufflinks. "You can learn a lot from simply observing."

He's so cryptic…it's driving me insane.

"Well, what exactly have you observed?" I ask with determination.

He rubs the back of his neck. "Oh…it's nothing. I apologize for my presumption."

But I can't let this go.

"Enlighten me, please."

He bites his bottom lip, his gaze glued to the wine glass in his hand. "Well…first off," he starts, hesitating a little, "when the maître d' didn't have a table for you, you didn't seem too upset. You seemed content, sitting there with your husband, which makes me think you're pretty easygoing. You didn't lose your composure or scowl in any way, like your husband did, which tells me you're patient. Even when the maître d' told you there was no table, you seemed concerned but not necessarily angry."

It's true. I *am* rather easygoing.

He ventures a look up at me and goes on, "When we sat down at the table, you doted on your husband and helped him with his jacket, and didn't seem to mind he wasn't paying attention to you. You like to take care of people, not be taken care of."

At this point, I am completely transfixed. This guy's better than that weird palm reader at the renaissance fair I went to last year.

He shifts in his seat and leans in a bit, the intensity not leaving his eyes for a moment. "You let your husband take over the conversation, so you don't like to be the center of attention. It's not about you, it's about others."

I am speechless at this point. Utterly speechless.

"When the server poured our water, you thanked her and acknowledged her. You don't consider yourself superior to her, or anyone else for that matter, merely of different life circumstances."

And suddenly, it's just the two of us in the room—his amazing green eyes boring into mine, my attention completely on him, and it shames me to admit, my panties are a little moist.

"And that quirky, rather interesting brooch you're wearing…it's very whimsical," he says, a hint of playfulness in his voice. "It tells me you love color. You love beautiful things, and you're young at heart. I'd wager you love to do crafts with your kids—you love to color and get silly with them. Am I right?"

Good God.

This guy *must* have a PhD in behavioral psychology. He's got me down pat. *I do* love to do crafts with the kids, and *I do* love to color. Everything he's said about me is spot on. I feel almost naked—like he can read my mind or something.

Oh shit! I hope he can't read the fact that I think he's the most gorgeous creature I've ever laid eyes on.

Damn.

I laugh a little nervously. "Wow…uh…you're good. You got me spot on."

He smiles without a word. I want to ask about him, but the waitress comes over and interrupts us.

She takes our order for drinks. Weston orders a bottle for the table—a red, something French and expensive sounding—it seems to be the usual. The waitress obviously knows him well, often addressing him as "Mr. Hanson."

Gabe, who usually drinks beer, doesn't order a drink—he never drinks and drives. But he'll probably have a small glass of wine. Bridget and I order martinis.

I'm glad when the waitress leaves us. I want to know everything about this man. Gabe and Bridget are still deep in conversation. She's talking about her alma-matter—Harvard…figures.

"So, how about you?" I ask. "Are you a psychologist? Let me guess… criminal psychology? You seem to be able to read people's minds."

He laughs. "No…I'm a developer," he says simply, without elaboration.

Then he's quiet again. There's such an intense look about him, like he's simultaneously having a conversation with me *and* trying to figure out how to solve global warming. There seems to be so much going on in his mind.

"Um…" I hesitate. I want to know more but don't want to appear too nosy. He's not giving me much to work with. I'll probably have to Google him. "What kind of development do you do?"

"Sustainable loft condos and housing. Sustainable energy is the way of the future. We're now building homes which create more energy than they use."

"That's great," I tell him, truly impressed. "Fascinating."

And we find ourselves in silence again. It seems he knows me down to my essence, yet I don't know a thing about him.

"How many children do you and your husband have?" he asks. How does he know I have children? I haven't mentioned it.

"Two. Two girls…Chloe and Claire."

"How old are they?"

"Eight and six," I wonder if he has children. I have no clue. "How 'bout you…do you have kids?"

He looks off into the distance and doesn't answer me. There's something odd in his expression—he seems to be working out his answer—which seems strange to me, since it's a pretty simple question. "We have two fantastic kids," he finally offers. "Ashton and Elizabeth. Ashton is ten and Elizabeth is eight."

I picture his children—they're perfect…of course. He has dark hair like his father, and she has her mother's light blond curls and blue eyes. And it goes without saying, they're both perfectly dressed—a picture straight out of a Brooks Brothers catalogue. They're not mismatched and disheveled like my girls—not in a million years would they ever have gum in their hair.

"Your daughter is the same age as my oldest," I point out. And before I can think, I add playfully, "We should have a play date."

And as soon as I say it, I regret it.

How foolish of me. We hardly know these people.

"I…I'm just joking, of course."

"Not a horrible idea," he says, his voice as soft as ever.

And I almost melt.

No, it *is* a horrible idea. We should definitely *not* have a play date—not with the feelings I've got going on inside me at the moment.

I stammer a little. "Well…you know…I'm sure we're all very busy."

And just then, the waitress comes back to save the day and take our orders. I've barely had a chance to look at the menu—much too preoccupied with the gorgeous man sitting across me.

I'm such a little tramp.

But then I notice Gabe hasn't figured out what he wants either—so it's not just me—he's guilty too.

Weston and Bridget haven't even peeked at the menu and have already made their choices.

I suddenly feel rushed. The waitress tells us she'll give us a moment. Gabe and I peruse the menu, quickly selecting our dinner choices. I realize that as much fun as we're having, we do have a show to catch.

Bridget orders a seafood salad, and I find myself wanting to emulate her. Maybe if I start ordering a few salads, I too, can squeeze into a size two.

The "wine guy" (I'm really not sure what his official title is—though surely this is the kind of thing Weston and Bridget know) holds up the bottle for Weston, who nods. He proceeds to pour him a sample. Weston tastes and nods again. There is a lot of nodding going on, and I find myself watching him curiously. I would have no clue if a wine was acceptable or not, but Weston seems to be an expert. My favorite wines can be found in eight dollar bottles.

"Wine guy" pours us all a glass, and I can't wait to have a taste—I need to take the edge off. Generally, the more expensive a wine, the more I hate it.

I wince as I take a sip. *Yep, this wine must be crazy expensive.* I do a rather monumental job at hiding my displeasure.

Bridget and Gabe are still immersed in conversation, laughing here and then.

"Where do you teach, Mirella?" Weston asks, my name rolling off his tongue so deliciously.

"I teach at Heron Heights. I like it. And where do you work?" I ask, curious. The more I know, the better.

He laughs a little. "Everywhere. I work everywhere."

Another cryptic answer. I hope he knows I'm not planning to stalk him anytime soon. Although it would be completely understandable if a woman were inclined to do so — he is totally stalk-worthy.

"You don't like to divulge much about yourself, do you?"

"You got me."

I will definitely need to check him out — a man like him must be all over Google.

We find ourselves listening to Bridget and Gabe who are going on about their college escapades. Gabe majored in business — his father wanted him to take over the family business management, but Gabe was never a paper-pusher. He wanted to get his hands dirty, work on the ground floor. We both went to Chicago State. I commuted, and I would often stay over at his dorm, even if it was against the rules — Gabe has always been a rule breaker.

Now those days seem so far away.

The waitress comes over with our meals. I'm always amazed how restaurants can coordinate completely different meals to arrive at almost the exact same moment. "Enjoy," she offers as she leaves us.

Weston pulls out a small plastic bottle from his jacket pocket, drops a dollop of clear liquid on his palm and rubs his hands.

I smile. This is exactly what I do, but I haven't brought my bottle because my fancy clutch is only big enough for my wallet and lipstick — and of course, lipstick takes precedence over hand disinfectant.

I extend my hand to him. "Can I have some?"

He smiles as he plops a drop on my palm. I catch Gabe's eye — he's looking at us like we're the two biggest nerds on the planet. Well, let's see how he feels when he gets the flu.

We enjoy our meal mostly in silence, with the exception of Bridget who manages a few words between every bite. I can't completely enjoy my pasta because I'm simply too worked up.

Worked up about what?

I'm not sure. I just feel this intense electricity in the air.

Gabe and I tell them we have to rush because we have a show to catch. Of course they've seen it—they've seen them all, Bridget informs us.

At this point, I don't want to see the show anymore—I want to sit with them all night.

The bill comes, and Weston insists he's got it, and Gabe protests, which is a little awkward. But when Weston points out he's ordered a three-hundred dollar bottle, Gabe smiles and says, "It's all yours." It's quite evident these two are not struggling to pay the bills like we are—the posh perfectly fitted clothing, his expensive looking watch, and the gigantic diamond on her finger tells me so.

When the waitress comes back with her payment gadget, Weston pays the bill. Gabe and I thank them profusely. And the waitress also thanks him abundantly when she sees her tip. From her reaction, you would think the guy has given her his left kidney.

"Weston always leaves an extravagant tip. I think it's too much. They're only doing their jobs after all."

"Well, you've made her day, that's for sure," I point out.

"Well, if I can make someone's day, then I suppose I've done my job."

What a sweetie…

We say our formal good-byes at the door since we are heading in different directions. Bridget hugs us both tightly and tells us how delighted she is to have met us. We thank them again for the wonderful dinner. Weston gives us both a firm hand shake, very business-like—he doesn't strike me as a hugger *at all*.

As we walk away, his eyes linger on me, and he seems…almost sad.

I wonder if he feels the same way I do. I'm a little saddened by the fact that I will never see these people again. We shared a wonderful meal and pleasant conversation, but now we're off in our own directions, to our respective lives.

Our paths will never cross again.

We race to the theater. Gabe pulls me through the crowds. His stride is much longer than mine, and I find myself actually running a little to try to keep up with him. Racing in my very high heels, I suddenly wish I had worn more sensible shoes. Thankfully, we make it to the box office, just in the nick of time.

The show is great, but as wonderful as it is, I have a difficult time focusing on the story—my thoughts are still in that restaurant, on that face. I replay all the words that were said, which really were not many.

I am shocked by the reaction I've had to this man, so sudden and powerful. Desire has struck me when I least expected it. I'm not a lustful woman but for a fraction of a second, I picture his beautiful face, and I long to touch it, and I crave the feel of his hands on my skin.

I shake my head a little. I've gone completely mad.

I barely know this man—he's a stranger.

But I can't deny the reality...I've *never* been so affected.

By anyone.

Chapter Four

Just imagine him…

"What did you think of the show?" Gabe asks as we walk back to the parking lot.

I don't know what to say. Hell, I don't remember the show. All I could think about was *him*. I might just be certifiably insane. "I… uh…it was great." It must have been—the set design and music were amazing.

"You seemed distracted." Gabe is nothing if not perceptive. He knows something's up. "Were you thinking about Mr. Perfect?" he jokes. He always teases me about my silly crushes—the hot guy who renovated our bathroom, the kids' optometrist. He joshes because he knows it's harmless—I've been faithful to him for almost twenty years.

I laugh a little, but somehow this time feels different. "No… who's Mr. Perfect?" I ask playfully.

"Oh, you know who I'm talking about." He smiles wide. "Don't play coy with me."

"You're referring to Weston?" I say casually with a little smirk. But for the first time since we've been together, I feel like I'm putting on a show, like I'm lying to my husband. There's just something about Weston…it's different this time.

"You totally have the hots for the guy, Ella," he says with a cheeky smile. "Ella" is what he calls me—unless he's mad at me—then it's "Mirella."

Who am I kidding? My husband knows me too well. There's no sense denying it. "Well…" I hesitate a little. "He is attractive, if that's what you mean."

He laughs. "Oh…it's more than that, he's totally your type… good-looking, charming, and well-dressed, with a little bit of nerdy."

Gabe is all smiles—he doesn't seem too concerned. And why would he be? We will never see Bridget and Weston again. And Gabe and I have always been open like this—I think it's what has kept us faithful to each other over the years.

I laugh a little. Yep…there are no secret crushes in this relationship.

"Well, you're one to talk," I say, trying to steer the focus off me. "You and Bridget were practically all over each other." I still can't get over how flirty she was with him—another woman's husband, a father.

"Yeah…she's *gorgeous*," he admits—like I hadn't noticed. "I'd like to tear that little prim and proper outfit right off her."

Unlike me, Gabe is not one to hide his thoughts. He usually spreads them all out on the table for everyone to see. We've been together so long, I've gotten used to his occasionally questionable sense of humor.

He grabs me by the waist. "I'm kidding. You know that, right? You're my only one, Ella."

"I'm sure she'd love it. She was all over you."

"You think?"

"Of course, look at you." I swear, sometimes Gabe doesn't realize how gorgeous he is. He's not traditionally handsome—he's a little rough around the edges, and he's definitely got that "bad boy" thing going.

"You're the sexy, rugged guy," I point out. "I bet she'd die to slum it with you," I add, a playful smile on my lips.

He laughs.

"I'm sure Mr. Perfect wouldn't mind slummin' it with you either."

I laugh nervously. He wouldn't. He couldn't possibly.

"I don't think so," I say, sheepishly. "He doesn't see me that way, I'm sure. Men like him go out with women like Bridget."

Gabe stops dead in his tracks and looks at me. Suddenly his beautiful hazel eyes are serious—they look almost black in the darkness. He grabs my wrist and pulls me to him. The heel of my shoe scrapes the sidewalk, and I look up at him, suddenly alarmed.

"Trust me, Ella, a man knows when a guy wants to fuck his wife."

I'm shocked and speechless.

Really? Is that what he saw?

Could he be right?

The thought arouses me. More than I care to admit.

We walk the rest of the way to the car, in silence, in utter silence.

As we're heading back home in Gabe's truck, I lean back on the soft leather of the seat, and close my eyes. I can't seem to get the images of the night out of my mind—Weston's face, his shiny silver cufflinks, Gabe in his sexy buttoned shirt, his hand on my thigh. I feel tense and restless.

And almost as if Gabe can read my thoughts, he slides his hand under the skirt of my dress. I don't protest this time—I want to be touched.

"I can't wait to get you home," he says, his voice hoarse. "I'm going to rip that sweet little dress right off you."

His hand slides further up, and I find myself spreading my legs for him.

Just a little.

"You want it. I can tell."

Gabe always seems to know what I want. He and I have a very sexual relationship...always have. I'm convinced that's one of the reasons our marriage is so strong.

He reaches my sweet spot and strokes me over my panties, and I can't wait to get home.

He's arousing me and he knows it. "You're primed."

He's right. I can't remember ever being so turned on. I just want him to stop on the side of the road and finish me off.

"Thank you, Mr. Perfect," he says with a hint of laughter in his voice.

He is so crass—has always been that way.

"He's probably the one who got you this wet," he points out, his voice playful. "But I'm the lucky one who gets to fuck you."

"Yeah…you are," I say, breathless, and I sneak a peek at the odometer—he's going ten to fifteen miles over the speed limit—he can't possibly go faster without getting us in trouble.

But I almost wish he could.

As soon as we walk up the steps, Gabe presses me against the door and kisses me. I can't quite remember the last time he kissed me like this.

"Hold on, big boy," I whisper, pushing him away, despite the fact that I don't want to. "We still have to pay Caroline."

Caroline welcomes us back with a friendly smile. "How was your night?" she asks.

I'm in no mood for small talk—I'm in the mood to screw my husband. I smile and fumble through my wallet. "Here you go. Thank you. See you next time," I say quickly as I hand her the cash.

"Everything went fine and the girls are fast asleep," she tells us, putting on her jacket and shoes—not fast enough.

And finally, she's on her way back home, across the street.

As soon as the door closes, Gabe grabs my face in his large hands and kisses me—his unshaven face scratches my lips.

His kiss is amazing.

He deepens the kiss. His ragged breathing is the only sound I can hear in the stillness of the night—he wants me. And he'll have me. Gabe never asks—he never needs to—he reads me too well.

His hands travel down my body and find their way under my dress. I run my fingers through his messy hair. I kick off my high heels and lose a few inches. He towers over me and hoists me up against the wall—my head knocks against a glass framed photo.

I reluctantly pull my lips from his. "Why don't we go kiss the girls good night," I whisper, my voice slightly breathless. As much as I'm enjoying this, I don't really want to have sex against the wall, in our entry hall.

He trails kisses down my neck. "We're kind of busy at the moment."

"Just two quick kisses," I insist. "Then you can have your way with me."

He laughs a little. "Oh…I will," he warns me. "Remember… *you* asked for it."

We tiptoe into Chloe's mess of a room, stuffed animals and books scattered everywhere. I kiss her softly on the cheek. Then we're off to Claire's butterfly filled room. Gabe gives her a quick peck on the forehead, and I linger awhile and plant a kiss on her sweet cherubic face. I watch her for a few seconds—she's so sweet.

When I finally make my way out of Claire's room, Gabe is waiting for me, leaning against the wall.

He's taken off his jacket. His hair is ruffled, and his eyes are intense. He scratches his unshaven jaw and looks at me.

He wants me to come to him.

Neither of us say anything as he studies me for the longest time. Finally, he's the first to break the silence. "I'm not sure if I'm in the mood, Ella," he says, the slightest hint of a smile on his lips. "It's kind of late. And I'm kind of beat."

I smile. I know he's joking. Gabe is *always* in the mood.

He's toying with me—teasing me.

I grab a handful of his shirt and start unbuttoning, from the bottom up. "Is that so?" I ask, my voice silky.

He bites his lip, an impish smile on his face. "I have a bit of a headache."

I almost want to laugh. He doesn't fool me for a second. I look him straight in the eye as I start undoing his belt.

He grabs my hand and stops me. "You want it badly, don't you?" His eyes seem darker, even more intense—almost angry. "But I'm not giving it to you. Because I know it's all about him."

My smile fades. I'm really starting to think he's serious, and I'm more than a little peeved. He's so wrong. It isn't just about the other guy—it's about him too. He's the one I want.

"I'm going to bed," he deadpans.

My stomach is suddenly tied up in knots. I didn't want this to happen. I didn't mean to hurt Gabe. It was just a stupid little crush.

"Okay…I admit," I finally manage. "I…I was attracted to him. But you're the one I want to be with." My voice is a little shaky. "Please don't be like this."

He turns to look at me, and his scowl slowly fades.

He starts laughing, and I'm confused. I'm not sure what kind of game he's playing, but I'm not impressed.

He grabs my rear. "Ella," he says to me, pulling me tight against him. "I'm just messing with you. I'll fuck you any which way you want, babe."

Bastard.

I punch him on the chest as hard as I can, but he laughs even harder. "You should have seen your face," he says, still laughing at my expense.

"Why are you always so juvenile?" I sneer at him as I walk to our bedroom where I plop myself on the edge of the bed. "We were having a special moment."

The room is dark. I haven't bothered to turn on the light.

He kneels in front of me. "Oh…is that what it was," he says as he slides a hand under my dress. "I thought we were just going to fuck."

"Well, you know what I mean," I try to explain. "But it doesn't matter now…you've ruined it. Now, I'm the one who's not in the mood."

He laughs out loud. "I can change that," he tells me, standing. He walks over to the bedroom door and locks it. As he makes his way back to me, he eyes me with that playful, intense stare I know so well.

He kneels in front of me again. "I'll get you hot…in no time," he says, his fingers playing with the lace of my panties.

"No, you can't. You're not that powerful." I am so mad at him—I really don't want to give in to him. I try to shimmy away, but he grabs my rear.

He pulls me to him. "I beg to differ." His hands are rough against my skin as he pulls my panties off.

And he's absolutely right.

I want this…so badly.

I lie back and completely give in.

"Now that's more like it," he breathes, burying his head between my legs, under the skirt of my dress. I dig my fingers into his dark, silky curls. And I completely surrender. I want him to kiss me like he has so many times before.

I want him…no one but him.

He starts off slowly, licking me softly, and it feels amazing. I want to get out of this dress. I want to be naked against him. I want to be touched all over, and I want to touch. But this feels too good, and I don't want him to stop.

In no time, my breathing quickens, and I am fully aroused. I rub my hands through his unruly hair as I press my sex against his mouth. He responds and moves his tongue faster.

He's *so* good at this.

I feel my body warm and reach that state of arousal I've been aching for.

My pulse quickens and my orgasm comes swiftly, long and intense. I stifle my moans on the fleshy part of my arm. And I can't believe I've climaxed already.

Gabe keeps going until my moans have settled down.

Finally, he pulls away.

"You don't waste any time, do you?" he teases, always the joker.

I laugh and cover my face with my hand, a little embarrassed.

"Don't be shy. I love it. You made my job real easy."

And I find myself laughing again.

He climbs up on top of me and plants a gentle kiss on my collarbone. I close my eyes and enjoy the state of relaxation I've fallen into, my body languid, heavy.

He studies me—a grin stretches across his face. "But I'm not quite done with you," he teases, my orgasm barely a thing of the past. Before I have a chance to even react, he grabs me hard and flips me over. My face pressed against the bed, I hear the sound of him undoing his pants. He grabs my hips and pulls me up to him. I feel tender and tight, but I still like the feel of him when he sinks into me. As he presses against me, I close my eyes and enjoy him. His hands dig into my hips as his thrusts intensify.

He's gentle tonight.

Despite the fact that I've just climaxed, I still love every second of it. My body responds to him so easily.

He's usually a little rough with me—sometimes I think he's too rough, but tonight he's not rough enough.

"Harder," I moan softly, barely audible.

He feels so good. This is sex—it's what we do. We don't make love…we fuck.

He kicks it up a notch and slams harder into me. The headboard bangs against the wall, again and again.

He feels incredible.

He grabs a fist full of my hair tightly at my nape. "You can't see my face," he breathes against my ear. "Just imagine him. He's the one fucking you right now."

My breath catches.

I'm not shocked by Gabe's words. It's the way he is…a little kinky.

But I can't do it.

I can see Weston's gorgeous face, but I can't imagine him there.

"Don't feel guilty about it," Gabe presses, "just let your imagination go."

I can only see Gabe's face.

I turn my head toward him.

It's dark, and I can't quite see him perfectly. But a flicker of moonlight streaming through the window is enough for me to make out his body pressed against mine—he still wears his black striped button shirt—the image arouses me.

I feel myself getting closer and closer to another climax.

He can sense I'm almost there. "I want to hear you," he says, his voice soft. "I want to hear you scream."

And I let go. I moan louder and louder—louder than I probably should. And I hear the familiar ragged sounds of Gabe's climax, perfectly timed to mine—he has amazing control.

And at that moment, I think my husband might very well be the greatest lover on the planet.

He leans down and kisses me on the shoulder. "I love you, Ella," he whispers, like he always does.

I wake up with a smile on my face, and I'm still wearing my dress. Gabe is stretched out next to me. He's been watching me sleep.

"Stop doing that," I tell him, laughing. "You know I hate that."

"But you're very cute when you sleep." He tucks a strand of hair behind my ear. "Last night was quite a night."

I smile at him. "You know what's ironic and a little funny?"

"What?" he asks, one brow perked up.

"All night long, you were telling me how you were going to rip my dress off," I remind him, smiling coyly, "…and here I am the next morning, still wearing it."

He laughs a little. "But I still showed you a pretty good time, didn't I?"

"Definitely," I say, biting my lip.

"I can take it off now if you want," he offers with that look in his eyes—the man is insatiable.

I'm almost tempted, but giggling and the sweet voices of my girls are in the distance. It won't be long until we see their faces.

We take the girls to the park and go for lunch. Chloe asks me about our night.

"Did you have fun?"

I smile. "We did. We met some nice people and saw a show." I almost tell her about Weston and Bridget, but decide not to—they're already ancient history.

I love spending quality time with my family on Sundays—it's one of my favorite things to do. But today, I'm not quite there—my head isn't anyway. I can't get Weston out of my mind, and I still can't believe how affected I was by him. I barely know him—he hardly gave me anything—didn't talk about himself at all.

Then a light bulb goes off.

That's what it is, I tell myself—he's still a mystery. If I could just know a little more about him, maybe I could finally get him out of my system.

I start typing his name in the search box. I get as far as "Weston H," and his name pops up, and I suddenly feel panicked.

And a little creepy.

I am a stalker after all—a cyber-stalker.

I tell myself I'm being ridiculous and close the browser. As I slam my laptop shut, I vow to stop thinking about the guy—he's just a good looking man I met at a restaurant, for heaven's sake.

That's all he is.

A good looking man with the most incredible eyes I have ever seen.

It's Monday, and I'm so happy to be back at work. I can't wait to talk to Gwen. Gwen's my best friend, and a fellow teacher at my school. She teaches sixth grade. She has to deal with attitude and burgeoning hormones, and she still has a smile on her face every minute of the day—she's fantastic.

My kids seem happy to see me. Lilly, a sweetheart of a girl, with golden curls and bright green eyes, hugs my leg when she sees me.

"Good morning, Lilly. How was your weekend?"

"Great. How was your weekend, Mrs. Mirella?"

"Fantastic," I say with a smile. *And that's an understatement,* I almost want to add.

"I like your earrings today."

"Why, thank you." The fun thing about kids is they notice *everything*—a new haircut, a new dress, a new necklace. I could be wearing a whole new outfit, and Gabe probably wouldn't notice.

Lilly is so sweet, and she speaks like she's just leaped off the pages of a Jane Austen novel—I think it has something to do with her British nanny. But anyway, she's my favorite.

Today, we're learning about the four food groups. I've brought some grocery store flyers from home, and we're cutting out various foods and gluing them onto paper plates. The activity teaches them about nutrition and lets them practice their dexterity. Even at this age, kids today don't get enough manual play—all they seem to do at home is play video games and watch television.

My hands are on the task in front of me, but my brain is full of Weston.

This is getting damn annoying.

I'll never see you again. Please get out of my head.

When the bell finally rings for lunch, I let Wanda take over. Wanda is great. She's one of my kids' moms who volunteers to help out every day for lunch. There was a rumor a while back about her and the principal being a little *too friendly*, but who am I to judge?

I run over to Gwen as soon as I spot her. She looks fabulous, as always, her dark complexion striking against a pale yellow sheath dress. I hug her tightly, my face full of her thick black tresses.

"How was your weekend, sweetie," she asks, all smiles.

"Mind-blowing," I gush, my face lit up like a fourth of July display. I can't wait to dish.

"That good, huh," she says, a coy smile on her lips.

"It's really warm today. You wanna eat on the bench outside?" There is no privacy in the lunch room—twenty or so teachers huddled together at small round tables—conversations usually start to mix.

"Sure," she says as I grab her by the arm—she really has no choice.

I'm thankful it's a wonderful sunny day…I love the month of May.

As we eat our very bland sandwiches, I tell her all about Saturday night—the restaurant, the fabulous couple we met, and the even more amazing sex. Gwen and I are very close. We share almost everything.

"So was it love at first sight with this man?" she teases, her eyes curious.

"Well, I don't know about that, Gwen. Let's just call it lust at first sight. And besides, we are all married, you know…"

She throws a playful, little jab at my shoulder. "Yep. You might want to be careful."

I smile. "You don't have to worry. It was a one-time encounter. We'll never see them again."

"That's probably a good thing. Temptation can be tricky, and you wouldn't want to mess things up with Gabe."

We sit in silence for a beat, both biting into our sandwiches.

"But…you can't help how your mind and body react to someone," she adds knowingly. "Don't feel guilty about it. It's cupid's fault."

"Cupid really messed up this time. I think he sleeps on the job."

She laughs, her big toothy smile *almost* brightens my mood.

"But it's all good," I reassure her...and myself. "Like I said, I'll never see him again." And sadness washes over me...a sadness I hadn't expected.

My students cheer me up—they always do. No matter what's bugging me, their energy is almost contagious—everything is new, something to be discovered and studied.

I feel pretty good, and I've almost all but forgotten about Weston, when Sylvia, our receptionist, walks into my classroom.

I stand, suddenly curious and concerned. When I see Sylvia in my classroom, it usually means something's wrong—issues with one of my kids, disciplinary problems, absence, illness, injury, or worse than all that...lice!

But today, Sylvia has a huge smile on her face—it must be something good.

"Someone's got a secret admirer," she says.

"What?"

"Flowers were delivered for you at the front desk. They're gorgeous."

I'm shocked. Gabe and I did have a great date night, but it wasn't quite worthy of celebratory flowers. Then again, Gabe has sent me flowers before—he's sweet that way. Although it has been a while. I'm quite excited to see them.

"I was going to bring them over, but Michael doesn't want them in the classroom...something about kids' allergies."

"That's fine. I'll fetch them on my way out."

Michael is our principal, and he's a little bit of a stickler for rules. Gwen always jokes about him—she says he has a thing for me. I tell her he's married, and she says, "What does that have to do with *anything?"* Who knows? Perhaps she's right. Maybe he doesn't like the idea of my husband sending me flowers.

When I finally make it to the front office at the end of the day, my mind is blown away. Sylvia wasn't exaggerating—the flowers *are* gorgeous. Gabe has outdone himself—a dozen of the most beautiful roses I have ever laid eyes on—lavender. I didn't even know lavender roses *existed.* But as wonderful as the roses are, the gorgeous vase is what my eyes are drawn too—hand blown glass, a rainbow of colors. I just know I will cherish it for years to come.

"Does Gabe have a brother by chance?" Sylvia jokes. It's a well-known fact that all the ladies at work think my husband is delicious. And Sylvia is probably the one with the biggest crush.

I laugh as I rip the tiny envelope open.

And as my gaze settles on the small card, my stomach drops.

Chapter Five

Love...at...first...sight.

Dear Gabe and Mirella,

We had a wonderful time on Saturday night. We would love to hear from you again.

Weston & Bridget

My eyes glance at the telephone number on the bottom of the card, and I can't believe what I'm seeing. I was not expecting this at all—it's all so absurd.

"What's wrong Mirella? You look like you've just seen a ghost."

"It's just...it's..." I'm at a loss for words.

"Oooh," Sylvia perks up. "Are the flowers from someone else? Do you have a secret admirer?" she asks, curious. Yes, I'm sure she'd love that. Then, she could tell Gabe all about my torrid secret affair and snatch him right out from under me.

With an uneasy laugh, I explain, "It's just a wonderful couple Gabe and I met on Saturday night." I really don't need her starting some unfounded rumors.

She reads the card and her smile fades. "You must have really made quite the impression."

Yes...it appears so.

I've set the flowers carefully on the floor in front of the passenger seat, and I try not to drive too fast or make sudden turns. The girls are quiet in the back and seem a little tired—Mondays are always hard on them.

The card tucked in my pocket consumes me. *Who wrote it?* The handwriting could be female or male, but the words almost sound like Bridget...But how would she know where to reach me? Well, of course, I did tell Weston where I worked.

I don't know what to think.

I don't need this. I don't need this man in my life.

I realize I'm at a crossroads—this is one of those "big moments." There's a fork in the road. If I go one way, my life stays as it is, wonderful and simple. If I choose the other path, my life could possibly get *really* complicated.

I just know it.

But I *really* want to go down that other road...even though I shouldn't.

I'm sitting at a red light, and I have the sudden urge to rip up the card and throw it out the window. That's what I should do. It would be so easy—it's sitting in my jacket pocket.

But I don't.

"I told you," Gabe says, all smugness. "The guy wants to fuck you."

"You don't know that."

The girls are sleeping. We're sitting on our bed. I'm painting my toenails a bright red—I've finally decided to pay a little more attention to my feet. "Maybe it was Bridget's idea. She did seem to have a pretty good time. You guys were chatting away like the best of friends," I point out, realizing that I'm making a lot of sense. "Weston and I barely spoke, or Bridget and I, for that matter. I would hardly call that 'a *wonderful* time.' It was all about you and Bridget."

As I say the words, I realize I should probably have thrown the card out the car window. I need a flirty, gorgeous supermodel lawyer after my husband like I need a hole in my head.

Fuck.

How could I have been so stupid—this isn't about Weston and I—this is about Gabe and Bridget.

She wrote the card.

Panic washes over me. Like I've stumbled on a merry-go-round and am spinning out of control. I can't jump off and can't stop the damn ride. Suddenly, I don't want to ever see Weston or Bridget again.

"I really don't think we should call them," I say, putting on my best all-business face. "I don't think it's a very good idea."

Gabe seems disappointed. "You don't think having fun with a cool couple is a good idea?"

Right. I know where he's going with this—the woman looks like a *Maxim* cover. Gabe always talks me into things. But *not* this time.

"Not *this* couple. Not with the way she was looking at you all night." If he thinks I hadn't noticed, he's sadly mistaken.

He smiles and closes the distance between us. "C'mon…You liked the looks of him too," he points out as he wraps his arms around my waist. "It could be fun," he adds, his expression playful.

"You know exactly what fun like that leads to."

"I'll behave," he promises.

"Oh…it's not you I don't trust…it's her."

"I promise I'll be good…if you promise to be good too."

And we both laugh a little.

Maybe I'm being a little neurotic. I'm always blowing things out of proportion. I'm sure they're not interested in playing naked Twister together. All we're talking about is probably a nice dinner out. And Gabe's right—we are completely anti-social—we need more friends.

Damn, part of me wants this, despite every bone in my body telling me not to.

"I heard about the flowers," Gwen tells me the first chance she gets. "Sylvia told me all about them."

Yep…Sylvia has a big mouth. She's probably told the whole staff.

"They were from that couple you met on Saturday night, right? That gorgeous lust at first sight guy," she whispers.

I can't hide anything from Gwen.

"Yes," I mouth, looking nervously over my shoulder. I'm kind of embarrassed about this silly crush. It is utterly ridiculous—I'm acting like a foolish teenager.

"And they left their number?" she asks, her eyes bright. "Did you call them?"

That Sylvia sure didn't skimp on the details.

"No," I say with conviction, "of course not."

"And I hear they were purple roses. How fun."

"Lavender actually. I didn't even know those existed."

"That's interesting." Her brows arch together, in deep thought. "I wonder what that means."

"What do you mean?"

"Well, red roses mean romantic love," she explains, her big brown eyes staring out into the empty school hall. "And yellow roses mean friendship. But I have no clue what lavender roses mean."

"I don't either." I'd never thought about a hidden meaning in the flowers. But now I'm curious.

"We are *so* Googling this," she shrills.

"Uh…I was kind of hoping to eat my lunch."

She drags me by the arm. Our heels click loudly against the tiled floor. "This is way more important than sustenance, sweetie."

I stand there, chomping on my wrap, admitting to myself the truth—we are shameless—acting like giddy junior high girls. Gwen is definitely guiltier than I am. She's even bouncing up and down a little on her chair, her long tresses dancing. She types in "lavender roses meaning," and in no time, she finds what she's looking for.

"Oh…my…God," she whispers, in slow motion. She turns to me, slack-jawed "Love…at…first…sight." Her words are carefully measured. "That's what it means."

My breath catches. My heart pounds. I feel my face flush. "It… d-does not," I struggle to say as my eyes devour the screen.

"I wonder if they have any clue what they just sent you," Gwen says, eyes still fixed on the screen. "Most people don't realize that colors have special significance when it comes to roses."

"You're right. Probably doesn't mean anything. It's most likely just a coincidence. I'm sure they just like lavender," I add, not quite convincing myself. "I told you he was wearing a purple shirt and tie." This makes it too real. This needs to be a coincidence. A silly one-sided crush is one thing, but a strong mutual attraction is another altogether. This spells t-r-o-u-b-l-e.

Gwen turns to me, wide-eyed. "Are you going to call them?"

I can't. I just can't.

"God, I want to," I confess. "But what about the whole 'I shouldn't mess up what I've got going with Gabe' thing?" I ask, almost pleading her to talk some sense into me and convince me to do the right thing. "I shouldn't, right?"

She bites her lip, pondering my question for a beat. "Yep, you should probably just ignore the flowers," she finally says. "But jeez, that's going to be practically impossible. I know you…"

"You're right."

She twirls a lock of hair and perks up. "But then again…we're probably just talking about dinner here. They're married…you're married. But…you *could* be playing with fire…you just never really know with these things."

I start to wonder if Gwen is living vicariously through me. She wants to see where this goes. It's her own little live-action soap opera. But unfortunately, soap operas always have drama, and the last thing I need in my life is drama.

"So you think I should throw out the card?" I ask, still convinced that if anyone can steer me in the right direction, it's probably her. She truly wants the best for me—she's my best friend.

"Yep, I think so," she says, turning to the screen. "That's what you should do, sweetie." But then, she turns to face me again. "But one thing I do know is," she says, her voice soft. "You'll always wonder if you don't call."

She's absolutely right.

"Let's do it," I tell Gabe as soon as he gets home from work. "Let's call them." As I'm saying the words out loud, I feel like I'm jumping into a cold lake in the middle of October. I can't help but wonder if I'm crazy.

"Are you sure?" he asks, a grin stretched across his face. He's into this as much as I am.

I tell myself I'm being way too dramatic—I've been reading too much into things. We'll probably get together and share a lovely meal. And once the initial attraction fades, we'll get to know each other and become great friends.

"Why not? We always complain we don't have enough couple friends."

"That's true. Are you calling them tonight?" he asks, hanging his jacket.

I'm putting the final touches on supper—spaghetti and meatballs and a garden salad. "Later tonight, after we put the girls to bed."

Claire and Chloe are sitting at the kitchen table, drawing on blank sheets of paper. Gabe walks over to them and kisses them both on the tops of their heads. "I know two little girls who are going to bed early tonight," he teases, with that mischievous smile I love so much.

"We are not," Chloe says with conviction. "No way."

"Yeah, we are *not*," Claire echoes her big sister.

I laugh a little—there's no way these two are going to bed early.

Gabe and I are simply going to have to wait to see how this little soap opera pans out.

Telephone receiver in hand, I open my desk drawer and retrieve the card. I've asked Gabe to give me five minutes—the last thing I need is him hovering over me. I can't believe how nervous I feel. It seems ridiculous that I should feel so on edge. I've done this before…it's just a phone call, for heaven's sake.

As I stare at the gorgeous bouquet of roses on my desk, the line rings repeatedly and relief washes over me—yes, I can leave a message—so much less awkward.

But then, he answers.

Damn.

"Weston Hanson." His tone is very formal and business-like, and I realize I'm probably calling his cell, not his home phone. I'm still reeling from the shock of his voice when he says, "Hello," with slight irritation in his voice.

"Oh...hi..." I stammer. "Hi, Weston, it's Mirella...from the—"

"Hi, Mirella." His voice is soft and sweet, just as I remember it.

"Uh...hi," I hesitate. I'm not sure where to start. "Thank you for the flowers. They're beautiful."

"I'm glad you like them."

"I do." I say, wishing this conversation wasn't so damn nerve-racking. I've got nothing more—my brain is off the clock.

After a few awkward seconds, he's the first to break the dreadful silence. "Bridget and I...were wondering if you'd like to go out with us...again?" he asks, his words hesitant. I can tell he's a little nervous too, and it helps me relax a bit.

"Of course. We would love it," I reply, trying to sound unaffected.

I am *so* affected.

"Great," he says, his voice cheerful. "Do you two like Malaysian food?"

I'm not quite sure how to answer that. I know I like Chinese food, and Thai, but not Japanese. But I've never had Malaysian food, and I don't really want to admit that and confess that I'm just a plain, boring, unworldly suburbanite—I *am* speaking to Mr. Sophisticated & Worldly here.

"We love it," I finally say.

He laughs softly. "You certainly had to think about that one for a while," he teases. "Are you sure you love it? Because—"

"Well, you know...I just haven't had it for a while," I explain. Geez, we've barely said three words, and I'm already making up crap, trying to impress this guy.

I can't start off like this.

"I'm sorry. I've never had Malaysian," I finally admit. I hear laughter on the line, and I am mortified. I feel like such an idiot.

"Well, would you like to try it? It's quite good." His voice is sweet.

"Sure, why not," I say, hoping I'll like it. "As you can probably tell, we haven't been around as much as you." I'm unexpectedly very comfortable talking to him.

"Not a problem. We look forward to introducing you to new things."

Wow.

What does this guy have in mind? I'm curious.

"Do you enjoy art?" he asks.

Now this, I know about, probably not nearly as much as he and Bridget do, but still, I know a few things. "I do. I love a good painting," I tell him before I can take the words back. *I love a good painting?* Who says that? I sound like an imbecile.

He laughs a little. "Well, I love a good painting too, Mirella. We can enjoy them together. I'm sure we'll have a great time."

Is he mocking me? I'm not sure I like that. But his voice is so damned sexy, I don't care.

"Bridget has a friend who has a showing not far from the Malaysian place we like. We thought it could be a fun night."

"Sounds great. We'd love it."

"I know this is short notice," he says, hesitating a little, "but the show is next Saturday...are you available?"

I think about it for a second.

We're not available. We're having dinner with Gabe's parents. But we have dinner with them *all the time*. I'm sure they can take a rain check this *one* time. But...we'll have to make an excuse. We can't just tell them we're blowing them off to go do who-knows-what with the hottest couple we've ever met. That might just sound a little depraved.

"Uh...hello?"

"I-I'm sorry," I stammer. "I just had to think about it for a minute." I twirl a strand of hair—an old nervous habit of mine. "Yes...I believe we're free."

I am such a little tramp.

"Great, sounds like a plan. We'll call you with the details."

"Sure."

I give him my cell number and say a quick good-bye.

And as soon as I hang up, I long to hear his sexy voice again.

"Drop it, Gwen," I snap, between bites of my grilled chicken pita.

Gwen, who is munching on an apple, doesn't seem to care what I think. When she wants to do something, she does it. "Let's go to the office and satisfy your urges," she says playfully.

"Let's not," I deadpan.

"I know you're just dying to know more about him."

She's right. I am.

I down a sip from my neon pink water bottle. "But it would make me feel like such a creepy loser. I'm not Googling him. I told you before."

A smile slowly stretches across her face. "But you want to, don't you?"

I smile.

She knows me too well.

I want to so much…it is literally driving me bonkers.

"C'mon. *Everyone* does it. It doesn't mean you're a creepy stalker."

"Well, maybe a little peek…"

"Atta girl," she squeals.

"What's up?" Sylvia asks as she walks into the lunch room.

"Uh…" I stammer. "Nothing."

"We just have a few things to catch up on in the office," Gwen tells her as she gathers our lunches off the table.

We're glad to see no one is in the office. I gather we wouldn't look very professional Googling crushes. But heck, *everyone* does it…

Gwen has officially taken over. If *she's* the one sitting at the keyboard and doing the actual typing, I can theoretically say I've never cyber-stalked him. She enters his name in the field and lets out an, "Ooh."

There are a lot of entries. I want to take it all in quickly and then sprint off. I am so mortified at myself.

"He's a popular man," she says, clicking on the first link. "Sustainable initiatives to help your bottom line…keynote speaker… Dr. Weston Hanson," she reads out loud. "He's a doctor? Did you know that?"

No I didn't. What?

"Are you sure you've got the right guy?" I ask, confused.

She clicks on the photo attached to the article, and my heart does a little cartwheel. It's definitely him, dressed in a sleek suit, looking *delicious.*

"Yep...that's him."

"He is...gorgeous," Gwen gushes. "I totally get the obsession now."

I am *not* obsessed. Well, maybe a little. A *little wee* bit.

"Geez...the guy's got about a million letters after his name," Gwen says, still clicking away like a wild badger. "Practically the whole alphabet...a Bachelor and Masters of Architecture, a PhD..."

Oh...that kind of doctor.

"He's really smart," I add, like I actually know the guy.

"Yeah," she concurs. "Went to MIT...Harvard."

God...this guy is *so* out of my league.

Which is fine.

Because I certainly don't have any intentions.

It's just a *little* crush.

Okay...a *big* crush...I admit it.

"Dr. Weston Hanson, in collaboration with MIT engineering students," Gwen goes on, seemingly proud of her very efficient cyber-stalking skills, "is overseeing a mentorship research program on applying solar energy technology in loft development building."

"That's cool," is all I can think to say. I want to stop her, but I can't help wanting to know more.

"Building a Greener Future," she goes on. "Sustainable Urban Development. Panel of Experts. Weston Hanson, Architect, President and CEO, Hanson and Hersch Developments..."

She's clicking away at lightning speed—the woman should have been a court transcriber. She finally lands on a Wikipedia page. I lean in to get a closer look. I can't help but be curious—the guy's got his own Wikipedia page, for crying out loud. What stands out to me is the bit about him entering college at the tender age of twelve.

"He was some kind of kid prodigy," Gwen points out the obvious. "His IQ was tested at one-sixty-eight," she adds. "Is that high?"

"I would say so. Einstein's was estimated to be in the one-sixties or one-seventies."

"Incredible."

"I think we've seen enough," I finally manage to say, feeling a little ridiculous. I know *way* too much about him. I will live in constant fear throughout dinner—he might know I've cyber-stalked him if I spill something I know about him that I shouldn't.

I start to feel nauseated. "Let's stop, okay?"

"Oh…look at this. He's on the Board of The Children's Hospital of Chicago," she reads aloud, clicking away. "Gorgeous…brilliant… and altruistic too. This guy's a gem."

I know.

"Ooooohhh," she swoons. "Look at this. He apparently donated five million dollars to some Cancer Research Center…*five million dollars*," she repeats for emphasis, her eyes practically bulging out of her head.

Wow. I can't wrap my mind around that much money.

"Gorgeous…brilliant…altruistic…and *rich*," she gushes.

Enough. Enough.

"Okay, enough already Gwen. I think we know all there is to know. This is really reaching the point of cyber-obsession."

"What are you girls looking at?" Sylvia chimes in. I didn't even hear her come in. I can't help but wonder if she's spying on us.

"Oh…nothing," Gwen tells her, quickly clicking off.

"You girls look like you're up to something."

"Of course we were," I joke. "Aren't we always?"

Sylvia smiles and eyes us suspiciously.

"I love your skirt," I add, trying to distract her. Anyone who knows Sylvia knows a conversation about fashion will do the trick.

"Thanks," she says, beaming. "I had an impossible time trying to find a top to go with it…"

And she goes on.

And I barely hear a word.

All I can think about is Weston.

Chapter Six

I want to see you again.

"Did you eat anything at all today?" Gabe asks. "I saw you make lunch for the kids, but I haven't seen you eat anything."

He knows me too well. He knows I can't eat when I'm nervous.

"I've been sustaining on lemonade and gum all day," I confess.

He shakes his head a little. "Bad girl." He reaches over me, opens the glove compartment, one eye still on the road, and hands me a granola bar.

I take it but have no desire to eat it. "I can't eat."

"Why are you so on edge? They're just people. Just relax and have a good time. It'll be fun."

I'm sure it will, but still, I can't seem to calm my nerves. I fiddle with the hem of my dress—I've worn the quintessential *dinner with friends* piece—the LBD—or "little black dress" for the layman. The chunky, amber, Bohemian necklace I picked out to accentuate the dress is nice. It seems like a fitting outfit for dinner at a Malaysian place and an art showing. I was kind of going for that *I just threw this on* look, but really…I spent a gazillion hours putting it together—like I was prepping to be on the cover of *Vogue*.

"You look nice, by the way," Gabe tells me, and I light up. I was hoping he'd noticed.

"Thank you."

"Nice dress," he says, looking me over a second too long.

"Watch the road," I say, a smug smile on my face.

"I just have one problem with it. I don't think it's short enough."

I laugh. "It falls just above the knee. How short do you want it?"

"Shorter."

I smile, catching my reflection in the side mirror. "I'm not trying to be sexy, just sophisticated."

"Well, if you're trying *not* to be sexy, you've failed miserably."

I laugh. My chances of getting lucky tonight are probably pretty good.

We park near the restaurant, and I wobble in my heels a little. Why does restaurant dining always involve heels? I could have worn more sensible shoes, but Bridget is likely to show up in stilettos, and then everyone will tower over me. With the four inch heels, I stand at a proud five-foot-eight.

There's no sign of Weston and Bridget when we get to the restaurant.

"Let's go in," Gabe says, resting his hand on the small of my back. "They're probably inside."

The warm atmosphere is cozy. The walls are lined with striking rosewood paneling set against stained glass windows. The filtered sunlight creates a warm glow.

The hostess welcomes us and we tell her we're meeting friends. She informs us they haven't arrived.

Surprisingly, I don't care. I just want to stand here and take in the room. Large paper lantern lighting fixtures hang at varying heights, casting a soft orange light. I stretch my neck to peek into the dining room—people enjoying their meals, seated at white linen covered tables. I spot booths in the back—they look so fun and comfy. I really want to sit in a booth—I'm like a child discovering a new playground.

I love this place.

"Check out those booths," I tell Gabe. "Don't they look cool?"

He laughs. "You're such a kid."

I hear the doorbell clang, and I turn to see Bridget and Weston enter. He's holding the door for her, and they both smile warmly at us. He looks very sleek in a cream-colored fitted suit and flashy orange shirt.

And suddenly, the room gets a few degrees hotter. I've never seen a man in a suit like that, and he certainly makes it work. I'm so busy looking at Weston, I barely notice Bridget who happens to be wearing a little black dress too, under her cream-colored pea coat.

"You look fantastic," she says, kissing me on the cheek.

"You too," I reply. I'm sure she hears that a *lot.*

Weston speaks to the hostess, and she takes our jackets and leads us to the dining room, to our table. Weston pulls a chair for Bridget, and Gabe does the same for me—apparently, the boy is learning some manners. I smile up at him.

"Booth next time," he says.

"Next time," I say, a little disappointed.

Weston looks at us, a quizzical expression on his face. "Would you rather sit in a booth?"

"No, we were just saying...they look cozy."

He looks over. "Yes. Actually, they do. I'm sure we can make that happen."

The hostess smiles at us warmly as she walks us over to one of the booths. Like all the others, it's an enclosed space—a little room of its own. Plush orange patterned cushions are meticulously lined up against the rosewood benches.

I slide easily along the wood bench and set my purse beside me.

Bridget smiles at Weston and signals him to slide in and sit across from me—the woman sure likes to share her man.

I'm not complaining.

She gingerly sits next to him and tilts her head, her blond curls bouncing slightly against her shoulder.

The server hands us our menus and takes our drink orders. Bridget and Gabe fall into conversation—and it flows so smoothly and effortlessly. There doesn't seem to be tension between them, like there is between Weston and me.

Bridget asks me how my week was, and I tell her all about my rambunctious kids.

"But at least I'm not dealing with accused murderers, like you do," I add, a pathetic attempt at conversation.

She laughs. "I think a class full of five-year olds is a lot scarier."

I like her…I like her sense of humor.

Bridget tells us about the menu items and gives us her recommendations. I tell her I'm having what she's having. I realize I'm trying to emulate her a little, but who wouldn't?

I bury my face in my menu, checking out the dessert choices. I look up at Weston. He smiles and opens his menu.

I was right—the booth is cozy…real cozy—it's very intimate.

The atmosphere is charged.

And sensual.

I don't think Weston could have picked a sexier restaurant if he tried, and I wonder for a second, if he did so on purpose.

Of course not. Of course he didn't.

Get your mind out of the gutter.

Obviously, I really don't mind sitting across from Weston—there are worse things to look at. I take in the details of him for a second—crisp orange button shirt, tiny black fish dotting his tie, a silver-trimmed, amber tie clip, and matching oval cufflinks. It's all in the details, they say. He may be the most stylish man I have ever met.

My fingers trace the edge of my own silver-trimmed amber pendant, a larger version of his cufflinks.

We look at each other, but we don't say a word.

I finally summon the courage to speak. "I like your cufflinks."

"Thank you. I like your necklace," he says, his gaze intense. "We make quite the pair."

Oh…I wish.

"Did you purposely color coordinate with the restaurant?" I tease, looking up at the soft orange light fixtures above us.

He laughs, looking up. "No. It's purely coincidental." His laugh is soft…beautiful.

"Well, you look very nice." Geez…is this my attempt at flirting? Well, if it is, it is a feeble attempt at best.

"Thank you. You look quite nice yourself."

I smile at him, and I suddenly feel shy.

"I confess," he says. "I really can't take the credit for my appearance."

"Bridget picked it out?"

"Actually, my stylist did."

Wow...the man has a stylist. I thought only movie stars had stylists.

"Trust me," Bridget chimes in. "He needs her."

I hadn't realized Bridget had been listening, and I'm a little embarrassed—because of the despicable flirting. But then again, *she* has been flirting shamelessly with my husband too.

"He is such a nerd. He has no clue when it comes to style."

"She said she wouldn't be seen with me in public if I didn't hire a stylist," Weston explains.

"You should have seen the looks of him," Bridget tells us between giggles. "He used to wear these horrid tweed jackets."

I find her words a little harsh. Geez...give the guy a break. Weston seems mildly uncomfortable—she's probably shared too much, and I get the feeling she does that a lot.

"Well, the stylist did a great job."

He blushes a little—which makes him even sexier.

God help me.

The truth is...he fascinates me.

He first comes off as hard, sleek, cool, and collected, but underneath the armor hides a sweet, sensitive introvert. I shift my gaze to Bridget—bubbly and outgoing. They are perfectly suited to each other—she's the yin to his yang.

Gabe looks over my menu and decides he's having the beef. He suggests I try the red curry chicken. I'm not sure why he always feels the need to order for me. It's probably about him wanting to eat my food too and making sure I'll order something he likes.

The server takes our orders and leaves us. Bridget digs for something in her flashy purse, creating a lull in the conversation.

"Thank you again," I tell them. "Thank you for the beautiful roses." I know I've thanked Weston already, but I feel the need to thank Bridget as well.

She smiles, pulling out a tissue from her purse. "It was our pleasure. You should really thank Weston. He was the one on top of it."

I'm thrilled to hear it. I don't know why. Just the thought of him picking the flowers and…

"You wrote the card?"

He pulls out the familiar small plastic bottle from his suit jacket. "Yes, I wrote the card," he informs me, his expression neutral, "or rather, I dictated it. The woman at the flower shop wrote the card." He rubs his hands with disinfectant.

He's put on his "all-business" face again.

Which is fine.

I decide to drop the subject.

But…

Just one more thing.

"The flowers she chose were beautiful. Please thank her on my behalf."

He smiles and looks over at Bridget and Gabe who are discussing the restaurant's furniture…I think—I'm not sure—I'm not really listening to them.

"I chose them," he corrects me, his eyes are dark and absolutely devastating. "I chose the flowers."

This is where I should offer a simple thank you, but my intuition tells me we're having a between-the-lines conversation.

I bite my lip and after a long, intense moment I ask, my voice quavering, "Why lavender?"

He doesn't answer me. He doesn't even look at me. Instead, he fiddles with his place setting, readjusting the cutlery just so.

The man is driving me insane.

I seriously start to think he might be missing some synapses in his brain, particularly in the lobe responsible for social interaction skills. Or something like that…

And just as I look away, he says, so softly, I barely hear him. "You know why."

The server comes over to top off our water glasses, and my head is spinning. Suddenly my senses are heightened. I'm overwhelmed by the clatter of dishes and utensils and the buzz of the conversations around the room.

I'm smothered, suffocated, trapped in this wooden hell of a booth.

I can't breathe.

And I seriously worry I'm about to have a full-on panic attack—I'm very prone to them. I close my eyes and suck in a deep breath. I nudge Gabe who's still in conversation with Bridget and completely oblivious.

"I need to get out. I need to go to the washroom."

He slides out, not even taking his eyes off Bridget—I might as well not even be in the room. I glance at Weston as I leave the table.

He's noticed my sudden panicked reaction.

He looks mortified.

I've overreacted. I press my back against the cold hard tiles of the bathroom stall. I'm safe here, relaxed.

Away from the situation.

But something is happening between Weston and me.

And it's scaring me to death. I've never faced this kind of situation before. Yes, I've found some men attractive, but never like this. I'm simply not equipped to handle this. I vow to keep my composure around him, from now on.

All business—no more flirting, no more between-the-lines conversations.

Surprisingly, the rest of dinner flows smoothly. We talk about our children, our families, and our lives. I bore them with stories of my Irish Catholic upbringing. Bridget can't believe Gabe and I have been together for eighteen years, and I'm shocked to learn Bridget is actually a year older than Weston.

Weston and Bridget met in Boston. He was doing his Masters, and she was a freshman. Despite this, he was actually a year younger than her—he had skipped six grades.

"A real mathematical prodigy," Bridget comments. Weston's mouth curves up at the corners as he looks away, and I can't quite tell if he likes the attention or not.

"He was such a cute sweet little thing. I absolutely had to corrupt him."

"Well, I'm sure he didn't mind," Gabe chimes in.

Weston smiles a little, still not quite looking at us.

"Then I fell in love," she says, looking over sweetly at Weston. "I never thought I would fall for a nerd."

Well if he was a nerd, he surely isn't anymore, I think, eyeing the clean smooth lines of his build and fantastic head of hair.

"I bet you liked the jocks," Gabe ventures, flirting with her.

"Oh yes," she tells him.

"You would have liked me," he says, completely serious.

He is *so* arrogant.

"For sure," she laughs.

I decide to change the subject—enough with the flirting already. "So tell us about your kids."

Yes, you are married with kids, remember?

A smile lights up her face. "Well, Ashton is just like his father, a real whiz." She rolls her eyes, like this trait irritates her somehow. "They spend hours building things, gadgets."

"It looks like you have *two* nerds on your hands," I tease.

She laughs. "I do."

Weston smiles in my direction, taking it all in stride.

"And Lizzie's my little girly-girl. We do everything together… shopping, shows, mani-pedis."

"Sounds fabulous," I say, realizing I've never gone for a mani-pedi with my girls. We should try it out sometime.

"But Weston spends a lot of time with her too. He's such a good dad." Somehow, that's easy to believe. He seems tenderhearted. I'm not sure why—maybe it's just intuition.

"When she was little, they'd play tea party for hours."

I smile at the vision—absolutely adorable. I look over at him, and he averts his gaze, a sweet smile on his face. I'm not sure he likes all this talk about him.

"Our two girls love to have tea parties too," I tell them, redirecting the focus. "We usually have iced tea and animal crackers."

So the conversation goes, the usual small talk—nothing electrifying. But somehow, there seems to be a charge in the air. My intuition is telling me we should all be very careful.

Learning so much about Weston and Bridget, and the reality of their lives, makes whatever happened between Weston and I seem insubstantial.

Which is a good thing.

A *great* thing.

The gallery décor is very "urban country"—exposed brick walls, large reclaimed wood beams, ultra modern chrome light fixtures, and white walls accentuated with bursts of color as far as the eye can see. Wine is flowing, and conversations are filling the room. I've dressed appropriately—it seems almost everyone is wearing black. I spot a woman in red, and my gaze is drawn to her, like the focal point in a painting.

The artwork is incredible—rich colors, impressionist style, splatters and diluted washes mixing together beautifully. It's messy and loose and somehow breathtaking. This is what true talent is, I muse, standing next to a painting of an old man pulling a rickshaw, the sun beaming hard on his back. I'm in awe. Gwen and I take a watercolor class on Saturday mornings, but I am nowhere as good as this, and I realize I never will be. It's an innate talent I just don't have. I try too hard, according to my teacher. I need to loosen up, she says. Apparently, it comes from the soul.

Bridget spots her friend and practically runs to her. "Hi, Simone. These are fantastic," she says, hugging her delicately, trying not to spill her wine glass.

"Thanks for coming, Bridget," Simone says. "Where's Weston?"

"Somewhere," Bridget tells her, and we all turn and scan the gallery.

He's standing there by his lonesome, staring at a piece, glass of wine in hand, looking very introspective.

"That suit is fabulous on him," Simone says without reserve. Obviously these two are close.

"I know…right?" Bridget agrees with a sly smile. "And lucky me, I get to take it off tonight," she adds, laughing.

They both giggle like junior high school girls, and I want to vomit a little.

Yeah, I'm jealous.

I'm jealous she gets to take that suit off. There is something fundamentally wrong with me, I realize as I gaze at the colorful paintings lining the walls.

"Oh my God," Simone suddenly blurts out. "Who is he talking to? He's gorgeous."

I peel my eyes off the paintings and turn my attention back to Weston. He and Gabe seem to be in deep conversation. What could they be talking about?

Bridget laughs under her breath. "That's Gabe, a friend of ours," Bridget answers. "Mirella's husband," she adds. "I'm sorry I haven't introduced you two."

Simone offers her hand, and I notice how beautiful she is, European features, dark complexion, long silky black hair.

"Well, your husband is gorgeous," is all she says—very forward, in my opinion.

"Uh…thank you," I stammer a little.

It isn't long before Bridget ends up on Gabe's arm, walking through the gallery, introducing him to people. He's so friendly and charismatic—he's enjoying every second of it. I notice how, occasionally, he puts a hand gently on the small of her back. It doesn't bother me too much—he's a very touchy-feely person. And I notice how he whispers things in her ear, and she laughs out loud.

I'm standing next to Weston. We've been walking together, discussing the art—which pieces stand out and which pieces evoke emotion. He seems genuinely interested, and I discover he's quite the art aficionado, unlike Gabe who seems more interested in the women and their sleek little black dresses than the art.

I tell Weston all about the watercolor class Gwen and I take on Saturday mornings.

"We're the youngest there. We're in a seniors' class."

A grin stretches across his face. "How did you manage that?"

I smirk at him. "Oh…I have my contacts. I like it, but it's kind of strange."

"You don't like seniors?"

"I didn't say that."

"You'll age too one day," he points out.

I stare at him, mildly irked.

"And those big, beautiful brown eyes of yours *will* get droopy."

My heart does a little skip. He thinks I'm "beautiful."

Well, not really.

He likes my eyes. Too bad about the rest of my face—my teeth and my horrid freckles. "Oh...the horror."

"Don't worry. I'm sure your husband will always love you."

The mention of Gabe brings me back to reality.

I lighten the conversation and tell him all about Cecilia. Cecilia is an eighty-ish year old woman in our art class who's completely deaf, or so the word goes.

"But I swear, sometimes she is totally listening to our conversation. When Gwen and I start talking about anything juicy, like sex, her little wrinkled face seems to perk up."

Weston laughs. "Be a little considerate. Give the old lady something to live for."

We both laugh, and I instinctively turn away.

"Why do you do that?"

"Do what?" I ask, confused.

"Cover your mouth every time you smile."

"Oh, I don't know." I shrug, not quite looking at him. "Nervous habit, I guess."

"You should really knock that off," he says simply. And I'm amused by his choice of words. "Knock that off" doesn't sound like something Mr. Prim and Proper would say.

"How old were you when you and Gabe met?" he asks, a hint of a smile. "Eighteen years together...you don't seem old enough."

He's been doing the math.

"Are you trying to determine my age, Mr. Hanson? You know it's very rude to ask a woman her age."

He laughs. "I wasn't asking." I love his laugh. It's soft, but still infectious.

"We were seventeen. He was the popular basketball player, and I was the new girl...I was terrified."

"And he was your knight and shining armor, I gather."

I smile, remembering those days so long ago. "He sure was."

We stand silent for a while, looking at the pieces displayed on the wall…or maybe *pretending* to look.

"Thirty-five," he says with a coy smile. "You look younger."

God, I love this man.

"And how old are you?" I ask, surprised I don't know, despite all my cyber-stalking.

"Isn't it rude to ask?" he teases.

"Oh…it's fine for a woman to ask a man, just not the other way around."

"Seems like a double standard."

We move along the narrow hall, toward the back display.

"You still haven't answered my question," I point out.

"I was born in nineteen seventy-five."

Great, now he has me doing math in my head. *Um…let's see… it's 2012…*After a long, rather embarrassing moment, I venture a guess. "Thirty-seven?" I ask, not sure I've calculated right—I've never been great at math.

He gives me one of his trademark make-you-melt smiles. "Not quite…I'm still thirty-six."

Damn.

We keep moving toward the end of the gallery and find ourselves in a small room—just the two of us.

I press my palm against the support beam, trying to steady myself since I'm suddenly a little light-headed. Looking down at my glass, I decide to ease up on the wine.

"Have you two ever broken up in *all* those years?" he asks out of the blue, catching me off guard.

"No," I reply, with a certain sense of pride.

"Was he your first love?" He seems very preoccupied with my relationship with Gabe, but I don't mind the questions.

"Yes."

We are clearly no longer looking at art.

He walks toward me. "Have you ever been with anyone else?"

His line of questioning has now *officially* gone too far. "I'm sorry," I blurt out as I try to pull myself away from him. The beam presses against my back. "That's a very personal question."

He turns from me. "I apologize."

But I don't want him to turn away. "No. He's the only one."

He turns back to face me. "Really?"

I resent the implication in his tone. The walls have been torn down, and the small talk is officially over. "I have never cheated on him," I snap. "And I've never wanted to."

He closes the distance between us. "You're telling me you've *never* been attracted to another man."

I can feel the heat from his body, and I can smell him, a delicious clean woodsy scent. And I'm seriously concerned I'm going to faint. I close my eyes and take a deep breath. "I didn't say that. I'm married, not dead," I say, trying to lighten the mood.

He smiles.

My heart is sprinting, and I find myself staring at him.

And wanting him.

"I just have never felt a connection with another man…before."

"Before?" he asks quietly. He knows too well what I'm trying to say.

I turn my head away. I can't look at him.

He inches closer. "I want to see you again," he breathes against the shell of my ear.

I can't do this.

I so desperately want to. But I can't. I can't do this to Gabe.

I turn to look at him. His beautiful eyes are fixed on me, threatening to melt my resolve.

Chapter Seven

Suddenly, it all falls together.

I steady myself against the beam. I feel like I'm about to fall. This moment…this moment is key. I can't fuck up my life. I can't let him get to me.

"I'm s-sorry, Weston," my voice cracks as my gaze settles on the vibrant art on the wall. "I won't cheat on Gabe, not under any circumstances." I'm trying to sound strong and business-like, but in reality, I'm so weak, I could break apart any second.

"Mirella, that's not what I'm asking," he says, his voice soft. "I'm very well aware you will not cheat on your husband."

I will myself to look at him. "Then…what…are you…asking?" My words are staggered, lost between labored breaths.

His eyes on my mouth unsettle me. I wonder if he sees my lips trembling. My whole body is shaking.

After a long pause, he speaks again with great effort, his words measured. "I want to meet with you and discuss something," he says, but does not elaborate.

"Discuss what?" I scoff, even more confused. "Let's discuss it right now." Maybe *he* can read minds, but I certainly can't.

"This is neither the time nor the place," he says, his eyes darting from me to the couple beside us, "the atmosphere is already too charged."

What in the heavens is this beautiful man speaking of? I'm dying of curiosity. "What is it about?" I ask, desperately wanting an answer.

"We'll discuss it at a more convenient time, just the two of us."

This sounds like a very bad plan to me. I bite my lip, mulling it over for a second or two. My stomach feels like lead…if he could only tell me. "Are you planning to get into my skirt under the pretense of this oh-so-mysterious 'meeting'?" I ask, my voice still unsteady. My crack at humor is a poor attempt to cover my emotions—he can surely see how messed up I really am.

He laughs his soft infectious laugh. "No. I promise I will *not* seduce you," he vows with his sexy trademark grin. "Well, not on purpose anyway." Oddly, this conversation doesn't seem to faze him—he's so cool. Meanwhile, I'm a ball of nerves, bouncing off the walls.

"I don't trust you," I confess. The fact is…I don't trust most men, especially those who look like Greek gods decked out in ten-thousand-dollar suits. "You'll take me to this wonderful place and somehow manage to kiss me."

He cocks his head, a huge smile on his face. I am amusing him thoroughly.

"And if you kiss me, Weston…I'll completely fall apart."

His smile fades. He is suddenly without words and looks at me—at my eyes, at my mouth.

He wants to kiss me.

I want him to kiss me. I'm frozen under his stare.

But he doesn't kiss me.

He jolts back in a sudden move, and I jump a little. Relief washes over me. A disquieting tingle runs up my spine at the thought of what I almost did. I know I would have kissed him.

"This is what we're going to do." He is all business. The walls have been built up again. "You will meet me at my office," he explains and then pauses for a moment, "…or I can come to you if you wish."

I listen to him, not saying a word.

"We'll meet in a neutral environment, and I promise I won't lay a finger on you."

He makes it all sound so formal, and I wonder if I'm reading too much into things again. We set the meeting for Tuesday at five o'clock. I ask him again what it's all about, but he refuses to tell me.

Finally, I pull away, still unnerved and determined to stay as far away from him as possible for the rest of the evening. I find Gabe buried in conversation, three beautiful women draped all over him. Not one or two…but *three*—that's Gabe for you. I lace my arm around his in an effort to find comfort…protection. Or maybe I'm just trying to mark my territory. I'm not sure. All I know is I need him right now. I need everything to be normal again—just us, Gabe and Mirella, like it's always been.

But despite being stuck to Gabe like gum in a kid's hair, I am intensely aware of Weston. He's far, yet he feels so close. I try not to look at him, but I see him from the corner of my eye, being pulled into conversation, drifting away, and back again…a reluctant extrovert…a true lone wolf.

Almost *three whole days* until I see him again, and he explains what this is all about.

I may very well die of curiosity.

As we walk back to the truck, Gabe takes my hand in his.

I have to tell him. I can't hide this from him.

I stop in my tracks, dead in the middle of the sidewalk. Gabe eyes me with a "what the hell" expression.

"I should tell you something," I say, my words heavy. I don't know exactly how to go on. I know he'll be angry.

I pull my clammy hand from his, my heart beating a little faster than normal. I'm scared he'll go into one of his little fits. Gabe has a short fuse. He can be the sweetest man, but is also very volatile. When something sets him off, watch out—random objects will go flying.

"What is it, Ella?" he asks, concern written all over his face.

"Weston and I…" I trail off. I just can't seem to utter the words.

I catch a brief glimpse of fear on Gabe's face—pure, unfiltered terror.

"Oh no…no," I'm quick to say. "It's just…we're meeting on Tuesday at his office."

"What?" He glares at me, confused. "Why? About what?"

"I don't know," I admit, knowing he won't be happy with this answer.

"What do you mean?" he snaps, his mouth a hard line. "You don't know?"

"He wouldn't tell me," I explain, my words strained. "He wouldn't tell me. It's all very mysterious. I wish I knew."

He grabs my wrist and pulls me to him. "I don't like this at all, Mirella. I've seen the way he looks at you."

I reach out to him, his unshaven jaw is rough against my fingers. "He told me it will be a formal meeting," I reassure him, not quite convinced myself.

We both stand there, in eerie silence, for what seems like an eternity.

Finally, he sucks in a long breath. "Well, I trust you, Ella. I always have," he says as he starts walking away.

I scurry up to him and lace my hand in his. "Thank you."

"The guy's kind of weird," he says as we reach his sleek black truck.

"I know."

I rest my hand on the car handle, waiting for the beep of the key fob, but it doesn't come.

Gabe wraps his arms around my waist, and I turn to face him. "Not so fast," he says and he leans in to kiss me.

My lips open against his, and our tongues tangle. Despite the coolness of the night, all I can feel is Gabe's heat—his warm arms around me, his scorching kiss. The kiss feels amazing, but as great as it is, I feel inhibited, standing there in a public lot. I try to tear myself away, but his kiss is wild.

"Gabe," I breathe, pulling away from him. "Let's wait till we get home."

"I don't want to wait," he breathes into my neck, warming my cool skin. "I want you *now*."

He's arousing me. I admit it to myself, but there's no way we're having sex against his truck in a public parking lot.

He reaches in his pocket, and I hear the beep I had been waiting for. But oddly, I don't move.

He trails the tip of his finger along the side of my face, his intense gaze not leaving me. "Get in the back."

"I...I don't think—"

He slides his hand beneath the hem of my little black dress, slowly up high, between my thighs. "Get in the back," he breathes into my ear. "I want to fuck."

I'm speechless...and really turned on.

I admit it—I like dirty talk. And Gabe knows this all too well.

I open the back door and hop in the truck, do as I'm told, and slide in the back.

He joins me and presses his weight between my legs, a hint of cologne filling my nostrils. His tongue finds mine. His kiss his wild—it wanders—traveling from my mouth, to my chin, my cheeks, all over.

He and I haven't done this kind of thing in a while—sex in public. I suppose we're not completely in the open, but it's certainly public enough for me. I feel so wanted.

The rough sensation of his unshaven jaw sends chills through me. The warmth of him heats me, and I can barely feel the coolness of the night. He's all over me—his hands sliding up my thighs under my dress, his mouth on my neck. I reach for his belt.

It's fun to act like a wild teenager, without a care in the world, when you're really a respectable, suburban working mom.

I want him inside me.

And I suddenly don't care about the public lot, or any person walking by for that matter. His lips travel down the edges of my face, and he lingers there, biting gently—his prickly whiskers brushing against my skin. I love the sensation of him against me. My fingers are tangled in his unruly hair, and my legs are spread wide against him. He slides his hand up my thigh and reaches for my panties.

He pulls away and slides my panties off slowly...leisurely. I can barely see his sly smile in the darkness, but I know it's there—he's such a tease.

Finally, as he pulls my panties over my strappy heels, he whispers, "What do you want me to do to you?"

So many things...

"Nothing," I whisper with a coy smile. "I'll take it from here."

I move up against him and climb on top of him. He leans back against the seat with a delicious smile on his face.

I straddle him, filled with anticipation. As I kiss him, I slip his belt out of its buckle in a swift move and free him from his pants. I take him in my hand. He's hot and hard for me.

He closes his eyes.

And I take him inside me.

Where he belongs.

Chapter Eight

We just clicked, didn't we?

Well, I'm still alive.

I haven't died of curiosity, after all.

I slide one leg over the other, mildly tempted by the bar wedged in the middle console of the town car. I'm not much of a drinker at all, but my nerves are shot. I take in the interior of the car—sleek taupe leather interior, television screen and satellite radio, dark windows.

Weston has arranged for a car to pick me up after school. I've sent the girls with Carla, a mother at the school who lives near our house. Chloe was beyond excited because Carla's daughter Maya is one of her best friends at school.

I grab a water bottle from my briefcase, wondering if I'm properly dressed for the upcoming events. I am wearing my usual "school uniform"—a pencil skirt, a white blouse, and tortoise framed glasses. I spot my reflection in the window and regret not taking the time to put in my contact lenses—I look positively librarian-ish.

I've brought my laptop and my notebook, not knowing what to expect. Not knowing what to expect is kind of exciting, but extremely annoying as well.

I spend the hour-long ride trying to figure out what this meeting might be about, fantasizing about Weston and wondering what he might be wearing today. I could be making the most of my brain cells and coming up with a genius business idea—a solution for dripping juice bottles, a kid's jacket zipper which is actually easy to zip up, or something like *Baby Einstein*—that was genius—I wish I had thought of that. I could be coming up with a revolutionary business idea right at this moment and become rich and famous.

But no…I prefer thinking about Weston's arms in a fitted button shirt.

We all make our choices.

Edward, Weston's driver, a red-cheeked, cheerful man in his fifties, drops me off in front of Hanson & Hersch Developments, Inc. Edward and I share an awkward moment when he sprints out to open my door, and I'm practically outside the car already when he reaches me.

"Let me take care of that for you, Miss."

I smile up at him, slipping out of the car. He addresses me as "Miss," not the dreaded "Ma'am." I like him already. I just really don't know how it's done—this way of life the one percent are so used to.

"I'm sorry. I've never had a driver before," I confess. "This is all new to me."

"It's easy…really," he replies with a cheeky smile. "Just let me wait on you, hand and foot."

I laugh. "I'm the one who's usually waiting on others. This is going to take some getting-used-to."

He laughs as he closes the car door behind me. "Call me Edward," he says, offering his hand.

I smile up at him and shake his hand. "You can call me Mirella… or Miss, if you prefer," I add with a playful smile. "I like the sound of that. It makes me feel young."

"Miss Mirella, it is," he says with a mischievous smile, his cheeks a deeper shade of crimson.

Hanson & Hersch Developments, Inc. is an impressive structure—about twenty stories high, slick and all glass. I shield my eyes with my hand, stretching my gaze to the top—the glass reflects the rays of the sun, and the effect is blinding.

I'm a little intimidated when I enter the lobby and make my way to the receptionist. I have the sensation of having traveled in time, and it seems I find myself in 2050—modern, curvaceous shapes surround me—futuristic chrome lighting fixtures hang from the ceiling, and everything is white. The walls are white. The curvy plastic chairs, which look extremely uncomfortable, are also white. The weird bean-shaped front desk is...yes...white.

I hate white...it is so sterile. I want color. I want warmth.

The receptionist, an ultra-skinny hipster type, greets me with a smile. I introduce myself and inform him Mr. Hanson is expecting me. The receptionist speaks into a mouthpiece as he taps away at a computer. "A Mrs. Keates is here to see you. Can I send her up?"

"Yes, Mr. Hanson," he says. "Yes, that's great."

"Mr. Hanson would like to come down and greet you," he informs me, and directs me to take a seat on one of the uncomfortable-looking chairs.

I sit down, surprised to find the chair to be extremely comfortable. I look around. This is not what I had envisioned. I've pictured Weston in his office before, dressed in his sleek suit, surrounded by colleagues, making important business decisions. I've always pictured the walls mahogany, the furniture stuffy, the lamps Tiffany, and the lighting dark. But yes, this fits Weston better.

This is very "Weston."

I spot Weston right as he rounds the corner. He's all smiles and gorgeous as usual. I jump to my feet, giddy as a school girl.

Settle down.

Right...not likely.

"Hello, Mirella," he says as he offers me his hand. I shake it, maybe a little too enthusiastically. I can't quite keep eye contact—my eyes drift to his sleek, black suit vest and fitted checkered button shirt, open at the collar. No jacket. No tie today. I like this casual look.

His gaze sweeps over me. "How was the ride here?" So he's checking me out too.

"Wonderful," I answer as we enter the elevator—all mirrors.

What a job it must be to clean this thing.

He presses a button and turns to look at me again. Our reflections stare back at us from every angle. Weston's presence is so much more imposing than mine—I look like a little church mouse, standing next to his tall frame.

He doesn't seem distracted by the mirrored walls—he hasn't taken his eyes off me since we've entered the elevator. "I like your glasses," he says, a slight curve to his lips.

I don't think he's purposely trying to be seductive…but he is. And I want to tell him to stop it. This instant.

The elevator chimes, and he motions me out. He leads the way to a receptionist desk.

"Please hold all my calls for the moment, Kathryn, if you could."

"Not a problem," Kathryn says, smiling at me. She seems like a jovial woman, and well put-together—hair in a bun, slightly graying at the temples, a classy red suit perfectly hugging her slim figure.

Weston promptly introduces us. "This is Mirella Keates."

I stand a little straighter and extend my hand. "Nice to meet you."

"This is my assistant, Kathryn," Weston explains. I remember he's mentioned her before, although he probably doesn't remember the conversation at all. Unlike me, he most likely doesn't have *every single word* I've ever said, catalogued in his memory, retrievable at any time.

His office is similar to the lobby—very bright, contemporary, and highly organized. Books and publications, contemporary sculptures and models are wonderfully displayed on glass shelves. His desk is all glass. All glass! And the items resting on it are aligned in perfect symmetry. The pens in his glass pencil holder are all black and identical, tops pointing up—no ugly plastic white pens from *Don's Supersaver Drycleaner*.

He rubs the back of his neck as his gaze travels to the two retro, white tufted leather chairs by the large window. "Please take a seat."

I've seen those kinds of chairs in fancy decor magazines, and I've always wanted to sit on one. As I make my way there, I walk past his glass desk and slide my fingers along its edge, itching to grab something and mess with it. I reach for one of the black pens and flip it upside down.

He smiles at me. "I see you've come to make trouble."

God, he is beautiful.

I smile back at him as I head to the sitting area and plop my rear on one of the fancy chairs.

Comfy.

I take in the Chicago skyline as I gingerly set my briefcase on the floor and cross one leg over the other, trying to appear sophisticated.

"You look very charming today."

Well, "charming" wasn't quite what I was going for, but I'll take it. "You too," I say with a sly smile.

Okay, this is definitely not a business meeting. At least, it doesn't feel like one.

He paces back and forth across the room and finally stops at the well-stocked bar and coffee station. "Can I offer you anything to drink?"

"No, thank you."

I'm not thirsty. I'm not hungry. I'm simply dying of curiosity—I can't wait to find out what this mysterious meeting is all about.

Finally, he takes a seat—not on the sofa, but rather on the coffee table, right in front of me. He rubs his hands on his fitted charcoal pants, and his right knee bounces up and down—I can't help but notice. His leg stills when he catches my wide-eyed stare. Whatever this meeting is about…it has turned him into a bundle of nerves.

He's so close…I can see the gold speckles in his eyes.

Yes, this is *so definitely* not a business meeting.

I have a tiny momentary lapse of judgment and itch to kiss him. But still having my wits about me, I tilt my head away.

He closes his eyes for a second and clears his throat. "First, I feel I must warn you…" he starts as he rests his hand lightly on my knee. My heart unexpectedly hammers in my chest, and I stop breathing for a second. His touch feels wonderful. I don't think he's ever touched me before. He jolts his hand away, as quickly as he's put it there. "You'll probably be shocked," he starts, the pitch of his voice uncharacteristically high, "by what I'm about to say."

Shocked?

I'm insane with curiosity, and my stomach is completely tied up in knots.

He rakes a hand through his hair. "Feel free to ask me any questions. I'll try to answer as efficiently as I can."

"Yes," I say, completely attentive. Heck, if I had been this attentive in school, I could have become a doctor.

He bites his bottom lip. "First, I want to tell you how much Bridget and I enjoyed meeting you and your husband."

"Us too."

You have no idea.

"The truth is," he carries on, not quite making eye contact, "we were truly amazed," he adds, pausing for a second, perhaps searching for the right words, "by this connection we seem to all have."

He's felt it too. It wasn't just me.

My heart beats at rocket speed, and I wonder, for a fraction of a second, if a heart can beat too fast. "Yes…I agree. We just clicked, didn't we?"

"Very much so."

I find myself staring at his mouth, aching to run my fingers along his five o'clock shadow. I could never. And I shouldn't.

I definitely *shouldn't.*

"First…first off," he says, scratching his brow. I can sense whatever he's about to tell me is not easy. "As you know, Bridget and I have been in a committed relationship for many years. And we love each other."

My heart sinks.

He's brought me here to let me down gently, to tell me to back off—complete with car service. How classy.

"I feel I must tell you before I go on," he says, looking out the window. I wish he could just settle his eyes on me and say whatever it is he wants to say. He stares down at a copy of *Architectural Digest* on the table and presses a finger against the cover.

Seriously?

There is no way in hell he's looking at pictures of crown molding and marble floors right now.

Thankfully, he isn't—he just can't seem to make eye contact.

"Look at me," I whisper. "Whatever it is, I'll understand."

He gazes up at me and smiles. There's such vulnerability about him, I just want to reach out and hug him.

"Well actually, this might be hard for you to understand," he finally manages. "I know from our conversations that you were raised in a Catholic family."

I have absolutely *no idea* where he's going with this.

He stares off into the distance, yet again. "Well, the truth is," he trails off, his knee still bouncing up and down frantically. "Hell, I'll simply get right to it. No sense in beating around the bush…"

He takes a long breath and doesn't utter a word for the longest time, and I sit on the edge of my seat, barely able to contain myself, waiting for him to tell me.

Tell me what, I'm not sure.

But I want to know.

"Bridget and I…" he starts. "Bridget…she and I…are in an open marriage," he finally confesses.

I think my eyes actually bulge out of my head for a second, like that guy in the *Guinness Book of World Records*. And I *still* don't quite understand what he's telling me.

It seems he senses my confusion because he goes on. "I like you very much, Mirella," he tells me, his gaze soft. The nervous energy seems to have faded. "I'm very attracted to you."

My heart hammers in my chest.

He wants to sleep with me. But I thought we'd covered that already. I've already told him I could never cheat on Gabe.

He rubs the back of his neck—he seems almost pained. He wants me to understand what he's telling me. But I still don't. I'm so confused.

"And Bridget is also strongly attracted to Gabe," he adds, his gaze not leaving mine.

Suddenly, it all falls together.

My heart drops, just like it does on one of those roller coasters at the amusement park. I feel nauseous.

I'm no idiot—I've put two and two together.

Two and two together.

That's exactly what we're talking about here.

I can't hide the shock from my face. "You want us all to—"

His leg starts to fidget again. "I realize you and Gabe most likely don't have the same arrangement Bridget and I have."

Of course we don't. Most normal couples don't.

I have no words. He's taken them all.

"We simply want you to discuss it, consider it." His tone pleading. "Even if it's just for five seconds."

A hundred questions come to mind, like a tidal wave.

"A foursome?" I ask, my eyes wide. I am definitely *not* into that, if that's what they have in mind.

"No," he says with a smile. "More like…uh…an exchange."

"Couple swapping?" I ask, knowing this is exactly what he's talking about.

He smiles again. I swear, that smile of his might just completely do me in one day.

"Bridget and I don't like the term 'swapping.' We prefer to think of it as a 'couple exchange.'"

Of course, Bridget and Weston don't *swap*—they're much too classy for that.

"But how does that work?" I ask, another million questions working their way into my mind. Where? When? Why?

"Well, I won't lie. It's a little complex."

I wonder if they've done this before, if we're just another notch on their fancy, expensive bed post.

"You've done this before? You do this a lot?"

His smile is warm, and he puts his hand on my knee again. "No… not a lot, but yes…we've done this before…twice."

I feel his hand on me. And I almost forget this might be the most horrible idea ever conceived.

"And what happened with those couples?" I ask him. The whole thing suddenly seems very sordid.

"I'm sorry," he says, his voice soft. "I've scared you."

"Yes…I'm a little scared," I admit. "Honestly, Weston…I don't know what to think."

"I understand. The concept is completely unfamiliar to you."

I sit motionless, speechless and stare into his striking eyes. I truly don't know what to think.

"We don't take these arrangements lightly, Mirella." His gaze soft—finally, he's making eye contact. "They must be approached with caution, and rules and agreements must be in place. Thorough discussion is absolutely necessary."

My eyes are a little lazy as I listen to his smooth voice. I don't think I've ever been so turned on by a conversation. In fact, I'm positive of it. It seems my whole body is throbbing, hanging on to his every word.

Gabe was right. He wants to fuck me. Most men would stick their hands under my skirt and whisper a few dirty words in my ear. But Weston Hanson is not "most men." He's a strange one.

And unfortunately…sexy as hell.

I start to think about the logistics of this whole thing, and suddenly, my questions become more concrete. "Where would we do this? Do we all go out together and split up? At your house?"

He smiles. He seems slightly amused by my questions. His smile irks me—these are legitimate, serious questions.

He scratches his brow. "Well, first, we would schedule individual dates. You would contact my assistant Kathryn, coordinate and schedule a convenient time. She knows Bridget's and my schedule inside out."

What?

"Are you kidding me? This is not a dentist appointment, Weston," I blurt out before I can stop myself.

"I'm very well aware of that, Mirella," he says, his eyes downcast. It seems I'm making this harder than he anticipated.

"Kathryn is quite efficient at what she does. She'll coordinate and schedule our dates. The meetings will take place in the city…if we…uh…go ahead with the exchange," he adds quickly, flustered.

Why does he call them "meetings"? Call them what they are, I want to scream—hook-ups, booty calls…whatever.

"Both Bridget and I keep suites in the city."

How convenient. They both have their own private little shag pads…how quaint. I'm not sure if my disdain is obvious, but I kind of hope it is.

"When scheduling our meetings, Kathryn will take into account our individual schedules, our respective family plans, as well as your menstrual cycle."

My jaw drops. I want to scream.

He did *not* just say that.

I take a breath and reach for my briefcase. I get up to leave but he stills me with his hand.

"Mirella," he says softly. "Please let me finish. Let me go through this with you. And then you can decide."

His eyes. His beautiful eyes do me in every time. I don't think he realizes the power he has over me.

I stay seated. "Well, I bet that part wasn't in the job description when Kathryn first applied for the position," I joke, the sarcasm evident in my voice.

"No, it wasn't. But she's great at it. She's very discreet."

"Don't you think it would be less weird if we just all went out and let the chips fall where they may? Play it by ear?"

He sighs. He doesn't seem to agree. "I know it may seem a little strange to you," he admits. "We could very well go the traditional route…all go to a club together, get drunk, seduce each other, and we'd probably all end up in each other's beds," he adds, a smile curving at the edge of his mouth. "I think that's how most people do it."

Yes, that's how normal *people do it.*

"But that's not my style," he says plainly, he eyes fixed on me. "I don't like chaos, I don't like uncertainty. I don't like the unexpected. I feel in control when I can foresee the course of circumstances and specific regulations are in place."

Are we still talking about sex?

Part of me hopes so.

And part of me is absolutely horrified.

"Don't you get jealous?" I ask. This question has been on my mind since he uttered the words "open marriage."

He shakes his head, his mouth a hard line. "No," he says matter-of-factly. "We don't."

I stare at him, speechless.

"If you think you might be jealous, this kind of arrangement is completely unsuited to you," he adds, his words clipped.

"I see," I say, looking down at my pencil skirt, and wondering if I could do that…not be jealous.

"This is about sex, Mirella. There's no room for emotional attachment in these arrangements."

I lift my gaze to his and study him for a few seconds. Yes, I can see how this would be easy for him—he's so rigid, pragmatic, distant and cold…almost inhuman.

"The sole purpose of this agreement is mutual sexual gratification," he says plainly.

His words are so business-like, like he's in a board meeting, going over the yearly profit predictions.

My heart sinks.

Well…if he's trying to sell me on this, this is definitely *not* the right approach.

"Please remember, I'm telling you this because I don't want you to have any illusions, or come into this unprepared for the reality of such a situation," he explains. "I want you to know exactly what to expect. If you do this, I don't want you to regret it."

"How very considerate of you," I offer, not hiding the sarcasm in my voice.

Yes, it's decided…I'm definitely *not* doing this.

We sit in silence for what seems like eternity. His gaze studies mine, and I think he understands I don't want to do this. His hand reaches for my face and cups my cheek. The warmth of his hand on my skin sends shivers through my spine.

"I anticipated this," he says, his words almost inaudible. "Someone like you…you're not cut out for this," he adds as his hand leaves me.

I want his hand on my face again. I want his touch again—it makes me feel so alive.

"I shouldn't have even asked," he says, staring down at his shiny black dress shoes.

If his hand on my face can evoke this sensation within me, I can only imagine…I've *never* wanted a man this much.

"I want you," I say, my words soft.

He looks up at me and fixes me without a word for the longest time.

"Are you sure?"

"Yes."

"Considering all I've just told you?"

"Yes."

"And you can remain emotionally distant?"

"Yes. I'm very physically attracted to you, Weston. I want to touch you. And I want you to touch me. I want your body against mine. But that's it."

He swallows hard—I think I've caught him off guard. His gaze is fixed on me, his eyes dark.

"I love my husband. And I don't want to jeopardize my marriage."

Gabe.

Oddly enough, I hadn't been thinking about Gabe.

"You and your husband should discuss this thoroughly. *Must* discuss this thoroughly," he clarifies. "You must *both* be completely sure you want to do this. And if you both agree, we'll all meet to go over the details."

"There's more?" I almost snap. "I thought we *just* went over the details."

"Like I've mentioned," a little smile curving on his lip, "it's quite complicated."

Yes, I think…that's the understatement of the year.

Chapter Nine

The ground rules.

I'm standing on my doorstep, clutching my briefcase, not really wanting to go in and face Gabe.

I don't remember how I got here.

The ride from Weston's office to my house was a complete blur. So many things whirled in my brain on the way over here. How do I tell Gabe about this? Will he want to do this? Or will he want to go beat the life out of Weston? I honestly don't know how he'll react.

I hang my jacket and take off my shoes.

Claire runs up to me and gives me a big hug. "We missed you, Mommy." I'm flattered—I've only been gone for a few hours.

"Daddy made us pizza," Chloe informs me. "He put mushrooms on it, which I told him I didn't like. But he put them on anyway."

Gabe is standing, dish cloth in hand, with a curious expression. I know he wants to know everything. "So how did it go? What did he want?"

I close my eyes. I can't even get into it right now. "Did the girls do their homework yet?"

"Yes," he almost snaps. I can tell the suspense is killing him.

"Good," I say. "Listen. I can't discuss the meeting right now. We'll put them straight in their pajamas and put on a movie."

"A movie," Chloe squeals. "But it's Tuesday. It's not movie night."

I stroke her head, thinking this is definitely no ordinary Tuesday. "It's your lucky night, I guess."

"Yay! Yay! Yay!" Both girls squeal and literally jump up and down. Well, at least some of us will be happy at the end of the night.

Gabe looks at me with a quizzical expression. "That serious, huh?"

"You have no idea."

Gabe stares at me, slack-jawed. "Are you joshing me, Ella?"

We're sitting on our bed. I've locked the door. And I've told him all about the meeting and what Weston and Bridget have proposed.

"No, Gabe. This is the real deal."

He shakes his head. "I can't believe it."

I notice he doesn't seem upset, which is a great relief. Last thing I need is Gabe going over to Weston's office tomorrow, beating the shit out of him, and getting arrested.

A slow smile stretches across his face. "They really don't strike me as the foursome type," he says. "They're so conservative. And he seems so uptight."

"I know. He *is* uptight. God, you should see his office. And it's not a foursome…it's a 'couple exchange.'" I cringe a little—I'm starting to sound like Weston.

"Call it what you want, but it's kind of hot."

I smile. "Is it?"

"I'm hard just thinking about it, babe."

Well, of course you are.

I laugh a little, not sure if he's joking or not. "You're hard thinking about you and her having sex."

He stretches his long body on the bed, shirtless and looking impossibly sexy. Bridget wants him, and she hasn't even seen him naked—she'll go absolutely crazy when she sees his tattoos. "Sex. Exactly. That's exactly what it would be, wouldn't it, Ella?" he asks, his voice softer than usual. "Like Weston told you…it's just sex."

I can sense Gabe is very interested in this proposal. Part of me is shocked, and part of me isn't shocked at all. Who could blame him? Weston dangles a mighty fine carrot—I don't think I've ever seen a woman more beautiful than Bridget. Ordinarily, I would be insanely jealous at the thought. But my desire to be with Weston has rendered me temporarily blind…and possibly mad.

"How would you feel, knowing I was intimate with another man?" I ask him. "I've only ever been yours." This is a big deal for me. Gabe is the only one I've ever been with. He had been with two girls before me. But I was still a virgin when we met.

He's quiet. He seems to be pondering my question with great intensity. "I'd be jealous, I won't lie," he admits. "But if it's just sex. Then, that's all it is."

"Of course you'd be jealous. That's what concerns me. Right now this isn't real. It's easy to say 'it's just sex.'"

He winces a little but doesn't say a word. I've given him something to think about.

"Wouldn't you be worried I'd fall in love with him?" I venture. "You know how sentimental I am."

"C'mon, the man's like a robot." He scowls. "To be honest, I have a really hard time picturing you two even having sex. I mean…that's why the whole thing shocks me."

I don't respond, but his words cut a little. He doesn't know Weston—he shouldn't say these things.

"You seriously want to be with him?" he asks. "I know the man looks like a *GQ* cover, but personality has to count for something too, doesn't it?" he asks me, not waiting for an answer. "I didn't think you were the type to fall for someone purely on looks."

I want to tell him I'm not. I want to tell him he doesn't know him. I want to tell him Weston is a sensitive, sweet, introverted, creative, cerebral man who seems to be lost in his own little world—and that's the part I find most incredibly sexy. But I don't say any of these things.

"Well, like we said, it's just about sex, isn't it," I say, trying to convince myself.

"You want to do this?" he asks.

I so badly want to do this. But I'm so scared. But if Gabe is willing to do this, maybe I shouldn't worry so much. Maybe I should loosen up and just go for it, live a little for once. But I worry that we're not thinking straight. We can't possibly put our marriage in jeopardy because of lust. He's says it's cool now, but how will he feel when he knows I've been intimate with someone else? And how will I feel, knowing he's been with Bridget? He doesn't realize what he's saying. I want to tell him all this, but I'm afraid he'll change his mind if I do. And I don't want that because I crave Weston so badly. I am out of my mind.

"Only if you do," I finally manage, the words small.

We spend almost two hours discussing the issue and what it would mean for us, for our relationship, for our family. And we somehow convince ourselves it might even improve our relationship, particularly our sex life, pointing out that ever since we've met Weston and Bridget, we've been boinking like bunnies. We convince ourselves of all this and completely disregard all the possible risks, because of only one thing—we're aroused by the idea.

We're horny…it's that simple.

That night, we make love, or rather, we have sex.

Because that's exactly what it is. Gabe and I rarely make love anymore. We mostly have sex, and I suppose I don't mind it either since I always climax. Sometimes we cuddle afterward, and that's probably my favorite part.

Tonight, we cuddle.

Weston has asked me to contact him directly on his mobile after I've spoken with Gabe. My fingers are shaking a little as I dial his number. As his cell rings, I hope to get him on the phone because there's no way I can leave a message about this.

What am I going to say?

Weston, Mirella here. Gabe and I have discussed your proposal. And the answer is yes. You have the official go to do with me what you will.

But seriously, I really don't want to leave a message. My legs are a little wobbly, and I take a seat in the desk chair. And thankfully, on the fourth ring, he answers.

"Hello, Mirella," he says. His voice is soft and almost brings me to my knees.

"Hi, Weston, how are you?" I ask, absentmindedly rearranging the objects on the desk, aligning the keyboard, mouse pad, pens, and papers at perfect angles.

"I'm well. Thank you. And you?"

Are we really doing this formal small-talk?

Aren't we past that?

My palm is sweaty against the receiver. I don't think any man has ever made me this nervous—any person, for that matter. "I'm…I'm good, Weston. I wanted to tell you Gabe and I spoke…" For some reason, I can't bring myself to say the rest.

"And?" he says, his voice hopeful.

"We'd like to meet to go over the details."

There's a pause on the line. And I fear he's changed his mind.

"I'm very glad to hear that, Mirella." I can almost hear the smile on his face—he sounds happy. "I'll have Kathryn call you and set up the details."

I don't know what to say. It all seems so formal. It shouldn't be so formal, should it? And for a brief moment, I have my doubts again.

I stare out the window. The kid from next door zooms by on his bike. "I'm looking forward to seeing you," I say, my words hesitant.

"Me too."

After a beat, he says, "Well, I should go. I'm in a meeting at the moment. We'll talk to you shortly."

"Yes, good-bye," I say, wondering what the hell just happened.

"Good-bye."

The line goes dead.

What?

We're about to have sex, and all he could spare me was ten measly seconds. We're about to be intimate, to see each other naked, for crying out loud.

This is a big deal.

Well, maybe not for him—he's done this before. This isn't a big deal at all for him, I finally realize.

And I almost want to call him again and call the whole thing off.

We meet at an upscale steak house on the following Thursday night.

"This place is impressive," Gabe says, as we wait on the banquette. The restaurant is very classy—high cathedral ceilings with dark wood beams stretching over us, mahogany wood paneling and rustic brick lining the walls.

Gabe is drawn by the classic details, the fine carpentry. "Apparently, the brick is repurposed from an old bank tower," he comments.

Gabe and I have dressed conservatively. I catch a glimpse of myself in the mirror lining the wall across from us and adjust my jacket. I'm happy with my outfit—it is very Jackie-O and classy. I've even brought along my sleek mini briefcase.

I really don't know what the dress protocol is for such an occasion. How do you dress for a meeting going over the fine details of a "couple swap?" Do you dress conservatively or sexy?

When Weston and Bridget come in, all eyes are on them. He's decked out in his usual tailored suit, and she's wearing a clingy red dress and black A-line jacket.

Damn, I think, I should have gone with "sexy"—that's how you dress for such a meeting.

Well, you live, you learn.

These two really stand out in a room, and I suddenly feel a little unworthy.

Bridget greets us with a wide grin and hugs, and for some reason, it doesn't feel strange at all.

Weston gives us both a tight-lipped smile. And his gaze holds mine for a second—this is where it gets strange. He seems to have a way of making me feel very odd.

"You look very nice," he offers with a hint of a smile.

I smile at him, not able to form words. And I wonder why he makes me so nervous.

We follow the hostess to a small room off the main dining area—it's dark, it's cozy and most importantly…private.

The server pours water, and we order drinks. I order a martini, and boy, do I need it. I almost want to order two. And I don't even usually drink.

Bridget hangs her chic purse on the table with some kind of fancy purse hook contraption. "How hungry are you two?"

"Not at all," I say. I am so nervous…I really couldn't eat a thing.

"I'm not too hungry either," Gabe says. It's shocking—Gabe is always hungry, especially when it comes to steak.

"We thought we would discuss the details before dinner and get all the formalities out of the way," Bridget suggests.

That's a great idea. Yes, let's get this out of the way, and I might be able to breathe again.

"We could order some appetizers if you wish," Weston offers.

"No thanks, we're fine," I say, looking over at Gabe who nods in agreement.

We seem to all want to get this over with. I hadn't imagined this would feel so strange. Suddenly, I want to make a break for it. I don't want to do this anymore. This is just too damn weird. I lace my trembling hand in Gabe's, hoping he'll look at me and be able to read my mind and get us the hell out of here.

Drinks are served, and Weston asks the server to give us a long moment. "We'll need about twenty minutes," he tells her.

"Yes, Mr. Hanson," the server replies with complete obedience. I have a feeling he's been here before. Who knows…maybe he owns the place?

"Come and get me when you're ready to order. I'll be out there," the server adds before leaving us.

The click of the door shutting leaves us in complete silence. And I just want to disappear.

I can still change my mind.

Weston clears his throat. "Well," he says, his voice soft, "where to start…" he trails off, not saying a word for what seems like a week.

"First, we'd like to tell you how much we appreciate you," Bridget chimes in. "You two are fabulous…smart, lovely, and so down to earth."

"The feeling is mutual," Gabe says, looking over at me.

I've yet to utter a word.

"And we don't take this lightly. We don't do this type of thing every day," he adds. "You were chosen with great consideration."

Wow, we were *chosen*.

I can't help but stifle a little laugh.

"What's so amusing?" Weston asks, his eyes curious—I guess he's caught me chuckling.

"I'm sorry. It's just that...you're so formal about it all."

"I know," Bridget chimes in. "He always speaks like that. Always. It's his way."

"Well, it does have a certain charm," I offer, looking up at Weston who smiles.

Flirting...now *that's* more like it.

"Well, essentially, I want to go over the basics." His tone has not lightened—it seems Mr. Hanson is not in the mood to play—he's all business.

He loosens his collar and clears his throat. "The ground rules."

The ground rules.

Sounds so serious.

I reach for my briefcase. "Should I be writing these down?"

Both Weston and Bridget laugh. And I feel like such a nerd. Geez, why don't I just whip out a *PowerPoint* presentation while I'm at it?

Weston still smiles at me. "I don't think that'll be necessary, Mirella."

Well, at the very least, I've managed to lighten the mood.

"There are five basic rules we like to follow. Sticking to those makes everything run smoothly." Bridget says.

"Yes," Weston echoes. "Five basic rules."

Gabe and I nod but don't say a word, perhaps trying to recover from shock—this is all so formal, so absurd.

"First off, we'll talk about monogamy," Weston starts.

I can't peel my eyes off him—he's so yummy in his sleek charcoal suit. His sterling silver cufflinks sparkle. I study his manicured hands and long fingers, and imagine what they could do to me.

"Within this arrangement, the four of us must be monogamous at all times," he explains. I watch him as he speaks. I notice his words are precise and deliberate, his palms are pressed together, fingers pointing toward us. I imagine this is what he looks like when he heads his work meetings.

"I can only have relations with Bridget and Mirella…no other woman. And conversely, Bridget can only be intimate with myself and Gabe…and so on." I notice he has difficulty keeping eye contact. His gaze often falls to the table, and back up again, looking at mostly me and rarely at Gabe.

"If one of us enters into a sexual relationship with someone outside our group," he continues, his words slow, "this person should inform us immediately of that fact, and an appropriate direction will be considered." His eyes fix on me. "It should be said…Bridget and I have no interest in such external relationships."

"Us either," I quickly add. And Gabe nods in agreement. "I mean, I've only ever been with him…" I trail off, my voice shaky.

"Good, that makes things simpler." And after a beat, he adds, "But nevertheless, we will insist on full STD screenings from both of you."

Bridget gives us a small "I'm sorry about all this…he's such a hard-nose" smile.

"And Bridget and I will both be subject to these screenings as well."

As I listen to his words, I realize this meeting is not at all what I expected.

It is not very sexy.

"I will wear a prophylactic at all times when with Mirella, no exceptions, as will Gabe when he is with Bridget."

A what?

"And in addition to this, both Bridget and Mirella will be on a form of birth control," he informs us, his words monotone. "I assume you're taking the birth control pill or a similar contraceptive, Mirella."

Oops.

"Um…no," I say, feeling like a third grader at the principal's office who has done something very naughty.

Weston studies me with a curious look.

"I got the old snip-snip last year," Gabe clarifies.

His gaze travels from me to Gabe, and back again. "Oh…I see," he says. "Well, in that case, you'll have to make arrangements. I hope that's not a problem."

"No," I say. It really isn't. I'll probably gain five pounds…but on the plus side, my breasts will be a little bigger. I just have to remember to take the darn things—I can be a little flaky sometimes.

I am *officially* no longer turned on. I was a little at the start of this meeting, but he's made everything so damned technical.

God, I hope he's not like this in bed.

Weston pauses for a moment and takes a drink, and it seems we all mimic him and down a sip—I think we all need it.

"We know this is a lot to take in," Bridget tells us, her expression warm. I get the impression she would rather approach the whole thing a little less formally.

"Secondly," Weston starts again, "we'll discuss discretion. Discretion is of utmost importance. For example, my relations with Mirella will be completely private." I find myself unexpectedly aroused by his words and looking into his eyes—they're so serious and intense. His gaze falls from mine again.

"I will not discuss our relations with Bridget, under any circumstances, nor will I discuss them with anyone else."

Good.

"Conversely, Mirella will not discuss our relations with Gabe or anyone else."

Damn, I can't even talk to Gwen about this. I'm not sure how I feel about that. I tell Gwen *everything.*

"Trust us. Talking only leads to jealousy. I really don't want to know what you two are up to," Bridget comments.

It makes sense. It makes a lot of sense. I wouldn't want to hear the details concerning Gabe and Bridget. And I really don't want Weston telling Bridget what my breasts look like.

"Number three is simple," Weston continues. "We treat each other with kindness and respect at all times. I do not speak ill of Bridget or Mirella or Gabe. And likewise, Mirella does not speak ill of Bridget or Gabe or myself and so on. This isn't about judging or complaining about our spouses. There needs to be a positive, respectful energy at all times."

Seems simple enough, I think. I like this rule. I glance over at Gabe who seems to be stifling a smirk. I know this because I know him too well. He's doing a rather impressive job looking attentive and serious, when all he probably wants to do is laugh. I glare at him and nudge him with my foot, just to keep him in his place.

"And of course, we respect each other's boundaries and do not force or coerce our partners into doing, or performing any act they don't want to do. Participation, desire, and gratification must be mutual at all times," Weston goes on.

I'm happy about this rule because, the truth is, I don't know Weston very well. I study him—the intense green eyes, the dark thick brows, the hard line of his jaw, the strong nose, and I wonder what he's like in bed, what he likes, whether he's kinky or domineering. The scary thing is…I don't know what to expect at all.

"Another rule we like to adhere to concerns the contact we have with each other," Weston adds.

I'm confused. I guess he can tell because he leans in and clarifies. "What I mean is," he explains, his words deliberately measured, "we cannot see each other outside the scheduled dates, in any other circumstances," he says, addressing Gabe. "For example, Mirella and I cannot contact or see each other any other time. We cannot call or text, or e-mail each other for any reason."

Gabe nods.

"And likewise, you and Bridget cannot contact or see each other outside of these agreed upon dates."

"I get it," Gabe says.

I'm confused by this rule. "How are we supposed to get together if we can't even contact each other?"

"Basically, all communication and correspondence will be done through a third party, my assistant in this case."

The woman sure has a lot on her shoulders.

"Poor Kathryn…does she ever go on vacation?" I can't help but ask. Everyone laughs. I really wasn't trying to be funny.

"Yes, Kathryn does go on vacation occasionally," he answers, a huge smile lighting up his face. He's so gorgeous when he smiles. I wish he'd smile more often. "Marilyn is her temporary replacement. And she's quite efficient and discreet as well."

"Can I ask why you have this rule in place?" I ask. "I mean, what's the big deal if I give you a call here and there."

He sighs and smiles at the same time. "Well, it brings us to the final rule, possibly the most important…emotional detachment."

"Yes," I say. "We've discussed that."

"Basically it comes down to this," he says, addressing everyone. "This is about sex. Pure and simple. There's no other way to spin it."

The room is completely silent.

"What I mean is it's a casual thing…it's about fun, excitement…desire. There's no room for emotional attachment here or intimate relationships outside of the agreed-upon dates. There will be no personal gifts or gestures. We will not introduce each other to our friends and families or even our children for that matter."

I notice his hands fidgeting a little as he speaks. He pulls his palms together again. "We can still socialize, the four of us, go for dinner before dates, or we can dine separately. It's important that we are all comfortable with each other before we become intimate," he carries on, his words measured. "Bridget and I are quite traditional…we like to converse over a nice dinner, build desire, loosen up. That's all part it. If it was just about the act itself, we'd all be better off going to sex club," he adds with a whisper of a laugh. "But that is definitely not our inclination, and I imagine it isn't yours either."

I nod, my gaze glued to him.

"However…having said that," he goes on, "we don't believe we should become the best of friends or enter each other's social circles."

His words get to me a little. He makes us sound like a "big dirty secret." I understand the need for discretion and distance as much as anyone, but…

"All this might sound harsh," Bridget chimes in. "But it really does work better this way. Our previous relationship ended because of social politics."

Interesting.

"And what about the first relationship you had? Why did it end?" I realize I'm being extremely nosy, but I'm dying to know.

Bridget hesitates. "The woman got emotionally attached. She became just about obsessed with Weston."

"Oh, I see," I say softly, looking down at my pencil skirt. I can see how that could happen. I *do not* want to be that woman.

I look up at him slowly, wanting to know, "Were you attached to her?"

"No, I wasn't," he replies. "Not in the least." His words ring true. And I can't help but think…he's a very cold man.

"And as mentioned before," he goes on, "all dates will be scheduled and coordinated by Kathryn."

"It makes things so much easier. Otherwise, we'd all be playing phone tag…it would be an absolute nightmare. And we'd be breaking rule number four," Bridget adds with a grin. And I get the distinct impression she's making fun of Weston a little.

But he doesn't seem to notice.

"Our dates will take place at our respective lofts," he says, addressing Gabe. "Both Bridget and I have places we stay, here in the city."

Gabe nods. I'm amused by the fact that Gabe hasn't said much at all so far, which is completely unlike him. I think he's just too shell-shocked.

"And we will pay for all dinners and related expenses," he adds. "In fact, we don't want to discuss this at all. It's our pleasure."

I'm glad he's clarified this because there's no way Gabe and I could afford all these extravagant dinners. I do feel a little strange about it—it occurs to me Gabe and I are officially "sugar-babies." The thought nauseates me a little. Not in a million years, would I have ever imagined myself as a sugar-baby.

"Finally, to sum it up," Weston says, his words matter-of-factly. "We have five basic rules. One is monogamy, the second is discretion, the third is respect, the fourth is appropriate contact, and finally, we have emotional detachment."

I nod obediently.

Got it, sir.

He's going over this like we're at a board meeting, and honestly, I'm very surprised he hasn't passed around a handout. I almost want to ask him where the coffee and donuts are.

But, I've learned to accept this as his style—it's just the way he is. And I find myself wondering for the umpteenth time what he might be like in bed. Will I have a checklist to follow? Will he make me sign a liabilities waiver? A confidentiality form? Will I go through a metal detector? I really don't know what to expect with this guy.

The thought concerns me a little.

And again, those same old familiar doubts show their worried faces.

Chapter Ten

Right now and right here.

With the "meeting" out of the way, the atmosphere lightens considerably. And we surprisingly find ourselves falling into easy conversation. Bridget is so cheerful and outgoing—she's a great catalyst for on-going dialogue. Weston orders a bottle of red for the table, and we order our meals. I decide to stick with a light shrimp salad, thinking I should really indulge in a steak. But I just can't… I'm still not very hungry.

Weston catches my gaze here and there, but his eyes always pull away. He can't seem to maintain eye contact. He can't even look at me, and he wants to have sex with me? I suppose we'll have to get over that if we're going to be intimate. But then again, I think, pushing my salad around, maybe we don't. If all he wants to do is screw me, he really doesn't need to look at me at all.

I look up at him, wondering if that's what he wants. He's said as much.

This is about sex. Plain and simple.

Maybe he's just nervous because of the strangeness of the situation—it's not every day you have a "swapping" discussion dinner-meeting.

I think he's handled himself pretty well. I think I've handled myself relatively well too, considering I was so nervous, I thought I might be sick the whole time. But somehow, I managed to not hurl or suffer a panic attack.

When we say our good-byes, Bridget hugs us both. And Weston shakes Gabe's hand. I consider going in for a hug, but I respect his boundaries. As he offers me his hand, I can't help but think, we're going to have sex soon, and I don't even get a measly hug.

As we walk away and wave, I wonder how this is going to work.

And again, I wonder what the hell I've gotten myself into.

"Wow, that guy's a few sandwiches short of a—" Gabe starts.

"Stop it right there." I cut him off mid-sentence. "You're already breaking rule number three."

He laughs out loud. "Oh yes, God forbid I break rule number three. Which one is that again?"

"Respect and kindness. You're being an asshole."

He looks at me, a smile still on his lips.

"Weston is pragmatic," I explain. "He needs order. He needs to have these concrete rules in place. I think it's a good idea. I can see how this whole thing could become a disaster if we didn't have these rules."

I don't know why I feel the need to defend Weston, but I do.

I go over the rules in my head. I know there are only five, but I'm afraid I'll forget one of them. I go over them in a way I can relate to a little better.

1. Don't sleep around.

2. Don't kiss and tell.

3. Be nice.

4. Don't text or call.

5. Don't fall in love.

Simple enough.

I don't think I'll have any problems with any of them. Normally, rule number five might be a problem because I'm a romantic. But it shouldn't be a concern with someone like Weston—he's so detached, hard, and cold.

"It's too bad about the privacy rule," Gabe says. "What is that… rule number four?"

"Rule number two."

His mouth stretches into a wide impish grin—trademark Gabe. "I was looking forward to hearing about all the kinky things he's going to do to you."

I laugh out loud. "You couldn't stand it. You would hate hearing about it. It would drive you insane with jealousy."

"You're probably right," he admits. "But I'm curious to see what he has in mind for you. Probably some wild stuff, babe," he warns me. "You might not like it at all. I know you're not really into that."

He's right.

What if…

"It won't be like that, I'm sure," I say, trying to convince myself.

But hell, I really don't know what to expect.

Gabe has me a little worried.

"It's always those strange, quiet, uptight types who like to do all sorts of weird shit," he says.

"Stop talking like that," I snap. "You don't know what you're talking about. And you're breaking rule number three again, by the way."

That night, Gabe and I make love. Actually make love. He's gentle and soft. We look into each other's eyes. It feels foreign…making love. He tells me he loves me, and I tell him he's the only one.

I think both of us know, deep inside…our relationship is about to change.

I study the magazines on the coffee table as I sit in Dr. Fisher's waiting room. It's quite the selection, news magazines, women's magazines, trash mags, and *Sports Illustrated.*

But I'm in no mood to read—I'm on edge. How am I going to address all this with Dr. Fisher? I've known her for so long. She was the one who first prescribed me birth control when I was just seventeen. She was the one who took care of me through my pregnancies. She's almost like family.

An old man sitting across from me, waiting for his wife, stares at me intently with what almost looks like disgust. He's watching me, studying me like he knows something, like he knows what I'm up to. He has big, dark out-of-control brows. I try to look away, but those big scary caterpillars keep drawing me in, and it turns into a staring contest.

What is his problem?

I close my eyes, thinking I'm losing my mind. I'm probably just projecting—he doesn't know anything about me—he's not judging me. I open my eyes to look at him. The scowl of disgust has disappeared. It was probably just the big crazy eyebrows.

The truth is…I'm ashamed.

I feel like a sexual delinquent. I've officially entered into a strange sexual arrangement. I would have never imagined myself capable of this. If someone had told me a month ago about the situation I find myself into today, I would have laughed and told them they were insane.

How do I talk to Dr. Fisher about this?

How are you?

I'm fine, thank you.

How are the girls and Gabe?

They're wonderful and growing up so fast, and Gabe and I are pretty good too, and having sordid swinging sex with sizzling-hot almost-strangers, which is why I'm here, in fact!

I walk up to the pamphlet display—breastfeeding, osteoporosis, tuberculosis, flu vaccine, herpes, HIV testing, HPV vaccination.

Oh shit!

Should I get the HPV vaccine? I've never had to worry about that before. There are about a gazillion pamphlets about STDs, and it kind of makes the whole thing a lot less sexy. If there was ever anyone trying to stick hard to abstinence, this is the exact spot where they should stand.

I feel my doubts creeping up again. I can still change my mind, can't I?

The receptionist calls out my name, and I'm a little hesitant. My feet drag as I make my way to the reception desk.

She walks me over to Dr. Fisher's patient room.

I'm comforted by the familiar room—the whimsical, colorful fish border lining the wall, a painting of a mother and child, the angel fish statue, and the cozy pink covers on the stir-ups. I quickly get out of my clothing, put on the paper robe the receptionist has given me, and sit on the patient bed.

And I wait.

I feel hot and a little sweaty…and I'm not breathing quite right. My blood pressure is probably through the roof. I try to organize the thoughts in my head—exactly how I'm going to go about this.

I hear a knock on the door.

Dr. Fisher looks cheerful. Her graying reddish hair is up in a severe knot, and she wears her usual white jacket. She looks exactly the same every time I see her.

"How are you, Mirella?" she asks, adjusting her dark framed glasses.

"Uh…good. How are you?"

"Great." She's always so cheerful—this is someone who truly loves her chosen profession.

"How are Chloe and Claire?" she asks.

It always amazes me that despite all the patients she sees, she remembers my daughters' names. "They're great."

"We're here for a physical today?"

"Yes," I say, hesitating. "Also," I pause for a second, trying to figure out how to say this. "I need to discuss…something."

"Sure. Let's discuss it." There's a hint of curiosity in her expression.

I think about it for a second. She knows I'm in a monogamous marriage. And she probably remembers Gabe got a vasectomy last year, since we discussed it at length at my last annual physical, when I got off the birth control pill. I can't very well say, "I need a bunch of STD tests and birth control pills," without offering an explanation.

"Nothing's embarrassing, Mirella. I'm your doctor."

"Well, the thing is," I say. My words feel like lead weights I just don't have the strength to drag out. "Gabe and I have been in a loving, monogamous relationship for almost twenty years," I start.

She listens intently, and I can tell she's intrigued.

I'm not sure how to tell her the rest. I decide to do it as fast as possible before I lose my nerve.

"The thing is…Gabe and I have met this wonderful couple. And we've become quite close," I add quickly. "We want to enter into a sexual relationship with them."

There. I've said it.

She looks shocked. I can tell. For a split second, her expression betrays her usual composure.

But I know I can trust her. She knows all my secrets. She's seen my "lady parts" after all. Only two people have seen my "lady parts" or my "privacy" as Claire calls it. Well, there were the nurses and doctors when I had the girls, but they don't count.

I suppose Weston will be seeing my "privacy" soon enough. I'm not sure how I feel about that. The thought unnerves me. Sex is such an intimate thing, and I feel like I hardly know him.

But as nervous as I am about it, the thought still arouses me.

A lot.

After the five seconds or so it takes Dr. Fisher to wrap her mind around what I've just told her, she finally asks. "And you and your husband have discussed this thoroughly?"

"Yes…thoroughly."

"And you *both* agree about this? One hundred percent?"

"Yes," I fib a little. Honestly, Gabe seems to be on board, but I'm not completely sure about myself.

"You two are consenting adults, and how you wish to live your private lives is entirely up to you. You would actually be surprised to know just how common these types of arrangements are today."

They are?

Dr. Fisher is amazing. This is exactly why I love her. I make a mental note to send her an extra special Christmas card this year—with glitter and gold embossing.

"But you will need to take precautions," she warns me. "We'll need to discuss birth control and STD prevention thoroughly."

And that's exactly what we do. We discuss STDs and the HPV vaccine, and she orders the STD screening I've requested. She writes me a prescription for birth control—the same pill I was on not so long ago.

I've broken rule number two already.

I couldn't help myself.

Gwen and I have been best friends since her first day at the school about seven years ago. I still remember that day so clearly. I came back from maternity leave and there was this new teacher everyone had been talking about—brash, sassy, and loud. I was sure I would hate her, but it was love at first sight, and we've been inseparable ever since.

And this new development is just too big not to share. I'm going to explode if I don't confide in someone.

So I cheat.

And I tell Gwen all about it on "Girls' Night" at our favorite dive. I still have that vision in my head—her face looms over her giant slushy Bellini—the thing is bigger than her head—and when I tell her, her jaw drops in shock.

"You're putting me on right now, Mirella," she shrieks.

"I'm not making this up."

She bites her lip. "I think Weston Hanson might be the sexiest man on the planet, and you lucky girl, are going to get to *tap that,*" she says, whispering the last words. "I am *so* jealous right now."

My breath catches thinking about him. "I know. He's so different, enigmatic, and intense. I don't know what to expect. I'm kind of scared," I confess. "What if he doesn't like me…once…you know…"

It feels so nice to get this off my chest, to finally share my fears with someone.

"He will love you, Mirella. How could he not? You're so beautiful."

"Thanks, Gwen. But you're my bestie…you almost need to say that."

She takes a sip of her giant Bellini. "Hey, you know me. I don't say crap I don't mean."

I laugh. "That's true."

"I say exactly what's on my mind."

"But…" I go on, exposing my vulnerabilities to the only person I can expose them to. "You should see his wife. She's perfection. She looks like a supermodel…tall, blond and not a single ounce of fat on her."

"Well, that *is* the kind of woman men like Weston Hanson marry, isn't it? The trophy wife. But I'm sure he's aching for a gorgeous, curvaceous bod like yours, you know what I mean?"

"Maybe you're right," I say, not quite convinced.

"Hey, he's the one who propositioned you, isn't he?" she points out. "Obviously, he wants to be with you. Just enjoy it."

We both sit in silence, sipping our drinks, looking over the menu. She's right. I should just stop obsessing. What will he think of me? Will I be good enough? Beautiful enough? I'm driving myself insane.

"This all seems very fun and exciting, Mirella," Gwen adds, looking up from her menu. "But don't you worry this could really mess up your relationship with Gabe?"

"Honestly, I prefer not to think about it."

I haven't. I've pushed those thoughts away, far away. I've wrapped them up in a box, and brought them to the dark, dingy back basement of my mind.

"And won't you be jealous, thinking about Gabe with that supermodel lawyer?"

"Maybe a little." I don't admit I'm just so insane about Weston, all I can really think about is him. This will remain my little secret. I don't even dare tell it to my best friend.

We spend the evening talking about nothing but the "swap." By the end of the night, Gwen knows about everything—the initial meeting in his office, the group meeting, and the rules.

She plops her credit card down in the leather bill folder, as excited as I've ever seen her. "We need to go shopping tomorrow."

"Shopping?"

A mischievous smile curves on her lips. "Naughty shopping," she clarifies, "you dirty little girl."

"Have you been waxed yet?" Gwen asks, as we make our way to her favorite lingerie shop downtown. It's a quaint privately owned little place. Gwen says the service is more personal, and the atmosphere is more relaxing than the big chain stores.

"No. You know me. I don't do that. I hate pain."

She smiles at me. "Weston Hanson sounds like the kind of man who likes his women primped."

I can't disagree. "He does. He's so pragmatic and orderly. He's almost obsessive about it…a place for everything, and everything in its place. You should see his office…it's sleek, clean, and freakishly orderly," I tell her, remembering our meeting at his office. "He's also a germaphobe."

"He probably expects you to be bare," she points out.

"Well, he can expect what he wants, but he's going to get what he gets."

"You go girl," she cheers.

"I'm not suffering through this crazy, modern day torture ritual for any man. He can take it or leave it."

She grabs me by the shoulders, taking me by surprise. "This is why I love you, girl," she almost screams out onto the street.

"I mean, don't get me wrong, I'm going to trim the hedges and make everything look pretty. Pick something lacy and pretty to wear, but that's as far as it's gonna go."

"Yeah…let's go pick out something cute," she cheers as we make our way into the old Victorian building.

Gwen was right—the atmosphere is very calming. The place is bright, airy, and smells of patchouli. Soft music is playing in the background. There's just one other client shopping, a young woman sporting a dark bob.

"How are you ladies?" the woman at the cash register offers, her flaming red hair flowing softly over her shoulders.

"We're good, Jasmine," Gwen tells her. "This is my best friend, Mirella."

"Hello, it's nice to meet you."

I shake her hand. "Likewise."

"Do we have a special occasion we're shopping for?" Jasmine asks in the softest voice.

"Ohhh," Gwen almost growls. "You could say that, Jasmine."

I am completely mortified. I bury my face in my hand, thinking I'm going to kill Gwen if she whispers a word. But thankfully, she doesn't. She tells Jasmine I'm looking for a few sets to spruce up my love life with my husband.

"You know what it's like, Jasmine," Gwen says, a mischievous smile on her face. "You have two kids of your own. Things can get pretty boring in the bedroom."

"Yes, the magic sure can disappear," she agrees. "Let's find you something fabulous."

I eye this beautiful white lacy set with delicate flowered embroidery. It's incredible and also very pricey. Gwen notices me look at the price tag.

"How 'bout if I get you a few sets," she offers. "My treat…an early Christmas present."

"I couldn't, Gwen. It's too much."

"I'm the one who dragged you here, knowing you can't afford it."

"You do make a good point," I half-joke.

"I do."

The thing is, Gwen is a little better off than I am, money-wise. Her husband Greg is a successful hedge-fund manager, and he keeps her happy in designer wear and a luxury home. Mind you, she's not a gold-digger by any means—she just happened to fall for a guy who has a way with money.

We pick out a few sets. Gwen is quite opinionated about the whole thing, but she has more experience in the bedroom department than I do, so I listen intently. She tries to push me toward the thongs.

"Men love thongs."

"But again, don't I have to be comfortable?" I argue. "You know me. Thongs are not me."

She looks me up and down, her gaze falling on my long skirt and comfy Mary-Janes, and she rolls her eyes.

"You're right," she concedes. "Let's look for sexy briefs instead."

We end up picking out the white pretty set I was eyeing, a sexy red lace set, and a black silky one.

I try on the white set, slipping the lace panties over my cotton undies.

Gwen sits on the pink Victorian bench, filing her nails. Her brow perks up as she looks up at me. "You have a really good body. Curves in all the right places. I've never really noticed before."

"Why, thank you, Gwen," I tell her, smiling a little.

"Why don't you ever wear bikinis?" she asks. "I've only seen you in those horrible mommy one-pieces."

"They're more comfortable for playing with the girls," I explain. "I don't want to fall out of my bathing suit."

"Oh, Mirella..." she sighs. "You're so uptight."

I laugh a little.

"Me...uptight? I *am* shopping for lingerie for my upcoming swap," I point out, slightly catty.

She laughs. "Yes. You make a good point. But I'm still getting you a bikini for this summer."

"As you wish," I say turning around, checking out my reflection in the mirror. I do look kind of pretty.

"That one's nice for the first time," she says. "It's demure and classy. You don't want to come off too horny the first time."

I turn to her and smile. She can be so funny.

"Save the red set for when you really want to get fucked hard," she says.

My jaw drops. "Gwen!"

"*What?*" she says with a quick shrug of her shoulders, one leg crossed over the other, still filing her nails.

I smile at her. Sometimes I ask myself how in the heavens she and I fit so well together.

Well, it's finally here.

The night I have been anxiously waiting for...our first "date."

Part of me wants it to be over before it begins. And the other part wants to discover it slowly...and all its possibilities.

Gabe seems as nervous as I am. I help him pick out an outfit—we settle on sleek black dress pants and a striped gray and black button shirt.

I stand next to him and study his reflection in the tall mirror hung in our walk-in closet. "I think Bridget will like this."

He doesn't say a word.

I look miniscule in my slip of a dress, standing next to his tall frame. "This is so weird."

"We are so fucked up," he says simply, a hint of humor in his expression.

"I still can't believe we're actually going through with this."

He wraps his hand softly around the curve of my hip. "Me either. Are we crazy?"

"Yes."

"Are you having second thoughts? We can still call it off, you know."

I think about Weston, about the last time I saw him, dressed in a charcoal tailored suit, the brilliant green of his eyes peering at me through gorgeous lashes as he went over the "rules" so diligently. And I think about his hand on my knee that time at his office and the electrifying current it sent through me.

I smile up at Gabe's reflection. "No…let's do this."

I smile at Edward as he opens the car door for me. I've got this down pat now—I'm supposed to wait and let him open the door for me. It kind of makes me feel like a movie star. I take his welcoming hand as I gingerly step out of the town car. I run my manicured fingers (today, both my hands and feet look amazing) along the lace on my dress (one of those impulse buys I thought I'd never get to wear—vintage-inspired, sheer, cream, delicate, lace-trimmed and tiny). The dress almost looks like a slip that could easily be torn off—and that's the point. I've worn the lacy white set underneath, the demure one.

The air is surprisingly hot and humid tonight. My up-do, sheer dress, and strappy sandals were a perfect choice. Weston is waiting for me when I enter the restaurant, a small, casual, intimate Italian place.

I clutch my beaded bag nervously. For a brief second, I worry I'm going to be sick and hurl all over the quaint black and white tiled flooring.

The expression on his face is unmistakable.

He likes my dress.

He leans in and gives me a light kiss on the cheek. "You look lovely." My knees almost give out.

He kissed me.

The food is delicious but I can't quite appreciate it—I'm just too on edge. Weston seems to have a healthy appetite—completely unaffected. What is it with men? Why do these kinds of things not affect them? Perhaps they just hide it better.

My gaze travels to the jars of pasta sauce and bottles of olive oil lined along the wall. I think about Gabe and Bridget and wonder what they're doing at this exact moment. And I push the thoughts immediately out of my mind.

Weston and I don't say much. And he doesn't really look at me—his eyes seem to be glued to the red and white checkered table cloth.

He occasionally puts his knife down and rubs the back of his neck or traces circles along the bottom of his wine glass. I watch him, fork mid-air, completely fascinated by his quirks.

He's just as nervous as I am.

Even on edge, he's gorgeous—dressed in a dark striped shirt, open at the collar. He doesn't wear his customary cufflinks tonight.

He sets his glass on the table and finally ventures a look up at me and puts his hand softly on mine. "I want you to know…"

His touch lights me up.

"I have no expectations. Let's just see where the night leads."

He's so sweet. I breathe a little easier, realizing there's really no reason to worry. Whatever happens, I know he'll treat me with respect.

I twirl my fork in my pasta repeatedly. "I can't eat," I confess. "I'm too anxious."

He smiles at me.

"You should try to eat," he presses. "You need energy."

For what?

I think he catches the look of horror on my face. "A walk would be nice later," he says, a smile playing on his lips. His smile always makes me melt. I don't want to go for a walk—I want to go straight to his bed.

He picks up his fork again and cuts into his veal. "What do think of this place?" he asks. "I know it's not much. I wanted this night to be casual," he adds. "Is it to your liking?"

I look around the quaint restaurant. It has a certain charm, but it's not quite as sexy as I would have liked. All I can think about is sex.

"Do you like Italian food?" he asks, fork mid-air.

"I do. Doesn't everyone?"

"I think so," he says. "Didn't you say you were part Italian?"

"Yes. One quarter Italian and three quarters Irish."

We've had this conversation before. Small talk isn't exactly what I had in mind for tonight. The vibe between us is way too formal. He's never going to make the first move—he's just too damned proper. We won't get *anywhere* at this rate. And I want to get *somewhere*. But unfortunately, I'm not quite sure how to elevate the conservation to the next level.

I put my fork down and take a sip of wine. "You are quite the gentleman, aren't you?"

"Always."

"Well...could you try not to be? Just for tonight," I say, attempting a sultry voice, but I'm no Marilyn Monroe.

A slow smile stretches across his face. "I'll see what I can do."

I smile and look away, feeling myself blush—I am so bad at this flirting business. I wonder if there are courses on the subject, maybe a *Flirting for Dummies*?

"Weston," I say, hesitating just a bit. "I love your smile. You should smile more often."

His lip curves up into a wide grin. "I can try."

It really isn't like me to flirt profusely or to make the first move, but I really want to be with him, and it seems all I can feel is this pent-up sexual energy within me—it's almost unbearable.

I lean in closer. "You know what your smile does to me?" I ask playfully.

He stares at me, his expression curious, and takes a sip of water, his movements slow and deliberate.

"It makes me want you," I tell him, my voice silky.

He swallows hard. His eyes linger on mine. I can see I've rendered him speechless. I don't think he was expecting this of me, but I can tell from his darkened gaze that he likes it.

"Right now and right here," I whisper, surprised at my own boldness.

He chokes a little on his water. But he smiles. He likes it. His eyes seem to get even darker.

He wants me too.

Now, this is more like it, I think. I'm sitting with this delicious man, and we're both into each other. We should be flirting, not making small talk.

"I don't think I ever answered your question," I say, looking off into the distance. "Yes. I like the restaurant." My gaze sweeps over the cozy space and its brick covered walls and framed black and white photos of Italy.

"I'm glad," he says, his eyes still intense.

I tilt my head, *trying* to be seductive. "You know what I like about it? It's small and intimate."

"It is," he agrees. "That's why I chose it."

"You know," I whisper. "These small places usually have private washrooms."

He swallows hard. His gaze is glued to mine. He's not stupid. He knows where I'm going with this.

I pause, take a sip of wine, and grab my clutch. "I'm going to powder my nose."

My eyes linger on him as I walk away.

The poor man looks absolutely flabbergasted.

My heart starts to hammer in my chest as I make my way to the back of the restaurant. Suddenly, I start to panic.

What am I doing? I can't do this. This isn't me. I'm not even sure there *is* a private washroom—what if it's just a bunch of dirty disgusting public stalls.

This was a very bad idea.

I follow the washroom sign and round the corner, wanting to die. I literally want my life to be over at this exact second.

That's it… *The End.*

But as I reach the washroom, I breathe a little easier.

It *is* a private washroom, and there seems to be no one around. I enter slowly and study my surroundings. It's not dirty, but not particularly clean either. It's simple—a lone pedestal sink and white toilet, waste basket, towel, and soap dispensers. A large gilded mirror catches my reflection…I look absolutely terrified.

What was I thinking? I wonder, my back pressed against the door.

He's hasn't followed me.

Weston Hanson hates germs. The man applies hand disinfectant religiously. He also appears to have OCD and a strong aversion to public displays of any kind.

Weston Hanson *does not* have raunchy sex in public washrooms.

I bury my face in my hands. I can feel the familiar lump in my throat, and I know the tears are coming.

Chapter Eleven

Better than good.

I hear a light knock on the door.

I turn around and open it slowly.

I see him.

He comes in and locks the door behind us, his gaze glued to mine.

His lips are on mine before I can say a word. His tongue is in my mouth. His kiss is hungry. He presses me hard against the door, holds my face tightly in his hands…he owns me.

I have never been kissed quite like this before—with such raw emotion, such hunger. I feel my entire core melting and a deep ache in my stomach, a wonderful ache.

I drop my clutch and reach for his skin. I want to touch him. I pull his shirt and slide my hand along the warm smooth skin of his stomach. He moans in my mouth and slides his hand up the inside of my thigh. I'm so aroused, I fear I might climax before he even touches me.

His mouth travels down to my neck. "I want you."

"Have me," I whisper in his ear.

He reaches for my panties. I feel him hard against me.

This is really happening.

He pulls them down. His hands are soft and gentle against my skin. I close my eyes, enjoying his touch. I am *so* ready for this.

But then…

Knock. Knock.

We stop. We don't make a peep. We don't move. Weston's face is buried in my neck, his hand still wrapped up in my panties.

We hear another knock. Louder, this time.

The handle jiggles.

We stay completely motionless, buried in each other.

The handle jiggles more loudly.

"Uh…one…moment," I say, my voice shaky. "I…I'll be right out."

Fuck.

I pull my panties back up. Weston looks absolutely mortified.

What have I got us into?

"There's no way out," I whisper. "This woman outside will see us. She'll know what we were up to."

My hearts pounds in my chest. And suddenly, I can't breathe.

I *really* can't breathe.

I'm familiar with this sensation—I'm having a full-blown panic attack.

"Are you all right?" Weston asks, genuine concern on his face. He rests his hands on my shoulders. "Breathe."

"I…I can…can't." I can barely get the words out. I kneel and bend my head down. I close my eyes and I hug myself tightly. I focus on my breathing. This will pass. It always does. It's been ages since I've had an attack, and I can't believe it's happening now. I'm sure I'm *real* attractive—Weston must wonder what the hell he's got himself into.

He grabs my clutch off the floor. "Will you be all right?" he asks. His voice is so soft, it calms me. And his eyes are so kind, full of concern.

He kneels down next to me and stays by my side until I can breathe again.

How did I ever think this man was cold?

Finally, I stand slowly, my breathing not quite normal, but good enough to undertake my "walk of shame."

"Let's do this."

I turn the door handle slowly and open the door to a very annoyed, tiny, middle-aged woman. I'm not saying a word, I decide. I don't owe this stranger any explanations. Weston walks out behind me, and I spot the look of shock on the woman's face.

"We're very sorry," he offers. "My girlfriend was having a panic attack."

Well, it's true. He didn't lie.

Except for the "girlfriend" part.

The tiny woman scowls. "Oh…is that what we're calling it these days." She's clearly annoyed, but she doesn't seem too scandalized.

It's not the end of the world, after all.

No, the end of the world comes shortly after, when Weston and I take our seats again. It is so uncomfortable—I will remember this moment for the rest of my life, the most excruciating minutes of my existence.

Such a situation would be uneasy for any normal couple on a first date, but this is Weston and I—we're already socially awkward in the best of circumstances.

He pulls out the familiar bottle of hand disinfectant.

"Can I have some," I ask. We both disinfect our hands. I smile at the sight of us—we make quite the odd couple.

"That bathroom wasn't super clean." I point out.

"It wasn't the worst I've seen."

"I'm sorry," I say, "for making you do that."

He smiles at me—a sly smile. "You didn't make me do anything. I admit it…I'm generally quite preoccupied with the billion or so microscopic creatures lurking on the surface of everything we see, but trust me…they didn't enter my mind for a second when I followed you into that washroom."

His words arouse me.

I'm curious. "What was on your mind?"

He pauses for a beat, his eyes thoughtful. "Touching you," he says, his words soft. "Kissing you."

And suddenly, I want to be in that washroom again—touching him, kissing him.

I spot the tiny woman returning from the washroom. She shoots me the evil eye. I'm mortified—I want to bury my face in my pasta.

And to add insult to injury, this one's a gossip. As soon as she sits down, I hear her whisper to her girlfriends. And they all turn to look at us.

"Don't look," she snaps.

But it's too late.

"I'm sorry, Weston," I say, head down. "But…can we leave?"

He looks at me, fork over his half-finished veal. "Sure, Mirella. If that's what you want."

I'm surprised by his reaction. If I pulled this kind of thing with Gabe, he'd tell me to shape up and finish my meal.

As we leave the restaurant, I'm still a little uneasy.

"I'm so sorry, Weston. You didn't even get to finish your meal."

"I understand. It was a painfully embarrassing situation. I wanted to leave as well. And besides, my veal was kind of cold."

"I've completely messed up our entire date."

He takes my hand. "No you didn't," he argues, pulling me to him. "You've made it wonderful."

"Are you sure you want to do this with me?" I ask, not quite able to look at him.

"Positive."

I look up at him. His gaze is fixed to mine. He still holds my hand in his, his thumb traces soft circles on the flesh of my palm.

"Can I take you to my place?" he asks. I can tell he wants to finish what we've started. And I want to.

But I'm just too frazzled. My breathing's not quite right. My nerves are shot. And I desperately want to retreat to a quiet place.

I realize I need a little more time.

"I want to, Weston. Believe me. But tonight doesn't feel right."

"You're not ready," he says. And I see unmistakable disappointment in his eyes. "I can wait for you." His expression is gentle.

He's so sweet…I feel something for him. Something I know I'm not supposed to feel. I try not to think about it…to not even go there.

I reach up and wrap my arms around him. He stiffens a bit and hesitates.

But I don't let go.

His arms wrap slowly around me and tighten. A wonderful heat spreads through my core…this is one *amazing* hug.

We hold each other for the longest time, standing on the street, and he doesn't let go. I'm shocked he doesn't let go. And it feels so intimate, even more intimate than our washroom tryst…and I tear myself away at the realization.

"I'm sorry Weston," I say, dashing to the sidewalk. "I know I'm not supposed to—"

He runs after me. "It's fine, Mirella."

He stills me with his hand. "Hugs are," he pauses for a beat, "acceptable."

I laugh a little.

"Really?" I tease. "Are hugs *acceptable?* You don't seem too sure."

He cocks his head with a playful expression. "Well, let me check the manual when I get home."

My jaw drops. "There's a *manual?*"

He laughs. "I'm jesting, Mirella," he tells me, with a gentle poke on the tip of my nose. "You're very gullible."

He's being playful, and I like this version of him. Very much.

Well, what do you know…perhaps there *is* a man under the suit of armor after all.

Weston sends me home in his car. Edward is courteous and discreet as always.

In the refuge of Weston's car, I can finally breathe. I close my eyes and relive the events of the night—the good parts—Weston's face, his smile, his hand on the inside of my thigh, his lips on mine, the taste of red wine, his arms tight around me.

I chide myself.

I'm already doing it…I'm already falling for him.

Why can't I do this? It's not that complicated…just have sex with the man and go on with my life, no strings attached. Just enjoy a good fuck. Why can't I just do that?

This was a colossal mistake, I can't help but think, tears running down my cheeks. I reach for a tissue.

I am so glad to be alone.

My thoughts drift to Gabe and Bridget. I shouldn't think about them, but I can't help myself. They are probably going to town on each other at this exact moment. My husband is balls deep in another woman right now. And then, I officially start to blubber like a small child. I don't think Edward sees me—he's trained to be discreet.

I don't even care if he sees me—I'm just that far gone.

Just a few weeks ago, I was a normal happy suburban wife and mother.

"And now, look at me," I mutter as I grab another tissue and blow my nose. "I'm a complete disaster."

When I get home, Caroline is playing a princess board game with the girls. She seems surprised to see me back home so early.

"I wasn't expecting you till much later. You're early."

"Yes," I say, knowing full well I probably look like something the cat dragged in. "I'm sorry. I'll pay you for the full night."

"You don't need to do that," she says, a concerned look on her face. "Are you feeling okay?"

"I'm fine," I assure her. "Here. I insist." I give her the full amount.

"You sure?"

I just want her to leave. "Yes."

Claire is attached to my leg. She seems glad to have me back home. "But, Mommy, we weren't finished with our game."

"I'll take Caroline's place." I think this might just be the distraction I need.

But it doesn't work. At all. Visions of Gabe and Bridget twirl around in my head. I'm so messed up. Why did I ever agree to this? I've never regretted anything more in my life.

I kiss the girls good night and tuck them in. I even kiss Bitzy, Claire's stuffed monkey, and Cookie, Chloe's favorite stuffed dog. As I tuck the girls in, a big part of me is happy I didn't go through with it. I can't do this to them—jeopardize my marriage, our lives. My panic attack was truly a blessing in disguise. I don't want to do this.

I take a long bath, and try not to think.

Gabe finally comes home at around eleven. I bound down the stairs in my plush pink bathrobe to see him.

And as soon as I see his face, I know.

He's slept with her.

My heart sinks.

I don't know what to say to him. I know we can't discuss it, but I want to know everything. I *need* to know everything.

"How was your night?" I ask, my voice soft.

He hesitates, taking off his jacket. "It was fine."

I stare down at the floor, not wanting to see his face, to see the truth. "Just fine?"

He turns away from me. "Mirella," he says. "You know we're not supposed to talk about it. It's a bad idea."

"Did you…"

He swallows, avoiding my gaze.

"Did you?" I snap. "Look at me."

He rakes a hand through his hair and turns to look at me. "Why are you doing this, Ella?"

My throat closes up. The tears rush out. "Because…"

He nods, his eyes downcast.

I sit down on the stairs and hug my knees. The tears flow. Part of me was hoping he'd had a change of heart too, that he'd also realized this was one big, giant mistake.

He wraps his arms around me, holding me tight. "Ella," he whispers, "you agreed to this. I thought we both wanted this."

I bury my swollen face in his chest. "I thought I wanted it too," I cry.

"You've changed your mind?" he asks. "You still can, if you don't want to do this."

"Oh great," I hiss, pushing him away. "You would just love that. You've already got your jollies. You're good to go."

"Ella," he pleads, reaching for my hand. "I know I can't say anything, but I can tell you one thing," he says, his gorgeous hazel eyes fixed on mine. "It was just sex. Just sex."

Just sex. Plain and simple.

"How did you fuck her?" I hiss. I want to know all the sordid details.

"Mirella," he snaps, grasping my hand tighter. "The girls are upstairs…don't be like this."

"How?" I ask. "More than one way, I bet."

He grabs my face in his hands. Hard. "Don't do this," he pleads with me. "Let's end this right now. Call everything off."

I tear myself away and stand, wiping my face with the sleeve of my bathrobe.

He reaches from behind and wraps his arms tightly around me, holding me captive. "What happened with Weston?" he asks, his words sharp and edgy. "He didn't hurt you, did he?"

"No. He was good."

Better than good.

"Did you two…" Suddenly, Gabe is the one who's curious.

"No," I say simply, not really wanting to talk about the details.

"Wow," he says. "What was he waiting for? You're gorgeous…I would have nailed you within the hour."

He almost did, I want to say.

"What's wrong with the guy? I told you he was strange."

I turn around to look at him. "It was me, Gabe," I cry. "I wasn't ready."

"Oh…" he mutters, and I see joy in his eyes. He's happy I didn't go through with it.

I bury my face in my hands. "I actually had one of my panic attacks," I confess.

"You didn't!"

"Full-blown, baby. It was mortifying."

"I'm sorry, babe," he says, hugging me tightly. "This was a bad idea."

I know.

"I love you so much," he adds in a whisper, squeezing me tighter.

I hold him tight, thinking maybe there's still a chance to end all this.

Maybe there's still a chance for us.

I'm sure Weston will understand.

Life is strange now.

I know Gabe hasn't technically cheated on me, but it still feels like he has. I can't be with him. There's too much anger in me. I need time.

He's been very patient and kind. He says he understands how I feel. But I don't think he really does.

We talk and officially decide to not go through with the exchange. We both agree it was a terrible idea in the first place. But I want to tell Weston in person. I don't think it's the kind of thing I should tell his assistant—and that would be way too awkward.

I pace around the house for days, dreading the confrontation. I don't eat. I don't sleep. Weston is a wonderful man, and the last thing I want to do is hurt him.

But I really can't do this.

I dab a touch of lip gloss, looking at my reflection in the bathroom mirror. My hair is up in a hard bun—no tendrils framing my face, not the least amount of softness. I've worn one of my outfits usually reserved for school—a simple black A-line skirt, a white buttoned blouse with a red Peter Pan collar. My makeup is minimal, and I haven't bothered with accessories.

It seems an appropriate outfit for a break-up. I definitely don't want to show up in a sultry dress, fuck-me heels, and then tell him I don't want to see him anymore—that would just be cruel.

I put on my glasses and grab my red briefcase on my way out.

Weston has sent his car to fetch me again—it's much better this way. I don't drive very much in the city, and I'm likely to get lost or develop an ulcer trying to find a parking spot.

As I sit, looking out the window, my emotions are at odds. I don't really want to do this. I've made my decision, yet I cannot imagine never seeing Weston again. And I know I'll never see him again once I tell him I don't want to do this. I wonder how he'll react—I know he'll be disappointed.

We meet for lunch at *Sixteen*. I've requested a lunch meeting instead of our usual dinner date—the last thing I want is a dark, moody restaurant—I don't want to lose my resolve.

I'm ending this.

As I leave the elevator, I'm confident I can do this.

But then, sure enough, I see him standing against the wall at the entrance. I've never seen him look so gorgeous—his tall frame sleek in a snug chocolate brown V-neck shirt and slim fitted khakis. A brown distressed leather satchel hangs loosely over his shoulder, and dark hipster glasses frame his eyes.

The man looks like a friggin' Gucci ad.

Damn.

Just when I thought he couldn't possibly get sexier.

He flashes me that insanely wide smile of his when he spots me. He seems so happy to see me, and I'm about to dump him. My heart is filled with guilt.

He kisses me on the cheek. "I love those glasses."

I was trying to be unsexy, but I think the glasses have backfired.

"I like yours too. Are they just for show?"

"They're the real thing. I like to occasionally give my eyes a break from contacts."

I take in my surroundings—wide open spaces, white linen tables, wood veneered walls as tall as the sky, and a view of Chicago to die for.

"Do you have a big prescription?" I ask as the hostess leads us to our table.

"I don't see too well. I've considered Lasik eye surgery, but honestly, it scares the hell out of me," he says, pulling a chair for me.

"I have a pretty small prescription. Point five in one eye, and point seventy-five in the other. What's yours?"

"About two point five in both eyes."

Splendid, I muse…we're just two nerds having a really geeky conversation about our eye prescriptions—this isn't sexy at all.

This is exactly the mood I was hoping for.

But then, he turns on a dime.

"I like your skirt," his says, his green eyes as striking as ever, even behind those heavy dark frames.

"Thank you," I say, trying to not be affected.

But it's no use. He looks so good.

Water is poured and menus are handed out.

I barely browse the menu—too much on my mind. "Listen, Weston, thank you for meeting me today," I start, trying to keep the mood formal. "I hope it wasn't too much of an inconvenience changing the time."

"Well," he says. "I did have plans with my children."

"Oh no," I say and suddenly feel like I've trampled a puppy. "I didn't want to take you away from your kids."

"It's fine, Mirella. We're actually having an early dinner tonight instead and going to see a movie. They hardly ever get to spend Saturday nights with me. They're quite excited about it, in fact."

"Oh, I'm glad to hear it," I say, looking down at the lunch menu. I decide to opt for the leek and truffle soup and salad. Weston decides on the beef pot au feu.

"Listen," I say, gulping a sip of water. "I wanted to meet today…" I trail off. This is a lot harder than I anticipated.

"Yes…what?"

I sigh. "Oh nothing…"

I am such a coward.

"I have something special planned. I thought it might be a good idea for us to do something fun together, get comfortable around each other," he says. "I certainly don't expect you to jump into bed with me right after dessert."

I sigh. He's making this really hard.

"You don't want me to have another panic attack?" I joke.

He laughs. "Yes, hopefully we can avoid that today."

"Where are you taking me?" I ask curious, thinking I can break up with him at the end of our outing. I know I'm procrastinating, but I can't help it. I just want to spend a little more time with him before we say good-bye forever.

"It's a surprise," he replies, as excited as a school boy going on a field trip. "But I can tell you…it's one of my favorite places in the world."

I am officially intrigued. What could it be? What would be one of Weston's favorite places in the world? The theater? The museum?

"Do you always spend Saturdays with your kids?" I ask him, enjoying a spoonful of my soup.

"I try. Before we had them, I was a real workaholic. I worked twenty-four seven. But the kids have changed me."

"Kids will do that," I point out with a smirk.

"You must really love children."

"I do."

"You are probably a great mother," he adds, cutting into his beef.

I laugh. "I like to think so. I strive to be."

"Did you have a good mother?" he asks, and I'm taken aback by his question. He occasionally has an uncanny way of jumping from small talk to more intimate conversation, skipping all the stuff in between, and completely ignoring social decorum. But I kind of like that about him.

I don't really want to answer his question, but I feel I almost need to, since he asked it.

"My mother was a good mother until she fell madly in love with another man."

"Tell me more," he says, probably not realizing he's being very nosy.

"She met him at a café. He was a professor of French literature, guest lecturing at the university. His name was Gilles. He was French and handsome, impeccably dressed, and he swept my mother right off her feet. She was thirty-three." I hesitate a bit before telling him the rest—it's not often I talk about this. "I was only six. My youngest brother was only one. I met the man just once, but I remember him clearly. She ran away to live with him in New York...and took the baby."

"I'm sorry. That's horrible," he says with wide eyes. "Did your father raise you?"

"Yes...me and my two older brothers. My dad's great."

"Yes," he says, fork hanging mid-air. "He would have to be."

"What were your parents like? What's your family like?" I ask, realizing I really don't know much about him. In my mind, I've already concocted my own story—and it involves a sprawling mansion, a successful family business, impeccably dressed parents and siblings, possibly a game of croquet—a real Kennedy-esque picture.

"Well," he starts, pausing to take a sip of wine. "Coincidentally... speaking of professors...my father was also a university professor. At

Oxford. Physics. Apparently a genius mind, according to my mother. He also owned dozens of patents. He was an inventor of sorts," he explains, trailing circles along the bottom of his glass. "My parents were both academics. My mother was just a student when she met him, and before long, she was pregnant."

"With you?" I ask, fully engrossed in his story.

"Yes. With me. And my father didn't want a thing to do with me…or with her, for that matter."

His childhood was not the one I had imagined at all. In fact, it sounds even worse than mine.

"What's worse?" I venture. "Your parent leaving you when you're six…or before you're even born?"

He ponders my question for a beat. "Six, I would venture," he says, his voice soft. "I never knew him. I never had a chance to even form a connection. You on the other hand…" he trails off, putting down his fork.

"What happened to you?" I ask. For some reason, I want to know every detail.

"Well, my father supported us financially—he was a wealthy man. My mother hired a British nanny…a real Mary Poppins type." A smile curves his lips. "Her name was Elizabeth."

"Like your daughter?"

"Yes. We named Lizzie after her."

"She meant a lot to you?"

"She did. I loved her more than my mother," he says, without the slightest indication of guilt.

"Was your mother not kind?" I'm prying, but the intimate feel of the conversation allows it.

"She was very distant. She was very independent. Sometimes I sensed she wasn't very fond of me."

"What would make you say that?"

He sets his glass down and looks out at the Chicago skyline. "Occasionally," he pauses for a second, "she would look at me with contempt in her eyes, and tell me I looked and acted exactly like my father."

"I'm sorry," is all I can say. I'm no child psychologist, but even I know something like that could really mess up a little kid.

And suddenly, I feel I understand him a little better…and I want to offer him my affection…my love. I don't want to leave him. And I certainly don't want to hurt him.

I was concerned I wouldn't be able to go through with the break-up. I worried his striking eyes or his drop-dead gorgeous smile would pull me in. But I never realized *he* would pull me in…*him*.

I drop my fork and gulp a mouthful of water. I am officially royally screwed.

"I apologize," he says. "I really didn't mean to be so somber… but you asked."

"I did," I say. "I'm sorry. I didn't mean to pry."

"It's fine."

I smile thinly at him and neither of us utters another word.

We opt out of dessert and head toward Weston's secret destination, whizzing in his town car. I am getting very used to being driven around.

"You don't drive much, do you?"

"I really don't like it. I like to multi-task and work, and I can't very well do that if I'm driving."

"Time is money right?" I say, crossing a leg over the other. And I notice him glance down at my stocking clad legs.

"Exactly."

"So, how much money are you wasting with me right now?"

He gives me that sexy smile—the one which makes me crave him. "A lot. But it's not wasted. Some things are worth it."

I bite my lip.

I want him.

I shake my head a little.

"So, you're not a car guy?"

"Not really. I have a few. But I consider them a necessity rather than a luxury. Occasionally, if something is weighing on me, I like to go for a drive to cool off, but that's about it."

"Wow. You're really not like other guys, are you?"

"That's what I like to think."

"How far?" I ask, curiosity killing me.

He reaches for my hand. "About ten minutes." I intertwine my fingers in his, thinking this day is not turning out as I had planned. I decide I'm going to commit, or not commit, but a decision needs to be made. And if I do what I really want to do, I'll be having a rather explosive conversation with Gabe.

I can't seem to peel my eyes away from him—I like this version of him—casual, more laid-back, less rigid. He seems more human.

"C'mon," I urge him, giving him my sexiest smile. "Tell me where we're going."

He presses a finger against his lips. "I'm not saying a word."

He looks happy. *I've* made him happy. And suddenly, I feel so powerful.

When we get to our destination, I recognize the place as soon as I see the large pillars standing tall at the front of the classic building. I've been here with the girls…they love Shedd Aquarium.

"Well, that explains the fish tie and cufflinks," I say as he leads me up the stairs to the entrance.

"You've noticed those? You're very observant."

He has no idea that I've mentally catalogued practically every detail of him—what he's said, what he's worn…everything.

"So, you like fish," I say as we stand to buy tickets.

"All sea life really. All underwater creatures. It's another world."

"Do you dive?" I want to know more about this obsession.

"I try as much as I can. And I go snorkeling with Bridget and the kids. Do you snorkel?"

"No." I laugh. "I'm a decent swimmer but breathing out of a tube really freaks me out. It panics me every time I try."

He looks at me and smiles but doesn't say a word.

"What?"

"Well, maybe one day, I can teach you," he offers.

I laugh. "I think I'll pass on that. Where do you do all this snorkeling?"

He pulls out his wallet to pay for the tickets. "Mostly Hawaii. We have a place down there."

Of course…they have a place in Hawaii.

"Well, if you're going to teach me in Hawaii, I think I've changed my mind," I joke, knowing very well he'll never take me to Hawaii.

He laughs. "Have you ever been?"

"Nope," I tell him, not elaborating. I've never been anywhere it seems.

The cashier hands him our tickets, and we make our way to the exhibits.

He leads me, occasionally putting his hand on the small of my back as we walk through the Caribbean exhibit. We're surrounded by colorful fish, beautiful coral, sea turtles, green eels, and rays. He's right…it is quite magical when you take the time to appreciate it.

I enjoy walking along with him as he tells me about the sea life. I can tell he's very passionate about it—he's a walking encyclopedia, telling me interesting facts occasionally. I like seeing him this animated—he's usually so subdued. He's like a little kid…an adorable little kid.

"You've always liked ocean life?"

"Since I was about two, according to my mother," he says, not quite looking at me. "It was an obsession. Apparently, I amassed a giant collection of all the sea life books in existence."

"The whole Jacques Cousteau collection?"

He laughs. "Of course."

Every now and then, he looks over at me with the slightest hint of a smile, his beautiful almond shaped eyes driving me insane. It seems no matter where we are…I am hopeless when it comes to him.

"Which sea animal is your favorite?" he asks.

I've never considered it. After a moment's thought, I decide. "The sea turtles, I guess."

"Good choice," he says, taking my hand in his. "They're beautiful. You should see them in their natural habitat…they're incredible."

I sigh a little. I would love to see that with him, to see all those wonderful creatures he loves. Bridget is the one who gets to share those experiences. And unexpectedly, I feel a little pang of jealousy, and I try to shove the thoughts away. I've mentally trained myself to not think about her…but sometimes, it's very challenging.

We finally make our way to the jellyfish exhibit, and I'm absolutely mesmerized—mushroom-shaped, almost transparent creatures, glowing, bopping and swaying against the glowing background, pumping like hearts—it's a magnificent display of nature.

We stand there for the longest time, just the two of us, watching them, not saying a word. I sense Weston's presence behind me with every cell in my body—his breath on my shoulder, his hand on my waist. His lips brush softly against the back of my neck. I close my eyes and suddenly feel limp, like one of those jellyfish, bouncing, floating…

I think about what I vowed. About everything I promised myself. I shouldn't be doing this. I don't want this.

But I don't just want him…I need him.

I turn toward him, and his lips meet mine. My mouth opens for his, and his tongue teases. His mouth tastes like spearmint. His kiss is soft and incredibly sensual. I feel myself melt into him and completely lose sense of my surroundings.

We hear voices in the distance, and I jolt away. He looks at me, his eyes filled with longing.

A mother and her son walk over to the display. The chubby boy looks about twelve or so, and I'm not sure if he spotted us. He might have. And I suddenly feel kind of embarrassed. He flashes us a metal-filled, mischievous smile, and it's confirmed—the kid caught us.

Weston looks over at me, and we both smile.

I pull him to me. "Take me to your car."

Chapter Twelve

He owns me...

Weston opens the rear door for me, and I slide in and take a seat.

We're really doing this.

He sits next to me. And God...how I wish the console separating us would magically disappear. He buckles his seat belt, not taking his eyes off me. I mimic his actions, wishing we weren't shackled by these safety devices. I really couldn't give a hoot about my safety at the moment—all I really want to do is climb all over him.

"How far to the suite?" I ask.

"About ten minutes." His eyes are dark and heavy. I honestly don't know if I can bear that long.

He reaches for my hand and takes it in his. His fingers are so soft and warm. His eyes don't leave me for a second.

"I didn't even get to show you the rest," he says, "the Amazon exhibit, the Oceanarium, the aquatic show. There's so much to see."

"We *could* go back?" I suggest with a sly smile, knowing very well what his reaction will be.

He bites his lip. "Not in a million years." His gaze lingers on me. "Are you sure about this?"

I feel I might explode without his touch. "Yes."

We look at each other for a beat, both knowing we'll be together soon.

"We should go there again someday," I suggest.

"Yes, I'd like that."

I think about our kids. Wouldn't it be nice to go there together with our kids? They would absolutely love it. But I know that could never happen. It would be a very bad idea. I sigh a little at the thought.

"Do you want a drink?" he asks.

"No, thank you," I answer. All I want is him, his hands on me, all over me.

Thinking about it is arousing me. And I wonder what he's thinking.

"Ten minutes has never seemed like such an eternity," he says, with a slight curve of his lip.

God...yes.

He looks at me but doesn't say a word.

We sit in silence for a while. My heart is beating so fast, and I wonder if his is too. I want Edward to speed up, but I know he's helpless against the traffic.

I'm throbbing with anticipation—the sensation is both delicious and painful. Weston's intense stare is not helping. I close my eyes and imagine us together—his lips on mine, his skin on mine.

"I want this so much," I say, feeling that desire in every part of my body—my heart, my stomach, my sex.

"Me too. You can't imagine."

I close my eyes and imagine us together.

I nervously cross and uncross my legs, trying to remember what underwear I'm wearing—I hadn't planned for this. My mind wanders back to this morning. Yes...I'm wearing something decent—a black set covered in cream lace, one of the few luxurious underwear sets I own. Maybe my subconscious knew this would happen—knew what a little tramp I really am.

I smile and pull my hand away from his. "I think..." I whisper, reaching under my skirt, "we should get things started." I'm surprised by my own boldness, but then again, I don't think I've ever been so turned on. Ever.

He looks at me with a strange mix of desire and curiosity. "What are you doing, Mirella?"

I don't answer him. I stare at him as I slowly pull my black panties over my knees and over my sensible black shoes, not breaking eye contact.

I see the desire in his eyes. The way he looks at me…I can't get enough of it.

"You wicked girl," he whispers.

I scrunch my panties in a ball in my hand and lie back on the sleek leather seat, my lids heavy. He might as well pounce on me right now, because I'd let him.

He's fidgeting again—that bouncing knee is going crazy. He bites his lip. "Give them to me."

I smile. I wonder what he wants to do with them—he probably wants to get a better look. I hand them over, trying to be subtle. Edward doesn't seem to be paying us much mind, but I'm not taking any chances.

Weston takes them. He holds them in his hands, traces his long fingers along the lace, and he studies them for the longest time. He seems so intense.

What is going through his mind?

Then he brings them up to his face and closes his eyes as he hides his nose in them.

I'm shocked.

His face is still buried in my underwear when he says, "I can't wait to get you alone."

His behavior is so unexpected. God…he's turning me on.

I bite my lip and I look over at the driver. "Weston…"

He smiles and shoves my panties in his pocket. He looks outside the window, his body edgy and full of nervous energy.

He takes my hand again—I wonder if he can feel it tremble. "We're almost there."

I look out, and there it is—it's so grand, a modern day castle nestled between the skyscrapers of Chicago.

We coast along the drive, and I notice it's busy today—limos, town cars and luxury SUVs. We maneuver slowly between the vehicles.

Finally, Edward leaves us at the entrance. Weston opens the door and pulls me out of the car as fast as I've ever seen a man handle a woman.

He takes my hand and leads me with gusto. He knows exactly where he's going.

I try to take in the grand entrance, but I barely have a chance.

Weston's strides are so long, I can barely keep up with him, and find myself sprinting—the man is in a hurry.

And I know we've passed the point of no return.

I almost want to stop and take in the lobby, with its white walls and cascading silvers, a bursting snowflake light fixture lights up the space—it's stunning—it seems like a mirage.

We reach the elevators, and Weston presses the button. There's no one around. We wait, and though it's probably just a few seconds, it seems like *forever.*

Finally the doors open, and it's just us two. As soon as we're inside, Weston quickly pushes a button and presses me again the mahogany wall. His lips are on mine. He slides his hand between my legs, and I just want to melt into him.

In no time at all, we hear the ding, and we're at his floor. He takes my hand and leads me down the hall to his suite. He pulls a card out of his jacket and shoots me a mischievous smile as he slides the key card in.

We are finally doing this.

And I can't think of anything else. Suddenly, the reasons we shouldn't be doing this don't matter. Not Gabe or the girls. Not Bridget, Lizzie, Ashton—they don't exist anymore. It's just us two.

He motions me to go in.

I barely have time to see where I am before his hands are on my waist. There's a sense of urgency about him I like—he's so uninhibited, out of control—it doesn't seem like him.

He presses me against the wall. My briefcase falls to the floor. He reaches for my hair, and he manages to undo my bun, very slowly. The movements of his hands are languid, and his eyes are fixed on mine. There's a moment of hesitation in me. I want him so much. But part of me is terrified. Once I fall, I'll never be able to recover. I'll only want him more. And I haven't quite fallen completely…yet. Almost. There's still time for me to stop this and go back to my life.

My simple, uncomplicated life.

My hair tumbles over my shoulder. I'm almost motionless. I've wanted to touch him so badly, but now I find myself still, anticipating what he will do to me.

I've never been so scared. "Weston…" I whisper.

He presses his finger to my lips—like he knows I'm teetering on the edge and if he lets me speak, we might never do this. He reaches for my glasses, gently pulls them off, and sets them on the console table. And still, his eyes don't leave mine. I smile up at him and reach for his adorable hipster glasses. I mimic his actions. There's something incredibly erotic about this moment. My mind wants me to stop and run, but I consciously disobey it.

He leans in to kiss me, and my breath catches.

But he doesn't kiss me. He trails his nose over my cheek, down my neck, taunting me. He buries his face in my hair, his familiar woodsy smell filling my nostrils. My hand glides along the edge of his jaw, feeling his five o-clock shadow on the tips of my fingers.

He brings his hand to my cheek—the warmth of it sends shivers through me. I suck in a breath and work up the resolve I need to not go ahead with this.

"I'm…I'm not sure…" I whisper. I can barely find the words—I feel like such a tease. I've let things get too far. "I'm not sure we should do this."

He seems to not have heard me at all. Maybe he doesn't want to hear me. His lips sweep over mine, but are gone in a flash, down to my neck. The warmth of his mouth spreads a heat deep through my whole body, a pulsing pounds deep in my sex. I close my eyes. This is the moment…the moment I let go. I let go of all my worries, my reservations and decide to just enjoy him. My hands travel to his stomach, and I pull his shirt, sweeping my palm against his hot skin. I want his skin on mine.

He's taking things slowly, I realize.

He likes to tease. And I like to be teased.

"Taking…your time," I whisper, my breathing shallow.

"I want this to last forever," he breathes.

And I think I'm going to die if he doesn't speed things up soon—he's killing me.

But I do hold a certain power—he's a man, after all. I bring my lips to his neck and bite him gently—I'm suddenly feeling a little feisty. He laughs, and the sound vibrates into my ear. I pull his satchel over his head and throw it on the floor. He smiles, a slow, delicious grin. I reach for his belt and undo him as fast as I can. I manage to undo his pants button and fly with one hand—my other one refuses to leave his warm skin.

I hear his muffled moan, and I smile—I love arousing him.

I reach into his silky briefs and slowly wrap my fingers around him. He's big and hard…and hot. I've never touched another man in this way before, and fear overtakes me again.

"Mirella…" he moans softly. My name is barely audible on his lips.

His lips sweep over mine, and I open my mouth for him. My whole body warms. This is the kiss I've been waiting for. Ever since the one in that little Italian hole-in-the-wall, I've been waiting for this kiss—uninhibited, passionate. I could do this all night. Just this…might be enough. If we just kissed, I might not jeopardize my marriage, I might not fall so hard. If we just kissed…

His tongue plays with mine softly, and I'm completely lost in him. The length of him is still pressed against my palm. His kiss becomes needy…wild, and I realize it's inevitable—we can't go back now—we want each other too badly.

I've never wanted a man more.

His finger traces a line up my thigh over my thigh-highs, and when he reaches my skin, he makes me shiver. I know when he gets there, he'll find me wet…drenched for him. His finger slowly glides between my legs.

I ache for him to touch me.

He pulls away to look at me, his eyes fixed on mine with an expression I've never seen—a strange mix of desire, playfulness, and domination.

He owns me…and he knows it.

His fingers draw circles up to the edge of my thighs, sweeping my curls lightly, but not quite touching. I catch an impish expression on his face. I cannot stand this anymore…he's driving me insane. He keeps playing with me, and he smiles, just slightly.

He's enjoying this.

"You want this?" he asks, with a sly expression.

I throw my head back and nod a big yes, not finding the courage to utter the words.

His finger sweeps between my lips, but only for a fraction of a second. And he goes back to trailing circles. I can tell he plans to make me suffer.

"Perhaps you shouldn't have made me wait." His words are playful. "My ego is fragile," he whispers in my ear, his breath warming my neck. "You need to learn to know what you want."

I moan out loud, stunned by the sound echoing off the walls. "I know what I want."

"You need to *ask* for what you want."

Damn, I wish I still had my panties on—maybe I wouldn't be so out of control, so vulnerable, so pliable.

He wants me to ask. He wants me to beg.

"I want you," I whisper. "I want you to touch me."

His fingers trails back to my sex, and he toys with me a little, that obnoxious grin still plastered on his face.

And then he slides his finger inside.

Finally…

I close my eyes and let myself enjoy the sensation. He's so wonderful at this. I can feel myself responding to his touch, so strongly, so quickly. I don't want to climax like this, but I let him tease me a little more, enjoying the building pressure.

And finally when I'm nearing the edge, I force myself to pull his hand away. I want to be with him. "Weston," I whisper. "I want *you.*"

His kiss trails down my neck to my shoulder, and he grabs my rear. He pulls me up against him, and I wrap my legs around his hips.

He carries me across the room, and everything's a blur—the living room, the dining room, the entire space. I feel light in his arms—my body fits perfectly against his—like it belongs there. He throws me on the bed and leans down on me, his body heavy. My legs are still in tangles around him, and I don't want to let go.

He tucks a strand of hair behind my ear and looks at me, his gaze soft. I stare at his beautiful eyes, his sensual mouth. His touch is suddenly gentle as a feather as he undoes the pearl buttons on my blouse, not taking his eyes off me. We're in slow motion—time seems to stand still. Finally, he leans in to kiss my collarbone. I pull his face to mine, and kiss him...completely caught up in him.

Desperately wanting him inside me, I tear my mouth away from his. "Do you have..." I ask him, my words breathless, my hands buried in his boxers, the warm smooth skin of his rear on my palms.

He doesn't say a word and reaches into his pocket.

I realize I've never used a condom. I've always been on the pill, and I've only been with Gabe. I struggle and Weston helps me—he seems to sense my lack of experience. Finally, I gently slide the condom on, my heart pounding.

He buries his face into my neck, and touches me again, sliding his fingers in and out. I don't want to come just yet. I don't know how long I'm going to last. I want to make love.

"Please," I plead. "Now..."

He pulls his hand away from my sex and wipes his wet fingers along my thigh. He trails kisses along the lacy edge of my bra and pulls my breast out of its cup and kisses it with such gentleness, I almost melt.

His kiss travels softly to my neck as he sinks into me. His heat fills me. And it seems my whole body sparks. But as wonderful as it is, it does feel somewhat foreign—another man inside me.

He buries his face in my hair. "You are beautiful."

He's slow and gentle at first. We kiss softly, hands tangled in each other's hair.

But before long, his grasp pulls at my hair, his lips tear away from mine, and he pushes into me harder, driving deeper and deeper into me—I love every thrust. I moan so loudly, I am practically screaming. I want him to hear how amazing he makes me feel. He breathes hard into my ear, and I think he whispers my name—his voice is so soft, I'm not sure.

I'm coming closer and closer to the edge. The louder I moan, the harder he pushes, my climax building.

He owns it. My pleasure is in his hands.

Finally, the tension in me releases in waves of pure ecstasy. I cry out and dig my nails into his back, the cashmere soft against my fingers. He pushes hard into me and stills as his climax follows mine. His moans are slow and soft, his breath is warm against my ear.

I feel slightly numb.

And wonderful.

His face is still buried in my neck. I don't dare look at him. I realize we are both still fully dressed. I hadn't imagined our first time like this—in my fantasies, we were both completely naked, exploring every single inch of each other's bodies. But reality is never quite like fantasy. Reality, in this case, was still pretty amazing, I tell myself, still recovering from one of the best orgasms I've ever had.

His weight suffocates me.

I push him off me. "Weston..."

He slides out of me slowly and pulls away. I almost reach for him. But he moves swiftly to the edge of the bed. He stands and turns from me. I catch a glimpse of his ass as he pulls his pants back up—he has a great ass. He leaves for the washroom without looking back.

I sit up, pop my breast back into my bra, and smooth down my skirt. My heart sinks. I don't know what to think.

What was I expecting? Cuddles?

I should have expected this—he warned me.

This is about sex. Plain and simple.

I hear the running water.

No words. No kiss. I still can't believe it.

He comes back and his pants are done up, his hair is smooth, and he's wearing his glasses.

He smiles at me and grabs his satchel off the floor. "You were wonderful."

Well, there's *something.*

He kisses the tip of my nose. "I'm sorry, but I do have to run. I'm running late. My date with the kids..."

I button up my blouse and stare down at my sensible black ballet flats—sex with my shoes on—how wild. "I understand."

My heart sinks even deeper. I want to cry. But I can't let him see me crumble. He has warned me about this. And I promised him I could handle it.

He reaches into his satchel. "Feel free to stay." He pulls out his wallet, and for a brief moment, I have this horrible vision of him giving me money.

"Here's a card for my car service. Call them when you're ready to leave," he hands me the card, "You can order room service if you wish. You barely ate a thing at lunch."

"I might." I try to act normal, even though I'm dying inside.

"Good, I was starting to wonder how you keep your curves," he teases. "I've barely ever seen you eat a thing."

"What are you trying to say?" I ask, a little self-conscious.

He laughs. "You're beautiful," he assures me. "You're perfect. Please don't ever lose an inch."

"You've never seen me naked."

He scratches his chin. "Yes…" he says, "we'll have to rectify that, won't we?" he adds as he walks away.

"Next time, I want to *see* you," he says as he reaches the door, "every inch of you."

And just like that, he's out the door, and I'm left with a business card in my hands and no panties.

I feel like such a whore.

When I get home, I kick off my shoes and practically sprint to see the girls. They're lying on the sofa downstairs in the rec room, eating potato chips and watching a movie they've seen a million times before. I hug Chloe tightly and guilt washes over me. How could I have done this? To her…to Claire? This kind of thing never ends well. And they're the ones who will probably suffer for it…I feel the familiar lump in my throat.

Claire pops a potato chip in her tiny mouth. "What have you been up to, little lady?" she asks, her voice as sweet as ever. It's the same question she's asked me a hundred times before, parroting her father, saying it just the way he does.

Sweet heavenly days…I have been up to no good.

I bite my lip and slump on the sofa, not quite looking at her. "Nothing." I have officially starting lying now. To my own daughter.

"Well, it must have been something, Mom…you were gone for hours," Chloe pipes in, not taking her eyes off the TV. I'm glad she's not looking at me. If she were, she'd probably know I'm lying through my teeth.

"I was checking out some stores I like in the city." *When I should have been spending time with you.*

Gabe bounds down the stairs. I can't quite look at him.

I don't want to do this.

"Ella…" he says.

I venture a look up at him. He stands there, motionless, today's newspaper dangling in one hand.

He knows. I'm not sure how, but his expression says it all. He looks like he's been kicked in the gut.

Damn it, I didn't want this.

He throws the paper at the wall and bounds back up the stairs. The loud bang stuns the girls—Chloe finally takes her eyes off the TV, slack-jawed. It's what he does when he's pissed—he throws things.

I run after him, wanting to explain. "Gabe, I…"

When I finally reach him upstairs, he turns to me and grabs my wrist, pulling me to him. I can tell he has no intention of letting go. He drags me to the powder room and slams the door shut behind us. He definitely knows what I've been up to.

He glares at me. "What happened?"

I can't seem to form the words I need to answer him.

"Did he hurt you?"

Did he hurt me? Yes, he did. "No."

"Why have you been crying then? What happened?"

I don't say a word, knowing my silence will be his answer. The truth is, I can't find the words. I can barely breathe.

"Did you fuck him?" he snaps. I'm not sure why he's asking since he seems to already know. He grabs my waist and buries his head into my neck. "I can smell him on you."

Tears make their way down my cheeks. "I'm sorry," I whisper, my voice ragged, "I planned to end things with him, but then…"

He presses closer against me. I want to escape. I don't want to have this conversation. "But then…you begged him to stick it in you…I get it."

"Don't be like that," I plead as I catch a glimpse of my reflection in the mirror. No wonder he knew; running mascara, flushed face, just-fucked hair—I'm a dead giveaway.

"How was he?" he breathes in my ear. "Better than me?"

I don't answer him of course. He wasn't better, I want to say… just different.

He presses me against the wall. "I'd be surprised if he was," gently biting my earlobe, "there's no one who can fuck you better than I can."

He trails his mouth along my collarbone. "Tell me something," he says, his words playful. "Did Mr. Stiff-Upper-Lip make you fold your panties after you took them off?"

I don't know what possesses me, but his arrogance gets to me. And I know I'll regret the words as soon as I say them. And I know I'm not supposed to talk about what happens behind closed doors, but the words come out before I can stop them. "No, he buried his nose in them…and shoved them in his pocket."

He jolts back, a scowl on his face. He turns from me, grabs the hand towel off the hook and throws it at the mirror, so hard, the "smack" bounces off the walls.

There's a good reason for the rules, I chide myself.

I have such a big mouth.

Surprisingly, his expression softens and his anger seems to dissipate.

His hand reaches for the collar of my blouse. He undoes the buttons slowly, surprisingly gently. "Wow, I'm impressed." He trails his hand down my chest. "Did he use a condom?"

I can't believe he would even ask me that question. "Of course."

He slides his rough hand up my leg. "Good. I'm putting my stamp on you. I'm completely erasing him."

He can't possibly want me here, now, in the powder room?

I can't do this.

This is not the time or place.

And he's not thinking straight.

His hand stills when he reaches my hips and realizes I'm going commando. "What the fuck?"

"Uh…" I stammer. I want to disappear. "Still in his pocket," I tell him, my words barely a whisper.

He looks at me with an expression I've never seen before—anger mixed with pure desire. "You are a little tramp, aren't you?" he whispers in my ear. "So, you'll probably like it when I treat you like one."

He's still fuming.

The grasp of his hand is hard.

This doesn't feel right.

His reaction shocks me—I've never seen him quite like this. I *can't* let him treat me like this. No matter how angry he is.

I push him off me. "Back off, Gabe. I don't want to play this game."

His face softens—apparently, I've finally knocked some sense into him. "I'm sorry," he says quietly.

I don't know what to say. I make an escape and run up the stairs, holding my blouse tightly against my chest.

I plop myself on the bed and fall into a puddle of tears. Gabe doesn't come to me. And I don't want him to.

God...what a hot mess.

Chapter Thirteen

Settle down...little butterfly.

Gabe and I are lying in bed. My head rests on his stomach, and he strokes my hair.

"I'm sorry, Ella," he says softly. "I was angry. It was the initial shock. It won't happen again, I promise. I just...I expected you to break things off with him, but then..."

Gabe's reaction wasn't completely unexpected. I knew he would be very upset. I've never been with anyone else before. I've only been his. And now, someone else has had me—someone he's threatened by. Gabe was angry, and he acted out of anger, and that's all there is to it.

I decide to let it go.

"I forgive you." I lace my fingers in his.

"You know I love you, right?"

"I love you too."

That night, although we know we can't go into the details, we talk about the exchange—about our feelings.

We discuss how strange it feels to be with someone else—the doubts, the fears and the excitement. We also confess the feelings of anger and jealousy we both experienced when we realized the person we love had been with someone else. And we talk about the guilt—the battle between remorse and desire.

I tell him I don't really want to do this again with Weston, but I don't tell him why—I don't admit Weston managed to make me feel like a whore. If Gabe knew, he would be livid and would probably do something very stupid.

After much prodding, he finally admits he enjoyed himself with Bridget and wouldn't mind seeing her again, but he also tells me he's happy I want to end the arrangement. I let him know I'd like to see Weston again, perhaps just one more time. Part of me wants to see him again, despite the fact that part of me hates him.

How can a person want to be with someone who makes them feel terrible? I don't understand my emotions. I don't understand him. He was so sweet and warm…and then, he just turned cold.

I so desperately want to understand him.

We don't see or connect with Weston and Bridget for what seems like an eternity, communicating with Kathryn exclusively. She lets us know Weston is out of town on business. And I wonder if he's avoiding me. His behavior was so strange after we had sex—he couldn't get out of there fast enough. Of course, I start obsessing, wondering what he thought of me. He did say I was wonderful. I chide myself for thinking this way and tell myself I don't give a rat's ass what he thinks. But I do.

I wish I didn't, but I do.

I want to see him. I want to talk to him. I want to know why he behaved the way he did. I hate these rules. I want to call him. I realize how convenient this little arrangement of ours is for him—he gets to sleep with me when the mood strikes but keeps me at arm's length. He gets a little on the side, and still, his perfect idyllic life is left unscathed. He's managed to turn me into a miserable, pathetic excuse of a woman—I need to stand up for myself. It's probably a good thing to keep some distance for the moment, because I might throttle him.

But despite this, I can't help thinking about him, about the way he made me feel. As much as I hate to admit…the sex was amazing.

I kind of wish he had been terrible in bed—then maybe I could just walk away. He still has my underwear, the bottoms of a very expensive set. And I can't exactly call him up or text him about it. I can only communicate with Kathryn. A smile stretches my lips as I compose a note for her.

> Dear Kathryn,
>
> Please inform Weston that he is in possession of some of my personal property. I would like to see it returned at a convenient time.
>
> Thank you so much.
>
> Cheers,
> Mirella

I have no clue how Weston will react to this playful e-mail, and I'm not sure if I even care. The next day, I receive a reply from Kathryn.

> Dear Mirella,
>
> I have informed Weston about your personal property. He is indeed in possession of it, is personally overseeing it, and will return it to you, in intact condition, at your next meeting.
>
> Best,
> Kathryn

I laugh at the formality and absurdity of it all. It seems Weston does have a sense of humor after all.

Weston and I meet at the restaurant at his building.

My brain has been playing a very explosive reel—a constant loop of alternating images of me telling him to shove it where the sun don't shine, my words laced with very colorful language. I'm still so angry at him, but I'm determined to not let it show. Under no circumstances do I want him to know I care.

Because he obviously doesn't.

The hostess leads me through the sleek space—glowing amber pendant lights, glossy leather seats, wrought-iron accents. One of my favorite Adele songs is playing in the background. The mood evokes something in me—something I can't quite put my finger on. But when I see him seated at the table, wearing a fitted paisley button shirt and dark wash jeans, it comes to me…yes…the mood is *all sex*.

He waves and stands when he sees me.

I take a step back when he kisses me on the cheek. He pulls a chair for me. I don't care how polite he is, I'm still livid. How could he just leave me like that, not call me for over two weeks, leave me hanging, and let me spiral into an obsessive-compulsive state of near-madness. I really should end this…right now.

I must admit though…the man does look good.

He folds up his *Chicago Tribune* and tucks it away in his satchel. "How are you?"

I take a seat, my body as stiff as a frozen shovel. "I'm fine, thank you."

I notice he's put on his armor again—it's evident in his rigid stance, his tone is even, his smile seems fake. This is the face he shows most people. But I've seen that softer, more human side of him, when we've been intimate—his eyes locked on mine, soft words whispered in my ear. I ache for that side of him again. I love when he loses his inhibitions around me, and I can truly *see* him. But that's all an illusion.

The server pours water and takes our drink orders. I opt for a simple cranberry and soda. She leaves us with a smile.

He looks off into the distance. "I wanted to apologize to you for the last time I saw you."

I shake my head a little. I don't say a thing. I'm not sure what to say.

"I want you to know," he's still not quite looking at me, "it was wonderful for me."

It was wonderful for me too…except.

"You were—"

"Yes, we covered that already," I scoff. "I was *wonderful*, amazing, a great lay."

He bites his lip and pulls at his collar. "I've been thinking about it endlessly," he goes on, "about how we left things off," he adds. "I'm afraid I left rather abruptly…"

You did.

"I fear I mishandled the situation," he says, regret in his eyes. "I hope I haven't upset you."

You did, I want to say…*I wanted to crumble and die.*

I cross my arms. "It was fine," I say, my words clipped. "You've told me. This is about sex. Pure and simple. I understand how this works."

"I shouldn't have—"

"You were in a hurry. You had to get back to your kids," I point out, my eye drawn to the intricate paisley pattern of his shirt.

"But still, I could have spared you five minutes."

He's right, but I don't say a thing.

"It's just that…"

"That what?"

He looks down at his glass, his mouth a hard line. "There was something…when we had sex…it seemed almost…too intimate."

Too intimate…

I lean in close, glaring at him. "We had sex, Weston. We still had our clothes on." I feel the color rise in my cheeks. "We still had our shoes on, for heaven's sake."

"I know, but—"

"But *what?* You fingered me, threw me on the bed, slipped on a rubber, and pounded me." I want to shock him. I want to anger him. I want him to react, not just sit there, acting cool and collected, like this conversation isn't getting to him. But as I say the words out loud, I know I'm full of it. He's right—it *was* more than sex.

He sucks in a breath. "I'm sorry…but that's not quite how I remember it," he says, resting his hand gently on mine.

I jerk my hand away. "Don't."

He closes his eyes, and I can see he's upset. Finally…I'm not the only one who feels something.

He turns his gaze away. "Next time I'd like to lie beside you for five minutes or so."

I snort. "Oh…is that the acceptable post-coital resting time?" I can't believe him. I want to give him a lesson is social decorum. "Is that listed in your manual?"

He sighs and pulls away. "Please, don't mock me, Mirella," he says, his tone serious. "These kinds of situations are not easy for me. If you haven't noticed, I'm not exactly full of social graces."

"I've noticed."

"It's the way I am. I can't change it. I'm not myself around others. I don't quite know how to behave."

His armor has been stripped. He gets to me—his words, the expression on his face.

"I'm sorry," I relent, my words soft. "My tone was harsh."

"And I didn't want to lead you astray. I'm walking a slippery slope with you, Mirella."

I'm not sure what he's saying.

"You've done this before. Haven't you walked this slippery slope before?"

"No," he says, not quite looking at me. "I never have."

I want him to make eye contact. I want to see those stunning eyes of his. I want to understand what he's telling me.

He finally ventures a look at me. "I need to be careful with you. The last thing I would ever want to do is hurt you."

The server comes back with our drinks, so friendly, so cheerful, and so obviously oblivious to the drama between us.

I lean in and take a sip of my cranberry soda...my mouth is so dry.

"I like your dress," he offers. I think he's trying to lighten the conversation.

I look down at my sleek sheath black dress and stiletto heels. "Thanks," I say, finally smiling at him. "I was going for sexy."

He takes a drink of his scotch, his eyes not leaving me. "Well, you've certainly succeeded." He's doing it again—practically undressing me with his stare.

My heart pounds. Damn him...it's so easy for him to completely undo me.

He reaches into his leather satchel. "I have something for you." He pulls out a small silver box and hands it to me.

My mouth hangs open. I wasn't expecting this.

I hesitate and finally take it. "But isn't this against the rules, Weston?" I ask, confused. "You specifically said...no gifts."

"It's something very small," he explains. "I was shopping with Lizzie when I saw it. It made me think of you," he explains, an adorable smile plastered on his face. "Please think of it as a peace-offering for my clumsy behavior."

I open the box and a smile stretches across my face as I stare down at the fun bejeweled turtle brooch nestled in the white cotton pad.

"I love it."

"You said the turtles were your favorite."

"I did."

"And I know you like brooches."

I take the brooch gently out of the box and pin it on my dress, an inch above my heart. Damn, now I can't be mad at him.

"It suits you." He's still looking at me with that unnerving, intense stare.

He leaves me speechless.

I don't know if it's the restaurant, or the sexy way his hair refuses to be tamed—that one unruly lock sticking out at an odd angle. Maybe it's the five o'clock shadow, the brilliant green of his eyes, but I want him.

Or maybe it's the fact that his suite is just a quick elevator ride up. I know I've told myself I would end it, but…

"I still have your panties in my pocket."

His words arouse me. "Have you had your nose buried in them?" I tease, realizing I've been defeated.

"Here and there," he says with a wicked grin.

"Such a dirty boy," I say, a smile on my face. I don't care if it makes me feel like a whore again…I still want him. As much as I wanted to end this, I'm still willing to put everything on the line—my sanity, my marriage, my heart.

I lean in close, my hand buried in my loose curls. "Take me to your room."

He swallows and puts his drink down. "You're not hungry?"

I brush my finger along my neck, feeling suddenly hot. "No." I am so turned on—I'm just about to short-circuit.

"Neither am I," he confesses, his words soft.

He gets the server's attention, tells her an emergency has called us away, and leaves a hundred dollar bill on the table.

He holds my hand as we walk to the elevators. Two older couples are standing, waiting. They seem to be friends, chatting about a local restaurant. They smile at us sweetly.

The elevator chimes, and we follow the couples in.

"Which floor?" one of the ladies asks.

"Forty-two," Weston tells her. His hand rests on my waist. This slight touch lights me up, and I close my eyes imagining what is to come.

My hand is in his as he leads me to his suite. I realize that despite how he might make me feel, or whatever happens, I can't free myself from him. I've had a taste, and now I can't do without.

As soon as we walk into his suite and the door closes, his lips are on mine. I promised myself I wouldn't let this happen again. But the sensation of him against me is so wonderful. He pulls my jacket off, trailing kisses down my neck. I pull his satchel over his head and bury my hands in that beautiful hair of his—it's so soft against my fingers.

I'm just about ready to devour him—just like those calorie-filled red velvet cupcakes they sell at my favorite bakery—the ones that go straight to my hips.

He pulls his lips away from mine and rests his head against my forehead. He tucks a strand of my hair behind my ear. "Remember," he whispers, "when I told you I wanted to *see* you?"

I smile at him, a little nervous.

What does he have in mind?

"All of you," he adds, his eyes dark.

"Yes," I whisper, my voice small. "I remember."

He pulls away and walks slowly toward the bedroom. He looks back and shoots me a soft smile, urging me to follow him. I trail behind him eagerly, taking in the space. When we reach his bedroom, he heads to one of the arm chairs sitting not far from the bed. I catch a glimpse of his shoulders in his fitted shirt. I don't want to be naked for him—I want *him* to be naked for *me*. He takes a seat, his movements slow and deliberate.

I stand there, taking in the room—the contemporary lines, soft lighting, crisp white linens, upholstered velvety headboard, soothing caramels, and breezy blues. The décor is soothing, but I am anything but relaxed. He stares at me without a word. He's making me anxious again.

His gaze sweeps over my body and rests at my stiletto-clad feet. "I'd like you to undress for me."

I stand still, speechless, but he offers no other direction.

"Uh," I say, caught off guard. "Where? Here?"

He scratches the edge of his jaw, still not quite making eye contact with me. "Come over and sit on the bed."

I can't do this—not when he's not even looking me in the eye.

I don't want to do this.

I want *him* to undress me. I'm a very private person—almost no one has seen my body in its entirety. I've had two children. I'm thirty-five years old and far from perfect.

I can't do this.

I walk slowly to the bed, and I hesitate a little before sitting. I'm petrified. I realize I probably look like a deer in headlights. We've discussed boundaries and limitations, and he's mentioned that I shouldn't do anything I don't want to do.

I smile as his eyes finally meet mine. "Why don't *you* undress for me instead?" I tease.

He smirks. "Next time, perhaps."

My gaze falls to the floor as I trace my finger along the scoop neckline of my dress.

"Please don't do this if you don't want to," he says softly. "I won't be upset."

I look up at him, still not sure.

"It's…something I've fantasized about," he confesses, "since the first night I met you."

"Really?"

"That pretty little pink dress you had on? I wanted it to disappear."

I can't deny him this one small fantasy…maybe he'll make mine a reality too.

I tilt my head ever so slightly.

I have no idea where to start.

I stand, trail my finger down to my leg, and slowly hike the hem of my dress, giving him a peep of my thigh-high stocking and garter. Part of me knew this was going to happen. Why else would I have dressed like this? Who was I kidding?

He leans forward on his forearms, a smile on his face—he seems to like what he sees.

This might not be so bad.

I throw my head back, trail my hand to the back of my neck and reach for the zipper of my dress.

But I can't quite undo this dress by myself. For some reason, I can manage to zip it up, but not down. I hadn't expected an impromptu striptease. If I had, I would have worn something more strip-friendly—like a wrap dress or a shirt dress.

Something I could undo easily and seductively.

This isn't sexy at all.

Weston seems amused by my struggle. A big grin stretches across his face as he watches me.

Yes, I knew this might be embarrassing—but so early on? I've barely gotten started.

He wears a devilish smile as he walks toward me. "Need a little assistance?" he asks as he grabs a hold of my waist.

"Yes."

He pulls me to him and turns me on my feet. His hand brushes my skin as he sweeps my hair over one shoulder, sending shivers through me. I close my eyes and wonder why his touch is so electric—it lights me up every time. He kisses the back of my neck as he slowly pulls down my zipper. He's taken over, and I'm officially in seventh heaven. "I've done my part," he whispers. "The rest is up to you."

Damn…I'm not off the hook.

I turn back to see him sitting comfortably in the chair again. He leans in, his forearms on his knees, his shirt pulling against his shoulders. God…he's gorgeous. The faster I get this done, the sooner I get him all over me.

I pull a strap slowly over my shoulder, and slowly pull the dress down to my waist, exposing my black silk bra.

He swallows hard and nods in approval, leaning back in his chair. His smile has faded—his face is serious and intense.

I'm turning him on.

And I love the idea of turning him on.

I shimmy my hips a little, pull the dress over them, and let it fall to the floor, revealing the matching silk panties, garter, and stockings.

He undoes the top button of his shirt. "I…love…it."

Yes, I almost scream…he's getting undressed. This is going exactly where I want this to go. "Do you approve?" I ask, my words silky.

His slow smile says it all. "Yes…definitely."

I sit on the bed and kick off my stilettos, throwing my head back. I trail my finger down my hips and slowly unhook the clips on my garter. He watches my every move, his eyes not leaving my body even for a second.

I start to lose my inhibitions, desperately wanting him to want me. I slide my stocking slowly down my leg. My eyes don't leave his—I want to see him react. His lids are heavy, and there's a hint of a smile on his face—barely discernable. His fingers trail down his shirt—he's down to the middle button, a white undershirt peeking through.

I can't wait for him to get that shirt off.

By the time I've removed both stockings, his shirt his off, and he's devastatingly beautiful in a tight undershirt, desire still in his eyes.

I bring my hand to my neck, knowing I need to kick it up a notch, but I'm so scared. I feel so vulnerable under his stare. I'm not sure if I'm ready to show myself completely to him.

I trail my hand to my breast and slide it under the silk of my bra. My skin is hot and my nipples are hard. I let my breast fall out over the underwire.

He closes his eyes for a second.

I'm arousing him.

I'm arousing myself.

"I want to touch you," he says, his words soft. "I want to taste you."

He has no idea how much I want that. "Come and touch me."

He studies me for a beat, and he smiles. "Settle down…little butterfly," he whispers, the words flowing off his tongue deliciously.

I laugh a little. "What?"

He leans back in his chair. "You're beautiful and colorful, and you do get quite eager and fluttery when you're aching to get off."

I bite my lip, suddenly a bit self-conscious. "Oh…do I?"

"You do. It's rather adorable, actually."

I laugh again but don't say a word, aching for him to come to me.

"I'll come to you soon enough, but I want to see you completely naked first. And feel free to speed things up," he quickly adds, his smile playful.

My inhibitions are completely gone. I want to be naked for him. I want him to touch me. I arch my back and reach for the clasp of my bra. It falls to the bed, as I reveal myself to him.

He bites his bottom lip, his gazed fixed on my breasts. I think he likes what he sees.

He peels off his undershirt, revealing a set of gorgeous shoulders. The sleek lines of his body under his fitted shirts gave me an idea, but I had no clue he was so ripped. He leans back in his chair with a sly smile, showing off his toned abs—he knows exactly what he's doing to me.

I quickly slide my hand down my belly and toy with the lace trim of my panties.

I can tease too.

He watches me intently, tapping his foot. I linger, tracing my finger back and forth along the waistband.

He sucks in a long breath. "Take them off."

I hesitate a little.

I'm not sure he's going to like what he sees. I've cleaned up for him, but I'm a natural woman. And he strikes me as the type who appreciates a nice Brazilian. But…he's touched me there before—he knows what to expect.

I peel off my panties, slide them slowly over my knees, and let them fall to the floor. I'm motionless in my birthday suit. I've never felt so vulnerable, so exposed. He stares at me for the longest time without a word. My heart hammers in my chest, and I wish I could dissolve into thin air.

"You're perfect," he finally says.

And I smile at him, relieved he likes me the way I am. And also very relieved my little show is officially over.

Except…it isn't *quite* over.

Not as far as Weston is concerned.

He bites his lip, a hint of a smile on his face. "Sit back on the bed."

I sit on the edge, waiting for him to come to me, the crisp white bed cover cool on my rear.

But he doesn't.

He sits there comfortably and kicks off his shoes. I'm just about ready to bolt at this point, but I'm stark naked. I've done my part, and I wonder what he wants from me.

"Come over," I tell him, wanting him all over me.

A wide smile stretches across his face, ever so slowly, doing sinful things to me. He's being playful again. "Open your legs for me. I'd like to see you," he whispers. "If you're comfortable..."

My heart pounds in my chest as I spread my legs for him, very slowly. I spread them wider and wider, surprisingly not feeling exposed at all, but rather extremely aroused.

"Mirella..." he whispers.

I feel like I'm going to die if he doesn't come to me soon.

Finally, he stands and walks slowly over to me, his eyes glued to mine.

He leans over me, and he kisses my neck softly. I close my eyes as he trails his lips down my chest and kisses my breast, licking circles around my nipple but not quite touching it. He's teasing again.

I run my hands through his soft hair, breathing in the wonderful scent of him. I want this moment to last forever.

Finally, he takes my breast in his mouth. My breathing quickens, and I slide my hands against his smooth shoulders. I make my way down and reach for his fly. I want him naked against me.

He stills my hand. "Uh...no," he laughs softly. "We're not doing that, quite yet." His tongue ribbons down my stomach and around my belly button...and below. I ache for him to venture south and lick me there. He tangles his arms in my legs and kisses the inside of my thighs, his tongue sliding against my skin, along the edge of my curls.

"You...are...such a tease." My words are ragged.

He plants soft kisses on the fleshy part of my thigh. "Just ask," he whispers.

He wants me to beg again.

"Please."

His warm breath lands against my sex, and I feel like I've died and gone to heaven. His tongue slides back and forth against me.

It's so good.

I'm climbing quickly.

I grab a handful of his hair, the soft, thick locks tangled in my fingers, my moans louder and louder.

I'm almost there. I want this to happen. There is no way I can stop him—it just feels too damn good.

But then, he pulls away.

I could just kill him.

I lean up on my elbows. "Weston," I cry out.

"I'll bring you there..." he promises with a sly smile, "but I have yet to see every inch of you."

What in the world is he saying? He's seen *everything*.

He pulls away. His eyes are intense and serious. "I'd like you to kneel for me."

He wants me on all fours.

"But only if you're at ease doing so," he adds.

At this point, I would do anything he asks—I want him so badly. I turn around, do as I'm told, and settle my knees on the soft bed, feeling extremely exposed. Suddenly, I'm in someone else's body—someone bold, sexual.

He stands behind me and trails his fingers softly along my spine, down to the base of my back.

He traces a line to the edge of my crack. "You are a work of art." His fingers dance lightly along my ass, my sex. Neither of us utters a word. I am too aroused to speak. I just want to close my eyes and enjoy his touch. His fingers linger for an eternity, trailing back and forth, nearing, but not quite touching.

I'm not used to this.

Gabe is not like this. His style is fast and furious—he plows on through and hopes I can catch up with him. Weston, on the other hand, likes to take things slowly. He likes to explore. He likes to tease. He likes to hear me beg. I had never realized being with another man could bring such a different experience. And I eat it up. I love being teased, taunted, and brought to the edge of desire. I love being explored and adored and handled softly.

"Touch me, Weston," I finally beg.

His fingers glide between my lips.

And I want him so badly.

"I want you inside me," I say softly. The ragged words escaping from my mouth shock me.

His hand leaves me, and I open my eyes. I tilt my head over my shoulder to look at him. He reaches into his pocket.

I throw my head down, close my eyes and wait for him, my body anticipating his. This magnetic pull he has over me is beyond comprehension. I've never seen myself as a very passionate person before—I've always been ruled by my good senses, not by lust.

He teases me with his shaft. I want to beg him to stop and to enter me—I want him inside me. I bite my bottom lip as I enjoy the feel of him against me.

He finally eases into me, and I want the sensation to go on forever. He moans as he stretches into me. I cry out, knowing I'm going to come, fast and hard. His thrusts are slow and intense, and he moans louder and louder. As he comes, he pushes harder into me and brings me to my own climax.

When I'm finally brought down from the waves of pleasure, I turn to look at him and smile. Thirty seconds—I think that's all there was to it.

He laughs. "In my defense you worked me up quite a bit."

I laugh. "I didn't even touch you."

He kisses the back of my neck. "What can I say," he says softly. "You have extraordinary powers."

He eases out of me, his hands still on my hips. "I'll be back in a moment." And he's gone again.

I bury myself under the covers and wait for him. I definitely don't want a repeat of last time.

I want him to stay.

He comes back, a plush towel wrapped around his waist. He is magnificent, and I just want to rip that towel off.

He lies next to me, pulling the covers over both of us.

"You were great," I tell him, remembering all the sensations he's brought on in me.

"It's easy to be great with you."

I trail my finger along his smooth chest, tracing circles around his nipple, and venturing further south. "You have a great body." I slide my finger all the way to his belly button. "How do you manage that?"

His smile is bashful. "I train religiously. Two hours a day, five days a week," he says matter-of-factly, like this isn't completely impressive.

"Wow. That's a lot of training. When do you find the time?" I ask, suddenly a little self-conscious about my complete lack of exercise.

"I work out from five thirty to seven thirty, Monday to Friday."

"In the morning?" I blurt out. "When do you sleep?"

"I sleep six hours a night. That's pretty standard I think," he says, his hand against mine, his thumb playing with my fingers.

I realize we are so completely different. "You are very regimented."

"It's what feels most comfortable to me. I like to follow a set schedule. I like to know what's coming."

I smile at him. He's such a nerd. A really hot nerd.

"What do you do at work all day?" I ask, wanting to learn more about this beautiful nerd.

"Ahhh..." He lets out a sigh. "A lot of meetings with suppliers and engineers, conference calls, meetings out of town occasionally, site visits, and quality control," he explains, looking half-exhausted. "But thankfully, I have a few men to cover most of it. I delegate a lot."

"You basically tell people what to do all day," I tease.

"I suppose you could put it that way."

"I tell people what to do all day too. But they're all five years old, and they never listen to me."

He laughs, fine lines edging the corners of his eyes.

"I guess what I do isn't very exciting and important compared to you. Gabe likes to say I get paid to make zoo animals out of toilet paper cardboard rolls all day."

I think this is kind of funny, but Weston doesn't seem to agree—his smile has completely faded.

He studies me for a second with a serious expression. "You shouldn't say that," he chastises me, trailing his finger along my hairline. "Your vocation is most likely a lot more important than mine. You are molding the minds of our future leaders. You probably spend more time with these children than their own parents. Do you realize just how pliable the human brain is at that age? How much it takes in? How much your presence in their lives will affect who they become?"

I'd never thought about it like that.

"Don't sell yourself short, Mirella." I don't think I've ever seen him look more serious. "What you do is *very* important."

"Oh...okay," I say, sheepish. "I'll try to remember that."

"You do that," he says, kissing the tip of my nose.

I kind of like when he does that. He seems obsessed with my nose. It's sweet.

"Why do you do that?"

"Do what?"

"Kiss my nose and stuff?"

He smiles, staring at my nose for what seems like an eternity. I almost start to feel insecure—I don't exactly have the daintiest of noses.

"It's that adorable freckle right here," he taps it with the tip of his finger, "I love it."

I laugh out loud. "I hate it. I've always hated it," I confess. "I hate them all. But that one…it's the biggest. And smack in the middle of my nose. I hate it the most."

"I think every single freckle on your face is exactly where it belongs. Especially that one."

I think I'm going to melt.

And I guess he can see right through me because the next second, he tells me he has to go.

I sit up on the bed, wrapped up in the crisp white sheets. "My five minutes are up?"

"Something like that," he says, dropping his towel—accidently, on purpose, I'm not sure—what a tease. I peep at the sleek hard lines of his naked body as he makes his way to the en suite, wishing we could have another go.

Damn…this is like the same movie playing all over again. I went to the city, hell-bent on breaking up with Weston and ending this once and for all. And now I find myself standing on my doorstep, staring down at the potted geraniums, not wanting to go in and face my husband. Because I certainly don't want to admit what I've just done…again!

I suck in a breath, and I slowly turn the doorknob. My fingers seem to be made of lead—they feel so heavy.

As soon as I get in, Claire runs up to me and hugs my hips tightly. "Missed you," she says, and her sweet little voice brings out emotion in me. Gabe comes out of the den, papers in hand, and as soon as his gaze meets mine, he knows—it's as if we communicate telepathically—I suppose that's a result of almost twenty years together. But surprisingly, he doesn't seem angry. He simply walks up to me, gives me a big bear hug, and rests his chin on the top of my head. "You've changed your mind?"

I can barely croak out the word when I say, "Y-Yes."

Chapter Fourteen

We don't belong to each other...

"He asked you to do what?" Gwen asks, a little too loudly. We are at our Saturday painting class and I'm recounting my latest meeting with Weston for her.

"Shush," I whisper, finger over mouth, looking over at Cecilia who seems completely focused on her task, meticulously adding crimson red to a bouquet of tulips with the tip of her paintbrush.

But I know better. I know she's listening.

She's *always* listening.

I dab a little cerulean blue, adding color to my sky, a little pizzazz to my scenery of Old Montréal. "You heard me right." I'm copying the image from a photo I took years ago, when Gabe and I went there for a romantic getaway—we had so much fun—all we did was walk, eat good food, and make love.

"He really asked you to strip for him?" Gwen asks, *trying* to whisper—but there's no whispering in Gwen's range—it's conversation volume, loud, and louder.

A smile curves on Cecilia's lips. And I decide I don't care if she's spying on me. If I can add a little excitement to her life, then so be it.

I stretch my arm out to get a look at my artwork from a distance. "I was so nervous." To my dismay, my perspective is completely off. I should have been a little more focused on my art and a little less on dishing about Weston.

"I couldn't even get the dress off," I whisper. "I was all twisted up like a pretzel, trying to unzip it."

Both Gwen and Cecilia giggle.

"Ah," I say, pointing a finger. "I knew you could hear me, Cecilia."

She looks away and swiftly focuses on her tulips, pretending to be innocent.

But I know better.

"So what happened?" Gwen asks, completely intrigued. She's stopped painting—her half-finished cow stares blankly at us, waiting for her spots.

"He helped me out," I say softly. "He unzipped me. He was so tender about it, kissing me on the neck, undoing me really slowly. I think it might have been the most erotic moment of my life."

"Wow," is all Gwen manages to say, her mouth agape.

I look over at Cecilia—she's staring at us again, jaw hanging.

"You should see this man, Cecilia," Gwen tells her. "He's absolutely gorgeous."

I can't believe I'm sharing all these details...but, I can't help it.

And I don't care if Cecilia listens. And everyone else is at the far end of the room. I wonder what Cecilia thinks about all this. Although we've sat beside each other for a few classes, we've never actually spoken. Does she know I'm married? If she has any observation skills, she would have noticed my wedding ring.

But I don't care.

"How far did you go?" Gwen asks.

"All of it." I confess. "He wanted it all off."

Gwen bites her lip. "What underwear did you wear?"

"The black silky ones," I whisper, "with black thigh-highs and a garter belt."

"God...that's hot."

Cecilia is still staring, jaw still hanging, eyes bulging out of her head. I think I've thoroughly scandalized her.

I almost want to apologize.

"Okay," I finally say. "That's enough talk about that." I'm not about to tell anyone about spreading my legs wide for him, and kneeling on all fours to give him a VIP view of my ass.

That would be going too far.

"You're such a tease," Gwen pouts, picking up her paintbrush.

And Cecilia smirks.

I'm filled with nervous energy as I sit on the sleek leather seat of Weston's car. I'm not sure where I'm heading. All I was told in Kathryn's e-mail was to dress up—something red.

I've picked the shortest of my three red dresses, a classic flowing, silky dress, snug at the waist. I've paired the dress with strappy red heels and a chunky silver necklace.

Edward drops me off at the Lake Point Tower on the peninsula. As he opens the car door for me, I gaze up at the sky, trying to see the top of the spectacular building, but my eyes can't seem to reach high enough.

Weston meets me at the entrance, dressed in a tailored two-button gray suit, with striped navy shirt—he looks as splendid as ever.

He touches my elbow ever so slightly and kisses me on the cheek. "You look wonderful. I love the dress."

"I'm glad you approve," I reply, noticing his red tie—we make quite the handsome couple.

"Why red?" I ask as he leads me toward a private elevator.

"I wanted to see you in red." His eyes have that look again—that look which makes me want to just rip his clothes off. But I settle for a light touch of his tie, which is peeking through the bottom of his jacket. I notice he only has one button done again—it gives him a casual, very sexy vibe. I don't know who his stylist is, but she must be the best in the business—she definitely has sex-appeal down to an art.

My touch doesn't go unnoticed. I can see it in his eyes. I get a thrill out of the fact that my touch seems to affect him as much as his affects me.

"I thought red would suit your complexion—your dark hair and dark eyes."

"And?"

He smiles, taking my hand. "I was right on the money."

We make our way into the elevator, and I hope to steal a kiss, but the ride to the seventieth floor is so fast, we barely even have a chance to look at each other, let alone get frisky.

The hostess takes my jacket and leads us to our table. The restaurant seems to be glowing—candlelight, plush seats, mirrors, steel and polished copper. The panoramic views of the city and lakefront completely mesmerize me. As I look out at the city lights stretching for miles, I understand why Weston insisted on a late dinner.

We sit down at a quaint cloth-covered table right by the window. The atmosphere is so classy and romantic.

It's perfect.

I feel like a princess. Weston makes me feel like a princess, I muse, looking up at him in his fabulous suit.

"This is one of my favorite restaurants," he says, unfolding his cloth napkin. "I wanted to share it with you."

"Thank you." I take in my surroundings. "It's wonderful."

"I like the logistics, the design," he explains. "It's very streamlined. It was designed by a mathematician."

"A very brilliant man I'm sure."

"A woman actually. I think it's what makes it so unique."

I smile up at him. He has got to be the most adorable geek I have ever met. "But what about the food?" I tease.

"Delicious. Best scallops in town."

The server takes our drink orders. Weston orders a bottle of white.

I order a martini—I want to be languid, without a care in the world.

I want to get lost in this night.

"This place is spectacular." I want him to know I appreciate his efforts.

"I want to make you feel special, Mirella." He's not quite looking at me. "I want you to know how dear you are to me," he stresses, his fingers toying with his tie clip. "I don't want you to feel like…"

"Like what?" I ask, curious. But he doesn't answer. "Like a high class escort?" I venture, a smile on my face.

But I can see from the expression on his face—my words have stung.

"I don't want you to ever feel that way, Mirella," he says, his words strained. "But I understand if you…I wine and dine you, and then I take you to my suite, and…"

"I don't feel that way, Weston," I assure him. "I get as much from this as you do."

He looks up from his glass, a hint of a smile on his face.

"Do you have any idea how beautiful you are?" I ask him. But I think I know the answer—I'm not sure he sees what everyone else sees. "Do you have any idea how much I want you?"

He smiles, his expression soft and sweet.

And I want him even more.

I enjoy a delicious lobster bisque soup, a wonderful watercress salad, and scallops. Weston has the lamb. And we share a crème brûlée. I'm glad I've finally found my appetite. In the early days, I couldn't eat a thing around him.

We talk about our lives. I tell him about my last day at school and the fun and quirky presents the kids gave me—lots of brooches—everyone knows I collect them. He tells me about a new loft development he's undertaking and the upcoming trip to the south of Italy he's taking with his family. I don't really enjoy hearing about the trip—feelings of envy and jealousy consume me every time he speaks about Bridget. This part is so hard—knowing this wonderful man is not mine.

But I put on a smile and listen intently.

As we make our way back to the suite, I remind myself why I'm here—to have sex with this Greek god of a man. I'm very lucky, I tell myself. How many women like me would die for this chance—the sex, the excitement, the magic.

Don't think too much. Just enjoy the moment.

He trails his fingers down the small of my back. "I have yet to undress you, Mirella. I want to take everything off you."

I smile, liking the idea very much. I desperately want him to undress me.

He trails a finger along my neck, and reaches for one of my silver hoop earrings. With one hand, he manages to unclasp it and take it off, not taking his eyes off me.

His movements are so very slow. He's teasing again. And I know this is going to take a long time.

It will be a late night.

I wish I had *all* night with him.

He leaves me to set the earring on the desk. And as he walks back to me, his gaze locked on mine, looking brilliant in his suit, I suddenly want to undress *him*.

I reach for the button of his jacket.

He stills my hand and smiles at me. "Not yet," he says with a playful expression. "I get *you* naked first." He reaches for my other earring and repeats his little dance. At this rate, this process is going to take *all* night. I sigh at the thought—I don't know if I can be that patient.

He walks behind me, sweeps my hair over to the side and kisses my shoulder softly. I take a deep breath. His sexy woodsy smell lingers around me.

The slight touch of his fingers on the back of my neck sends shivers through me. He takes off my chunky silver necklace, unclasping it gently. I look out at the beautiful view of the city as he lingers behind me—the twinkling lights are magical. He sets the necklace delicately on the desk. He reaches for my arm and slips off my matching bracelet, his fingers trailing slowly along the inside of my wrist. He takes my hand in his and rests his thumb on my wedding ring.

"Of course, this stays," he says. "But I want everything else off." I almost wish he hadn't spoken—his words have brought me back to reality—I'm married, he's married, and we don't belong to each other.

He's not mine.

Then, his hands are on my waist, turning me on my feet. His hands move slowly as he undoes the back of my dress. He gently pulls it off my shoulders, letting the material pool softly to the floor. But he doesn't touch me.

And I so want him to touch me.

"Nice," he whispers in my ear, his body pressed against my back.

"What?" I ask, smiling.

"The red lacy underwear. Very sexy."

"I thought you might like it." Yes, this is the *when you want to get fucked hard* set. And I definitely want to get fucked hard.

"You were right," he breathes in my ear. The warmth of his hands wrapped around my waist is wonderful.

I'm in heaven.

"But as much as I appreciate it—it has to come off." He hooks his thumb into the waistband of my panties and pulls slowly, kneeling behind me as he does so. It is amazingly erotic.

I gingerly step out of my panties. I'm down to my red lacy bra and heels.

He stands back up to tower over me, his hands at my back, unclasping my bra. It falls to the floor, my breasts exposed to the cool air. He kisses my shoulder as he slides his arms around me and takes my breasts in his hands. My nipples are hard against his fingers.

His touch is sending me through the roof.

He slides his body along my back and trails a finger down to the back of my leg, then reaches for the strap of my heel. His hand lingers there for the longest time, undoing the clasp. I realize there have been a lot of clasps he's had to undo. And I make a mental note to not be so shackled next time—things might move a little faster.

This sloth-like pace is absolutely killing me.

He slides the shoe off, his thumb stroking the top of my foot and teasing the tip of my toes. He moves to the other foot and repeats the excruciatingly slow ritual, but his lips linger on my ass this time, and he trails kisses there, teasing me.

As soon as my shoe is off, I turn to him. I want to kiss him. I pull him to me, and his lips touch mine but just ever so slightly.

He's teasing again.

"Undress me first," he breathes. "It's your turn."

I reach for his jacket button and pull his jacket off, moving as fast as I can.

"Slow down…little butterfly."

I take off his silver tie clip and set it on the desk. I reach for his tie but I hit a stumbling block—I'm not used to ties—Gabe never wears them.

Weston notices my clumsiness and smiles.

"Let me help," he offers, loosening his tie in one smooth move, making it look so easy. I pull the loop over his head, messing up his hair in the process.

I undo his top button and land a quick kiss on the edge of his jaw. He's looking sexier by the second.

Next, I reach for the buckle of his brown leather belt, unclasping it with ease—this I've done before. I run my hand down his crotch and explore a little. He's rock hard. He smiles and a soft moan escapes from his mouth. He's enjoying this just as much as I am.

I move my hand back to the top of his shirt, teasing him a little. I undo the buttons swiftly. I sweep my hand over his broad shoulders to take off his shirt.

"The cuffs," he whispers, his eyes heavy.

I take his hand in mine, and reach for the cufflink and undo the diamond-tipped sphere. So many restraints…

I just want to get this beautiful man naked.

I remove the other cufflink, and finally pull off his shirt and let it fall to the floor. *Finally*, part of him is bare. I slide my hands against his torso and reach for his undershirt. I stretch up on the tip of my toes to pull it over his head. And finally, I have him half-naked. I cannot resist bringing my lips to his chest, trailing kisses over his stomach, down his smooth skin, and back to his chest. I can feel his heart pumping hard…for me.

I close my eyes, and trail my tongue down his stomach again, traveling down below his navel.

He pulls me up, breathless.

"Mirella," he breathes, his words ragged, "you're driving me insane. Take my pants off."

I smile up at him. "Yes, back to work, sir," I say, my words playful. I pull down his pants, revealing tight black boxer briefs. I kneel down and take off his dressy brown leather shoes and slip off his socks, sneaking a peep up—those boxers are just about to burst.

And finally, I stand back to my feet and pull down his boxers, freeing his erection. I glide my hands against his ass as I slide the briefs down. I crouch as I pull them lower, letting my mouth slightly brush his erection.

He's not the only one who can tease.

The second his briefs are off, he pulls me up and hoists me up against the wall. My legs tighten around his hips as he presses into me. He grabs ahold of me tighter and carries me to the bed. He throws me on the mattress, and I bounce like a rag doll.

Then he pounces.

His kiss is wild and untamed. His teeth scrape against mine and trail along my cheeks and my jaw. His hands are all over me—in my hair, on my breasts, between my legs.

His naked body slides against mine deliciously. I wonder if I'll ever tire of this.

I reluctantly pull away from him, and reach for his pants on the floor, in the pocket, where he always keeps a condom.

When we find ourselves together again, he's over me, kissing me gently. He's heavy, but I manage to pull myself over him. I want to be on top. I want to look at him, at his beautiful face, at his amazing body.

I slide over him, and he eases into me. Our eyes lock, and it feels very intimate. I push back and forth slowly, looking into his eyes. He reaches for my hands, not taking his eyes off mine. Our fingers intertwine gently.

I ride him gently at first, but he feels so good, I soon go faster and harder. He grinds into me and hits just the right spot, over and over. And with each thrust, I moan as I'm brought closer and closer. He can see my face, and I can see his. We read each other—we know we are both nearing the edge.

And finally both of us are brought to orgasm, still looking at each other. As the waves crash through me, I feel like he's looking right into me—into my soul. And I feel I can almost see his.

I close my eyes.

We lie, tangled in the crisp white sheets. I stare up at the ceiling. Weston lies on my chest, and I cradle his head in my arms, running my hand through his thick dark hair.

"I can hear your heart," he says. "It's beating so fast."

I laugh. "It's because we just had sex."

"That will do it every time. It's good for the heart. Or that's what they say."

"Then my heart must be in tip-top shape," I joke, thinking about all the sex I've had lately.

He laughs, trailing his finger down my side, all the way to my legs. His touch arouses me every time, even as I lie here in post-orgasmic bliss.

"Did you have a nice evening?" he asks. "Sex notwithstanding, that is."

"I did. It was a wonderful dinner. Thanks for taking me there."

"I wish I could do more," he says, tracing circles with the tip of his finger around the small mole on my hip. "I wish I could take you to see the world."

My heart hammers in my chest, and I'm sure he can hear it.

"Where would you take me?"

"Everywhere…" he says softly. "Hawaii, Paris, Venice. Have you ever been to any of those places?"

"No," I reply, knowing he probably expected that answer.

"You would love it."

"You're going to have fun in Italy next week," I say with a sigh, thinking about the fact that Bridget is the one who gets to see all those places with him, while I sit home, watching television in my rec room.

"I wish I could take you, Mirella," he says again. "But you understand why I can't…right?"

"Yes, I understand." I work my way out from under him. "I think it's time for me to go. Our five minutes are up."

"Mirella," he says softly, his eyes pleading. "You're not upset, are you?"

I can see genuine concern on his face. I force a smile. "No, I'm fine. It's just getting late. I should be going."

He grabs my hand and kisses it. "I'll miss you."

"I'll miss you too." My words are ragged. And I feel tears coming on as I turn away.

I cry all the way home, burying my nose in tissues, trying not to sob too loudly. Edward minds his business and doesn't say a word. He must be wondering what the hell Weston is doing to me. But I suppose it's his job to be discreet and loyal to his employer.

When I get home, Gabe is already there, lounging in his sweats on the sofa, eating pretzels and watching a rerun of *Seinfeld*. He looks so relaxed, like he doesn't have a care in the world. Sometimes, I wish I could be a guy and not be so damn emotional.

"What's up?" he asks, knowing not to ask more. We never talk about our dates, with the possible exception of where we had dinner.

My body drags as I sit next to him, shoulders hunched.

He sits up suddenly and looks at me. "What's wrong, Ella?"

I reach for him and wrap my arms around him.

"Did the bastard hurt you?" he asks, his words clipped. "I swear I'm going to kick the shit out of him."

"No, no." I pull back. "He didn't hurt me. He was a perfect gentleman, as always."

"Then, what happened?" he asks, looking confused.

"I don't know," I say. I don't want to tell him I'm jealous—jealous of Bridget. That would be saying too much. That would be admitting I care, admitting I've crossed the line, and have actual feelings for this man.

"I just don't know if I can do this anymore."

His large hazel eyes contemplate me for the longest time. "We can put a stop to this whenever you want, Ella. Just say the word."

"I know," I say, and give him a small smile. The truth is…I don't want to put a stop to it. I feel I couldn't live without Weston in my life right now, which scares the hell out of me.

"I'm just tired. It's been a long night."

"Yeah, you're home pretty late," he points out, and I sense he would like some kind of explanation, but doesn't dare ask.

"Weston took me to this amazing restaurant," I explain. "The place has the most panoramic views of the city. And he wanted to have a late dinner so we could see the twinkling lights at night."

"Oh…I see," he says. "The guy sure knows how to show a gal a good time."

"Yes."

"It helps when you're filthy rich," he adds, not quite looking at me. And I can tell it bothers him—the fact that Weston probably makes more money in a week, than he might make in a year.

I reach for him, wrap my arms around him, and my mouth tugs at his ear. "Well, you know who's best at showing a girl a good time in bed?"

"Oh..." he says, laughing. "Weston couldn't get the job done?"

"Well, I had to do all the work. I'm exhausted. I want to be a little lazy with you now."

A smile plays on his lips. "You want it soft or rough?" he whispers in my ear.

I laugh out loud. "What I really want is to cuddle with you and watch *Seinfeld*."

"Well, you know I'm always available if you change your mind," he jokes, squeezing me into his arms.

I laugh again.

Who needs Weston when I have this?

This is a nice moment, I muse, my legs stretched across the picnic blanket.

It's a lovely day, hot and sunny, and Chloe and Claire are playing at the park just a few yards from where Gabe and I sit. I've brought along sandwiches, fruit, and chocolate cupcakes for dessert.

"Those look good," Gabe says, eyeing the cupcakes. "Did you make them?"

"Yes," I answer proudly. "This morning, with the girls. They loved it."

"I bet they did," he says, laughing, tiny lines forming at the edge of his eyes. "I bet it was a mess too."

"Oh...it was," I say playfully. And he smiles at me. And then it occurs to me I've forgotten how gorgeous he is—his curly, unruly dark hair brushes the collar of his white T-shirt, the black stringed hippie necklace he always wears falls at the top of his broad chest, his tribal tattoo as sexy as ever. When I first met him, he was ink-free, but over the years, he's practically become a human canvas—a large tattoo covers half of his torso and left arm—I think it's pretty hot.

I haven't been thinking enough about him, I realize. I've been thinking too much about Weston and what he might be doing with his family, driving myself insane in the process and forgetting to enjoy my own wonderful life.

"I love you," I say out of the blue, inspired by the moment.

He eyes me with a funny look, curiosity in his eyes. "I love you too, Ella," he replies with a sexy smile.

And just then, I think I don't need to see Weston again, just yet.

"Bridget and Weston are back from their vacation next Friday. But I don't think we should get together with them right away."

"Oh…okay," he says. "Why not?"

"Well, because I think we could use more time for us."

He smiles at me. I can tell he's happy to hear me say this. "I thought you were counting the days until he came back."

"I was not," I argue. But, he's right. I had been. And I realize I've been silly.

If we can wait for them…Weston and Bridget can wait for us too.

I contact Kathryn by e-mail, explain we can't make our arranged date, and tell her I will contact her about future plans. I realize this is leaving Weston in limbo, and he will absolutely despise this, being such a slave to routine and schedules. This is a man who likes to have his whole life planned ahead of time, practically down to the last hour. This will drive him absolutely bonkers, and I smile at the thought.

In the following weeks, Gabe takes some time off work, and we spend quality time with the girls, going on day trips to the beach, to the city, to Gwen's pool, and the zoo. We enjoy movie nights with popcorn, and Gabe and I get reacquainted, making love often.

We are happy, I realize, more than once.

Why are we messing with that?

Every day it seems Kathryn contacts me and asks what the status is on our next date. She tells me Weston would like to know for scheduling purposes.

Scheduling purposes, my ass.

He just can't stand this.

She sends me e-mail after e-mail, inquiring about our schedule openings and informing us Weston and Bridget have made alternate plans for the Friday and Saturday, asking if a weeknight might be more manageable. I ignore most of her messages. I'm sure she isn't offended—she's just the go-between.

I'm trying to hurt him.

But I'm also trying to hold on to Gabe.

Each day I don't see Weston is another day closer to sanity, to a simpler life. Gone are the feelings of insecurity and guilt, the petty jealousies. I feel lighter, free. Maybe if I never get back to him, he'll get the picture and we will have said good-bye without actually saying good-bye.

But the thought of actually letting go seems impossible to me.

I lie poolside at Gwen's place. The girls are splashing around in the pool. Chloe's a decent swimmer but Claire isn't—she's wearing her water wings, and I keep an eye on her while sipping an appletini. Gwen sure knows how to entertain—it's relatively easy with a fully stocked bar and pool. Pushing thirty, Gwen has yet to have kids—she and Greg are enjoying their freedom too much—traveling often and playing golf almost every day. Today is one of those rare summer days I get her all to myself.

She lies back on the blue lounge chair, black braids falling to the side, her large sunglasses pointing to the sky. She says she's working on her tan, and I laugh—her dark skin is in no need of a tan. My freckly, Irish white skin, on the other hand, is another story. I slather on more sunscreen at the thought. And I look over at the girls, wondering if I should touch them up a little too. But I don't worry too much about it—they've inherited Gabe's beautiful olive skin—every summer, I thank the Lord for that.

"So," Gwen says. "You and Weston haven't seen each other for a while."

"Nope." I simply say. Gwen knows the rules. She knows I'm not supposed to say too much about our dates. And it is just killing her.

"I'm making him sweat a little," I add, giving her a mischievous look.

"I bet he doesn't like that."

"No, I don't think he does," I say, quite satisfied with myself.

I hear the old familiar Beyoncé tune on my phone, and reach into my beach bag. I throw in a casual hello, not bothering to look who's on the other end of the line.

"Mirella," he says.

My breath catches. I recognize his soft-spoken voice instantly. "Hi," is all I manage to say.

"How are you?" he asks, his words sound strained.

"Uh…good," I stammer a little.

"I've missed you." My heart does another flip flop, but still, I don't tell him I've missed him too. Even if I have.

"Where are we at, Mirella?" he asks. "Why haven't you contacted us?"

"Well, you know," I say casually. "We've been busy."

"Too busy to send *one* e-mail?"

"Why are you calling me anyway?" I say. "I thought this was against the rules."

At these words, Gwen perks up and takes off her sunglasses, her mouth in the shape of an O.

"You've left me no choice," he points out. "I've missed you."

"How was your trip?" I ask, my words clipped.

"It was quite nice, but I couldn't stop thinking about you."

He's getting to me.

"Weston," I say. "You're breaking a few rules right now," I remind him, still keeping an eye on Claire. Gwen is too engrossed in our conversation to pay any attention to the girls.

"I know," he says. "I miss you. I miss your touch."

Now he's starting to arouse me. I should really end this conversation.

"Please, I need to see you," he adds, his voice soft.

"Listen," I start, my words business-like, "I'll contact Kathryn shortly and maybe we can set up something for next weekend."

"I'd like that," he says, his words barely a whisper.

"Bye, Weston," I say before hanging up.

"Holy cow," Gwen squeals.

"I can't believe he called me," I tell her, not able to restrain the smile on my face.

"Well, sweetie, it looks like you broke him," she says, her toothy smile as wide as I've ever seen it. "He begged, didn't he?"

A smile stretches across my face. "He sure did."

Chapter Fifteen

I wanted you to suffer a little…

Kathryn's e-mail is a little cryptic.

> Dear Mirella,
>
> All plans have been arranged for your date with Weston this next Saturday. Edward will pick you up at 4:00 p.m. Dress however you would like, but please ensure you are wearing a white or beige strapless bra and very high heels (five inch minimum).
>
> When you get to your destination, a girl in a red polka-dot dress will meet you.
>
> Weston looks forward to seeing you.
>
> Best,
> Kathryn
>
> P.S. Please forward your measurements: bust, waist, inseam (from waist to floor) and shoe size.

What the…?

I don't even want to ask.

I do as I'm told, curiosity filling every cell of me. I settle on tight white capris and a black breezy polka-dot blouse, with a strapless bra, as requested, and five-inch black pumps. I've styled my hair in a retro do and dabbed on some red lipstick. I'm quite happy with the results—I look classy, very "Audrey Hepburn." The shoes are not the most comfortable ones I own, but if history is any indication, there won't be much walking tonight.

As Edward drives me to the city, I try to pry information out of him. But he knows nothing. At least he acts like he knows nothing. He drops me off on some random corner, by a health food store. I have no idea where I am. I hold my black clutch tightly, realizing I'm a little on edge.

I look for a woman in a red polka-dot dress, but I don't see one. There are a lot of people milling about, but no woman in a red polka-dot dress. What is going on? I turn back toward the car, but Edward has driven off.

I pace back and forth, and my feet are starting to hurt. Finally, I spot a bench and make the trek toward it.

I'm extremely happy to sit down, but still wondering what the hell is going on.

I wait and wait, watching people go by, fidgeting, crossing and uncrossing my legs, my heeled foot dangling above the pavement. I look at my watch every two minutes, and finally it occurs to me—I've been waiting fifteen minutes.

That's when I see her.

She's wearing an adorable red polka-dot dress. She's not the woman I'd been looking for, but rather a cherubic little girl with adorable blond ringlets. Her mother holds her hand and seems to know who I am. I stand and practically sprint to them.

"Mirella?" says the mother.

"Yes," I reply, more relieved than I could have imagined.

"I'm Anika and this is Tasha," she says, tilting her gaze to the adorable girl, who's staring down shyly at her red Mary Janes. "We're friends of Weston's."

"Nice to meet you," I offer, extending my hand.

She digs into her chic black purse. "Weston has asked me to give you this note." Her gloved hand reaches to offer me the white envelope.

I take the envelope, still confused as ever. "Did Weston mention what this is all about?"

She laughs a little, looking down at my shoes. "Oh…he sort of did, but I can't tell you. He's a mystery, isn't he?"

The suspense builds as I tear the envelope open.

The note reads:

Meet me at Ann Santhers.

I sigh and look up at the sky. I'm as puzzled as ever.

"I'm not sure where that is," I confess.

"It's just up there. Take a left on Belmont Avenue, and keep walking. It'll be on the south side."

"Okay," I say. "Thank you. It was nice meeting you."

"Likewise," she says with a mischievous smile. Tasha waves goodbye. She is very adorable—she looks a lot like Claire. I turn and I make my way toward Starbucks.

I round the corner, hobbling on my feet. My shoes are already killing me, and I hope this place isn't too far. There are lots of restaurants and quaint establishments—I can't help but think it would be a nice stroll if I weren't wearing these blasted five-inch heels.

I pass a martial arts center and decide to lean against the window and peek in—it's really just an excuse to step out of my pumps and give my feet a break.

I rub the heel of my foot.

Sucking in a long breath, I head toward my destination. I don't understand why Weston's driver wouldn't simply drive me to this place. I spot a blue overhang, and I'm sure that's the place. But when I get there, I realize it's not.

I can actually feel my body drag. Completely defeated, I keep walking.

And finally, I spot it—Ann Santhers's big blue sign. I start walking a little faster, plowing through the pain, anxious to get to my destination. I spot my reflection in the restaurant windows and I am quite a sight, hobbling like I've sprained an ankle. I figure Weston is probably sitting in there, waiting for me, and I decide to give him a piece of my mind as soon as I see him.

When I walk in, I am delighted—the place is the cutest, quaintest place I have ever seen—Swedish atmosphere, turquoises and reds, mosaic tiled floor. The adorable folksy illustrations covering the walls beckon me to sit down on the cozy plump red leather chairs. I scan the place, but I don't see any sign of Weston. He must be running late.

A friendly brunette walks up to me. "Are you Mirella, by any chance?"

I perk up. I'm at the right place. "Yes. I'm supposed to meet someone…Weston Hanson."

"He actually couldn't make it," she explains, seemingly apologetic. "He asked me to give you this note."

Another note?

C'mon.

I pinch the bridge of my nose and close my eyes, willing myself to settle down—I feel I could dive into a tirade of expletives at this moment.

Please meet me at Anette's Vintage Wear,
up on Clark Street, north of Belmont

What? I can't help but be livid. I was just up that way. Now, I have to backtrack. I can actually feel myself slouch.

"I'm sorry," says the friendly server.

"This place looks yummy. I wish I could stay and eat."

"Sit for a second. Rest your feet. I'll get you a glass of water."

I sit for a moment, cursing Weston. What is this? I'm really mad at him, but the more I sit there, staring at the adorable mural of a milkmaid dancing with a little girl, I can't help but relax a little.

I drink a few sips of water and thank the server. I leave and wave good-bye as I set out to find this place, my energy drained.

It seems my feet get achier with every step. I'm fuming. He better have a good explanation for this unfortunate turn of events, making me run around like a headless chicken.

I just can't take it anymore. I take off the heels and hold them by the strap, delighting in the sensation of my bare feet against the concrete. I look down, making sure there are no broken shards of glass. Thankfully, the streets are pretty clean.

When I get back to the corner of Belmont and Clark, I head north and look up at all the store signage. I need to look on both sides of the street since Weston didn't bother to tell me which side this place is on. I strain my eyes a little since I don't have my glasses on.

I walk past quaint stores, nestled within impressive architecturally detailed historical buildings. I walk past a spot of greenery, still keeping an eye out.

This place is nowhere in sight.

My feet are killing me.

I'm starting to wonder if it even exists. Is this Weston's twisted idea of a horrible joke? And then, just when I think I'm just about to officially have a nervous breakdown, I finally spot the bright pink sign—*Anette's Vintage Wear.* And it's like I've reached an oasis in the middle of the desert. I'm hot, I'm parched, and my concrete scraped feet feel raw.

And also…I am *so* mad, I could strangle the next person I see.

But as soon as I walk into the cozy store, I breathe a little easier. The air is cool, and there's a slight smell of vanilla…it's very pleasant. The space is incredible, cramped with beautiful vintage pieces. The charming, shabby-chic Victorian décor is very welcoming. My eye is drawn to the brass antique chandelier, and I can tell it's the real thing—not one of those horrible replicas. Soft scone light fixtures, silk hangers, and Victorian velvet chairs add to the charm. I was wrong—this isn't an oasis, but feels rather more like heaven, my own personal version of heaven.

And then I see it.

The most breathtaking dress I have ever seen, in the middle of the room, draped on a silk hanger. It's flowing, sheer, soft pink. I trail my fingers gently along the embroidery—the detail of it is exquisite.

"That's a vintage nineteen thirties Jeanne Lanvin," a cheerful voice calls out. I look up. An elderly lady with a short black bob smiles at me. I was so mesmerized by the space and the dress, I hadn't even noticed her standing there.

"In mint condition," she adds. I can't peel my eyes away from it. I trail my finger down to the hand-written paper tag.

Jeanne Lanvin, 1930s

There's no price listed. And I know I can't afford it.

"You like it," she says.

"I do," I say, smiling at her, thinking she will most likely be disappointed with my next words. "But I could never afford it. Not in a million years."

"It's not for sale," she says.

I laugh. "Oh…I see. It's bait," I venture.

She laughs a little louder.

"You should hang it in the front window. Get the customers in."

A huge smile stretches across her face. "It's yours."

"What?"

"Mr. Hanson wants you to have it."

My stomach is suddenly filled with butterflies. Weston has done this. This dress is what this whole wild goose chase was all about.

"I'm Anette, by the way," she tells me, offering her hand.

She then leaves me to contemplate the dress. "I'll get you a glass of water. You look thirsty."

"Oh…thank you."

I take the hanger in my hand and drape the dress over myself, looking at my reflection in the mirror. It looks beautiful. The color really suits me. How romantic of him, I think, sliding the delicate soft pink material between my fingers.

He's breaking the rules again.

I hang the dress back on the old vintage coat rack.

Anette returns and hands me a cold glass of water. "I think you should try it on."

"Here?"

"Why not?" she says with a playful smile. "I have a spacious changing room at the back."

I smile back at her. "Why not?" I'm dying to try it on—the size looks just about right.

She takes my glass of water, clutch, and shoes and sets them behind her counter. She comes back, her walk graceful in delicate red heels, and grabs the hanger with her red-tipped, manicured fingers—this woman is all class.

I follow her down the narrow store. The space is filled with wonderful fabrics. The walls are covered with Victorian gilded mirrors, reflecting the light from the gold chandeliers over top.

The place is magical.

When we reach the changing room, she pulls the flowery curtain open for me, and I spot a velvet Victorian chair. The most fabulous shoes I have ever seen, sit on top, sparkly and perfectly matched to my dress.

"The shoes are yours too."

Wow.

My gaze travels from the shoes to the gilded mirror. It's massive and rests on the oak planked flooring, reflecting dark red painted walls and…

Weston.

He's sitting at the back of the changing room, on a green velvet bench. He looks up from his iPad and smiles at my reflection in the mirror. I look over at Anette, whose red lips stretch across her face—she's obviously in on it.

He looks delicious in a fitted tux, one leg propped up on his knee. He gives me that all too-sexy smile of his—it's that rare mischievous one I don't see often—he knows he's been up to no good.

"Well, I'll leave you to try it on." Anette hands me the dress.

I'm careful to catch the fabric, not letting it fall to the floor.

"Take your time," she adds with a playful smile.

I walk in slowly and pull the flowery curtain closed behind me. His gaze is fixed on me—intense and hot and playful too.

I hang the dress on the large gold hook next to the mirror. "What are you reading?"

He sets his tablet on the bench and doesn't answer me. He stands, and his lips are on mine before I can say another word. His wonderful smell fills me, and the sweet taste of his mouth makes me want to eat him up.

I realize how much I've missed his kiss.

His large hands cup my face as his kiss grows in intensity. I don't want him to ever stop.

But he does.

He pulls away.

And his hands drop to my hips, making their way around my ass. "I've missed you so much, Mirella." His words are soft in my ear. "You cannot imagine."

My breath catches. He makes me feel so desired.

So adored.

"I've missed you too." My words barely a whisper.

I have…so very much.

He trails kisses along my jaw. "You could have fooled me. You've been ignoring me for weeks."

"I have?"

"Don't play coy with me," he says, trailing his hand up my back, under my blouse. "I like what you're wearing."

"Thanks. I had no idea what to wear. Kathryn's e-mail was a little vague."

"Yes, I know."

"Why did you want me to wear ridiculously high shoes? What's up with that?" I ask, curious. "And what about the wild goose chase?"

I want answers.

He laughs. "I confess…I wanted you to suffer a little."

I jerk away from him. "You're telling me my bleeding feet were all part of an evil plan."

His smile fades. "You had me running in circles, trying to find out when I would see you next. Wondering what in the heavens was going on with you. Wondering if you had a change of heart about us?"

His eyes are so soft, filled with pure emotion, with a hint of pain—I can hardly be mad at him. "I didn't appreciate that one bit," he explains, trailing his finger along my cheek. "I thought you deserved a good lesson."

"Who knew you were so vengeful," I say, my lids heavy. I could just throttle him right now but still, I want him.

"I certainly didn't," he whispers, his finger tracing the outline of my lips. "You drive me insane, Mirella."

I reach for his belt. I want him…now. I've missed his touch, the taste of his skin, his beautiful cock.

But he pulls away.

He pushes me against the wall and reaches for the fly of my capris. He undoes it in one smooth move. His hands glide over my hips and against my legs, pulling at the fabric, dragging my pants down along with my panties. When he gets to my feet, he kisses the top of my left one.

"I'll give you a foot massage later," he promises, looking up at me. "You've earned it."

As he pulls my pants and panties over my feet, I feel so exposed… and wild. I can't believe we're doing this…here.

He stands up and towers over me, pulls my face to his, and kisses me again.

We feverishly work together to undo his pants, and free him—his erection brushes against my belly. There's a sense of great urgency, and I don't think I've ever seen Weston so unrestrained.

He props me up and takes me against the wall.

"You feel incredible," he breathes as soon as he's inside me. "I've missed this."

He pushes into me over and over again. I tighten my legs around him as his hips press harder against me. He breathes hard into my ear. I moan softly, enjoying him thoroughly, my head thrown back toward the ceiling. The small room shakes, as does the gilded mirror and the small chandelier on top. And I pray it doesn't come crashing down.

Weston's breaths come faster and louder, he plows into me harder, and I can sense both of us reaching climax. I bury my orgasmic moans into his neck, trying not to make a sound.

But it's obvious—we're not fooling anyone. I'm sure Anette knows what's going on. But she's just sold a very expensive dress—I imagine she'll let us get away with it.

Up against the red wall, he still holds me in his arms. My face is buried in his warm neck, my nose marvels in his woodsy scent.

The moment is perfect.

"Fuck," Weston whispers, the word barely audible in my ear. I'm shocked. I've *never* heard the man curse before.

"What? What is it?" I ask, the words spilling out of me. "Did we break something?" I ask, looking up at the chandelier.

"No. I forgot the condom." His voice is coarse.

"Oh," is all I manage to say.

He buries his face in my chest. "I can't believe I've been so irresponsible."

"It's fine, Weston," I try to reassure him. "I've been on the pill. And as you know, I'm clean and I haven't..."

"I know you're clean. It's just that..."

"That what?" I want to know why he's so upset.

"I'm losing my bearings with you," he confesses. "It seems I'm breaking all the rules."

I can't argue with that.

He has been.

"Well, that was a really nice quickie," I say with a sly smile, trying to lighten the mood. "Shall I try on my dress now?"

As Weston helps me into the dress, his touch is soft and delicate. I look at our reflection in the gilded mirror—his tall frame in a tailored tux and mine in my soft flowing gown. I can't help but feel like Cinderella.

He trails his finger along my exposed neck. "You look as exquisite as I'd imagined. It fits you like a glove." His gaze lingers on me. "I'm glad. I was concerned it wouldn't be quite right."

"It's really me. You chose wisely."

He wraps his hands around my waist, warming my insides. "I thought something old might be appropriate. I know you love vintage...you're an old soul."

I smile.

I've always considered myself an old soul. No one has ever noticed before. No one has ever really noticed *me* before. For some reason I can't seem to quite understand, Weston gets me.

And I get him.

We eat at The Signature Room at the 95th—it's sleek and contemporary. I'm not sure what I would call the décor, but it almost feels like modern art deco to me—glowing, cubist, hanging light fixtures abound.

As we take a seat next to the window, looking down at the fantastic views of the city, it occurs to me that I never truly appreciated the beauty of Chicago before I knew Weston.

"You're making me love this city, more and more every day," I tell him as the server pours our wine.

"It's a beautiful city."

Sitting across him by the window, up high, looking down at the landscape filled with tall buildings, I get a sense of déjà-vu.

"You like to eat up high," I point out, enjoying a sip of my wine.

He laughs. "I do. I love to see a sea of buildings beneath me."

"Well, you *are* an architect. Makes sense that you would love buildings."

"Sitting up high like this…feels amazing to me."

"Sitting across from you like this, feels amazing to me," I say light-heartedly.

He smiles at me—that bright charming grin. And I have to remind myself not to let myself fall.

Because I could really fall hard.

We share a nice meal. I enjoy the salmon, and Weston has the New York strip. We share the French crêpes for dessert—the most fantastic peach and blueberry crêpes I've ever had. Our conversation is light, mostly about the city and our work. I've noticed Weston often shies away from more intimate subjects, and I fully respect that—he wants to keep a certain distance between us, and I think we're both better off for it.

Edward brings us to a secret destination. I laugh at Weston when he refuses to tell me where we're going. It seems he's always playing games, teasing. He likes to keep me on my toes. And I love that about him.

I stare at my fabulous sparkly shoes, which are surprisingly comfortable, as I hold Weston's hand.

"Thank you so much for the dress. I love it."

"I thought you'd like it. It's very feminine. Just like you."

"But you shouldn't have, Weston. You're not supposed to offer me gifts."

"You deserve it," he insists, squeezing my hand. "It really isn't a big deal, Mirella."

I try to justify it to myself. It's not a big deal. It's just a dress. It's not like he's bought me a car.

"Did you pick it out?"

He laughs. "Well, I did have a little help from Anette. I dragged her to an auction. She was leaning toward a silky sleek dress. But I saw this one, and I knew it was you."

I smile at the thought of him picking out my dress—it's so erotic.

"How do you know Anette?" I ask, curious. "She…uh…knows about us?"

"She's a dear friend of my mother's. I've known her forever. She used to look after me occasionally."

"Does she know…you and Bridget…about your lifestyle?"

"She does. She's a very modern, liberal woman. She's one of the few people who knows, in fact." He pulls my hand to his mouth and kisses it. "And the little girl in the polka-dot dress," he adds. "That's her granddaughter."

"She was cute," I say. "And her mother was so elegant."

"I think it runs in the family. Anika's just like Anette."

I purse my lips, curious. "You and Anika?"

"No…she's always been like a sister."

I breathe a sigh of relief, not sure why I even care about his past. I suppose I don't like the idea of yet another woman in his life. I have enough with one woman to contend with.

"Do you see your mother often?" I ask, not sure if he wants to talk about his mother.

"No. She's back in London these days," he says without emotion. And I let it go.

I rest my eyes on him…he's splendid in his tux. And I suddenly wish we had more privacy.

When Edward opens the car door for me, and I set my eyes on the majestic historical building with the large arched windows, I instantly recognize where we are—he's taken me to the symphony.

"You'd said you've never been."

"I did say that," I confirm, hiking up my dress—there's no way I'm letting it drag on the concrete.

Weston leads me to the first row on the first balcony. I am absolutely stunned by the beauty of Orchestra Hall—the light open space, warm sparking glow of lights, and arches surrounding us. I marvel at the incredible architectural details.

The concert is wonderful, the music reaching deep to my very bones, it seems. The orchestra members seem so small—streaks of black, working in perfect unison. Weston's fingers are intertwined in mine, our hands resting on the fabric of my dress. He holds my hand throughout and squeezes it occasionally. I smile at him, enjoying the sight of him lost in something so wonderful.

I plop my rear down on the bed, my beautiful dress floating around me, and I slip off my sparkly shoes. "So, Weston," I say, with a coy smile. "When do I get my much anticipated foot massage?"

He kneels at my feet, undoing his bowtie. "I was hoping I'd get to kiss you a little first."

I laugh. "No…I want a foot massage first. You're not getting out of this."

He slides his hands under my dress, and drags his soft fingers against the skin of my legs. "You obviously don't know what kind of kiss I had in mind," he says, his grin playful.

I'm officially intrigued.

"What kind of kiss did you have in mind?"

"The naughty kind." His eyes darken.

My stomach flutters. And in a matter of a second or two, I'm fully aroused. I feel the familiar heaviness in my belly and the pressure in my sex. I ache for the feel of his tongue.

His gaze is locked on mine, his eyes intense. He toys with the lace of my panties. "I've never made you climax this way before. Would you like that?" he asks, ever so politely.

I almost want to scream, "Of course I would like that!" but I settle for a quiet yes.

"Lie back," he orders and buries his head under the organza of my dress. He pulls my panties slowly off, and I open up for him and close my eyes.

He holds my thighs softly in his arms, sliding his tongue along the inside of them, up and down slowly. The heat of his mouth comes so close and pulls away, over and over. He's teasing again.

And he's driving me insane. "Weston," I moan. "No games, please."

My body is so aroused, it's almost in pain—I don't care if I have to beg.

The sensation of his warm tongue finally sweeping gently along my lips feels mind-blowing, and I know it won't take me long to come. He licks me in a back and forth motion, teasing me. And I spread my legs wider, pressing my hips into him.

I want more.

"I love the way you taste," he says softly.

I reach for his head under my dress and rub my hands through his hair—it's so soft.

His mouth finally moves up to my clit, and his tongue softly swirls around it.

"Harder," I moan, knowing I'm almost there. He builds pressure, and I groan lightly as he brings me closer. I'm louder and louder until I finally explode into his mouth. He carries on until my moans quietly disappear into the stillness of the room.

He drags his face along the length of my thigh and makes a sudden reappearance.

"You enjoyed that immensely." He smirks, looking quite happy with himself. "I gather I didn't do a horrible job."

"You gather right." My body is still limp and numb. I reach for him and bury my face in his chest.

I kiss him, sliding my tongue along his jaw, and I pull him under me.

"Your turn," I whisper, trailing kisses down his neck.

He looks down at me and smiles.

I reach for his belt and undo his pants, freeing him.

I lick circles around his navel, teasing him. I look up at him every now and then—his eyes are closed, and there's just the slightest hint of a smile on his lips—he's clearly enjoying it. I love bringing him pleasure as much as I enjoy my own pleasure.

Finally, I trail down and take him in my mouth. He lets out a soft moan.

And all I want to do is rock his world.

Chapter Sixteen

I know. . .how you like to watch.

I squeal and jerk my foot away. "You're doing a horrible job."

Weston laughs. "It's not my fault you're so ticklish. How can I give you a foot massage when you won't let me touch your feet?"

"Just take it more slowly. Don't just pounce like that."

He smirks. "Well, usually, you quite enjoy it when I pounce," he says with a sly smile.

I laugh. "Well, that's another matter entirely."

"I'll be gentle," he promises as he takes my foot in his hands and rubs softly in a slow motion. "I'll stay away from your toes for the time being."

He rubs gently, and it feels so nice. It's wonderful, being here with him. I don't think I will ever tire of it. I can't believe the night we just shared—the dress, the amazing changing room quickie, dinner and the symphony, the best oral sex of my life, and now a foot massage!

I lie back on the bed, close my eyes, and decide life couldn't possibly get any better.

"Why did you pull away, Mirella?" he asks, still rubbing my foot. His words are sudden and unexpected.

I lean up on my elbows. He doesn't look up at me—his eyes are still focused on my feet.

"What do you mean?"

"You shut me out for weeks and left me no other choice but to contact you and break the rules."

"I was busy," I say matter-of-factly, knowing very well I'm full of it.

He's certainly not stupid. "Don't lie to me," he pleads. "I know there was more to it than that."

He's right, but I don't want to tell him the truth—the emotions of envy, jealousy, and anger I experience regularly, the way I drive myself crazy thinking about him when he's not with me.

I feel so unhinged.

But I can't tell him all this.

"I needed a break."

It's true—I did need to pull away—for my own sanity.

"A break?" he asks, finally looking up at me. "Why?"

I hesitate before answering, careful not to cross any lines with my reply.

"Well, for starters, sometimes it feels like you're always in control. I'm always the one waiting for your signal, asking myself a million questions. When will I see you next? Where will you take me?" I explain. "I wanted to be the one who made you wonder, for once."

"Well, you certainly achieved your goal. Do you not like the way our arrangement works?" he asks, genuine concern in his eyes.

"It's fine. But, when you're jetting off to who-knows-where, I'm left back here, waiting for you."

"It bothers you when I go away with my family?"

I hesitate before telling him, "I get a little jealous…the thought of you and her in all these exotic places."

The color drains from his face. He closes his eyes and lets out a huge sigh. "Mirella," he starts. "We discussed this a long time ago. There is no room for jealousy in this arrangement." His tone is condescending—I feel like a child being scolded.

I'm just human, for fuck's sake.

"If you can't—"

"I'm fine, really." I realize I'm threading a line here. "No, really, I'm fine, Weston," I lie. "I just miss you, that's all."

"I miss you too. Very much."

It's Sunday morning, and Gabe has gone out to train at his club. He usually trains and spars with his buddies, Jason and Rob. He also hangs out with Stephen, an old friend from high school. But mostly, he likes to spend time with the girls and me.

I've made a late breakfast—pancakes, eggs, and cut-up strawberries.

I'm still on a high.

As soon as I get the chance, I call Gwen and tell her all about the dress. She asks me to describe it, but I can't really do it justice. How do you describe something so beautiful?

Gwen shows up at my doorstep an hour later.

She storms into the house, not even taking off her wedges. "Let me see it."

I laugh. "Come to my room."

We run up the stairs like giddy school girls.

I slowly drag the dress out from the back of my closet. I've hidden it from Gabe. When I came home, after my date, he wasn't home yet. This bothered me somewhat. I came home relatively late—Caroline had fallen asleep on the sofa. I wondered what he and Bridget were up to. Anyway, I don't want him to know Weston has given me such a wonderful gift. Gabe will never notice it in my closet—he's not very observant when it comes to my clothes. If I ever choose to wear it again, I can simply tell him I bought it myself—a little white lie.

I hand the dress to Gwen.

Her jaw drops.

She eyes the label, and her eyes practically pop out of her head.

"Holy hell, Mirella," she almost yells. And I kind of want to scold her for cursing in my house, but I let it go.

"What?"

"This is a Jeanne Lanvin dress."

"Is that good?" I ask. I don't know nearly as much about fashion as Gwen does. I don't really care about labels—I just like pretty things.

"You can't even buy a dress like this," she explains, her eyes still wide as saucers. "This is the kind of dress they hang in museums. This dress is worth like ten, twenty grand...or probably even more."

My heart drops.

It really isn't a big deal, Mirella.

He might as well *have* bought me a car.

"Who knows exactly...I'm not sure," she says. "I'm no expert," she adds as she trails her fingers along the embroidery. "Do you know how old it is?"

"The lady at the shop said nineteen thirties."

"Wow..." she says, looking over at me.

Her gaze softens, and there's a hint of concern in her eyes. "Mirella...I don't know..." she trails off.

"What?" I ask, eager to know what's bothering her all of a sudden.

"You should probably be careful with him."

"Why?" I ask. "What do you mean?"

"I think he might be in love."

I've been thinking about Gwen's words. I really don't think Weston's in love with me. He's just fond of grand gestures—everything has to be grandiose with him. And since he's filthy rich, a ridiculously expensive gift might not represent as much to him as it might for the rest of us lowly middle-class civilians.

I tell myself I'm not going to dwell on it. And I act like everything is just as it was before.

Weston and I are scheduled to go out next Saturday, the day after his birthday. He never mentioned his birthday was coming, but I know since I've done more than my share of cyber-stalking.

I really want to get him something. But what do you get for the man who has everything? He gives me a priceless dress, and what do I get him…a lame tie? I've been racking my brain about it for weeks.

And I know I'm breaking the rules—giving him a gift.

But he did.

Therefore, so can I.

I decide to contact Kathryn.

> Dear Kathryn,
>
> I am looking to get a little something for Weston's birthday.
>
> Could you please ask him for any advice?
>
> Cheers,
> Mirella

I pace all day, impatiently awaiting her reply. I wonder if Weston could even give me an idea. He seems like the kind of person who is very particular.

Finally, toward the end of the day, I'm surprised to receive an e-mail, not from Kathryn, but from Weston himself.

> Dear Mirella,
>
> I was amused to receive your message from Kathryn. How did you even know it was my birthday? It appears someone has been doing a little spying.
>
> There is only one thing I would like—a photo of you. Framed or unframed.
>
> Looking forward to seeing you,
>
> Regards,
> Weston
>
> P.S. Clarification: Although I would most likely immensely enjoy a boudoir photo of you, what I would really like is a simple photo of your beautiful face. And I want to see that smile.

My breath catches as I read the message over and over again—*your beautiful face*. His words are so sweet and his needs are so simple—all he wants is me.

I'm almost tempted to reply with something flirty, but I know that's against the rules. He might be breaking the rules, but I'm desperately trying to stick to them. So I do not reply and content myself with the knowledge that I will see him shortly.

I print the e-mail, fold it into a little square, and hide it in my jewelry box.

I dive into the photo albums and look for a nice photo of myself.

I feverishly dig through all the albums and the photo collection on my laptop.

But there are none.

The only nice ones are from my wedding day, taken by our wonderful wedding photographer, and I'm sure this is not what Weston had in mind.

I can't believe I do not have *one* single nice photo of myself.

Gabe and I take a lot of photos. We actually have a nice camera—a high-end Canon digital camera with a few lenses. But we reserve the use of it mostly for trips and photos of the girls. We barely ever take photos of ourselves. And I really don't think Weston wants a photo of me cradling Claire or Chloe in my arms or smiling cheek-to-cheek with Gabe or standing in front of the Statue of Liberty with a backpack, wearing ugly sneakers.

I sit on the plush carpet in my bedroom, shoulders hunched, surrounded by a mess of photo albums and my laptop. I feel completely defeated.

I lie down in the middle of it all, and I think of Weston—the way he looks when he smiles at me, his funny quirks, what he likes.

And an idea hits me.

Then another…

And yet another one…and that last one brings a mischievous smile to my lips.

Quite a sight I must be when Chloe walks in.

She looks at me like I've gone off the deep end. "What's so funny, Mommy? Why are you smiling? What are you *doing?*"

"Looking at pictures."

"Can I see?"

Chloe, Claire, and I spend over two hours looking at photos, and I forget to make dinner. When Gabe gets home, he's mildly annoyed, and we order a pizza.

It's no roast beef, but it's still pretty damn good.

To date, Weston has planned all our dates, and I don't mind it that way—he knows the city better than I do, and he's the one footing the bill. I also get the impression he likes to be in charge. As he's told me more than once, he doesn't like the unexpected—he likes to know what's coming. I'm sure the idea of a date he knows nothing about would not sit well with him.

But just this once…I type a message to Kathryn.

> Dear Kathryn,
>
> How are you?
>
> I'm not sure if you and Weston have already planned our evening this next Saturday, but I would like to suggest a walk in Lincoln Park at around 5:00 p.m., followed by dinner at Mon Ami Gabi.
>
> Please let Weston know and get back to me with his opinion on the matter.
>
> Cheers,
> Mirella

Kathryn's reply is short and curt.

> Dear Mirella,
>
> I'm very well. Thank you. Weston is fine with your suggestion and will meet you at Elis Fountain at 5:00 p.m. Edward will pick you up as per usual.
>
> Best,
> Kathryn

I wear a flowery summer dress and sensible pumps. I've always loved this particular dress—the vibrant colors bring out the color in my cheeks. I curl my hair, take more care than usual with my makeup, and finish things off with a classic red lipstick. Today, I really want to look good.

I stuff Weston's birthday presents in a large red purse, along with my camera.

I kiss Gabe and the girls before I leave.

"You're going out early tonight," Gabe points out. He's the one in charge of dinner tonight, and I smile at the thought—the girls will most likely be eating boxed pizza.

"We're going for an early walk in Lincoln Park and then dinner. I won't be very late. What about you?"

"We're going to eat in the Theater District. That's all I know."

Chloe looks up from her drawing, pencil in hand. "You're going to see your friends in Chicago again, Mommy?"

"Yes. And Daddy too. Caroline will come over later."

"Yay," she says, cheerful.

I'm amazed at how smoothly this arrangement is running. We had a rough time at the get-go, but now it's simply become our "lifestyle." I convince myself everything's fine. The girls are happy. Gabe and I are happy. I delude myself into thinking we're not hurting anyone. I even convince myself we're not taking a huge risk.

And I convince myself I'm not ashamed. But of course, no one knows…with the exception of Gwen. I'm sure that even if we told our friends and families, they wouldn't believe us. And if they did, their opinion of us would surely change drastically—as far as everyone is concerned, we've always been the sweetest couple there ever was.

I sit on the concrete bench at the fountain and turn my head to study the statues of flocking geese and strange half-cherub, half-mermaid mythological creatures wrestling fish. It's bizarre, but lovely nevertheless. I'm so enthralled by the fountain I don't even notice when Weston walks up to me.

He smiles at me, and I stand up to greet him. He looks handsome in a dark fitted top and slim gray chinos. His hair is perfectly smooth as always, with that one unruly lock of hair sticking up—the sight of it always makes me smile. I can't believe I hadn't noticed it the first time we met.

"You look lovely," he says, and no other words pass between us. From his expression, I can tell he means it. He's not just being polite—Weston is not one for pretense. I've noticed he only says what he means—and that's another thing I like about him.

I reach into my bag. "I'm sorry. I don't have a nice photo of myself to give you."

"Not even a single one?" he asks, his expression a mix of surprise and disappointment. "I find that hard to believe."

I pull out my camera. "It's true, but I have something even better." I hand him the camera.

"You want me to take photos of you?"

"As many as you would like," I say. "And I'll print the best ones for you and burn you a CD."

"Sounds good. But I don't know too much about photography."

"It's easy. It's set on auto. Just click."

As we walk through Lincoln Park, Weston clicks away and captures my image against the greenery, the cityscape in the background and the lovely fountains and ponds.

I admit—this was not a completely selfless idea—I manage to snap a few photos of him as well—capturing his gorgeous smile, the spark in his brilliant green eyes, even that rebel lock of hair.

He takes one or two selfies of the both of us, stretching out his long arms, the camera looking down on us. As I smile at the camera, I can't help but realize this is probably one of the unspoken rules—no "loving couple" photos. But I push away the thought from my mind almost as soon as it makes its appearance. I want a photo of him and me. No matter what happens, I know I can look back at the photo when I'm ninety years old and remember him and this absolutely tumultuous time in my life.

"Nice choice," Weston says as we sit comfortably on the terrace at *Mon Ami Gabi*, a French bistro style restaurant. "This place is quite charming."

"It kind of feels like we're in Paris, right?" I say playfully. "If only I knew what Paris feels like," I'm quick to add. "I've never been."

"I'm sure you'll get to see it someday," he tells me, looking at me in that way he always does—like I'm the cutest thing on the planet.

"I sure hope so," I respond, scanning the menu.

Weston orders a glass of red from the rolling wine cart, and I order a white since I plan to have the roasted chicken with frites.

"Happy belated birthday," I blurt out when the server finally leaves us.

He smiles shyly and doesn't quite look at me. "Thank you. Although, I think I'd rather forget all about it."

My fingers are trembling as I reach into my oversized purse. "Here, I got you a little something." My nerves are tied up in knots as I hand him the small wrapped package. I'm not sure why I'm so flustered. I just hope he likes it.

"Thank you," he says, clearly surprised. "This isn't a picture of you, is it?"

He tears the wrapping off and smiles when he sees the CD I made for him.

"You've made me a mix-tape, I see," he says, a grin stretched wide across his face. "Very old-school."

"It has some of my favorite songs…some stuff you've probably never heard of," I explain, a little nervous. "I'm always looking for new music."

He studies the list of songs scribbled on the cover paper. "I love it. I like a lot of these songs. I'll listen to it when I work out."

I smile, happy he likes my gift. Then, I swallow hard and stare down at my dress. "I also have something else for you."

He tilts his head. "Oh…" is all he says. He seems curious.

"Which I'll give you at the hotel."

A slow mischievous smile spreads across his face. "I'm intrigued."

I smile at him, not wanting to divulge more.

And I hope he can't see just how petrified I am.

When we get back to the hotel, Weston asks me about the second gift.

"It's not really a gift," I tell him as we walk into the elevator. "It's not something tangible."

"I am bursting with curiosity."

I start to doubt myself—maybe this was a horrible idea. I don't even know if I can pull it off.

I take my shoes off once we're in the suite, and sit on the sofa. My nerves are in knots—I'm so anxious.

He pulls his satchel over his head. "It's a shame I don't have a CD player here. But I'll have Kathryn transfer the songs to my iPod as soon as she can."

"I hope you like them," I say, my voice barely a whisper.

He takes a seat next to me on the sofa and takes my hand in his. "Thanks for the CD."

I look away, ill-at-ease. "It's not much," I say. "But it's really hard to get a birthday present for the man who has everything."

He laughs. "I do have everything," he confesses as he trails his finger along the edge of my face.

I know what he wants. And I want it too.

But I need to stick to the plan.

I pull his hand away. "Uh..." I stammer. "About your other present..."

He perks up. "Yes?"

I stand and walk toward his bedroom. Once I make my way there, I pull one of the arm chairs and position it to face the bed.

"Here. Sit here."

He does as he's told, pausing to examine me, eyeing me with a suspicious smile. I'm sure he's wondering what the heck I'm up to.

I clutch my bag against my chest and sit on the bed, right in front of him. He studies me intently and tilts his head to the side.

I'm surprised at how nervous I am. Weston and I have been together a few times now, and we've become quite intimate, yet he still manages to unnerve me—in many ways, it's still like being with a stranger every time I'm with him.

I finally summon the courage to speak. "Well...Weston," I say, sucking in a long breath. "As I've said already, you're not exactly easy to shop for..."

He smiles, his elbow propped on the arm of the chair, his chin rests on his thumb, and his gold-speckled green eyes fix me intently. I'm sure he's not trying to be sexy, but he *sure* is.

I reach for my bag slowly, my eyes locked on his.

He leans in. "What do you have in there?" he asks. His eyes have an energy about them—I can tell I'm driving him a little crazy.

"I've racked my brain thinking about what I should get you. I wondered about the things you like, what you like to do..." I go on as I retrieve a silver case from my purse. "And an idea came to me."

I slide my fingers along the hard edge of the case, and slowly open it. My breath hitches. "I know...how..." I bite my lip. "You like to watch," I quickly add, my words barely a whisper. I can't believe how difficult this is. I thought it would be easier. I thought I was comfortable enough with Weston but..."I thought I'd give you a little show."

My heart hammers against my ribcage as I turn the case toward him and show him my vibrator. I look up at him to see his reaction—it matters so much to me.

He smiles—that wicked smile which I only see when we're about to do something delicious and naughty. He bites his bottom lip. "I must say…I love this gift so far."

I smile. "It hasn't even started yet."

He leans back in his chair. "What are you going to do exactly? What will this little show entail?"

"I'm going to pleasure myself in front of you while you watch," I inform him with a sly smile. "And you're only allowed to watch… you can't touch."

He smiles, a fire in his eyes. "That's a little cruel, but fair enough."

I look at him and set the case on the bed, reaching for the side zipper of my dress.

His smile fades. He's serious all of a sudden—intense. He's aroused. "Do you do this often?"

I swallow hard. This is a conversation I've never thought I'd have with *anyone*. "Enough. I think about you."

He closes his eyes. "I like that," he says. He opens his eyes again to see my purple lace bra exposed. I've worn a tasteful set under my dress. I want this show to be classy—well, as classy as a masturbation show can be. A small part of me can't help feeling a bit like a porn star. I still can't believe I'm doing this. I'm completely under his spell.

"And that's your tool of choice?" he teases.

I slide my dress down and expose my matching lacy briefs. "It's pretty effective. It's about the same size as you. I like to imagine it's you inside me."

"Only I don't vibrate," he jokes. "It's even better than me, I imagine."

I shoot him a sly smile. "It's *never* as good as you."

I reach for the case and pull down the covers.

He scratches the edge of his jaw. "Take off the bra. I'd like you fully naked."

I unclasp my bra and let it fall to the ground. I feel the weight of my breasts drop. My nipples are erect—I've been aroused since I first took the silver case out of my purse. I reach for the band of my panties and pull them down slowly, revealing myself completely.

He groans a little—he seems to be enjoying the show. And I'm still scared as all get-out. So I try to take the focus away from myself—I'm feeling way too exposed. "Are you hard?"

"What do you think?"

"I can tell," I say, sitting on the edge of the bed, vibrator in hand.

"I can't touch you…not even one bit?"

"No," I say firmly. "But you can watch."

"Show me…" he says, tracing his index finger along his bottom lip.

The way he's looking at me is so damn hot.

I take out the vibrator from its case and hold it in my hands—the sleek see-through rubber is cold against my palm. I get right to it, turn it on, and spread my legs wide.

I glide it against my lips, slowly back and forth, delighting in the sensation.

"Sweet hell…" is all Weston manages to say.

I close my eyes. My other hand strokes my left breast. My fingers caress my nipple. "I like to imagine you're the one touching me."

"I wish." His voice is ragged, uneven.

The pressure is building—it feels so good. Usually, I climax really quickly this way.

But I want to give him a good show, so I drag the vibrator away from my sex, down my thigh.

"Teasing yourself?"

"I need to," I breathe, "if I want this to last longer than a minute."

"You're killing me."

I open my eyes to look at him. He seems so turned on, yet he's just sitting there watching me, behaving, like the good boy he is.

I sit up, still watching him—he's being so good. I turn off the vibrator and get up off the bed.

He jerks to attention. "What are you…"

I walk up to him and reach for his belt.

With a hint of a smile, he asks, "What are you doing?"

"I want you to touch yourself too, while you watch me."

"I don't hate that idea," he says as I free his erection, big and glorious.

I lean down and wrap my mouth around it.

"Mirella…" he breathes.

I suck him, hard and slow, enjoying the sensation of him. But I don't want to take it too far. "There…" I whisper, pulling back. "I got you started…nice and wet."

His hand grips his long shaft, in a smooth up and down movement. I sit on the bed and watch him—watching him masturbate is such a turn-on.

I spread my legs wide again, giving him a nice view—I'm quite uninhibited when I'm aroused. I slide the vibrating dildo up and down along my sex, loving the way my body feels…and builds—every cell seems alive. I bring myself to the edge, but then I pull away when I sense myself too near.

Weston's lids are heavy, and his breathing seems to grow shallow.

"Don't move too fast," I warn him. "The show's not over," I whisper and turn over on my knees, my ass facing him.

"God…I love that view."

"You and every single man."

I ease into the vibrator. It fills me deep. I slide it in and out, pushing my hips hard onto it, imagining I'm straddling Weston.

"You're beautiful." His voice is soft.

As the vibration hits my G-spot over and over, I feel myself nearing climax. I can't see Weston, but I can hear him—he's nearing too. And if I can hold off for just a second, I can time the grand finale perfectly.

But no can do.

Despite myself, I explode into waves of pleasure, my moans surprisingly loud.

When the pleasure finally recedes, I crash down on the bed, spent.

My body is numb.

"Incredible," he whispers.

I realize he hasn't climaxed yet, and I want him to.

"You can touch me now," I say playfully, looking back at him, "if you want to."

He jumps to his feet and lunges at me. His hands grab my hips, and he trails his tongue down my spine, all the way to the tip of my crack.

He puts on a condom as fast as humanly possible and presses into me—the sensation of him inside me is always so amazing—I can never seem to get enough.

He reaches his climax almost instantly.

We both crash onto the crisp white sheets, our bodies fused.

Chapter Seventeen

Tell me I'm better than him.

"I think this might be the most memorable present I've ever received," he whispers, his lips against my earlobe.

I laugh. "I think I enjoyed it more than you did."

He strokes my hair away from my face. "I sincerely doubt that. That was astonishing."

I turn over and reach for him. I wrap my arms around him—his shirt is soft against my naked skin. "Lie with me."

He lies beside me and presses against me, his arms hold me tight and keep me warm.

We lie like this for what seems like an eternity, without words. I think about how wonderful it would be to be snuggled in his arms like this forever. Almost as if he's reading my thoughts, he says, his voice soft, "I wish you could stay the night."

My heart fills with butterflies. "Me too."

"But…we can't."

"No, we can't," I agree.

I hate these damned rules.

"It would be nice to wake up next to you," he says.

It would be.

"You have no idea what I look like first thing in the morning," I joke, trying to lighten the mood before I start to cry. "And the morning breath…you have no idea."

He laughs a hearty laugh—the sound of it in my ear is wonderful.

"Trust me…it's better off this way." There is genuine emotion in his eyes.

"I trust you."

"Mirella," he whispers, hesitating. "It's been over three weeks since we last saw each other."

"Yes?"

"I've been concerned about the last time we were together," he says with uncertainty in his tone.

I know what he's asking.

"I've had my period," I reassure him. "There's nothing to worry about."

"Good," he says, squeezing me tight.

And I wonder…what if it hadn't been…good.

Would he have stood by me? Or would he have insisted I get an abortion? My intuition tells me it would be the latter. But I honestly have no clue. A baby would be pure chaos…and completely unexpected.

And I know how Weston hates the unexpected.

I receive a surprise e-mail from Kathryn, addressed to both Gabe and me.

> Hello Mirella and Gabe,
>
> Weston and Bridget were wondering if you would like to join them for dinner at Lake Point Tower this Thursday night, at six o'clock, followed by a visit to Adler Planetarium.
>
> If so, will you be needing the car service?
>
> Please get back to me at your earliest convenience,
> Kathryn

Gabe calls me from work at lunch time. I'm a little giddy when I answer—I love when Gabe calls me from work—it's a rare occurrence.

"So, this is unusual," he says, his voice upbeat. "A date on a school night."

"Yes," I agree. "It's been a while since we've all been together."

"Yeah, it has."

"You think it will be awkward?"

He laughs. "No…not at all."

I laugh too. Yes…how could it not be?

"I'm not sure it's a great idea," I confess. "Things have been running so smoothly. Why mess with that?"

"I don't know," he says. "Maybe it's a good idea. Maybe it will rein us in, in case any of us were entertaining delusions, getting carried away. Show us who belongs with who, you know what I'm saying?"

He leaves me speechless for a beat—his words shock me. Occasionally Gabe will say something insightful and eerily apropos, and I almost wonder if he's been spying on me.

"Maybe you're right. Listen, I need to go. I need to get lunch ready for the girls."

The thing is…his words have rattled me.

Gabe's words are still on my mind when I get dressed for our double date. I've chosen my favorite skinny jeans and a breezy, white Bohemian top.

Is Gabe right?

Do I need to be reined in?

Will seeing Weston with Bridget knock me back to reality? Because Gwen is right—I have been stumbling a little.

It will probably not be easy, I admit to myself. I've been very good at not thinking about her. When Weston and I get together, it seems there's just us two in the whole world, and I often forget he has a whole other life I'm not a part of—a whole family, children I've never met, a home I've never seen—multiple homes I've never seen.

And now I've managed to self-talk myself into a mood.

By the time I touch up my makeup and fix my hair, I'm officially bitchy. I don't want to go on a double date.

I want to see Weston…and *only* Weston.

And I remind myself, this is exactly *why* I try not to think about these things.

As I slip on my open-toed wedges, I kiss the top of Claire's head. "Promise you'll be good for Caroline?"

"I promise," she says in her sweet voice. I can't resist kissing her on both cheeks.

"You too, Chloe." I kiss her cheeks as well.

My two beautiful girls.

"We won't be late."

A wide smile stretches across Caroline's face. "Have fun," she tells us, adjusting her dark-framed glasses.

"We'll try," I say, half-rolling my eyes, still a bit cranky—I just can't seem to shake it.

We ride to the city in Gabe's truck. There's no way on earth he would ever accept a ride in Weston's car—probably not even if we were stranded in the middle of nowhere, dying of dehydration.

Of course, I'm not about to argue with him.

"You don't look happy," he points out, his eyes fixed on the road.

"Hmpf," I grunt.

He laughs a little. "What's the problem?"

"I don't know. I'm just not looking forward to it."

"But we had fun with them before, didn't we?"

"We did," I agree. "But that was before…"

"Before we all fucked each other?"

"Well, I wouldn't have put it quite that way, but yes," I say, trailing my finger along the seam of my jeans. "I just think it'll be awkward."

"Yes, maybe," he agrees. "I've been thinking about how I'll react. I'm sure I'll want to punch the guy in the face."

I laugh a little. "Please restrain yourself," I plead, half-serious. "He wouldn't stand a chance."

"He wouldn't. I could kill the guy."

My smile fades. "You could."

And I think about it for a second.

He could.

Weston works out two hours a day but is nowhere as big as Gabe. And Gabe is a brawler—it's in his blood. In his younger days, he was arrested twice for assault—a few too many drinks resulting in a few ill-advised bar fights—messed both guys up pretty good. But in recent years, he's taken out his aggression in MMA training, and it has been a godsend. With his training, and his primal taste for blood, he could definitely do some damage.

Yes…Weston should definitely not get on his bad side.

We meet Weston and Bridget at the Lake Point Tower.

I spot the familiar sleek town car drive up and get butterflies in my stomach—not the good kind. Edward walks around the car and waves. I smile brightly at him—my first smile in a while. My smile fades as he opens the door for Bridget and Weston. Bridget looks fabulous in a cream fitted suit and stiletto pumps, and I suddenly feel frumpy in my jeans and cheap top. She flashes her megawatt smile at both of us as she walks in our direction. Weston is dressed more casually—designer jeans and a dark fitted V-neck shirt. As he walks behind her, he almost looks like a little boy clinging on to this larger-than-life woman.

Wherever she is, Bridget owns the place.

She air-kisses me on both cheeks. "It's so nice to see you again."

The whole thing is surreal—our exchange is so ordinary—so typical—there's no indication whatsoever we've been with each other's husbands. She certainly doesn't seem to be holding a grudge.

She gives Gabe a quick hug, and I cringe inwardly, visions of their naked bodies intertwined. My gaze travels to Weston who gives me a sheepish smile—I can tell he's in agony—the strangeness of the situation is not lost on him. He offers his hand, and I smile up at him as he smiles at me, both of us on the same page.

"Gabe," Weston says as he shakes his hand firmly.

"Weston," Gabe says.

And that's as far as that conversation goes.

We ride up the elevator in a flash, and thankfully, we're up on the seventieth floor before we can even start a conversation.

We sit by the window and enjoy the magnificent view.

I find myself sitting across from Weston, and he can barely look at me—it seems like it was on our first double date—we had ended up in front of each other, and we had barely been able to look at each other then too. Every now and then, Bridget leans in, smiles, and touches Weston with the affection of a woman who loves her husband. I try not to look at them. I don't understand her—she seems to love him. Why is she sharing him? But then again, I love my husband too. Why am *I* sharing?

We are one messed-up bunch.

The server takes our drink orders and leaves us. Bridget asks me how I've been. I tell her about my summer break and ask her if she's been busy over the summer. But her words barely register, disrupted by this intense déjà-vu.

It wasn't so long ago when Weston and I had dinner here—the memories clog my mind—the twinkling lights, my red dress, Weston taking off that dress and everything else, as slowly as humanly possible, teasing me. The recollection arouses me, and as I catch a glimpse of Weston, I see he's looking at me with that intense expression, the same expression he wore when I stripped for him, when I masturbated for him.

This was such a bad idea, I think, trying hard to focus on Bridget's words. But it's hard to carry on a conversation with a woman when her husband is looking at you like he wants to devour you.

The server comes back with a bottle of Merlot Weston has ordered and pours us all a glass.

Weston finally breaks his stare. And I take a drink. God knows…I need it.

With his eyes off me, I can finally manage a decent conversation. Gabe, Bridget, and I talk mostly about our kids, she goes into great lengths about their recent trip to Italy, and I don't want to hear it. I try consciously not to scowl or let my bitterness show.

We enjoy a nice enough supper.

I have the scallops again since I enjoyed them so much the last time. And I'm thankful dinner is going relatively well. I mentally pat myself on the back—I haven't made a scene, I haven't hurled insults, thrown things, or stormed out, which is impressive, considering the emotions I'm having.

Weston is mostly quiet, but that's the way he is when it's the four of us. He's as arresting as ever—his large almond shaped eyes are just as striking as ever. Part of me wishes we could sneak away in a dark corner of the restaurant and steal a kiss. It feels strange being so close to him and not being able to touch him. It makes me want to touch him even more. And judging from the way he's been looking at me, he feels the same way.

This is undue torture.

"I didn't even realize the Planetarium was open at night," Gabe tells Bridget.

"Yes. Once a month, it's after dark night. It's great geekish fun," she jokes, resting her hand on Weston's shoulder. "There's a bar and everything."

"Well, it should be lots of fun," I add, trying not to look at Weston.

"Weston loves it there. He's into all that astronomy stuff," she comments, taking a sip of Merlot. "And robotics too, but I don't want to bore you with that."

I smile. I could never be bored hearing about Weston.

"And he's really into sea life."

"Yes…I know," I say tightly, swallowing the urge to prove how well I know him. Weston raises a brow and looks away.

It's true. I do know a lot, but I'll never know as much as she does.

Despite the fact that I've had only two glasses of wine, I feel a little lightheaded as we exit the tower. Bridget and Weston hop in their town car, and we head to the parking lot.

"Meet us at the south entrance," Bridget instructs us as Edward opens the car door for her.

We wave good-bye as we make our way to the parking lot. I'm glad I've dressed comfortably.

"I don't like the way he looks at you," Gabe says as we head toward the island. "He's kind of predatory."

I laugh a little. "He is not."

"Maybe someone should remind him that you're *mine*, not his," he sneers, not taking his eyes off the road.

"Now who's being predatory?" I tease. "Or rather territorial, I should say."

"Maybe you were right, Ella," Gabe concedes. "I think it is a bad idea...all of us getting together."

"You *think?*" I tease a little.

"I can't stand seeing the two of you together," he confesses, "even just talking."

"Well, I don't particularly enjoy seeing you and Bridget together either," I reluctantly admit. "These feelings are normal, Gabe."

Gabe doesn't say another word. Neither of us do. We sit in silence, probably both uneasy about the night ahead.

As we near the planetarium, I am awed by the astonishing building, as I always am whenever I come here—the rather fascinating contrast of historical architecture of the dome topped Grainger Sky Theater—it seems so old to me—enclosed in the cool sleek glass modern structure. It always takes my breath away.

We meet at the VIP south entrance. Weston shoots me a smile as we near them. I gather they've been waiting for a while—we've had a little more walking to do than they have—how does Bridget keep up those fantastic legs when she never seems to *walk?*

"This place is wonderful, isn't it?" I venture, trying to make small talk as we head inside. Weston seems to have arranged for everything—I appreciate how he always seems to be on top of things.

"It's one of my favorite examples of amazing architecture. Designed by Ernest Grunsfeld, Jr."

I spot Gabe rolling his eyes a little, and I almost want to elbow him in the ribs.

We *actually* have fun...sort of.

First we visit a solar system display—it's quite fun walking under the huge solar system floating above our heads—the space is airy and bright, the twilight of the evening reflected in the wall to wall skylight windows.

We learn all about the planets—I'm proud I already know a thing or two—as I should, as a teacher. We explore the surface textures of the different planets and touch a real piece of meteorite, its surface rough.

Weston is the ever-charming guide, answering any questions I come up with easily. He seems truly fascinated by all this stuff—I think it's kind of sweet.

Gabe, on the other hand, doesn't seem too interested in his surroundings, but more taken with his touring partner. I can't help but wonder if he's purposely trying to make me jealous. I decide I won't give him the satisfaction. I'm not going to act jealous, but I am more than a little annoyed by his behavior. Weston and I are behaving ourselves and acting like proper adults—not shamelessly flirting and behaving like horny teenagers.

There's a time and place, people.

I try to ignore them. I'm just happy to be with Weston.

We enter another exhibit, dark and moody with oddly shaped screens everywhere—thousands of pixels making up strange images. Weston tells me they are telescopic views of galaxies, stars, planets and atoms—the story of the universe.

"Gabe seems to be enjoying himself," Weston points out, looking over at Bridget who is practically wrapped around my husband. It seems odd to me that Weston doesn't seem to care. I know I do. They must have a very strange relationship—but then again, they've been doing this longer than we have.

"They're certainly not shy about it," I tell him as we enter this futuristic, glowy pink and blue tunnel, feeling like a young college kid at the hippest club in town. I kind of wish loud music were blasting. "This is so cool."

"Thirteen thousand linear feet of aluminum siding and two thousand square yards of fabric." He sounds like Wikipedia—if Wikipedia came in a gorgeous, live-male version. He is such a nerd.

He cocks a brow and looks at me. "I see I'm amusing you again," he says, a sheepish smile.

"You are. I love when you share your little blurbs of knowledge. Tell me more."

He laughs.

And I take his hand. I was afraid to do so—afraid he was going to pull away, but he doesn't—he simply looks at me with that sweet smile of his. We hold hands as we watch video greetings from famous astronauts. I feel oddly normal, but a little nervous. What if we run into a couple Gabe and I know—with my hand in Weston's and Bridget wrapped around Gabe—just how would we explain that one?

We watch the Cosmic Wonder show, all sitting together in a row. I end up sandwiched between Gabe and Weston, lying back comfortably, looking up at the night sky above us—the universe. Billions of galaxies, Weston explains, but all I can think about is how lucky I am to be sitting between two gorgeous men who both care about me. I can't help but think—if my younger self were here to catch a glimpse of my older present-day self, she'd be impressed—how did this happen, to little old me?

We end the evening at the bar. It's magical—the Chicago skyline reflected in the skylights, twinkling, sparkling lights—not stars, but man-made buildings, and amazing nevertheless.

Weston comes back with imported beers for himself and Gabe and girly cocktails for Bridget and me. We chat awhile about the exhibits and the show. The energy between all of us seems erotic and palpable. I'm pretty sure we're all in the mood for sex, but of course, no one dares to talk about it—instead we make polite small talk, and I laugh inwardly at the absurdity of it all.

I catch a glimpse of Weston and shoot him a little grin—a playful smirk.

He smiles back and takes my hand.

"We're going to head outside," he tells Bridget and Gabe. "I want to show Mirella the amazing view."

They both smile, seemingly unaffected. I think it's understood we are all heading toward a known conclusion.

He leads me to a secluded spot on the observatory, wraps his arms around my waist, and kisses my neck softly. "I've missed you."

"I've missed you too."

My heart heavy, I pull away and turn to smile at him. "It's only been five days, Weston."

"I know," he says, looking absolutely defeated, "but I can't stop thinking about you." He pulls me back to him. "The vision of you, naked on my bed," he whispers in my ear, "legs spread wide, pleasuring yourself…is etched in my brain."

I smile, feeling that familiar energy between my legs. But this isn't the time or place.

"Stop it, Weston."

"Why?" he asks, his tone playful. "Am I arousing you?"

"Yes," I admit, looking up at him. "Big time."

"I like that," he says, his delicious wide grin teasing me.

"Well, now's not the place."

His hands travel to my rear. "I couldn't stop thinking about it all week. I had to excuse myself a few times to go take a shower. Thankfully, it's pretty handy having your own washroom at work."

"The perks of the powerful," I say with a sly smile, trying to tear away from his grip.

"I want you," he whispers in my ear, "as soon as possible."

I look up at him, my gaze heavy.

I want him too.

He's really turning me on. "When you say you want something as soon as possible, I bet you usually get it."

"Always."

"Well, I don't know if you'll be so lucky tonight," I can't resist saying. "Your beautiful wife and my husband are here too, remember?"

His lips press into a tight smile. "You're jealous."

I jerk away. "I am not."

"Oh yes…you are. You've been surly all night," he points out. "You've been sneering at Bridget like you just want to tear her head off."

He's right. I do want to tear Miss Universe's head off. But there's no way I'm admitting that. He is so full of it, and suddenly, I want to tear his head off too.

"You can't be jealous, Mirella," he deadpans. "I made that explicitly clear from the onset."

"Yes, sir," I scoff, turning on my heel. "Let's go."

He grabs my arm and pulls me to him. "Bridget wants to leave with Gabe. You and Gabe should discuss."

"Oh…she does, does she?" I snap. "No, she can't have him tonight."

He laughs, but his laughter is edgy. "Seriously?"

I smile. I'm enjoying every second of this. "I want him all to myself tonight," I say and walk away.

He darts after me. "You can't be serious. You've been looking at me all night like you just want to tear my clothes off."

"You're delusional." I pull away.

He grabs my arm again. "Mirella…"

I glare at him. "Let me go."

He lets go.

"It's nothing personal, Weston," I tell him as I walk away. "I'm just in the mood to be *properly* pinned against a wall tonight."

Weston calls me on my cell, the next day, at seven thirty in the morning. I don't answer, of course. He calls again at ten forty-five and then again at twelve thirty. I finally relent.

"Mirella, this is the third time I've called."

I gaze out the kitchen window, trying desperately to remain unaffected. "I know."

"You've been avoiding me."

"I thought this was against the rules," I scoff. "You can't call me."

I can hear the sound of a deep sigh. "I can call you if I want to speak with you, Mirella."

I scrunch a dish cloth, my hand a fist. "Oh…how convenient. You can bend the rules, at your leisure. But when I might have a problem with them, it's a big to-do."

"Obviously, I've upset you. I didn't—"

"I'm sorry, but I've gotta go."

As I press "end call," I look up to see Claire, juice box in hand, staring at me, slack-jawed. And I realize she's overheard everything. I try to replay my end of the conversation in my head.

"Oh…it was…just…grandpa," I stammer. "You know…*grandpa*."

She stares at me, wide-eyed. "Why were you screaming at him?"

"Uh…" I stammer. "It's okay now. It's all better, sweetie."

My cell rings again. The man is really starting to annoy me.

"Hello."

"Mirella…just listen to me…"

I don't dare scoff, in Claire's presence. "Yes."

"I miss you." His words are soft. "I was so torn-up last night."

Please.

"I'm sending a car later tonight, and I want you at my loft."

Who does he think he is?

I look over at Claire, who's at the table drawing funny faces on people in my *Redbook*. "I'm not a pizza. You can't just order me to be at your place whenever you get a craving."

"Don't you want to be with me?" he asks, his tone laced with uncertainty, vulnerability.

I do want him. I'm not only hurting him…I'm hurting myself.

"I do," I admit, my words a whisper.

"Then you'll come?"

Suddenly, I'm so easy. I've *never* been easy.

I bite my lip. "Yes."

Weston kisses me in the elevator, a hungry kiss, but soft. His tongue explores my mouth, and I moan at the sensation. I don't think there's anything on earth I enjoy more than his kiss. I could kiss him for hours.

When we're finally in the privacy of his suite, he presses me against the wall, and pins my arms above my head with a hard grasp. His kiss takes on a whole different dimension—it becomes more aggressive, wilder. He bites my bottom lip—it's deliciously painful.

"How's this for *properly* pinning you against a wall?" he asks me between kisses. He's pushed all my buttons. I'm just about to explode.

He trails his tongue along my jaw line. "Tell me I'm better than him."

I want him to kiss me, just like this all night long. I'm torn—I don't know if I'd rather just make out all night or go all the way.

He pulls at the waistband of my dress pants. "Tell me," he almost growls.

"You are. You're amazing."

"I wish you were mine," he whispers in my ear. "I could have you anytime."

I am taken aback by his words. I wish he were mine too. I've wished he were mine a thousand times.

I reach for his soft cashmere shirt and pull it over his head, revealing his delicious body. I slide my tongue down his chest to his navel and swirl it around his belly button. He moans, and I love the sound. He's so delicious—I just want to eat him up.

I pull his belt and reach for his fly.

"You're eager again, little butterfly," he says, his voice playful. I free his erection, and take him in my mouth. He groans a little. I revel in the sensation of giving him pleasure.

He drags his fingers in my hair, pulling—the pain deliciously bearable. "That feels amazing," he breathes, barely audible, "but," he says, pulling me back up, "I want to be inside you."

I want that too.

I pull his pants down all the way and slide off his shoes, even his socks. He's completely naked for me, a specimen of a man. "I like you like that."

He laughs. "Well, one of us has too much clothing on." He kneels down and grabs my waist in his arms. He kisses my belly—his lips fall on the soft material of my frilly top.

He undoes my fly in one swift move, and peels my pants down, taking my panties along. He lands a sweet kiss on my curls.

"You don't need to worry. I'm not jealous. I know this is just sex."

His hands glide along my legs. He slides off my wedged heels. The feel of his soft hand around the heel of my foot lights me up. I want him so badly.

"I'm just here for a good fuck..."

He smiles up at me—a wicked smile. "At your service..."

I hold his face, the hard angles of his jaw feel solid in my hands. I pull him for one last kiss before I reach for his satchel where he keeps condoms.

I put on the condom, and he tries to assist me, but I bat his hand away. "I've got it. I'm in charge of this ride."

He laughs. "Are you, now?"

I trail my hand across his stomach and push him against the wall. He's absolutely right...this is just sex. And I should start to act like it. "My turn to be in the driver's seat." I smirk.

He's so much taller than me—I need to stand on the tip of my toes to kiss him. His lips are soft and warm. I reach for his shoulders and push him down. "Slide down...all the way."

His back glides down the wall. He looks up at me, desire in his eyes.

I kneel down and straddle him.

I rub myself along his shaft—it already feels so good. "I know this isn't the most comfortable position. But this is about my pleasure tonight. And you're going to rock my world."

He laughs a little. "I'm feeling a little used, Mirella."

"Are you complaining?"

"Never," he insists, his lids heavy. "Not at all."

I look straight into his eyes and ease him into me slowly. He closes his eyes, and I close mine. I push into him deeper, and we're completely connected.

"I love it like this." I rock back and forth slowly. "You're so deep inside me."

He mumbles something unintelligible, nibbling at my ear. He's hitting just the right spot, and it drives me to ride him harder and faster, my legs rubbing against the scratchy carpet. The floor is so hard, but the resistance is what makes it so damn good.

I ride him intensely, chasing that mind-blowing orgasm I see in my near future.

"Mirella..." he breathes.

"Take me there," I beg, my teeth trailing along his jawbone. I can feel myself so near, and I can tell it's going to be explosive.

"Kiss me," he pleads. "I want to be kissing you when you get there."

He holds my face in his hands. My lips search for his, and our tongues tangle.

He pushes harder into me and finally brings me to the edge.

I moan into his mouth.

The waves of ecstasy hit me, and it's so good, it's almost painful. He moans into my mouth loudly, reaching his own climax. His fingers dig into the flesh of my cheeks, but the pain feels wonderful.

I will never get enough of this.

I bury my face in the crook of his neck, trying to catch my breath. My legs hurt like crazy, and I'm sure he's completely uncomfortable too.

"Are you all right?" I ask, slightly embarrassed.

"Glorious," he replies with a hint of laughter in his voice. "You like it down and dirty, don't you?"

"There's nothing like a good old romp on the floor once in a while."

He pulls the sweaty strands of hair from my face and kisses the tip of my nose. "You sure gave us quite a workout."

"I know," I say, exhausted, lying on him. And as uncomfortable as we are, I don't ever want to move. "I love the way you make me feel," I whisper, my face still buried in him.

"Me too, Mirella. Sometimes I feel like I can't live without it. You're like a wicked itch I just can't seem to scratch enough."

I don't respond to his words—they're too powerful.

He couldn't have said it better.

That's *exactly* what this feels like.

We move over to the bed, and Weston insists on taking my top and bra off and having me completely naked in his arms. He kisses my moles and spots—every single one of them—I think he's obsessed with them. I love it, but I don't understand. One minute, he's treating me with such tenderness, and the next, he's telling me to back off. This push and pull is so confusing.

He nibbles at my hipbone and trails kisses along my side, moving slowly up to my shoulder. "I wonder how many freckles you have. This perfect little mole right here," he tells me as he kisses it, "I was obsessed with it the first time we met."

I smile at him. "Really? Why?"

"I don't know. It just kept disappearing and reappearing, hidden under the strap of your dress. There it was. Or it wasn't, depending on the way you moved, almost like it was dancing."

I laugh, thinking he's completely lost his mind.

He traces circles around the much-loved mole on my shoulder. "You know, it was me…it was me who chose you and Gabe."

My breath catches.

I look over at him. His eyes are serious. "What do you mean? I thought it was Bridget. She was all over Gabe."

He nods. "Bridget was the one who chose the first two couples. She's always initiated the whole thing in the past. But this time, it was me," he confesses. "I wanted you."

His words manage to make both my heart warm and my sex heat up—there's something so erotic about the admission.

"I know I shouldn't tell you this," he admits. "But I wanted you to know."

"When did you know you wanted me?" I ask him, curiosity filling me.

"The first time I saw your smile. Before we even sat down together."

"Wow," is all I manage to say. I can't quite believe his words.

"You tried to hide that lovely smile, covering it with your hand. I could tell you weren't quite at ease with yourself. And I thought that was such a shame."

"I've always hated my smile. I have the hugest gap I've ever seen. You could drive a Mack truck through the thing," I joke. "I don't understand why you like it so much."

"Because it's what makes you beautiful, Mirella. It's the imperfections that bring character. It's what makes you interesting to me."

"That's easy for you to say, Mr. Perfect," I argue. "You are the most gorgeous man I've ever met. Your teeth are perfect."

"Please…don't remind me. Thanks to three years of orthodontics…head gear and everything."

I laugh. "You wore head gear?"

"Yep. It was horrible. It goes without saying I didn't have many friends."

"Poor boy. I've been thinking about fixing my smile," I admit. "The dentist says all I'd need is nine months in those invisible braces, and I'd look like everyone else."

At my words, his calm expression disappears. He grabs my face. "Tell me you will do no such thing, Mirella," he pleads. "Promise me."

My breath catches. His reaction has taken me completely by surprise.

"I…I guess I won't. I promise," I stammer, a little rattled. "I think I've changed my mind."

"Good," he says, releasing my face. "I don't want you to look like everyone else."

"I didn't realize you were so attached to the gap, Weston," I joke.

"I am. I'm very attached. I like the gap. I'm hopelessly in love with the gap."

We both laugh, lightening the mood, and he nuzzles his face into the crook of my neck. The moment is just perfect.

"When…did you know…you wanted me?" he asks, his words tentative. "The day I made the proposal?"

"No," I reply, thinking back to that first meeting at the restaurant and how stunning he was, how beautiful his eyes were—I'd never wanted a man so much.

"When you pinned me down. When you told me all about myself. You barely knew me, but it seemed you knew me better than my own husband."

"Is that so?" he says, his eyes happy. "I did peg you quite well."

"You certainly did. It was so damn hot."

He laughs. "Well, that *wasn't* my intention. I wasn't trying to excite you."

"Well, you did…in a big way."

"And I still do, I hope," he says, wrapping his arm around my waist, pulling me to him. I can feel his erection against me.

I smile at him. "Wow, you're ready for round two already?"

He kisses my shoulder. "You bet."

"You think we have time?" I ask. "Our five minutes are already up."

"Plenty," he says, and his body is on mine before I can protest.

Chapter Eighteen

You're not mine. You will never be.

"Stop hogging the blanket," Gabe grumbles.

"I am *not* hogging the blanket," I snap. "You're just so big. You should get your own damn blanket."

That's usually how it is on a Saturday night—Gabe and I huddled together on the sofa in the basement rec room, watching a movie and sharing a checkered fleece throw.

We should really get another throw.

But I think we like sharing.

Every once in a while…actually often, Gabe will slide his hand along my thigh under the throw.

That's the signal.

I usually shoot him a sly smile and make him work for it a little, but I'm always on board. But tonight, I'm still mad at him. I'm not sure if he even knows I'm upset with him, but I've been rejecting his advances for the last week or two.

And that's just not like me.

He sweeps his rough hand along the inside of my thigh—it feels nice. Part of me wants to, but the other part is still livid at him. I grab his hand and pull it away, not quite looking at him.

He's not happy.

"What is it with you these days?" he snaps. "You've pushed me away half a dozen times."

I don't want to talk about it. I know I'm being irrational and shouldn't even be mad at him. But I can't help it.

I get up from the couch, bowl of popcorn half-eaten, movie half-finished.

"I'm beat. I'm going to bed."

He grabs my wrist. "No, you're not. We need to talk."

I pull away from him and head up the stairs.

He follows me to the bedroom. "Talk to me," he pleads as we reach the top floor.

"I'm just tired," I fib as I step out of my yoga pants. "The movie was crap."

"It was," he agrees, "but that's not the problem here. What's up with you?"

I slip on my silky, yellow summer nightie. "I told you," I snap. "I'm just tired."

"It's more than that." He scowls. "It's about him, isn't it?"

I face the wall door-length mirror, and unclasp my silver hoop earrings. Gabe stands behind me and wraps his arms around my waist. There's something sensual about our reflection—his large, dark presence against mine, small and light.

I *do* want him.

He drags his hand under the yellow silk of my slip. "Don't forget," he whispers against my ear, "*I'm* your husband. You're mine." He toys with the lace of my panties. "And I should get to make love to you more often than he does."

I can feel my resolve dissolving as he kisses my shoulder. I know I'm going to give in. But I want to talk to him first. I think he should know what's bothering me.

I turn to face him. "I'm mad at you," I finally confess.

He jerks away. "What the heck for?"

"The way you behaved at the planetarium," I explain. "You and Bridget were shameless."

He stares up at the ceiling. "Oh…come on."

"Weston and I were well-behaved. It's not that hard to show a little self-control."

"Well, you know me," he scoffs. "I'm not quite as reserved and tightly-wound as Mr. Stiff-Upper-Lip."

"Well, I didn't need to see you all over her," I insist. "It made me jealous. I don't like seeing you with her."

"Do you think I like seeing you with him?" he snaps. "It drove me insane...maybe that's why I was acting like that. I was trying to make you as jealous as I was."

I bite my lip. "That's quite juvenile, Gabe."

He wraps his arms around my waist again. "I know. It was childish. But it's because I love you so much. You know it's just sex with her, right?"

I smile. "Yes."

"And it's just sex with you and Weston too," he says with conviction.

And my heart sinks a little. The truth is I don't know what it is. All I know is...Gabe is the one I want to be with when I'm ninety and complaining about my aching knees over a cup of herbal tea.

Gabe is the one.

Another adventure. Another night full of surprises.

That's one of the many things I love about Weston—he always keeps me on my toes. Kathryn's e-mail was curt—she told me Weston's car would pick me up at five and asked me to bring a sweater. I wasn't told anything else. I wasn't sure what to wear, so I opted for a simple A-line, white, summer cotton dress.

My body is filled with excitement as I fidget on the sleek leather seat of Weston's town car. Edward's not driving fast enough tonight it seems—I can't wait to see Weston, hold his beautiful face in my hands, feel his body against mine.

"Do you have any idea what Weston has planned for us tonight?" I ask Edward, hoping to get some information. But I know Edward enough to know he's a vault when it comes to these things.

"I know where I'm taking you, but that's about it, Mirella."

"And where are you taking me?" I ask, my voice playful.

He laughs. "Loose lips sink ships, don't you know."

I sigh a little as I realize I'm not getting anything out of him. As I look out the window, I notice he's not taking me downtown as per usual—he's taking me north of the city.

I try to focus on the direction we're heading, but all I can think about is Weston. The last time we were together was so perfect—the sex was out of this world. And I just haven't been able to stop thinking about all the sweet things he told me that night. *I wish you were mine*, he'd said before we'd made love.

A wicked itch I just can't seem to scratch, he'd said after. *It was me who chose you…*

The truth is, I've been driving myself absolutely insane, thinking about him, but I just can't seem to stop.

We finally reach our destination, and I realize I haven't even noticed how we got there. Edward drops me off in front of a tall, ultra-modern building. I wait for him to open my door since he always insists. At first, it felt odd every time he opened the car door for me, but now we've fallen into a routine, and it finally feels normal to me. He smiles at me as I step out. I smile back, a little nervous, my eyes pleading with him to tell me what the heck is going on.

"Just go to the lobby and introduce yourself to the concierge."

"Thank you, Edward." I look up at the building—sleek and mirrored, its shape curvy and almost seductive.

As I walk in, I take in the lobby, large and airy—stunning contemporary stainless steel water fountains greet me on either side. My gaze follows the streams of water falling into koi ponds filled with large red fish. I stop—it's so surprisingly beautiful—the odd combination of ultra-modernism and nature.

A woman at the desk with a short dark bob and cat-eye glasses smiles.

"Hello," I say, my voice soft. "I'm Mirella Keates."

"Yes, I've been expecting you. Just give me one second, and I'll contact Mr. Hanson. Please take a seat."

I sit on the tufted black leather sofa. The glass coffee table is bare, but there are a few glossy magazines laid out on the side table—I don't think they've ever been touched. A glass bowl sits next to them, a goldfish swimming lazily in circles. The sight almost hypnotizes me—sometimes, this is exactly how I feel—like I'm swimming in circles.

A young woman smiles at me as she sits on one of the leather chairs across from me. She sets her shiny briefcase on the floor and leans down toward the coffee table. She touches it slightly, and a screen image appears. I'm amazed. Here I thought this was just another boring glass coffee table, but it has a secret identity. She's checking the weather and looking up an address on Google Maps. I feel a little guilty spying, but then again, if she wanted privacy, she would have used her own tablet or laptop. This is so cool!

"So, what do you think?" a familiar voice asks.

I look up at Weston, who I hadn't even noticed standing beside me. He's looking as gorgeous as ever in fitted, beige khakis and a tight, plaid button shirt, opened at the collar. And all those old familiar desires come to the surface again—so fast, it's like lightning.

"Hi," is all I manage to say as I stand up.

"So, what do you think of this place?" His face seems eager for my reaction.

"It's beautiful," I say. "I like the fish."

I'm still not sure where I am.

His wide sexy smile does me in every time. He stands with his hands on his hips, looking at his surroundings, an expression of pride on his face. "This is The Onyx. They're all very similar, but this is my favorite."

And it *finally* occurs to me—this is one of Weston's loft condos, from the advertisement posters in his office, his pride and joy. "You do incredible work."

"You want me to show you around?" he asks, eager.

"Of course," I reply and take his hand. I can't wait. I'm so excited. The warmth of his skin on mine, no matter how small his touch is, drives me crazy. He leads me to the modern-looking elevators.

The interior is all shiny stainless steel, and the buttons are aglow.

"We are riding green," he tell me as he pushes the P button.

"Are we?" I ask, not sure what he's saying.

"This elevator is sustainable. It uses thirty to forty percent less energy."

"That's great," I say. "So this is one of your LEED certified, sustainable buildings?"

"You've been paying attention," he says as he leads me out of the elevator on the top floor. I catch a glimpse of the view outside the building—it's amazing.

"Of course, this fascinates me."

You fascinate me.

"How does it work?" I ask, genuinely interested.

"With radio frequency identification technology, tenants can use a pass card to call an elevator before they even leave their suite," he explains as we walk toward his suite door. "This results in fewer stops, shorter wait times, lower energy use. It's good for the environment and everyone's happy," he adds as he swipes his card. "The use of LED lighting and sleep mode saves energy as well."

He is such a nerd. But definitively the sexiest nerd I've ever met.

We walk into a suite, and it's mindboggling—I get the sensation I've walked into the future.

"Welcome to the penthouse at The Onyx," he says, his striking green eyes more brilliant than ever.

I stand there, motionless, speechless.

"Come in," he urges. "Make yourself comfortable."

Despite the contemporary design, the space manages to look cozy, accentuated with warm tones and textures. The streamlined white sectional looks inviting with its myriad of throw cushions, some furry.

But I don't dare sit—I want to explore. This is my first time here, and I can see his essence in this space. A collection of artsy black and white photographs of buildings elegantly set in contemporary white frames hang over the sofa. And to the left side of the room, there's a large aquarium filled with colorful coral and tropical fish.

"Do you spend a lot of time here?"

"No, not really," he admits.

"Who takes care of your fish?" I ask, concerned, although they look plenty healthy and cared for.

"I have a service. I also have a cleaning service, which is why the place looks spotless."

"You have a lot of services, I bet."

"I do," he admits. "I do employ a lot of people to keep my life running smoothly."

"Honestly, your life gives me a headache just thinking about it."

He laughs and wraps his arms around my waist. His touch sizzles, and my breath catches. I sometimes wish he would suddenly lose all his power over me. I know it would certainly make my life a lot simpler.

"I've missed you," he tells me, his lips searching for mine. He kisses me softly and tears himself away, leaving me hanging. "Do you want a tour?"

"No. I want you to finish what you've started. You just can't kiss a woman like that and walk away," I almost snap.

He laughs at me again. "Good things come to those who wait. I've got something planned for us."

My ears perk up—I want to know all about it. But he doesn't tell me. He walks over to the kitchen—all smooth white and stainless steel surfaces, a cool industrial-style light fixture emitting a soft warm glow. He slides his finger over the refrigerator door, and a screen pops up, just like the one on the coffee table in the lobby.

"Wow," I say. "Is everything interactive in this building?"

"Yes, state of the art. The best in glass technology."

I can't quite see what he's looking at on the screen. He opens the door and grabs some grapes.

"Would you like a glass of water or an iced tea? Or perhaps a glass of wine?"

I'm pleased—he's been paying attention too. "Red wine is fine… thanks."

He presses a digital button on the refrigerator. Coldplay's "Till Kingdom Come" fills the room. It's one of the songs I included on the mixed CD I made him.

For some reason, I'm on edge. Maybe it's the foreign surroundings or him looking so delectable. He's perfection in every way.

He washes the grapes. "That mixed CD you gave me…quite the eclectic mix."

"I know, right? They're all songs I love." I don't tell him it's all about the lyrics—lyrics that make me think of him—that Coldplay song says it all.

He walks over to the wine fridge and pulls out a bottle of Shiraz. "Everything from the Cure to Beyoncé."

"Well, I couldn't make you a mixed CD without a little Beyoncé, could I? I love her."

He laughs. "I've noticed. I've heard your ringtone."

"Have you listened to all the songs?"

He fetches a dish from the cupboard. "Of course…I love them. Thank you."

"You're welcome," I say with a shy smile—I know it wasn't much.

He plops the grapes on an ultra-cool serving dish. "That Melissa Etheridge song…quite clever."

I smile. "I thought it was fitting. 'Your Little Secret'…that's what I am, aren't I?"

He looks down at me. "I wish you weren't. In another life, I'd introduce you to everyone I know."

My breath catches at his words—my heart caught like a fish on a hook.

Me too.

He opens the Shiraz in a matter of seconds with some cool looking, ultra-modern bottle opener.

"You like gadgets, don't you?"

He fetches two wine glasses. "I do. I love them."

"What else do you love?" I ask. I want to know everything about him. I just don't know enough.

He seems taken aback and takes a few seconds to contemplate my question as he pours me a glass. "I love my children," he confesses with a huge smile. "I love my work. I love architecture and technology." He looks around the room. "I love the sea. I love quiet…I love spending time with you," he finally adds, his words soft.

My body warms at his words.

"I love spending time with you too."

And we stand there, looking at each other—the energy between us seems to heat up.

"I want to show you the master," he says with a playful smile, "but I fear you might just pounce on me when we get there."

I laugh. "Don't flatter yourself."

"Admit it," he presses, "you can hardly wait to tear my clothes off."

He's so arrogant. But he's so right.

"Guilty," I finally admit, slightly embarrassed, "but I promise I'll be good."

"Good," he says as he takes my hand and leads me to the bedroom.

He was right—as soon as we step into his bedroom, all thoughts turn to sex—his naked body on mine, mine on his. Now. The room is so sensual—tufted velvet soft brown headboard, crisp white linens, colorful retro looking pillows, and a few of those soft, white furry cushions. The whole room has a retro seventies vibe. I spot the sleek black music player in the corner.

"Do you like The Doors?" I ask him, "The band, I mean."

"I do actually. I have the greatest hits on my iPod."

A smile curves on my lips. "Why don't you put that on and make love to me on that deliciously comfy looking bed."

"You are a temptress, Mirella," he proclaims, his eyes dark. "I told you I wanted to wait. You promised you'd be good, remember?"

"You're driving me crazy, Weston. You are the king of delayed gratification."

He laughs his delectable laugh. "I've never thought about myself that way, but that's quite accurate, actually."

"It's maddening, is what it is," I almost scream.

"Sit down on the bed," he urges. And I do, thinking this could lead somewhere.

He takes a seat on one of the retro, white leather, egg-shaped chairs.

He stares at me, his gaze intense. He seems to want to tell me something. So I don't utter a word, and I wait for him to talk.

"Have you ever experimented with tantric sex?" he asks.

I bite my lip, not quite able to catch my words.

"Or the *Kama Sutra*?"

God, he's full of surprises. "Um…no," I say. "Why do you ask?"

"Do you know anything about it?" he asks me, his gaze serious.

"Not much," I admit. The truth is…I know nothing.

"Is it something you could see yourself doing?"

"Uh…maybe," I stammer a little. Where is he going with this? "Why? Is this something you're interested in?"

"Yes, very much so," he confesses, not a hint of humor in his expression.

I suddenly find myself very aroused by the conversation and the way he's looking at me.

I'm not sure if it's the conversation, the sensual room, or how delectably sexy he looks in his snug-fitting plaid shirt, but I find myself in serious want.

"Tell me about it," I say, my words soft and raspy. "I want to know more."

From the way he's looking at me, I can tell he knows I'm turned on. And he is too. There's no denying it—it's palpable.

"Well, it's all about bringing awareness into the sexual act, a consciousness, a certain level of intimacy between lovers."

"Interesting..."

"It's about being in the moment, breathing it in, and appreciating each other. There are many sexual positions which foster intimacy."

"I see," I say, "and you've done this...with Bridget?"

His smile is barely discernable. "Well, Bridget's not really into it. We've dabbled. But I've always wanted to explore it deeper."

"I see." And I can't help but play the devil's advocate. "But you mention it's about increasing intimacy...isn't that exactly what you and I should be avoiding?" I'm quick to add, "Isn't this arrangement between us supposed to be purely physical?"

He looks slightly offended and takes a deep breath. "What I'm talking about is physical intimacy, not emotional intimacy."

"But doesn't physical intimacy translate into emotional intimacy?" I ask, confused.

"Damn it, Mirella," he snaps as he stands to his feet.

I stare down at the bed linens. "I'm sorry."

He kneels in front of me and tilts my chin to face him, straight in the eye. He's so beautiful. "Are you afraid of me?"

"Yes," I confess. But I don't tell him I'm already falling for him and that *making love* to him might just throw me over the edge. I don't tell him I don't want to jeopardize the most important thing in my life—my family. And I don't tell him I don't quite trust myself to not go down that road. "You are a man of contradictions, Weston. One minute, you tell me to back away, keep my distance, to not be jealous. And the next, you kiss me with such emotion, whisper sweet nothings, and talk about fostering deeper physical intimacy."

He stares down at the floor, speechless.

"I'm serious, Weston. You're so mercurial. Make up your mind, already."

He looks up at me again. "I know," he says. "But...we are allowed a certain level of physical intimacy."

"Be careful what you wish for, Weston. I don't mean to sound cliché, but we're walking on thin ice, you and me, don't you think?"

He looks down at the floor, not able to face me. "Perhaps," he says matter-of-factly.

There's an uncomfortable silence between us, and I'm desperate to fill it and end this conversation.

"I want to go check out the bathroom. I'm sure it's fabulous," I venture as I jump to my feet.

When he joins me in the washroom, I'm glad to see the energy between us has shifted.

The space is sterile—sleek, clean surfaces abound. I'm intrigued by the toilet, which seems to float on the wall, the toilet handle sticks out of the walnut finish. There's no tank, no bottom. I've never seen a toilet like this—I'm fascinated.

"Where's the tank?" I ask, intrigued.

"It's built into the wall," he explains, seemingly amused by my fascination.

"And what keeps it up?" I ask, not waiting for an answer. "I'd be afraid to come crashing down."

He laughs. "A little thing like you," he says. "You'd probably have to be a thousand pounds to bring that toilet down."

"It's kind of freaky."

"You haven't been out much, have you?" he teases.

"You've noticed?"

"A little."

I laugh inwardly at the sound of our discussion. This is just what we needed—a conversation about a toilet—non-sexual, not intimate at all. Things were getting *way* too intense back in the bedroom.

I take in the rest of the bathroom—it is purely innovative. Two square, stainless-steel sinks sit side by side under a seamless mirror, which almost melts into the wall. The glass enclosed shower is accentuated with a dramatic mosaic backsplash — the tiny tiles making up an image of an oriental tree.

"I love the shower. What a nice touch."

"I can't take the credit, I'm afraid," he confesses. "That goes to our designers."

There are about a zillion shower heads, including a large overhead one, and a digital touch pad on the outside wall with LED display.

"That is one fancy shower. It looks complicated."

He laughs. "It is."

The large sleek soaker tub looks very inviting. "You and me, later," I say with a sly grin, "in that thing."

"Maybe," he says with a devilish smile. "But I think you might enjoy the shower more."

"Oh...would I?" I say. "I'm more of a bubble bath kind of girl."

"Trust me...you would like this shower."

I'm not sure exactly what he's saying, but he's turning me on, nevertheless.

I grab his shirt and pull him to me. "Well, let's try it right now," I venture with my sexiest voice.

He kisses me...another sensual, soft kiss. But then he pulls away again.

The man is driving me absolutely bonkers.

The intercom buzzes just as I'm about to beg.

A lady's voice tells him the catering crew has arrived.

"Please send them up," he says.

And I know I won't see any action anytime soon.

The crew arrives and the atmosphere becomes chaotic and loud. After we offer our initial hellos, they set up in the kitchen — boxes, crates, stainless-steel food heating contraptions, and dishware. A plump, middle-aged lady with sharp bangs seems to be in charge, barking out orders.

"Do you need anything from us, Rhonda?" Weston asks.

"Nope. I think we're all set," she tells him, smiling at both of us. "You two pretend we're not here."

The two assistants, a young man and woman, travel up and down the glass-encased staircase. I haven't even been to the second level yet, and I wonder what's up there. They seem to know what they're doing and where they're going—I gather they've been here before.

"You entertain a lot?" I ask, wondering if he's brought other women here before.

"Yes. We've had a few parties here. Mostly when the units first opened...showings, for promotional and marketing purposes."

"Let me guess," I say. "This is all being covered by the company? Isn't that an inappropriate use of company funds?"

"Who are you?" he jokes. "My accountant?"

"What's upstairs?" I ask, curious.

"Do you want to see?" he asks, taking my hand. I love it when he takes my hand. Unlike Gabe, Weston is not the most touchy-feely person, but when he *does* touch me, he usually lights me up.

He leads me up the stairs, and I follow eagerly. When we reach the landing, I am awestruck. The contemporary theme continues up here, warm shades and soft lighting. A window looks out to a wonderful view, and that's when I'm reminded we're in the penthouse.

"It pays to be the boss," I say casually. "This place is fantastic."

He smiles as he brings me into his den, furnished with a sleek walnut desk and white leather desk chair. Multiple large, flat screens cover the desk and a large TV stretches along the wall. Everything is meticulously ordered, groups of objects forming perfect lines and angles, books and display pieces arranged flawlessly.

I slide my finger along the edge of his desk, not daring to touch anything. "You must be the most orderly person I've ever met."

"Yes," he admits with a sigh. "I'm not sure if it's a virtue or an affliction, to tell you the truth. I feel much calmer when everything's in order."

I contemplate his words, wondering what kind of effect this arrangement of ours has on him—it is anything but simple.

"And...you and I," I say, my words soft, "that's not quite orderly."

"It's a great source of stress, to be honest," he confesses, taking a seat at his desk. "But also a great source of pleasure," he adds with a sly smile.

"I mess up your life a little, don't I?"

He laughs. "You have no idea."

I love his laugh. When he smiles, he seems more relaxed, more human, more approachable, and I have the urge to hug him and hold on forever.

"Do you want to see the rest?" he asks, getting up from the desk.

He leads me to the kids' bedrooms, which are immaculate, a far cry from my girls' rooms.

"My children have barely set foot here," he admits. Although I realize this isn't his main home, where he spends the majority of his time with his family, I still feel privileged to be able to see a small slice of his life.

Then, he leads me to the terrace—it's wonderful—a little piece of heaven nestled amongst the myriad of buildings surrounding it. We're surrounded by greenery, topiary type trees, large stainless-steel heat lamps, and sleek, contemporary outside patio furniture in shades of black and beige. There's even a matching lounging canopy bed, fully dressed in plush-looking, white linens.

The crew is busy at work—the young woman is setting the white linen covered table. The night is warm and there is a small pleasant breeze. I'm thrilled by all this—what a wonderful idea… dining under the stars.

"This is amazing."

"I was hoping you'd like it."

"Of course I love it," I almost gush. "I'm sure all the ladies love it."

He raises an eyebrow. "You might not believe this, Mirella, but this is a first."

"Oh…is it?" I ask, not quite convinced. "You've never had a romantic dinner like this out here with anyone?" I ask. "Not even with Bridget?"

"No."

Wow.

The food is wonderful.

We start off with a deliciously tangy, homemade vegetable soup. The crew, dressed in white, is very efficient and professional, and very discreet.

Despite the heating tower close to us, the air is slightly cool, and I'm glad I'm wearing a sweater. Weston seems at ease in his thin dress shirt. But then, I'm convinced his blood runs hotter than mine—every time we come together, his skin is sizzling. I long to reach out to him as I look at him sitting across from me. He's so near, yet he seems so far, untouchable—I can't very well jump him with all these people walking about.

"When does the crew leave?"

"A little impatient, are we?" he whispers with a wicked smile. "Patience is not a quality you have."

"That's funny. Some people think I'm the most patient person in the world."

"Well, not when it comes to sex apparently."

"You just enjoy teasing me, don't you? You've barely touched me at all, all night. Maybe you just don't want me as much as I want you."

"Trust me, Mirella," his says, his lids heavy. "I want you."

And his words almost make me melt.

The young woman appears and serves our main dishes. "Chicken with lemon sauce and capers with angel hair pasta and vegetables," she tells us in a delicate soft voice. Although it all looks very delicious, I'm not very hungry…for food anyway.

"Thank you, Jessica," Weston says and she smiles at him. She seems a little flustered, and I'm not sure if it's because he's her boss, or if it's because he's impossibly gorgeous. I would be willing to bet my next paycheck on the latter.

"What does it feel like to have women everywhere falling under the spell of your charm?"

He laughs. "I've never thought of myself as charming," he tells me, cutting into his chicken. His smile lingers—he seems to find my comment very amusing. "In fact, I've always been rather standoffish. Once initial pleasantries are done, I don't offer much of myself."

"Well, it's a good thing," I tell him, enjoying a sip of wine, "because you would have a million women falling in love with you."

He looks up from his plate and contemplates me in silence for the longest time. And I fear I've stuck my foot in my mouth. I really shouldn't have said that—it implies that I, myself, have fallen in love with him.

"Well, they might be a little smitten with me…but I would never return the sentiment," he deadpans. Just in case I didn't get that he's emotionally unavailable, he needs to drill it into me again.

I get it. You're not mine. You will never be.

And I don't want him to be. I'm a happily married woman. But sometimes, this pesky jealousy threatens to completely unhinge me.

I'm failing miserably at this casual sex thing.

An uncomfortable silence sets in as we eat our meals. The food goes down, but I don't quite taste it. Why couldn't I have kept the conversation light and fun? It *was* light and fun. But somehow, it took a sharp turn.

I really need to constantly remind myself of the fact that this arrangement is just about fun, excitement, and sex.

It's not about love.

"What's with the bed?" I ask with a sly smile. That canopy bed has been in my field of vision all through dinner, filling my subconscious with thoughts of sex and Weston…naked.

A slow smile stretches across his face. "That's where I plan to play with you a little, after dessert."

Oh my…please let's skip dessert.

"Who needs dessert really?" I joke. "Just empty calories."

He laughs. "You really need to work on your lack of patience, Mirella. And besides, those extra calories ensure those curves I love so much."

"You're going to force me to have dessert, aren't you?"

He nods at me, a grin stretched across his face. Jessica clears our plates and asks us if we're ready for dessert.

"Oh…you have no idea," I say. "Make it quick please. I just can't wait."

Weston and I laugh, and Jessica looks at us with a strange expression, obviously not privy to our inside joke.

"I'm serious, Jessica. Bring it as fast as you can, please," I call out as she makes her way back to the penthouse.

Weston laughs, clearly amused.

"I love the way you make me laugh." The motion of his long finger sliding up and down the stem of his wine glass arouses me. Everything about him arouses me.

"I'm glad I can amuse you," I say, my voice cool, trying to manage my out-of-control libido.

"You don't even try," he adds. "It's just the way you are. Your mannerisms and quirks are quite charming."

"I'm afraid most people wouldn't agree," I argue. "I think most people think I'm just a big spaz."

He laughs. "I suppose it's just me then."

Jessica returns with martini-type glasses filled with chocolate mousse, covered with whipped cream and a myriad of berries—blueberries, raspberries, and blackberries.

"I moved as fast as I could," she explains.

"Thank you. You have no idea how much I appreciate it," I say, looking over at Weston who wears his devilish smile.

The sight of the dessert makes my mouth water—I truly don't know what tempts me more—the dessert or Weston.

But lucky me, I get to enjoy both.

Chapter Nineteen

. . .tell me you don't love him.

Weston slides my sweater down over my shoulder as he kisses me softly. I can feel the chill of the night and can't wait to wrap myself in the heat of his body. His kiss is a little different tonight—tender, not hurried. Although I love his hungry, needy kiss, I enjoy this one just as much—somehow it feels more intimate...real. I slide my hands under his plaid shirt, feeling the heat of his skin on my fingers.

His breath hitches. "Your hands are freezing," he mumbles into my mouth.

"Your body is so warm," I say, a smile on my lips. I can't wait to get him naked. I want him just as much as I did the first time we had sex. My body hasn't tired of his—the desire has yet to dim.

I pull him to the canopy bed. The sheets are crisp and cold. The sensations of the cool sheets under me and his hot body over me are at odds, but the contrast is delicious. I enjoy the weight of him on me as he slides his hand under the skirt of my dress, his fingers toying with the lace of my panties. He pulls them down slowly as he trails kisses down my neck and at the top of my breasts.

"You are so...soft," he whispers as he undoes the side zipper on my dress. He always seems to know exactly how to undress me. I see him observing me throughout the night, taking in every detail with his keen eye, probably visualizing how he's going to get me naked at the end of the night. He pulls my dress off hungrily. He wants me—he's losing his resolve. I'm almost naked, down to my pink cotton lace bra—and I'm freezing.

I rip his shirt open, the snap buttons giving in easily. I pull it off in a rush, aching to feel his warm chest on me. When he finally presses against me, it feels so wonderful—nothing could beat the sensation, short of having him completely buried inside me.

He pulls down the thick duvet and we climb in, taking refuge from the cold under the blankets. I unbuckle him and pull off his pants along with his boxers in one languid motion, slithering like a snake along the bed, under the haven of the fluffy duvet, in our own wonderful cocoon. I trail kisses back up along his leg and hip bone, teasing him.

He laughs.

"I can tease too," I say with a cocky smile.

"Oh, I know."

I find myself on top of him, my sex brushing against his erection. My body is so ready for his.

My breath is slightly unhinged when I whisper in his ear, "I want to…try one of those *Kuma Sutra* positions." I have been thinking about it all night—the thought of it arouses me.

He laughs a little. "Kama *Sutra*," he corrects me. "You do?"

"Yes," I whisper.

"What position would you like to try?" he asks, his voice eager.

"I'm not sure," I say and finally confess the truth. "I don't know anything about the *Kama Sutra*."

"You want to try the 'Lotus'?" he asks, his fingers trailing the edge of my jaw. "It's my favorite."

"That sounds exotic."

"It's very intimate," he explains as he sits up. The duvet slides off and the cool chill of the night hits us. "Here, wrap your legs around me." He sets my legs tightly around his hips and crosses his own. He reaches behind his back and hooks my feet behind him. We are sitting, tangled, eye to eye. And despite the cool air, I no longer feel cold, in the comfort of his arms wrapped around me.

Looking into his beautiful eyes, I ease onto him, despite the fact that I know he hasn't put on a condom. I don't mention it and neither does he. I don't want anything separating us. I want to feel him completely.

He trails his finger along my spine, reaching the clasp of my bra and undoing it. My bra falls between us, and he leans his head into me, taking my breast in his mouth. I bury my face into the thick softness of his hair, delighting in the wonderful unique scent that is him.

We move in a slow sensual rhythm, kissing and occasionally pulling away to look at each other. His eyes seem to almost look through me, into my soul. I'm terrified.

That first moment, that spark…everything we've shared—every look, every word, every touch, culminates now.

I've always thought Gabe and I were soul mates, but now I don't know anymore. Can someone have two soul mates? I've never been so confused.

"I feel whole with you," he breathes into my ear.

My heart pounds.

I've fallen and have become completely unhinged—completely undone. I want him to know.

I know I shouldn't, but before I can stop myself, the words are out of my mouth. "I love you," I whisper, my words barely audible. Three little words. Three very powerful words.

He kisses me. His kiss is wild and frenzied, full of emotion and torment. He pushes into me harder, and I match his intensity, sinking deep into him.

We make love without a word.

I can hear his labored breathing, the climb to his climax. I've become familiar with his sounds and breathing patterns, and I hold him tight when he finally comes.

I don't climax, but I don't need to—the love making, in and of itself, is unlike anything I've ever experienced.

We hold each other, and we don't make a sound. He doesn't mention the words I've said to him.

And he doesn't repeat them.

My heart sinks.

I know I shouldn't have said them. And I regret my impulsive behavior, but part of me is glad he knows. Tears falls down my cheek as I realize he doesn't feel the same way. He's still holding me, and he can't see my tears as I wipe them away and will myself to stop crying—I can't let him see me like this.

I hate myself for loving him.

We retreat to the warm comfort of each other under the covers. Neither of us utters a word. I lay in his arms, looking out at the skyline—glittering dots of light against the darkness. We don't stay in bed too long before he tells me he's going to take a shower and asks me if I'd like to join him.

At first, I decline, telling him I want to lie in bed a little longer.

"Are you sure?" he asks me. "Like I said, it's an extraordinary shower…top of the line."

Suddenly, as the chill of the night hits my shoulders, the idea of hot water streaming down on me sounds quite tempting.

"You've convinced me," I announce, hopping from the bed. I wrap my arms around my breasts as I follow him to the penthouse—I'm pretty sure no one is looking, but I'm not taking any chances.

Weston fiddles with the digital buttons on the panel outside the shower.

"At my house, all I need to do is turn on the faucet and pull out the shower thingie," I joke. "Why do you make your life so complicated?"

He laughs. My gaze travels from his smile to his glorious naked body, and despite the fact that we *just* made love, I want him again.

"It should be about right," he says and urges me to walk into the spacious shower stall. The water feels wonderful and the pressure is just right, delightful in fact. It sure beats that poor-excuse-for-a-shower I have at home. I'm amazed by all the jets, including the large round stream over top. I mentally scold myself for falling victim to the pleasures of luxury. The incredible mosaic artwork draws my attention again, and as I stand admiring it, I feel Weston's hands wrap around my belly. His touch sends a current through me, and I desperately want him to take me, right here in the shower. I arch my back and rest my head against his chest, enjoying the sensation of the water falling on me.

His hands travel over my hips, my stomach, and my breasts. My nipples are erect against the palm of his hands. I wonder what he has in mind for this shower. Is he planning to make love to me again?

"You didn't climax earlier, did you?" he asks me, trailing his hand to the wet curls between my legs.

His touch feels so good.

"No," I confess, my voice raspy. "But I didn't need to. It was still amazing."

"But…that's simply not acceptable," he whispers in my ear, gently rubbing me. "We'll have to rectify that."

Please…yes, rectify that.

I am fully aroused and ready for whatever he has in mind. But then, he pulls away slowly and leaves me hanging.

"Weston…please," I plead. I can't believe I'm about to beg again—I'm shameless.

He pulls out the removable shower head and has me lean my back against him. He slides his wet hand under my thigh and props my leg on the shower bench.

"Now this shower head is top of the line…four zone-eight setting massaging feature." He teases my thighs and stomach with the jet stream. It feels fantastic, and I ache for him to bring it between my legs—my sex is almost begging for it.

But he doesn't…he teases me.

The stream hits about every part of my body but the one I desperately want it to hit.

"Weston," I cry out.

"I don't think we're fooling anyone though," he says. "We all know what this is really for." He aims the stream directly at my sweet spot, and I arch against him.

The sensation is fantastic.

"Please, don't *ever* stop," I breathe.

"You like this pressure?"

I nod, not quite able to speak.

"How about this?" he asks, and the pressure increases—the soft stream becomes a pulsating jet, and it feels mind-blowing.

"Oh…sweet heavens."

"You like that?" he teases. "I thought you might," he says, pulling the stream away.

Oh no…you don't.

"Don't you dare," I scold, grabbing his wrist.

He stops fooling around.

The pulsating pressure brings me to the edge at record speed. As I near it, I moan loudly, knowing it will be an incredible release.

"I want you to let go," Weston breathes into my ear. "I want to hear you."

What Weston wants, Weston gets.

I cry out loudly, like I never have—the sound of the shower muffles my moans.

Spent, I lean against Weston who wraps his arms around me.

"You enjoyed that immensely," he says softly.

"I did."

And as he holds me, I tell myself I don't care if he doesn't love me, as long as he keeps making me feel this way.

That's what I tell myself.

The radio is on, the reception scratchy as I mill about in the kitchen working on dinner—nothing special—chicken stir-fry. Gabe is reading the paper in the living room and I'm not sure where the girls are, but as long as I don't hear them fighting, I'm happy.

It's an ordinary day at the Keates household, but that's about to change.

I'm standing over the stove, stirring the vegetables and chicken, and I don't see Claire sneaking up behind me.

"Mommy, who's this man?" she asks, her high-pitched six-year old voice carries across the kitchen.

My heart stammers.

I turn around to see her holding a photo of Weston and I—one of the selfies we took at Lincoln Park—the one I printed and kept in my jewelry box, in the bottom slit, along with Weston's e-mail. I *thought* I had hidden them so well.

"Claire, what were you doing in my jewelry box?" I hiss. "I've told you before not to touch my things."

The pout makes its appearance, along with the teary eyes—she's about to cry—I feel horrible. Claire has never taken reprimand very well. I rarely yell or scold her.

"I'm sorry, Claire," I say, my voice soft.

Gabe dashes into the kitchen. "What is she talking about?"

I take a step back, my back pressed against the stove.

He tears the photo from Claire's pudgy hand. "Can I see that?" His face falls when he sees it—a close-up of Weston and I, huddled together, smiling brightly at the camera, our features soft, Weston's eyes a brilliant green.

"What?" is all he says—he's shattered. "When did you take this?"

"On one of our dates." I try to sound casual—like the photo doesn't mean anything at all.

But I think he knows better.

"We went to Lincoln Park, and I brought my camera to shoot photos of the park and we just—"

"Why did you print it?"

"Uh…" I'm without words.

He glares at me. "Why do you keep it in your jewelry box?"

I knew I shouldn't have printed it. I knew I should have just left the photos on my laptop, hidden carefully in a buried folder.

"You two look…" he trails off. "You look like you're in love."

I don't know what to say.

He darts off upstairs.

"Gabe," I yell after him, trailing him up the stairs. I know where he's going.

He turns the corner into our bedroom, into our walk-in closet where I keep my jewelry box.

It sits open on the floor, its contents poured out. Just as I feared, Gabe spots the folded up sheet of paper and grabs it before I can stop him.

"Gabe," I plead as he unfolds it. "It's not what you think."

But it is—it's exactly what he thinks.

He reads the e-mail from Weston—the one where he asks for a photo of me, and tells me I'm beautiful.

He rakes his hand through his hair, his mouth a hard line. I realize why Weston has these rules in place—no communication, no gifts, and no intimacy.

It all makes sense.

I see pain on his face like I have never seen before. Gabe is always so strong and stoic—he doesn't wear his emotions on his sleeve—but this…this has cut him.

"You two are in love," he scoffs. "You've gone and fallen for this asshole." His voice is loud and carries through the house.

"No, I haven't," I lie, my eyes tearing up. I can't tell him how devastatingly messed up I really am. "I haven't."

He grabs my wrist. "You're lying," he hisses.

I see contempt in his eyes. His grasp on my wrist tightens. He's hurting me. "Look me in the eye and tell me you *don't* love him."

I know I need to lie. I know telling him the truth could be the end of us—the end of our life as we know it.

"Tell me," he screams louder, his grasp not yielding.

"Mommy," Claire whispers, standing near the closet door. She looks afraid and so does Chloe, who stands just behind her.

Gabe finally lets go of me.

I pull my arm to my chest and slump back. "It's okay girls. Mommy and Daddy were just having a fight…like you girls do all the time."

Claire rushes up and wraps her arms around me, and Gabe hugs Chloe close against him.

We know we can't fight in front of them.

Gabe pulls away from me, and he doesn't ask again.

I think he doesn't want to know.

That night, I convince myself I don't love Weston. Sure, I'm obsessed and infatuated with him. I think he's the most stunning man I've ever laid eyes on.

But I don't love him.

And with those thoughts in my head, I tell Gabe I don't love Weston. I tell him he's the only one for me. My words are so convincing—even I believe them. Gabe believes them too—I can see it in his eyes—he seems so relieved. He says he couldn't bear the thought of me in love with someone else, and he holds me in his arms.

We lie together until we fall asleep.

A little white lie…for my family.

Weston and I sit at a quaint little Italian restaurant—the same spot where our first date took place. My mind is brought back to that steamy quickie we *almost* had in the washroom. I was so nervous that night.

That night seems so long ago now.

Although the atmosphere is warm and relaxing—red and white checkered table cloths, rustic brick covered walls, and friendly staff—the vibe between Weston and I is anything but. There's tension between us. It's not anything he's said or done, but I can tell something's bothering him, and I have a pretty good idea what it might be.

For the past two weeks, I've been scolding myself for uttering those three little words—how I wish I could go back in time and not tell him I love him. Not only have I broken the rules, I've embarrassed myself. But far worse than all that...I've betrayed Gabe and the girls.

I'm pretty sure I'm going to hell.

I sink my fork into my pasta, not really wanting to eat it, but shoving it down my throat anyway. Weston eats his homemade lasagna, head down, not uttering a word, avoiding my gaze. He shoots me a closed-lipped smile once in a while, making a conscious effort to be nice.

What have I done? He shouldn't need to make a conscious effort to be nice to me—he should *want* to be with me.

I consider apologizing for breaking the rules. I can tell him I was lost in the throes of passion and merely got a little carried away. But mentioning it at all would bring attention to it. I just want to forget the whole thing and pretend it never happened. It seems to be what Weston is doing.

It might just take a little time for us to get back to normal after this little set-back. And then, everything will be perfect again, just as it was.

Despite the tension between us, I can still sense electricity in the air. Although he doesn't quite look at me, his gaze falls all over me, scattered—on my lips, the cleavage of my tight little black cocktail dress, all the way down to my legs. And despite the fact that I kind of want to crawl under a rock and die, I still crave him, crave his touch—he looks yummy in a soft cashmere gray sweater and fitted black pants. He's wearing his dark framed glasses tonight—very sexy.

God…I hope he's not upset enough to not want to have sex—I don't think I could bear it.

We have tiramisu for dessert and make small chit-chat about the past two weeks. I talk about Chloe's mishap—we were having dinner at Gabe's parents, and she was carrying a large bowl of macaroni pasta salad. She managed to trip on her own two feet and the bowl went flying—pasta splattered everywhere, all over everyone.

"There was even a macaroni stuck on Gabe's dad's glasses," I finish, laughing at my own anecdote.

He gives me a tight-lipped smile.

"Well, I guess you had to be there," I say.

As much as I try to lighten the mood, it seems I just can't.

I take off my jacket as we enter his hotel suite—I'm a little warm. I'm also a little disappointed—unlike our usual custom, there was no tender hand-holding, no passionate kisses in the elevator. There's still a great divide between us. I realize it will probably need to be addressed if we're going to be intimate again.

Weston pulls his satchel over his head, drops it on the desk in the entry hall, and sits down on the chair, his elbow propped on the sleek surface. I find myself staring at my surroundings, taking in the clean lines and muted colors and the sleek contemporary furniture.

I can't quite seem to look at him.

This isn't how it typically goes—we usually practically attack each other as soon as the suite door closes, ravishing each other, pulling passionately at each other's clothes, delighting in each other's taste, smell…touch.

He slumps in his chair. "Mirella," he sighs. "We need to talk."

I look down at him. His eyes are full of torment—he looks burdened.

And I know.

I know he's planning to break up with me.

But he can't. He just can't.

What we have is too precious.

I walk seductively to him and shoot him a sly smile. I hike up my little black dress, lift a leg over him and straddle him on the chair. "I don't want to talk," I whisper.

"Mirella," he sighs, "please don't." His heavy lids and shallow breathing betray his words—I know he wants me just as much as I want him.

"Have we ever done it on a chair?" I ask, my voice smooth as velvet.

He shakes his head, and I can see his resolve melting—the desire pooling in his eyes.

I kiss him softly along his jaw. "I think you're right. I don't think we have."

He pushes me away gently. "Mirella, *please* stop," he pleads, his voice deeper, more forceful.

I pull at his shirt, my fingers skimming his hot skin. "You want this," I breathe into his ear.

"Mirella, please," he says quietly.

I run my hands to the band of his pants and start undoing his belt.

He grabs my wrist. "Mirella," he snaps.

He doesn't want me. He wants to be rid of me.

I can feel the tears coming, and I'm powerless to stop them.

The expression of anger on his face seems to melt into one of concern. "Mirella," he sighs. "Please, don't cry." He cups my face in his hands. The gesture is so gentle—I know he still cares.

"I just want to talk for a second. I'm sorry I was a little harsh, but I had to get your attention."

I nod, the giant lump in my throat preventing me from speaking. It's inevitable—this needs to happen, regardless of whether I want it to or not.

"I wanted to talk about what happened the last time we were together," he says, his words measured, "when we were having sex."

When we were making love.

I nod again, fearing my words might come out all strangled.

His gaze is soft—his eyes are as arresting as ever, which makes this all the more heartbreaking. "Remember what you said to me?" he asks, his gaze fixed on mine.

Of course I remember.

"I told you I loved you," I say without emotion.

"You did," he goes on. "And you know why that's a problem? You are aware of how this arrangement works, aren't you?"

"Yes, I am," I answer him matter-of-factly. "No emotional commitment. No declarations of love." I roll my eyes like a teenager. "I just had a temporary moment of insanity…so sue me." I realize I'm acting quite immature. I'm doing it purposely to push his buttons.

"Mirella," he says. "Don't make light of this."

I look away.

"Look at me," he snaps.

I don't look at him, determined to piss him off. He's being a real jerk.

He grabs my chin roughly and tilts my head to face him. "Look at me." I'm taken by surprise by his aggression. This isn't like him—Weston is usually so gentle.

"Regardless of how you might feel about me," he tells me, his gaze piercing into mine. "I don't want to hear it."

My heart sinks—he's so cold.

"Well, I want to tell you anyway," I hiss. "You're an asshole. That's how I feel about you, you prick."

His eyes darken, with what…I'm not sure. Anger? Passion? Desire?

"You think you can just bring me to a posh restaurant, drag me to your hotel room, screw me any way you want, and send me on my way in your fancy car, without the slightest of complications," I scoff. "Well, you're fucking wrong about that. Life is not that simple."

"Mirella," he scolds. "Stop it. You know I can't stand that kind of language."

"Oh yes…" I scoff with an exaggerated smirk. "I forgot. Mister Perfect doesn't like cursing. God forbid—"

He grabs my face and his gorgeous mouth takes mine, scorching my lips. His kiss is greedy. His hands trail from my cheeks to my neck. Our tongues dance wildly, sloppily. He teases and bites my bottom lip. The desire pools inside me. I want him so badly—even if I truly hate him at the moment. His hands travel to my back, he undoes the delicate buttons one by one, and I almost wish I'd worn a different dress, with a zipper—something easier to take off.

I pull his shirt over his head and trail my tongue all over his chest. He's turned on—his breathing labored and his erection pressing against me. I grind myself against him as I kiss him. It feels so good as I move back and forth, I could just climax like this. I almost want to, then just get up and leave him hanging.

But I also want to kiss every inch of him.

I could just fall into this and enjoy him without a struggle. But I'm just too mad at him.

I'm not done with this fight.

Chapter Twenty

Just maybe. . .he loves me too.

I jerk away from him, "You like that, sir? You're getting your money's worth?" I ask him, my eyes threatening to go farther.

"Stop it," he whispers.

"Well, that's what I am. Your whore. I want you to admit it."

"You're not my whore, Mirella."

I try to pull away, but he grabs my ass and stills me. "Besides, I haven't heard you complain."

I can tell he just wants to fuck.

"But that's what it feels like, Weston. Like I'm your little high-class escort. You don't love me."

"You're not my whore," he snaps.

"I am," I go on, determined to anger him. "You screw me, and then you practically throw me away."

"I'm always good to you," he argues. "You know I don't treat you like a prostitute. You can't say that."

"You pretend to be good, but you're not," I scoff. "You're a user."

He closes his eyes and sucks in a deep breath. I'm afraid I've gone too far.

"You want me to treat you like a whore…" he scoffs, his mouth a hard line. His eyes are dark—they almost seem foreign.

He stands up and pushes me off him in one swift move. I tumble to the ground. He looks down at me. "I can treat you like a whore."

My heart pounds.

He rubs the back of his neck as he makes his way to the bedroom. "Take off your dress."

I'm stuck, still frozen from the shock of being tossed to the floor.

I stand and do as I'm told. The little black dress pools to the floor. I step out of it and follow him to the bedroom. When I make my way there, he walks toward me, his gaze piercing. "Take it all off."

He stands over me as I undress, watching me. He's treating me like a whore and for some reason, it's arousing me—this is a different version of Weston. He watches me, his gaze intense as I take off my bra and peel off my panties.

His eyes are glued to me as I stand next to him naked, feeling vulnerable. He doesn't say a word for the longest time. He seems to be contemplating his next move. His expression hasn't changed—it's still a strange mix of anger and desire.

He undoes his belt, walks toward the bed and reaches into the nightstand, where he keeps condoms. "Get on the bed."

I can't believe myself when I do as he says. The rational me would grab my clothing, tell him to go to hell, and run to the bathroom. But this version of me is someone different—someone desperate, desperate to not love him. Maybe if I let him degrade me, he'll become a different person in my eyes, and he'll lose hold of my heart.

"On your knees," he whispers—there's a softness in his gaze—a flicker of the Weston I know.

I do as I'm told and kneel on all fours.

He grabs me tightly by the hips, and his fingers dig into my flesh. He's rough, and I'm not quite ready for him. But I don't make a sound. He pushes into me hard, and there's discomfort, but it dulls with every thrust.

I want this.

I've asked for this. I don't want him to be gentle, whisper sweet nothings in my ear, and make me fall in love with him. I want him to treat me like shit—like a whore.

Then…maybe I can get over him.

But…

Weston is Weston.

His pace slows, and he trails his finger softly along my spine. "I'm sorry, Mirella," he says softly. "I shouldn't treat you this way." He leans down against me and kisses my back, just between my shoulder blades. "I can't do it."

Heavy tears trail down my cheeks as a realization dawns on me.

I'm in love with this man—there's no escaping it. Nothing we can do will change that. I will probably always love him.

He pulls away.

"No," I say. "I want you this way…here."

He leans back over me and wraps his arms softly around my stomach. His touch warms me and makes me feel safe. He pulls my hips hard against him as he presses into me, and he starts off slowly.

He feels wonderful.

I close my eyes and enjoy him. He drops kisses on my back every once in a while, sending shivers through me.

"Harder," I breathe. I want to climax.

His pace intensifies, and he stretches deeper into me, reaching my G spot—I let out a whimper—the feeling is mind-blowing. He grabs my hips tightly and groans into my ear. I moan louder and louder, guiding him. He pushes into me, faster and harder.

And before long, he makes me come.

I rest my head against Weston's chest, tracing circles around his navel with the tip of my finger. I love the dark line trailing from his navel to his pubic bone—he's ticklish right there, and I can always get him going.

He laughs, pulling my hand away. "Stop it."

I smile up at him. "You like it."

"I do," he admits.

We lie in silence for a while, staring up at the ceiling, both of us lost in thought. I think about the way I've behaved—it was atrocious. "I'm sorry about my behavior. I was acting juvenile. It's just… this is so hard."

He kisses the top of my head. "I know."

I hold him tighter, realizing this arrangement is probably not exactly easy for him either.

"Did I hurt you?" he asks.

I look up at him, not sure what he means.

His eyes are dark, and I realize he's talking about the sex.

"Oh...just a little."

"I'm so sorry, Mirella." There's a foreign emotion in his gaze, something I've never seen in his eyes...shame perhaps.

"It's fine," I insist. "I could have stopped you, Weston."

"But...I still shouldn't have," he argues, his words soft. "I—"

"I'm fine, Weston. I promise."

He sighs. "It's just that," he says, his words slow, "you drive me mad."

I look up at him, shocked by his words.

"I'm usually always in control," he tells me, playing with a strand of my hair. "I crave control. I'm in charge at work, at home, wherever I go, it seems. I have hundreds of employees who do exactly what I tell them to do. I know what to expect from them. I even have a handle on Bridget, believe it or not."

"Now, that's hard to believe," I joke, trying to lighten the mood.

"But...you...you make me feel completely out of control."

Completely out of control.

That's what love feels like, I want to tell him.

But I don't dare say a thing.

I've been feeling a little uneasy since my last date with Weston. Memories of that night—the passion, the raw emotion, the confusion and pain on his face, swirl in my head on a maddening, endless loop.

To make matters worse, since school is still out, I find myself without distractions. I take the girls to the park, Gwen's pool, the library, but still, I am constantly bombarded by thoughts of him. Our last date has affected me more than all the previous ones combined.

I think Gabe has noticed something is wrong, but he hasn't said a word. I'm pretty sure he knows my mood has something to do with

Weston. But since our last fight, we haven't really talked, we haven't had sex…we've grown apart. I can't very well tell him my heart is in shatters. I can't tell him he was right—I *am* in love with another man, a man who doesn't share my feelings.

And I do still love Gabe.

I'm in love with two men.

I am *royally messed-up.*

It's Wednesday morning, and as I'm dashing out of the house for the girls' swimming lesson, my cell rings, and I absently pick it up, buckling Claire in her car seat.

It's Weston. He wants to see me.

"Can we see each other next Friday?"

I ask him why he's calling me. I tell him he's breaking the rules. He doesn't quite seem like himself. I ask him if something's wrong.

He says he needs to see me.

I'm so curious, I can barely contain myself. I'm as giddy as a schoolgirl. I can barely eat—and *forget* about sleep. I don't understand why he still has this effect on me, after all these months. I should be over this by now, but just the thought of him…

I wish I had more control over my emotions. I wish I could tell my heart what to feel, order my mind to stop thinking about him endlessly.

He's still all I can think about.

I decide to go a little sexy tonight—sexy but classy. I slip on a sweet, cream lace dress with a soft flowing skirt. The hem is probably too short for a woman my age, but I'm feeling daring tonight.

Claire strokes the velvety texture of my shoes with the tip of her chubby little finger and says I look pretty. She always loves to watch me get ready. I feel a little twinge of guilt knowing she has no clue I'm about to go out to meet another man. In her perfect little world, there's just Mommy, Daddy, and Chloe.

I've paired the rather innocent dress with a flashy pair of leopard print, peep-toed heels. My hair falls over my shoulders in wavy tendrils, and my eyes are smoky.

Gabe and I are two passing ships in the night. He's going out tonight too—with Bridget. I watch him fiddle with his phone, standing by the kitchen counter. He looks good in a fitted black top and stylish gray pants. I've noticed he's been dressing a lot better these days.

He turns around and notices me—*definitely* notices me.

"You look amazing," he says with that devilish grin of his. "You look *hot*."

"Not so bad yourself," I reply with a sly smile.

He drops the phone on the counter, makes his way to me, and wraps his arms around my waist.

He slides a hand under the hem of my dress. "Quickie?"

I laugh. I'm almost tempted. We haven't had sex in forever, and I miss him. "No time...Edward will be here any second."

"He can wait," he whispers in my ear.

The man is insatiable.

"You look very nice," I say, trying to distract him. "Very sexy. Did you go shopping?"

He pulls away and nods, not quite looking at me. I get the sense he doesn't really want to talk about it. I have a feeling Bridget might have taken him shopping—probably had a little fun with her "boy-toy"—another little Ken doll she can dress up. The thought annoys me a little, and I push it away instantly.

The doorbell chimes.

"Your car is waiting, madam." Gabe smirks and gives me one last kiss on the cheek.

The drive to the city seems long tonight, too long. It's the same duration as always, but the anticipation of seeing Weston makes me impatient.

And after what seems like an endless trek, we finally get there.

Edward opens the door for me as he always does. I take his hand and thank him. And then, I turn to see Weston waiting for me, standing tall in a sleek charcoal suit and bright pink shirt.

He's splendid...as always.

He smiles at me. It's that special smile, my favorite—the one he gives me just before he has his wicked way with me. God...I *love* that smile.

"You look *amazing*," he whispers as he kisses my cheek.

"You too," I say in a barely audible voice, my heart stammering. Geez...it's been barely five seconds, and he already has me flustered.

We eat at a French restaurant on the fortieth floor of the Chicago Stock Exchange. This doesn't surprise me in the least, with Weston's obsession with sky high views.

The atmosphere is sexy—contemporary, sleek chrome finishes, muted colors. But then again, I probably think everything is sexy at this point...I'm just so turned on. One slight touch from Weston, and I'm done for. It's as easy as the tap of a button—I'm completely pliable under his stare, his touch.

As the hostess leads us to our table by the window, I notice the breathtaking views of the Chicago skyline. But I'm not awestruck or surprised—I've come to expect this from Weston—the man knows how to entertain a woman and bring her to her knees.

"I can't wait to get that charming little dress off," he teases as soon as the hostess leaves us. His tone is even and business-like, without the slightest hint of playfulness, which makes his words all the more...hot.

My heart leaps in my chest, and I'm at a loss for words.

"Cat got your tongue?" he says, his words almost dancing. He knows what he's doing to me. And he loves it.

"Uh...I...I'm glad you like the dress, Weston," I finally manage, trying to sound coy. But it's no use—I'm *completely* flustered.

He smiles. *That* smile again.

I want him to take off the dress.

As soon as humanly possible.

Weston orders a bottle—a Bordeaux of some kind—I'm not paying too much attention, I'm just too distracted.

Something's not right.

Despite the playful smiles, Weston seems in a rather serious mood tonight, and I wonder what's on his mind. He's not quite as talkative as usual.

He looks at me...he stares, really. There's emotion in his gaze, something foreign, something I haven't seen before. I'm not sure what it is, and I tell myself I'm reading too much into it, as I always do, overanalyzing everything and everyone.

Weston orders the oyster appetizer, and I opt for the peekytoe crab. Taking my first bite, I'm happy with my choice—it's delicious.

Weston offers me an oyster.

I refuse without a moment's hesitation.

"Are you sure?" he asks, playful.

I nod profusely. "Yes, I'm positive. I don't like them. They look disgusting."

"I bet you've never even tried them," he says. And it's true—I haven't.

But still…

"You know what they say about oysters," he says, his words playful.

I laugh a little. "Yes," I reply, a little shy all of a sudden. "They make you horny."

He laughs. "Well, we both know you certainly don't need them."

My jaw drops. "What are you saying?" I ask, my words buried in laughter.

He flashes me his megawatt smile. "You know what I'm saying."

"I haven't heard you complaining," I point out rather coyly.

"Oh…I'm not complaining," he says. "I love the way you are. I love the way you respond to me."

His words bring on that old familiar feeling deep in my core—desire.

"I love the way you react to me too," I say softly.

He looks at me but doesn't say a word for the longest time. And his eyes fill with that foreign emotion again—I can't quite put my finger on it.

He pulls his gaze from mine and takes a drink of his wine. "We *do* fit well together," he says, his words soft.

What the hell is bothering him?

I desperately want to know.

We eat our meals mostly in silence. It isn't uncomfortable but rather intense, emotionally filled. I can barely eat the halibut I've ordered under the scrutiny of his gaze—his stare is passionate—I know he craves me as much as I crave him.

"You look quite different tonight. Very sexy…I like it."

I laugh. "I know…you've been looking at me all night like you want to eat me up."

"I do," he says, his voice soft, "I want to *feast* on you."

Good God.

He puts his knife and fork down—his steak half-eaten—his gestures slow and deliberate. He reaches into his jacket pocket and pulls out his cell, and I wonder what is so urgent all of a sudden.

"Hello, Edward," I hear him say. I take another bite of my fish, but I don't really taste it, my senses lost in Weston's conversation.

"Well, there's been a change of plans," he says with a soft laugh. "We'll need the car in ten minutes..."

He shoots me a playful smile and tucks his phone away. "I hope you won't mind," he says with a mischievous grin, "but we're skipping dessert."

"Are we, now?" I ask, my voice silky. I wonder what he's up to.

"Yes, we are. I need you."

And that's all he needs to say.

I undo his buttons and pull him between my legs onto the bed, my hands sliding down his torso and sliding off his suit jacket. He takes my face in his hand and kisses me softly.

He slips his hand under the sheer fabric of my dress. I reach for his belt and undo him. I slide my hands over his rear and pull down his pants, freeing his erection. I turn over him and straddle him.

"I like a woman in charge," he teases.

His playful grin is doing things to me again.

I undo his shirt buttons one by one, slowly, shooting him a sly smile every now and then. He grins up at me, not saying a word—he loves it when I undress him. I pull up his undershirt, trail kisses down his chest, and make my way to that dark line straggling under his navel. My tongue swirls around his belly button and travels south, teasing him. I hear grunts of pleasure—I'm probably driving him insane.

"You are so cruel," he breathes.

"Payback," I whisper...and finally take him in my mouth. He moans as he grabs a fistful of my hair. I want to give him the same sensations he's given me.

I delight in the sounds he makes as I pleasure him. As I go a little harder and faster—his breathing becomes labored—I can tell he's close, and the thought arouses me.

I'm shocked when he tenses up.

He slides his hand against my cheek, pulling me to him. "Mirella," he breathes. "I had something different in mind for tonight." His eyes filled with that same foreign emotion I had noticed back at the restaurant—I want to know what it is. "I want us to be together." He kisses my cheek softly.

I don't quite understand. What man doesn't want a blow job? I'd done it before and he loved it.

"But," I say, doubt suddenly filling me. "I wanted to…was I not doing a good job?"

"God…" he sighs. "You were doing an *amazing* job. It's just not what I want tonight."

He reaches for my back zipper and pulls it down slowly, his eyes fixing mine. He slides his hand slowly up my body, pulls the dress over my shoulders, freeing me of the sheer lace fabric. I'm left in my white lace underwear.

He gazes at me as he trails his finger down my stomach. "You are so beautiful, Mirella," he says, his words soft. "You're perfect. Don't you *ever* forget that."

I'm both flattered and a little uncomfortable—I've never taken compliments easily. But his words make me happy—no one has ever made me feel as beautiful as he does. "Thank you," I say, my words barely a whisper.

"And you are just as beautiful inside."

"You're beautiful too," I whisper as our lips meet. His kiss is soft and tender, his hands are gentle as he undoes my bra and explores my breasts with his mouth. He has always been gentle, but never quite like this—this is different.

He pulls me under him and slides my panties down, kissing the length of my thighs. His lips travel all over my body, and his gaze catches mine occasionally, his eyes full of longing. He kisses me again and again, softly…kisses my eyelids, my cheeks and the tip of my nose, the sensation of his lips soft on my skin. He looks into my eyes for an eternity—I sense he wants to say something—I can almost hear what he wants to tell me. His eyes don't leave mine as he sinks into me.

He's *making love* to me.

My heart swells up at the realization.

Just maybe…he loves me too.

Chapter Twenty-One

Oh. . .shut up, you stupid cow.

Kathryn calls me on Tuesday morning—I'm surprised—Kathryn *never* calls.

She tells me Weston and Bridget would like to meet with us as soon as possible at his office. I'm surprised and extremely curious. The last time we met at his office was when he first made us the proposal for the exchange. What could they possibly want to talk about now? This must be somewhat important—I can't imagine what in the world would require an official meeting at his office.

Different possible scenarios run through my brain—and the worst comes to mind—they want to end the arrangement. But then, I think about it for a second—things have been going so well—the last time Weston and I were together was...almost magical.

It can't be it.

Maybe they want to organize a trip for all of us...

"What is this all about?" I ask Kathryn.

"I honestly don't know. I was just asked to contact you and make arrangements for a meeting, as soon as possible."

I call Gabe and tell him about the meeting.

"Do you think they want to end it?" he asks, going exactly where I had gone.

"I don't know, Gabe," I say, my heart sinking a little. "How have things been with you and Bridget?" We're not in the habit of talking about this stuff, but the situation warrants the question.

"Good. She seems happy. I haven't sensed anything different. How 'bout you and Weston?"

"Uh..." I hesitate, thinking about the night I told him I loved him, the night we fought. But the last time we met seemed so perfect. "I think we're okay," I finally manage to say.

"That's probably not it. Maybe it's something good."

"Can you take some time off tomorrow afternoon?" I ask. I want to arrange this meeting as soon as possible, or the suspense might very well do me in.

"Uh...sure," he says. "Just let me know when."

Gabe has never been to Weston's office, and he seems both impressed and unimpressed—the sleek glass and chrome finishes probably don't appeal to him—he's more of a traditionalist—solid hard wood is more his style.

The receptionist tells us Weston will come and meet us in a minute. We sit impatiently on the ultramodern white chairs—Gabe's large frame seems out of place, tucked in the compact curved seat. He seems as eager as I am.

Finally, Weston appears and greets us, dressed in a fitted gray suit. He extends a hand to Gabe with a forced smile. He does the same to me, not quite making eye-contact. And suddenly, I feel strange—the moment is reminiscent of the early days of our relationship. We wait awkwardly at the elevators, my attention drawn to Weston's tapping foot.

He stares at the wall, clears his throat. "How was your drive here?"

"It wasn't too bad," Gabe tells him as we enter the mirror encased elevator. "But my truck is brutal on gas—it costs me quite a penny to make it to the city."

"You should consider a hybrid," Weston suggests as he presses a button. As we make the quick trek up to his offices, it occurs to me that he hasn't looked at me *once.*

Bridget greets us when we enter Weston's office, dressed in a tailored black suit.

We exchange one of those slightly uncomfortable, pretentious hugs.

"It's so wonderful to see you again."

"Likewise," I reply, forcing a smile. I'm not sure if I'm happy to see her yet. I just want someone to tell me what the hell is going on.

Weston paces across the room. "Take a seat," he urges us, pointing toward the contemporary, tufted, white leather seats. As I sit down, I'm brought back to that conversation Weston and I had long ago—when he told me he wanted to be with me—it was so erotic. I close my eyes for a second, remembering the delicious sensation I experienced when he touched me for the first time, putting his hand softly on my knee. That day, I made a decision that changed my life.

Bridget takes a seat across us. "Can we offer you a drink? Weston has quite the coffee selection."

"No, thank you," I say politely, my palms sweaty.

Let's just get this over with already.

"I'm good too," Gabe says.

I shoot him a quick sideways glance, curious to see how he's holding up—I think he's as edgy as I am.

Weston takes a seat across from us as well. Both he and Bridget sit upright, stiff, like they're accountants about to go over our income taxes. Bridget has one leg crossed delicately over the other, her heeled foot bouncing ever so slightly.

Weston sucks in a breath. "Well…" he starts, his expression heart-attack serious. "We might as well get straight to the point." His words are heavy, dragging like lead weights. "Bridget and I wanted to meet with you today to discuss our arrangement."

My heart sinks at the sound of his words.

I know what's coming—and I know it's not good—body language is an amazing thing—it speaks louder than words.

I look down at my black heels, not wanting to face them when they tell us they don't want to see us anymore.

"Weston and I have had a wonderful time with both of you," Bridget tells us, her voice sympathetic. I venture a look up at her, and she's as stunning ever and seems genuinely sorry. "But we think this might be the time to..." she hesitates, looking out the window at the Chicago skyline, "cool things off."

My heart fills with heaviness...a heaviness I've never felt before. My eyes tear up...I really don't want them to see me like this, but I can't help myself. I'm translucent—my heartbreak completely obvious.

Weston sees me. He sees the heartbreak. This is hard for him too—I can see it.

He rakes a hand through his hair. "Bridget and I have discussed this thoroughly," he explains, not quite looking at me. "And we both feel we have all gotten a little *too* close."

I have no words. I'm completely shattered. Oddly, I don't feel shocked—I just feel numb.

"This is...exactly when things...could start to get complicated," Weston says, his words caught between heavy breaths. "And I think we are both very dedicated to our respective marriages and families," he adds, his gaze catching mine. He seems truly heartbroken. Maybe he doesn't want to do this—perhaps this is all Bridget's doing—maybe she's jealous.

"Well, you guys are the experts, aren't you," Gabe scoffs, his tone drenched in sarcasm. "I guess you've had your fill of us."

Weston fidgets in his seat, clearly uncomfortable. "Please don't take offense," he says, his words measured. "We are simply trying to avoid both our families a lot of heartbreak."

"Believe us," Bridget chimes in, "this is for the best."

Oh...shut up, you stupid cow.

"How...can we not take offense," I finally manage to speak, my words shaky. "You're dumping us."

Weston sighs. "We are not *dumping* you, Mirella," he stresses, his gaze boring into mine. "We are merely making a well-advised decision for *all* of us."

I roll my eyes. This situation is getting to me—I can feel the anger building up. I don't think I've ever been so upset.

"And although we don't believe we should remain friends," Weston goes on, picking up his water glass from the coffee table. His words are business-like, without emotion. "We would be more than willing to help you out financially if you were ever in need."

This is it…

The exact moment.

The moment I absolutely lose it. It is one thing to dump us like we're nothing, like what we've shared was completely insignificant. But it is quite another to treat us like cheap whores.

"You little fuckin' shit," I scoff, flinging my briefcase at him—the sleek red one with the brass corner reinforcements and brass buckle.

And damn, if I don't get him right in the face.

He winces and throws his hand over his face. I think I may have taken out an eye. I hope I have. He's drenched too—empty glass on his lap.

"Mirella," he hisses.

Bridget looks absolutely shell-shocked, mouth gaping. Gabe loves it—a wide grin practically splits his face in two.

I tear my briefcase from Weston's grasp.

"Let's go," I tell Gabe, and he follows like an eager puppy.

That's how we leave off.

A horrible ending to a really fucked-up story.

It's Wednesday evening, and I'm still so angry.

I can hardly stand it.

Well, that's the first stage of grief, I think. No…actually that's the second. I realize I've completely skipped "Denial." I'm not in denial. I know I've been dumped. I suppose I still have Bargaining, Depression, and Acceptance to look forward to. I'm definitely skipping Bargaining—I'm way too proud to beg.

But, at this moment, it seems the "Anger" stage will *never* go away.

Gabe has taken this a lot better than I would have imagined. I think he's secretly happy—he wants me all to himself again.

But I do think his ego was slightly bruised. "Fuck 'em," he scoffed as we neared his truck. "They think they're too good for us. Fuck 'em." And that was it. That was all he said. And then, he went to the gym, back to his life, seemingly unaffected.

This makes me happy in a way. I know he didn't love her.

And that's my problem—unlike Gabe, I couldn't remain emotionally distant.

I fell in love.

The anger propels wild, outlandish behavior in me. I flock to my closet and haul the twenty thousand dollar dress off its hanger. Claire is trailing me with wild eyes—I think she can tell I've gone completely mad.

I bound down the stairs, sprint across the kitchen, drag the dress outside, and throw it in the steel fire pit sitting in the middle of our backyard.

Claire watches me, her mouth buried in pudgy hands, big brown eyes as large as saucers.

I want to burn it.

I am going to burn it.

"Claire," I hiss. "Go inside. Go to your room."

She stands frozen.

"Go now," I yell at her, and she scurries away, little legs bouncing frantically.

I feel awful. I didn't mean to yell at her. I *never* yell at her. This isn't like me. She's probably wondering why I'm so upset. Poor little thing has no clue what is going on. I want to go to her and explain.

But I'm still mad as hell…and I desperately need a release.

I run to the shed and shuffle through the mess, throwing everything in my wake. Finally, I stumble on lighter fluid and a lighter.

I grab the dress and pour lighter fluid on the charred bits of wood in the pit—just a small amount—I don't want to burn the neighborhood down.

I walk away from the pit, and hold the dress in my arms, stroking the delicate sheer fabric between my fingers—it is *so* beautiful—it is truly the most beautiful dress I've ever seen. Memories of the day he gave it to me flood my mind—our reflection in the mirror, his arms wrapped around my waist, the symphony, the soft stroke of his mouth on my thigh as he took it off.

I hold the flame of the lighter up to the bodice and my eyes linger on the dress as it lights up. The flame grows.

I throw it in quickly.

At first, the flames are small. And as I watch, the flames grow tall, gaining momentum, and I see the dress slowly disappear under my stare.

Tears run down my cheeks.

I *finally* cry.

It's what I've been wanting to do all along.

It's what I've needed to do.

I tuck Claire in, wrapping her tightly into her purple butterfly-covered comforter. She smiles at me—that sweet smile that always me so happy. I stroke the golden ringlets off her face.

I kiss her forehead gently. "Snug as a bug."

She looks at me, sadness washing over her sweet features. "Did you burn it, Mommy?" she asks. "The dress?"

"I'm sorry about that, Claire," I apologize, my heart heavy. "You shouldn't have seen that. It wasn't about you sweetie. I wasn't mad at you. I'm sorry I screamed."

"It's okay. But did you?" she asks, eager. "Burn it?"

I sigh, not wanting to tell her the truth. "I did," I finally confess. "I was mad, and I did it, and I shouldn't have done that. A person should *never ever* burn anything."

"A person should not even play with fire," she adds knowingly.

I smile down at her. "You're right Claire. That's absolutely right. You're a smart girl."

Smarter than your mother.

"It was pretty," she says, her eyes serious. "The dress."

"I know." My heart fills with sadness.

I shouldn't have burned it. Unimaginable regret washes over me. It felt good at the time, but now I just feel empty.

"Why did you do it, Mommy?" Claire clearly wants to understand. I realize this must be so confusing to her, and I struggle to find a way to explain it.

"It made me feel really sad," I start. "The dress reminded me of someone who's gone—someone I miss very much."

"Did they die?" she asks, eyes wide.

"No…" I hesitate, searching for words. "They moved away. And they gave me the dress. And if I looked at the dress, I would think of them."

"But you didn't *want* to think of them?" she asks, confused.

"Exactly, sweetie."

She looks at me for the longest time, seemingly in deep thought. And unexpectedly, her face lights up. "Maybe, you could get a new pretty dress."

I smile down at her. "Yes, that's a great idea, Claire. Maybe you and Chloe could help me pick it out. We'll go shopping. I'll talk to Chloe about it when she gets back from dance class."

She smiles and finally closes her eyes, apparently exhausted by the conversation.

I kiss her again on the forehead, on each cheek, and on the tip of her nose.

And my heart sinks, remembering Weston had done exactly this the last time we were together—he knew it would be our last time.

Chapter Twenty-Two

. . . it was a really, really, really long time.

I wave good-bye to my students, thankful my first week back at school is finally over. I've been in a particularly sour mood all week, and the kids haven't seemed quite as charming as they usually are at the start of the year.

I linger behind as always. On Friday afternoon, every teacher in the place practically sprints to get out for the weekend. But I like to trail behind, avoiding the rush in our cramped parking lot. I figure I'll probably be the last one out again as I fiddle with my notebooks. The girls trail behind me patiently, as they always do. They are in the habit of hanging around my class while I gather my things and tidy for the next day—on a good day, they actually help out.

As we make our way out, Chloe ventures, "We should go to McDonalds."

She always makes this suggestion on Fridays—she's nothing if not persistent. Who knows? One day, I might just pipe up and say, "Yes, let's go to McDonalds," but it has yet to happen.

I scrounge in my oversized purse for my keys.

I don't see him right away. He's standing against a brick pillar just at the entrance of the school—but he catches my eye for a split second—a tall, shaded, dark stranger, wearing sleek, silver-rimmed sunglasses.

And as I approach him, I recognize him. My hearts starts to pound…hard. I have absolutely no control over the damned thing—if it's anything, it's damned, this heart of mine.

"I thought you would never leave," he says, his voice friendly.

I'm at a loss for words—I am completely shocked to see him standing there—in the front yard, at my school.

The girls reach us, and Claire cozies up to me, hugging my skirt, as she always does when confronted with a stranger.

Weston seems surprised by their presence. "Uh…are…" he stammers. "Are these your girls?"

"Yes." Part of me is happy he finally gets to meet them. I've dreamed of this moment often…but it was never quite like this.

"I'm sorry," he says, his voice soft. "I didn't realize you were going to be with your girls. If I had—"

"It's fine, Weston. They go to school here, and they always ride with me. I'm much faster than the bus."

He smiles, extending his hand to Chloe, who's been studying him like she studies the little creatures she captures in her bug gadget. He pulls his shades up, and I notice his bruised eye—and there's a pretty nasty scratch just below his brow.

I got him good.

Satisfaction washes over me…he deserved it.

"I'm Weston. I'm a friend of your mother's…and your father's too," he's quick to add.

Chloe offers him a soft, "Hello," staring blankly at his bruised eye.

"What happened to your eye?" Claire chimes in.

"Well," he starts, his expression grave, "I had a rather nasty run-in with a crazy woman." He shoots me a sideways glance, his words playful. "But I kind of had it coming."

"Did she go to jail?" Claire asks, full of questions.

I smile, kind of wanting to laugh.

"No, I'm afraid not. The justice system simply isn't what it used to be."

Despite myself, a slow smile creeps up on my face—my heart betrays me.

Claire extends her chubby hand and says, "I'm Claire. It's nice to meet you, sir. You're tall…like my daddy." I smile a little—Claire has always had a way with people, just like her father.

Weston smiles at her—that huge genuine smile that makes me melt…*still* makes me melt. I don't think I've ever seen it directed at anyone other than me before. "Nice to meet you too, Claire," he offers, kneeling down to her level. "You are a very charming girl." He seems completely at ease. For all the socially awkward behavior I've observed from him in the past, there's no hint of it here—I'm taken aback.

Claire smiles brightly—she has taken a liking to him—who could blame her.

He stands and looks at me again. He looks delicious, despite the rather impressive black eye, and I almost want to apologize—but I don't.

"I'm not sorry."

His gaze is fixed on mine. He doesn't say a word. "Well, I am… sorry. I'm sorry we left off the way we did, Mirella."

Suddenly, images of the meeting in his office come rushing back to me…and the anger comes back in full force.

I take a step back. "Why are you here, Weston?" I ask, my words clipped.

"I…" he starts, "I wanted to apologize for the way things ended… how we left off. Perhaps I didn't go about it the right way."

The girls are listening carefully, confusion on their faces. I can tell they want to understand.

"Girls," I say. "Could you go sit on the bench while we talk?"

Chloe gives me a medal-worthy eye roll. "But, Mom, I wanna go home."

"We'll go in a minute," I promise. "I'm sure you have some stuff in your bags to keep you entertained for a minute."

They reluctantly leave us, shoulders hunched, feet dragging. They understand this is a "grown-up" conversation.

"God dammed straight…you didn't handle it right. How dare you break up with me like that. You should have talked to me. Just *you* and *me*."

"I'm sorry. When I told Bridget I wanted to end things, she insisted on doing it this way."

I jerk away, not wanting him to see my reaction. "Oh…of course… Bridget," I scoff.

"It wasn't just her. I just couldn't go through with it." His voice is soft. "I was planning on discussing it with you on our last date… but then, when I saw you…you were so beautiful and sexy." His expression is full of regret. "I just wanted to be with you one last time. I'm sorry…I was a coward."

I look up at him, understanding—remembering the time I met up with him to end things…when we ended up making love for the first time.

He rubs the back of his neck—he seems completely torn. "I want to say a proper good-bye. What we had was too wonderful to end things this way."

He doesn't realize what he's doing to me—he's making it harder. I much preferred when I hated him—when I wanted to never see him again.

I glare at him. "Well, it obviously wasn't as wonderful for you as it was for me," I hiss. "You have no idea how much I cared about you."

He reaches out to me. "I do. And I cared about you…*still* care about you."

He's being nice again. I can't stand it—I'm still mad as hell.

"I burned the dress you gave me."

He jerks back. He seems taken aback. "You burned it?" he asks, his eyes wide.

"Yep. I threw it in my fire pit and lit it up," I scoff, satisfaction filling me. "It was a hell of a bonfire."

He laughs a little. "You obviously have no idea how much that dress was worth."

His words rub me the wrong way…they scratch me.

"Oh…I do, but heck, there's a lot more where that came from right? Or did you forget your oh-so-generous offer to help us out whenever we needed." My words are filled with anger. "I could have sold it on eBay…but here's a newsflash, Weston," I say, closing the distance between us. "We don't need the money."

"I'm sorry. I shouldn't have offered. I seem to have struck a nerve. I was merely trying to be considerate."

"We don't need your charity," I snap. "What we really need right now is for you to leave us the fuck alone."

I rarely curse. But it seems when it comes to him, I do. I know he hates foul language, and I want to hurt him. I want him to despise me as much as I despise him.

"Mirella," he says softly, grabbing a hold of my wrist.

I jerk my arm away. "Do *not* touch me."

He backs away. "I'm sorry." I can't count how many times he's said he's sorry now—and it's starting to wear on me.

"You never loved me," I whisper, still aware the girls are sitting not far away.

He sighs and closes his eyes. "Mirella…" he says softly.

"You've destroyed me," I cry.

I see what I've been searching for in his eyes…pain. "The way I feel about you is the reason I had to do this."

His words get to me.

"I'm falling in love with you," he says, his eyes not leaving mine. "And I told myself I would break things off as soon as I could, if it ever came to that."

It's what I've wanted to hear all along, but somehow, it doesn't change a thing now. "Why didn't you tell me that earlier?"

He doesn't answer. He looks away, toward the girls.

"Does Bridget know about this?"

He shakes his head, not quite looking at me. "She doesn't need to know."

"She should know, Weston," I tell him, realizing I'm being a complete hypocrite. I haven't told Gabe about my feelings either.

"It's better for everyone if she doesn't," he stresses. "Trust me."

"Doesn't she wonder?" I ask. "Did she want to end things too?"

"No. Actually, we had quite the row about it. She really wanted to keep seeing Gabe."

His words shock me. I had never stopped once to consider how Bridget might be feeling about all this. "Do you think she has feelings for him?"

"No," he says plainly. "I think she just likes the sex, to be honest."

"I don't think they have what we have."

Silence lingers around us as we look at each other.

His striking eyes draw me in…there is so much sorrow in them.

I still crave him.

But I can no longer have him.

I need to move on.

"You're…right…Weston," I struggle to say, my heart heavy. "It's for the best. You made the right decision."

He pulls me into his arms and holds me tightly. "I will miss you so much," he whispers.

"I'll miss you too."

He holds me for a long time…for what seems like eternity.

We're having bowtie pasta with sausage. The girls don't particularly like it, but they seem to be making an effort to eat. I've been feeling uninspired these last few days. I've just been going through the motions, doing the bare minimum. Gabe hasn't seemed particularly upbeat either, but I'm sure he's doing a lot better than I am.

I think about Weston's visit today, and it makes me feel better, but also worse. I should really tell Gabe about it, I muse, stuffing a fork full of pasta in my mouth—forcing it down. I'm eating for the first time since the meeting at Weston's office—I've been sustaining on bananas and iced tea—heartbreak robbing me completely of my appetite.

"A man came to talk to Mommy at school today," Chloe suddenly blurts out.

"They talked for a long time," Claire pipes in. "We had to sit and wait on a bench. He was tall like you, Daddy…and he had a black eye."

Gabe eyes me with a curious look, his fork mid-air. I sigh. I was hoping to bring this up myself…but, it *just* happened, literally less than three hours ago.

"Weston…" I say reluctantly. "He came by the school after class."

"Why?" Gabe asks, his tone eager.

"He wanted to say a proper good-bye," I explain. "I swear it was nothing more. He didn't like the way we left off. You should have seen his eye…I got him good."

Gabe smiles a little but seems concerned. He glances quickly at the girls, trying not to reveal too much. "Has he changed his mind?"

Claire and Chloe listen intently—probably trying to figure out our conversation.

"No. He hasn't. It was actually good closure," I admit. "I think we both needed that."

"Did he tell you why they…ended things? They never really gave us a good explanation."

I shake my head and decide to not tell him about the details of the conversation, about what Weston had mentioned about Bridget not wanting to end it, about Weston's feelings for me, and about the true reason we had to let go of each other.

He doesn't need to know.

"He gave Mommy a big hug," Chloe tells him. "A really long hug that lasted like a million hours."

Nice going, Chloe, you little snitch, I think, feeling caught in the act.

Gabe cocks his brow and looks down at his plate, apparently deciding to let it go.

"It *wasn't* a million hours, you silly," Claire chimes in. Thank goodness for my sweet little girl.

"But…" she adds, tiny brows furrowed, little red mouth on bendy straw as she sips her chocolate milk, "it was a *really, really, really* long time."

It's been two weeks…and I'm getting better.

Although I've burned the dress, I've never destroyed the photos of us or the cute turtle brooch he gave me on our third date. I keep them in a secret box, stashed under my bed, hidden among a hodge-podge of boxes full of junk. I've only looked at the contents of the box once or twice, tears flowing down my cheeks.

I've been putting on a brave face for Gabe and the girls, and my kids at school, going on about my day, pretending I am completely fine. But every now and then, I lock myself up in my closet or in the bathroom, when no one is watching, and I cry.

This is so hard because I've never been heartbroken before. Gabe was my first love, and he's always been by my side. I feel so ill-equipped to handle this.

But I've been working hard, trying to forget him. And I just can't seem to.

I still miss him so much. I miss his touch…his smile…the way he makes me feel.

I don't hate him anymore.

I am grateful to him. For the decision he's made for both of us—for *all* of us. I wasn't strong enough to do it. I never would have let go. But I'm so glad he did. Sure it hurts terribly, but it will get better in time. It was the right thing to do. I was so angry when I slung that briefcase at him, but now I realize he was just trying to protect us.

Gwen tells me it's for the best. She says I'm very fortunate to come out of this with my marriage intact, she'd been worried about Gabe and me. She suggests I should forget about him and move on with my wonderful life and simply be thankful for having had the chance to have a little fun…a little adventure.

She's right. I am blessed. I still have the man I love and my two beautiful daughters. It's time to pour all my love and energy where it belongs—they need me. I've been so very selfish these past few months. And I came so close to messing it all up.

It'd been a while since Gabe and I have made love. As he holds me in his arms and strokes my cheek, I reach for him and press my lips against his. His tongue tastes sweet as he pulls me closer to him. And I know I have everything I need.

Right here.

I'm almost sure of that...

Excerpt from the second book in The Ground Rules series

I walk over the refrigerator and grab the carton of juice, busying myself. The last thing I want to do this morning is look at Weston.

"You and Gabe sure had yourselves a good time last night," Weston says without preamble.

"Uh…" Suddenly, I'm flustered and embarrassed. It had seemed like a good idea at the time—when I was a little buzzed and horny-as-hell. But now, in the light of day, stone sober, I'm really mortified.

"I'm sorry about that," I say, barely able to look at him. "We didn't—"

"It's fine, Mirella," he says, looking up at me through his dark long lashes. "I didn't mind."

His words shock me. There's heat in his gaze. He's looking good this morning in a soft grey T-shirt. His hair is mussed up a bit, and he hasn't shaved yet. He looks carefree.

He watches my every move. His eyes are glued to me as I twist the jar of jam open…as I pull a knife out of drawer…as I grab the loaf of bread.

I pull my eyes away from him, my nerves lit up. I can't quite bring myself to look at him, but I feel his gaze on every inch of my body. My heart pounds in my chest. I want to look up, but I just can't.

"You wanted me to hear," he says, his voice soft. It's not a question but a statement, delivered with one hundred percent conviction.

I blush crimson. Oh, God…I seem to have forgotten a little fact—Weston Hanson is practically psychic. He's very attuned to people's behaviors. I'm also convinced he can read my mind. Of *course,* he knows what I was up to.

He sets down his fork and knife. "And I did hear, you'll be glad to know. Loud and clear. The acoustics in this place don't leave much to the imagination."

"I'm sorry," I say again. You'd think I could come up with something more substantial to say, but he's rendered my mind useless.

His eyes fix on me as he drinks the last of his orange juice. He gently sets down the glass on the granite counter—a soft clank travels across the kitchen through the eerie silence. Still, his eyes don't leave me.

He bites his bottom lip like he wants to say something. He seems to be working it out. I don't take my eyes off him. I want him to say it—whatever *it* is.

He closes his eyes. "It was extremely arousing," he says softly, "hearing you with him."

I drop my knife with a loud clank on the granite counter. Strawberry jam splatters all over—the plate, the counter, my white T-shirt, my hands. But oddly enough, none of it seems to land on my piece of toast.

As he gets up from his stool, he smiles—a slow wicked grin. He sweeps past me to drop his dirty dishes in the sink as he shoots me a sly look, cool as a cucumber.

He smiles again as he leaves me…in an absolute fumbling mess.

Acknowledgments

A big thanks to my husband for always supporting me, and to my children for being so sweet. Another big thanks to members of my extended family for reading my first self-published book and offering feedback and encouragement. To my Mom (*un gros merci*) for being my #1 blog fan and for buying me my first laptop (on which, I promptly started working on my first romance, which I abandoned a month later for other creative pursuits and the Toronto bar scene). To my new writer friends, Emily, Kylie, Jennifer, Robin, and Carol for listening to my excerpts and being so encouraging. To Emily Sylvan Kim of the Prospect Agency (the first to read *TGR*) for offering constructive feedback and encouragement on Book 1. And lastly, but not least, to Traci, Robin, and everyone at Omnific Publishing for believing in my trilogy and giving me a chance.

About the Author

Roya Carmen is a book junkie, doodle addict, and self-professed chocoholic. A graduate of Ryerson University, she worked in Graphic Communications before becoming a stay-at-home mom. She has always loved writing, finding her passion for romance in 2008. She enjoys spending time with her family, camping, and painting. And of course, there is nothing she loves more than sitting down at her laptop and making up stories—and if those stories should include beautiful men, a little romance, and a few steamy scenes, all the better!

Roya Carmen lives north of Toronto with her husband and three children and is a member of RWA.

check out these titles from

OMNIFIC PUBLISHING

Contemporary Romance

Keeping the Peace by Linda Cunningham
Stitches and Scars by Elizabeth A. Vincent
Pieces of Us by Hannah Downing
The Way That You Play It by BJ Thornton
The Poughkeepsie Brotherhood series: *Poughkeepsie, Return to Poughkeepsie* & *Saving Poughkeepsie* by Debra Anastasia
Recaptured Dreams and *All-American Girl* and *Until Next Time* by Justine Dell
Once Upon a Second Chance by Marian Vere
The Englishman by Nina Lewis
16 Marsden Place by Rachel Brimble
Sleepers, Awake by Eden Barber
The Runaway series: *The Runaway Year* & *The Runaway Ex* by Shani Struthers
The Hydraulic series: *Hydraulic Level Five* & *Skygods* by Sarah Latchaw
Fix You & *Trouble Me* and *The Jeweler* by Beck Anderson
Just Once & *Going the Distance* by Julianna Keyes
The WORDS series: *The Weight of Words, Better Deeds Than Words, The Truest of Words* & *The Record of My Heart* by Georgina Guthrie
The Brit Out of Water series: *Theatricks* & *Jazz Hands* by Eleanor Gwyn-Jones
The Sacrificial Lamb & *Let's Get Physical* by Elle Fiore
The Plan by Qwen Salsbury
The Kiss Me series: *Kiss Me Goodnight* & *Kiss Me By Moonlight* by Michele Zurlo
Saint Kate of the Cupcake: The Dangers of Lust and Baking by LC Fenton
Exposure by Morgan & Jennifer Locklear
Playing All the Angles by Nicole Lane
Redemption by Kathryn Barrett
The Playboy's Princess by Joy Fulcher
The Forever series: *Forever Autumn* & *Forever Winter* by Christopher Scott Wagner

Young Adult Romance

The Ember series: *Ember* & *Iridescent* by Carol Oates
Breaking Point by Jess Bowen
Life, Liberty, and Pursuit by Susan Kaye Quinn
The Embrace series: *Embrace, Hold Tight, Entwined* by Cherie Colyer
Destiny's Fire by Trisha Wolfe
The Reaper series: *Reaping Me Softly* & *UnReap My Heart* by Kate Evangelista
The Legendary Saga: *Legendary* & *Claiming Excalibur* by LH Nicole
The Fatal series: *Fatal* & *Brutal* (novella 1.5) by T.A. Brock
The Prometheus Order series: *Byronic* by Sandi Beth Jones
One Smart Cookie by Kym Brunner
Variables of Love by MK Schiller

New Adult Romance

Three Daves by Nicki Elson
Streamline by Jennifer Lane
The Shades series: *Shades of Atlantis* & *Shades of Avalon* by Carol Oates
The Heart series: *Beside Your Heart, Disclosure of the Heart* & *Forever Your Heart* by Mary Whitney
Romancing the Bookworm by Kate Evangelista
Flirting with Chaos by Kenya Wright
The Vice, Virtue & Video series: *Revealed, Captured, Desired* & *Devoted* by Bianca Giovanni
Granton University series: *Loving Lies* by Linda Kage
Missing Pieces by Meredith Tate

Paranormal & Fantasy Romance

The Light series: *Seers of Light, Whisper of Light* & *Circle of Light* by Jennifer DeLucy
The Hanaford Park series: *Eve of Samhain* & *Pleasures Untold* by Lisa Sanchez
Immortal Awakening by KC Randall
The Seraphim series: *Crushed Seraphim* & *Bittersweet Seraphim* by Debra Anastasia
The Guardian's Wild Child by Feather Stone
Grave Refrain by Sarah M. Glover
The Divinity series: *Divinity* & *Entity* by Patricia Leever
The Blood Vine series: *Blood Vine, Blood Entangled* & *Blood Reunited* by Amber Belldene
Divine Temptation by Nicki Elson
The Dead Rapture series: *Love in the Time of the Dead, Love at the End of Days* & *Love Starts with Z* by Tera Shanley
The Hidden Races series: *Incandescent* & *Illumination* by M.V. Freeman
Something Wicked by Carol Oates
Chronicles of Midvalen: *Command the Tides* (book 1) by Wren Handman
Saving Evangeline by Nancee Cain

Romantic Suspense

Whirlwind by Robin DeJarnett
The CONduct series: *With Good Behavior, Bad Behavior* & *On Best Behavior* by Jennifer Lane
Indivisible by Jessica McQuinn
Between the Lies by Alison Oburia
Blind Man's Bargain by Tracy Winegar

Historical Romance

Cat O' Nine Tails by Patricia Leever
Burning Embers by Hannah Fielding
Seven for a Secret by Rumer Haven
The Counterfeit by Tracy Winegar

Erotic Romance

The Keyhole series: *Becoming sage* (book 1) by Kasi Alexander
The Keyhole series: *Saving sunni* (book 2) by Kasi & Reggie Alexander
The Winemaker's Dinner: *Appetizers & Entrée* by Dr. Ivan Rusilko & Everly Drummond
The Winemaker's Dinner: *Dessert* by Dr. Ivan Rusilko
Client N° 5 by Joy Fulcher
The Enclave series: *Closer and Closer* (book 1) by Jenna Barton
The Adventures of Clarissa Hardy by Chloe Gillis
The Ground Rules by Roya Carmen

Anthologies

A Valentine Anthology including short stories by
Alice Clayton ("With a Double Oven"),
Jennifer DeLucy ("Magnus of Pfelt, Conquering Viking Lord"),
Nicki Elson ("I Don't Do Valentine's Day"),
Jessica McQuinn ("Better Than One Dead Rose and a Monkey Card"),
Victoria Michaels ("Home to Jackson"), and
Alison Oburia ("The Bridge")

Taking Liberties including an introduction by Tiffany Reisz and short stories by
Mina Vaughn ("John Hancock-Blocked"),
Linda Cunningham ("A Boston Marriage"),
Joy Fulcher ("Tea for Two"),
KC Holly ("The British Are Coming!"),
Kimberly Jensen & Scott Stark ("E. Pluribus Threesome"), and
Vivian Rider ("M'Lady's Secret Service")

Sets

The Heart Series Box Set (*Beside Your Heart, Disclosure of the Heart & Forever Your Heart*) by Mary Whitney
The CONduct Series Box Set (*With Good Behavior, Bad Behavior & On Best Behavior*) by Jennifer Lane
The Light Series Box Set (*Seers of Light, Whisper of Light, Circle of Light & Glimpse of Light*) by Jennifer DeLucy
The Blood Vine Series Box Set (*Blood Vine, Blood Entangled, Blood Reunited & Blood Eternal*) by Amber Belldene

Singles, Novellas & Special Editions

It's Only Kinky the First Time (A Keyhole series single) by Kasi Alexander
Learning the Ropes (A Keyhole series single) by Kasi & Reggie Alexander
The Winemaker's Dinner: RSVP by Dr. Ivan Rusilko

The Winemaker's Dinner: No Reservations by Everly Drummond
Big Guns by Jessica McQuinn
Concessions by Robin DeJarnett
Starstruck by Lisa Sanchez
New Flame by BJ Thornton
Shackled by Debra Anastasia
Swim Recruit by Jennifer Lane
Sway by Nicki Elson
Full Speed Ahead by Susan Kaye Quinn
The Second Sunrise by Hannah Downing
The Summer Prince by Carol Oates
Whatever it Takes by Sarah M. Glover
Clarity (A *Divinity* prequel single) by Patricia Leever
A Christmas Wish (A *Cocktails & Dreams* single) by Autumn Markus
Late Night with Andres by Debra Anastasia
Poughkeepsie (enhanced iPad app collector's edition) by Debra Anastasia
Poughkeepsie (audio book edition) by Debra Anastasia
Blood Eternal (A Blood Vine series single, epilogue to series) by Amber Belldene
Carnaval de Amor (*The Winemaker's Dinner*, Spanish edition)
by Dr. Ivan Rusilko & Everly Drummond

coming soon from OMNIFIC PUBLISHING

Twice Upon a Kiss by Jane Susann McCarter
The Keyhole series: *Keyhole Kinklets* (short story anthology)
by Kasi & Reggie Alexander
A Nightingale in Winter by Margart Johnson
True Gold by Kathryn Barrett
Finding Parker by Scott Hildreth
Guardian of the Stone by Amity Grays
The Revenger by Debra Anastasia
Subject X by Emma G. Hunter

CPSIA information can be obtained
at www.ICGtesting.com
Printed in the USA
LVOW03s2016070318
568996LV00002B/236/P